WOMEN IN WAR

LIZZIE LANE

First published in 2018. This edition first published in Great Britain in 2023 by Boldwood Books Ltd.

Cover Design by Colin Thomas

Cover Photography: Colin Thomas and Alamy

A CIP catalogue record for this book is available from the British Library.

Paperback ISBN 978-1-83751-846-3

Large Print ISBN 978-1-83751-845-6

Hardback ISBN 978-1-83751-844-9

Ebook ISBN 978-1-83751-847-0

Kindle ISBN 978-1-83751-848-7

Audio CD ISBN 978-1-83751-839-5

MP3 CD ISBN 978-1-83751-840-1

Digital audio download ISBN 978-1-83751-842-5

Boldwood Books Ltd
23 Bowerdean Street
London SW6 3TN
www.boldwoodbooks.com

1

BENARES, INDIA, 1941

It was a week before leaving Benares School for Young Ladies that Nadine Burton came home expecting everything to be as it always was but found it had changed forever.

As always the air was humid and heavy with the scent of rotting vegetation, rich spices, and bullock droppings. In contrast, the veranda running along the front of the house was cloaked in shadow. But something, she wasn't sure what, was very wrong.

The house was the same, but there was no Shanti, no loving *ayah* waiting on the veranda to welcome her home. Ever since she could remember, her nurse had stood on the veranda waving a welcome, eyes sparkling, lips spread in a welcoming smile.

She frowned. Her hands turned clammy. Some ancient, womanly instinct clicked into place.

A small lizard ran across the floor in front of her, disappearing into a crack in the wall. This particular breed of lizard was common and harmless but today there was something ominous about the hollow sound of its scuttling in the shady house and there no response when she called Shanti's name, just the scuttling lizard.

Uneasily, feeling slightly sick, she walked swiftly towards Shanti's bedroom, the corridor so cool after the heat outside.

If her *ayah* had been sleeping, the door would be closed but it was open. The room was bare except for the familiar iron framed bed and a small yellow rug. The mattress was rolled up and placed against the iron bed head.

Nadine saw no trace of her *ayah*'s silk saris, her sandals decorated with silver bells, her bangles, her unguents, the heavy gold earrings with the fine chain connecting them to her nose ring.

A small earthquake erupted in her heart. There was no life in the room. No Shanti, though her scent still lingered on the air.

The soft rustle of a sari sounded behind her accompanied by the hushed padding of sandals upon stone.

For a moment her spirits soared then dipped again when she saw it was Myla, the housekeeper. Though her hair was black, a swathe of whiteness ran back from her temples which gave her a fierce look as if she was running into the wind.

'She is gone,' said Myla in a matter-of-fact manner.

'Gone where?'

'Away from here. You do not need her any longer. You are a grown woman now. Your father let her go.'

Nadine felt as though the ground had given way beneath her. The whole world seemed so much darker, her life destroyed.

'I shall kill myself if she doesn't come back. I mean it. I shall kill myself!'

'Foolish talk.' Myla shook her head emphatically. 'She would want you to live forever.'

Nadine's laughter was raw and brittle and tears stung her eyes. 'Nobody lives forever.'

'Life is precious. That's what your *ayah* always said.'

'Where has she gone?'

'Back to her place in the world,' said Myla, and hurried away, her calico skirt swirling as she went, her leather sandals slapping the hard floor.

Nadine sunk down against the whitewashed walls until she was sitting on the floor, her legs folded beneath her, her feet bare and dusty. Shanti was gone and the world seemed a much lonelier place. So where was she? Nothing is ever totally unknown.

'Nothing,' she murmured, springing to her feet on legs that had been coltish and were now firmly feminine.

Those legs now ran through every room in the house searching for the woman who had brought her up from babyhood. She demanded of the house servants, the gardeners, the cooks, and the grooms to tell her where she was.

'Tell me. Tell me now!'

Nervously, they shook their heads, dark lashes flickering over velvet brown eyes, their mouths firmly shut. Their jobs depended on them obeying orders.

The old house reverberated with the noise of slamming doors and running footsteps.

One door, dark mahogany and usually locked against the world, suddenly opened. Her father, Roland Burton, a severe personage dressed in well-tailored clothes, a gold ring on one finger, appeared at his study door. He was wearing a pale cream suit, the knot of his old school tie hard as a pebble against his throat. The stark lightness of his suit was angelically white against the dark mustiness of the study behind him, a place lined with books, the curtains dark, the furniture leather covered and unashamedly masculine.

'Stop this noise. I am trying to work.'

His manner was curt, each of his words delivered like the thwack of stick against ball on the polo field.

'Shanti! I can't find her.'

Seldom did she find herself face to face with her father. She was his child, yet over the years they'd seldom spoke or even ate together. Only in these last few weeks had she been invited to dinner when guests were expected. The rest of the time she'd dined in her room or with the servants, eating what they ate whilst sitting barefoot at the back door watching the sun go down.

'Forget Shanti. You are now a woman and have no need for a nurse.' There was no softness in his words, no sympathy or acknowledgement that there had been affection between the two women. 'And no more dancing. Not Shanti's style of dancing. You must be the prim young English lady and behave properly.'

'Where is she? I want to see her,' Nadine shouted.

He stiffened, his expression grim.

'You have no need of a nurse. You are now a young lady. A young *English* lady. In future you will behave as such and will forget everything Indian. The time has come for you to marry. An English gentleman requires an English wife, not one that acts like a native.'

He went back into his study, the door closing on him and the smell of musty books, tobacco, and masculine cologne.

Hours later, she was still sitting where she had last sat with Shanti, her eyes still heavy with tears and her nose running.

Though twilight lay heavy over the garden and the shadows were long, she kicked off her shoes, stepped onto the grass and began to move her body and arms in the way Shanti had taught her.

Tears streaming down her face she danced until it was too dark to see then went inside and went to bed, fresh tears staining the pillow.

* * *

It was the following day before she found out what happened.

A dim narrow corridor ran from the main one to the back of the school and the veranda where the caretaker kept his buckets and sweeping brush.

The corridor was empty. So many of the girls had been sent home at the outbreak of war in Europe. To Nadine, it seemed all so far away in a country she'd never visited. War would not come to India, surely? It was too distant and protected by its own army. Shanti would have reassured her that everything would be fine. Thinking of Shanti, she began to dance, imagined music guiding her movements. In her mind, Shanti was dancing with her.

None of her fellow students ever came here so she had not expected to be discovered, but today she was.

'You're dancing like a native! It's disgraceful. Absolutely disgraceful. I intend reporting you to Miss Clark.'

The speaker was Cecilia Renfrew, the red-headed daughter of a senior civil servant. Nadine stopped dancing, placed her fists on her hips, and faced the least popular girl in the school.

'Cecilia Renfrew! Why do you have to spoil things for everyone?'

'You shouldn't be dancing like a native. It's not seemly.'

The girl with the unruly red curls and a turned-up nose took a step backwards. Nadine concentrated all her anger on that nose. It was like a small snout, intruding pig-like into the secret world of her imagination.

'Seemly? What would you know about seemly? Come to that, what would you know about anything? Anyway, I was just exercising, flexing my limbs to improve my poise. A well-educated young English lady should always move gracefully. Which is more than you'll ever do! You have all the grace of an elephant. No. Less than an elephant. More like a water buffalo!'

Cecilia raised her least attractive feature that little bit higher, her oily chin blemished with faint traces of acne shiny in the noonday light. Most people sweated. India was like that. White hot summer. Humid winters. How could anyone not sweat?

'I'm going to tell Miss Clark. Now!'

Nadine paused in mid pose. She didn't care if she was reported. Shanti was gone and her world was shattered, but she would always dance. She owed it to Shanti.

In her mind she had been bending and weaving to the sound of a sitar in the vine-covered pergola at the far reaches of her father's garden.

The imagined smell of roses, perfumes and spices was wiped out by the musty stink of mothballs and old tweed as Miss Clark, the headmistress appeared.

Bull dog fashion, the headmistress's bottom lip curled up over the top one. 'I will tolerate half heathens, I will even tolerate full-blooded natives as long as they are Christian, but I will brook no heathen decadence in this school!' Her voice had a grinding quality as though she were mincing each word before spitting it out. She wasn't finished yet. 'Your father will know about this. Those dances are the Devil's work, Nadine Burton, and whoever taught you such things is the devil incarnate. A heathen practise.'

Hot tears burned at the back of Nadine's eyes, but she willed herself not to cry.

'Shanti is not a devil! She is – was – my *ayah*!'

Cecilia's eyes glittered. 'Well I heard she was your mother and that she lives in Alexander Street. I heard she was your father's floosie and that you are their bastard.'

'Enough of that!'

Miss Clark delivered a hefty whack to Cecilia's freckled cheek which instantly turned scarlet.

'It's true, miss. My mother heard from our housekeeper and my mother says that such as she make British men run round naked and...'

'Quiet!'

The word hit them like a slammed door. Miss Clark was incapable of saying anything quietly.

For a moment, Nadine's wide-eyed amazement stayed with the girl who now preened with cruel satisfaction.

The address in Alexander Street echoed cold as a tolling bell in her mind and gave wings to her feet. Kicking off her shoes, she ran from the school corridor.

Miss Clark's voice boomed after her. 'You little heathen. Come back here!

She ran all the way, uncaring that the first rain of the monsoon was bouncing off the ground and leaving deep puddles where garbage floated from the dumps and into the town.

Little more than an alley, Alexander Street was a place of ramshackle dwellings alongside tall houses ornately carved in centuries past but now showing signs of being infested with termites the wood brittle with sawdust.

Nadine slowed her pace, her eyes darting from right to left, seeking as if Shanti was likely to pop out of a doorway. How stupid she had been to think she could find her without a specific address, not that Cecilia, the ginger-haired harpy, with her superior airs and nose to suit, would have given her one! Not once she'd realised how desperate she was.

She searched with her eyes, darting to any woman who chose that moment to poke her head out of her dirt-floored house. A useless task.

A woman scouring a pot with dirt from the edge of what had been a drainage gutter and was now a muddy stream looked up.

Nadine greeted her respectfully, hands together, a slight bow of her head. 'I am looking for Shanti Bai. Do you know where she lives?'

The woman rested her iron pot against her side and pointed to the end of the street.

'Follow this road. You will find her by the Ganges.'

She saw pity in the woman's expression and heard it in her tone of voice.

Kicking splats of mud up and over her navy gymslip, she ran on. The rain was heavier now and soon her hair was plastered to her head. Moisture ran down her face, into her eyes, her mouth and dangled from the end of her nose. The feet of her black school stockings were soggy and spattered, the toes hanging like dead things on the end of her feet.

She ran out onto the top of the Burning Ghat in front of the mosque built by the Moghul Emperor Aurangzeb on a site that had once been a Hindu temple.

As the rain eased, the smell of smoke circulated more freely along with the more fetid odour of fermenting marigolds, carnations and other garlands, votive offerings floating on the river.

Nadine stopped to catch her breath, her eyes continuously searching the surge of humanity that was the ancient city of Benares, the sacred bulls, the naked holy men, and the flocks of crows circling above the corpses laid out for burning. Once the body was totally consumed by fire, the ashes would be scattered on the holy Ganges.

A ragged man brought out a pile of kindling from beneath a metal umbrella leaning against the wall of the temple. She watched as he set the logs beneath one particular pyre where the small feet of a graceful woman pointed out towards the water.

For a moment she couldn't breathe and her body trembled. How was it possible to identify someone by looking at their feet, and yet, she knew it was Shanti. Hadn't she seen those feet dancing many times?

She approached the ragged man.

'Please. That lady. Who is she?'

When he looked up at her she saw that he only had one eye. The other was tightly closed as though it had fallen asleep and never reopened.

His mouth spread in a toothless grin.

'She *was* a lady named Shanti Bai. A great *devadassi* in her youth. A *nautch* was good luck indeed when graced with her presence.'

A *nautch* was a party, a great celebration such as for a wedding or business success or for the entertainment of a great *maharajah*.

The bare feet were level with Nadine's face. She stared at the soles, her heart beating like a drum. Taking a brave breath, she walked slowly along the length of the body until she was level with the head. Hot tears squeezed out of the corners of her eyes, running down her cheeks to disturb the dirt accumulated on her run here.

'Did you know her?' asked the ragged man.

She bit her bottom lip and nodded without taking her eyes off the slim figure lying so still on the pile of logs.

'I would like to light the pyre,' she said firmly.

He looked taken aback. 'Are you a relative?'

She thought quickly and carefully. 'Not really.'

The old man made a sound of acquiescence and reached for the burning log he had stuck in an adjacent brazier.

'Then that is all right. She paid for things to be done in a professional manner. Someone who is not a relative must light the fire now that the world is finished with her. This is only her body. Her soul is long gone.'

Nadine understood. Some people believed it unseemly for relatives to gather and mourn or to light the funeral pyre.

His callused hand guided hers to the pyre.

'In there.'

She did as instructed and stood back as the flames began to lick up over the damp wood, the resin hissing and spitting as the logs cracked open.

The rain lessened. The crows wheeled and circled overhead, glutted on the smell and the feast of burning remains.

Nadine stood sentinel, needing to cry but unable to move. Her body was stiff and so was her face.

An old *fakir*, his joints knotted like tree trunks, joined them. They stood on either side of her watching as the flesh was burned from the bones.

A sudden thought occurred to her. 'Quickly. Don't let the crows have her.' She took off her broad brimmed hat and proceeded to fan the flames.

The two men exchanged looks of incomprehension.

'You should not be so sad,' said the *fakir*. 'She chose of her own right to finish with this body.'

'So I hear,' said the ragged man nodding sagely in an effort, so it seemed, to place his wisdom on a par with that of the holy man. 'But no matter. She will soon be ash. She chose to leave this life and her wish has been fulfilled.'

Not sure she understood correctly, Nadine looked at the *fakir*, then at the ragged man. What did that mean?

The *fakir* noted her questioning frown.

'She chose,' said the *fakir* more slowly now so that she might better understand. 'She took her life because she had no need of it any more.'

'If a life becomes empty...' added the ragged man.

A log crackled and tumbled. Morning turned into afternoon before the logs and their precious cargo became ash, and even then Nadine could not move. The truth was too terrible to bear. Her mother, distraught at being parted from her daughter, had killed herself.

The ragged man began to shovel the ash into the river where it mixed with the evening mist. Perhaps she was fooling herself, but she was sure that she had seen the mist dancing around the ashes, homage to a dead soul. Even Shanti's scent seemed to hang in the air above the stink of decomposition and human occupation. She was gone; gone forever, leaving Nadine feeling empty and uncaring of whatever happened next.

2

The house in which Nadine been born was as drenched as the rest of the world, but the shutters were tightly closed against the wetness outside, sealing the humid heat within.

Excess water gurgled along culverts and into storage tanks. The high walls enveloped a household untroubled by famine or deluge.

The soles of her sopping wet stockings left a watery trail all the way from the front door to her bedroom.

Myla, the housekeeper, left the job of pounding spices in the kitchen and shadowed Nadine's progress, dipping to pick up the clothes as she discarded them. With each dip a mist of cinnamon and other spices drifted from her clothes.

'I want a bath,' said Nadine, her chest tight, her head aching with the weight of unanswered questions. 'A very hot bath.'

Myla eyed her warily.

'A chill,' she said once she'd chewed over the facts and reached a conclusion. 'You are getting a chill. A bath would be good. I will see to it.'

The water was hot and simmering with the perfume of violet-scented bath salts.

The pain in her chest persisted and her face was wet with tears. Sinking herself deeper into the water, she closed her eyes, conjuring up Cecilia's superior expression. Gossip had been the lifeblood of the *cantonment* since the first *memsahib* had placed her booted foot on Indian soil. Children, as they grew older, began to better understand what was being said. Almost young women now, the girls she'd gone to school with were feeling their feet, their superiority and class snobbery. She was different and they'd decided she did not belong.

Back in her room, dressing gown wrapped tightly around her, head swathed in a soft towel, she looked at the photograph sitting on top the chest of drawers. It had a black frame and had sat there for as long as she could remember. This, according to her father, was her long-deceased mother. Every night, Shanti had bid her say a prayer for this woman.

The woman's hair was shingled and she was looking coyly over her shoulder. Nadine eyed her speculatively. Never before had she searched so diligently for some facial feature confirming this was her mother.

The contrast was striking. Shanti had been bright and colourful. The black and white photograph showed a stranger, a woman she had never known yet was expected to venerate, to remember as being someone special. She couldn't do that now. Cecilia had sown the seeds of doubt and they would not go away.

Quickly, without giving herself time to think, she prised the brass fixings from the back of the frame. They were stiff, but though her fingernail broke, she persevered, slid the photo out, turned it over, and read the faded inscription.

To my darling Freddie... sorry for turning you down, but until we meet again, much love from your darling Gertrude Unwin. Look after your little girl. No matter her mother's origins, she didn't ask to be born.

June 1926

Nadine felt as though her blood had turned to ice. 'Your little girl' had to be her. The reference to her not asking to be born cut the deepest. She read the words again, each one cutting into her heart, stabbing at her mind. The words were unchanged; had she expected them to be different? In time, she might live with what Cecilia had said, but this... this meant her whole childhood had been a lie.

In her mind, she went back over all the birthdays she'd ever had. Leaving the photograph out of its frame, she brushed her hair numbly and dressed automatically, not really caring whether her clothes matched or not.

'You will eat with your father?' Myla asked her later when she was sitting out on the veranda, staring towards the double gates at the end of the drive. She asked her again. 'Will you eat now or later?'

'I'm not hungry.'

Her eyes remained fixed on the gate. The photograph lay face down in her lap, her palms flat on top of it.

At the sound of a car horn, the gate *wallah* came out of his little hut at the side of the gates, sprinting across the patch of dusty grass to swing both gates wide open.

The air was fresh with the scent of raindrops hanging on blossoms and the air was filled with monkeys chattering in the trees.

The last rays of sunset flashed on the chromium headlights of her father's car. Due to his height and his turban, the chauffeur sat hunched over the wheel, his shoulders tight against his ears.

She stepped in front of him.

'Father. I need to talk to you.'

Her father, a slimly built man with sharp eyes and quick movements, looked disgruntled at being confronted the moment he got out of his car.

'And what could possibly be so important that you have to waylay me before I'm even through my front door?'

She felt the heat of him as he passed.

She held the photograph with both hands behind her back. 'Father. I want to speak to you.'

'And I want to speak to you.' His voice was a flat monotone and her stomach curdled.

'Good,' she said, more resolutely than she felt.

Myla held the door open for them to enter.

'The school sent me a note.' He shook his head as he passed his hat, his briefcase, and his walking cane to the houseboy. 'This will not do!' He made a hissing sound through his teeth when he was angry; he was doing it now.

'The dancing or lighting Shanti's funeral pyre?'

His expression froze. She had caught him off guard.

She pressed on regardless, knowing he would get angry but for once in her life not caring if he did.

'I want to know about my mother.' She brought the disassembled photograph out from behind her back. 'Not this woman in the photograph. I want to know why you didn't tell me who she really was. I want to know who I am, father. I want you to confirm to me that Shanti was my mother.'

The red veins that had started to scar the tip of her father's nose intensified. Feathers well and truly ruffled, he glanced around him.

'Not here,' he said his hand landing on her shoulder. Gently but firmly he pushed her in the direction of his study. 'Not in front of the servants!'

His study was a shrine to masculinity and the unflinching belief that the British Empire would last for a thousand years.

The shelves lining the study groaned with the weight of books on Robert Clive, Cecil Rhodes, and the *Illustrated History of the British Empire and Dominions*. The gilded spines of *Source of the White Nile*, *Cape Town Revisited* and *The Life and Battles of Lord Horatio Nelson* gleamed like battle honours.

Normally he presided over this room from behind his desk. This evening he was unnerved which in turn made him restless. Knuckles jammed onto his hips, head bowed, he paced the room. She could see the bristles of whitish hair stiff and upright at the nape of his neck.

'This is simply not good enough, Nadine. Not good enough at all!'

Her anger intensified. He had totally ignored what she'd asked him, treating her as he'd always treated, like a child who should be kept at arm's length.

'You didn't answer my question.'

'I am greatly displeased.' He took the note from the school out of the inside pocket of his coat and threw it onto the desk.

'Who am I?'

He frowned. 'What sort of a damned question is that? The answer is obvious.'

'You're my father.'

He cleared his throat before answering. 'Yes.' She sensed his disquiet.

'Did you hear me just now? I asked you about my mother.'

Despite the dimness of the room, she saw beads of sweat glistening on his forehead. He waved his hand dismissively as though he were considering swatting a fly.

'She died when you were born.'

'This photograph is not my mother!'

'You've broken it.'

'No. I took it apart after I lit the fire beneath the woman who loved me as no other.'

'You have no respect for your mother,' he said, totally ignoring what she'd said as his face turned red.

'Oh yes I do. I have the greatest respect for my real mother. But this isn't her.' She pulled the photograph from the frame and waved it. 'Gertrude? 1926? Father, surely you know I was born in 1924. So if she didn't die when I was born, she must have left me. And if that wasn't the case either, then I must draw the conclusion that she was not my mother, and if that is so, then who was? I've read what Gertrude wrote, that despite my mother's origins, I did not ask to be born and that you should look after me. Shanti was my mother, wasn't she! Shanti was my mother and all this time you've been too ashamed to admit it.'

'Now look here, my girl...' His expression eddied between guilt and anger. Suddenly, the anger overcame him. 'I am your father! That's all that matters and you will obey me!' His arm shot forward, his finger level with her face.

Despite her determination to stand her ground, she took a step back and he immediately took the advantage.

'You *will* act like a young lady! You *will* respect your mother's memory.'

What little fear she felt melted away, replaced by a cold indifference to whatever he chose to do.

Her voice was low, as hushed as the evening breeze. Her face, her whole being was sombre.

'This is indeed a day for respecting my mother's memory, for on this day her ashes were scattered on the Ganges.' She placed her palms together in the manner of a Hindu and bowed over her steepled fingers. She left him there, knowing he was staring after her totally lost for words.

* * *

Twilight was sliding into darkness and still Roland Burton sat at his desk, staring at Gertrude's photograph. She'd hated India, refused to marry him, and gone back to 'the old country' as swiftly as she could acquire a place on the *S.S. Uganda*. She'd died in a car crash shortly after the photograph was taken, racing around with some titled chinless wonder from Berkshire. That was when he'd moved Nadine and her mother into the house. Obviously he wished to preserve the façade of being an upright British gentleman and he'd wished his daughter not be regarded as anything less than British. He'd told everyone that her mother, Gertrude, was dead. In fact her mother was very much alive at the time and serving as her *ayah*, her nurse.

Shanti had been the dancer, the *devadassi* he'd seen at a *maharajah's* party and immediately fell in love with.

Gertrude had let him down. That was all he could think of; Gertrude had let him down.

'Sweaty lechers and shrivelled up old prunes, darling. Not for me, I'm afraid. I don't want to shrivel up with them. God, no wonder there are so many half-castes about! Though with those soft grey eyes your daughter is pretty, I must admit, and hardly a shade darker than either of us. You'll have no problem passing her off as full-blooded British, though I must admit Anglos are beautiful, don't you think?'

He'd understood her feelings. She was true blue British through and through, from the right family, with the right amount of money and just enough education to get by.

'I can't blame you for being besotted with your little dancer. A young man, out here, with all this temptation.'

The memory of that last night when he'd tried to explain things was as vivid now after fifteen years as after fifteen weeks.

'You have to understand, Gertrude. I was out here alone. Shanti was my comfort woman. I cared nothing for her. She was just a little something to warm my bed.'

'And your daughter?'

To some extent, it was at Gertrude's prompting that he'd taken the child in and raised her the English way. He'd insisted that the English way was the right way for Nadine to be brought up and to do that, Shanti must relinquish all rights to the child. He in turn, passed himself off as a widower.

Perhaps out of love for him as much as for the child, Shanti had agreed. However, he had discovered she had not kept all her promises. He'd seen them together, dancing in the garden and had felt uneasy, perhaps a little guilty. Breaking them up was the best thing he could do for his daughter. If she was to succeed in life, she must be uncontaminated by her Indian roots and be brought up a British girl, just like Gertrude. The world was her oyster, as long as her pedigree was untainted by foreign blood.

Keep calm. No confrontations. That, he decided, would be for the best.

Right from the start he'd decided not to become emotionally involved with the child conceived on his Punjabi mistress. Throughout her short life, he had avoided being alone with his daughter, staying away from the house, staying at his club, a place of leather chairs and dark wooden walls where superior servants of the weakening Raj smoked amid silence and echoes of dead glories.

Apparently his lack of presence had largely gone unnoticed.

He had not wished to become close to her, and she had never sought to become close to him.

School days were coming to a close and Nadine was glad that they were. She'd never fitted in, viewed as slightly odd by fresh-faced girls who knew the far-off Mother Country far better than they did the one they lived in. Her dark hair and skin had set her apart. Only the odd contrast of her grey eyes had halted their insinuations of mixed blood, until Cecilia Renfrew had thrown comments around that she'd overheard from gossiping *memsahibs*. Some of the girls now went out of their way to avoid her, though not all.

Girls in brown uniforms had filed in and out The Benares Academy for Young Ladies for over forty years. Most were destined to be wives either in this country or back home. Only a very few intended furthering their education and contemplating a career in 'something useful', such as becoming a secretary or a little nursing, though nothing too strenuous.

Someone asked Nadine whether she was going to England to continue studying. 'Seeing as Cecilia may have scotched your chances on the marriage market.'

Nadine had bristled. 'No. I'm going to study India – and the rest of the world if I get the chance.'

'Oh! How odd,' said the person who had asked. 'Still, as long as you can afford it. Anyway, not everyone needs a man, do they?'

'Will you get a job?' someone else asked.

'As what?'

Jennifer, a softly spoken girl who was as near to being her best friend as anyone, shrugged her narrow shoulders.

'Nurse, secretary, teacher...'

Nadine shuddered. 'Certainly not. What will you do?'

'Marry an eligible man as quickly as possible. That's what my parents hope for too. Have you considered marrying? I mean, I know some of the others think you've got no chance because of your pedigree, but let's face it, you're jolly pretty. Actually, the prettiest girl in the school.'

Nadine glanced at the slight sixteen year old. She had hips like a boy and the curve of her breasts barely disturbed the front of her blouse.

'No. I won't marry.'

'I see. Of course now there's a war on you could do something in the military I suppose – once you're old enough, that is.'

'I don't think so.'

'So what will you do?' said the girl, peering from beneath a floppy brown fringe as she awaited an answer.

Nadine eyed the sandstone yellow of the school building, the locked gates that kept the girls in and the world – an India viewed as decadent but tempting – firmly shut out.

Remember it was here that made you respectable young ladies, truly representative of all the British Empire stands for.

The school's mantra, dogged and basically unthinking. Nadine grinned as a deliciously naughty thought crossed her mind.

'I think I shall be a dancer.'

Jennifer gasped and clapped a hand across her mouth. 'You wouldn't!'

'Why not?'

Nadine spoke deliberately loudly. 'I'm going to be a dancer in the Hindu fashion. I'm going to twirl and twitch my hands and arms around all those exquisite temples – you know the ones I mean – those decorated with intertwining, naked bodies.' Jennifer's shocked expression fuelled Nadine's urge to shock and unsettle. She raised her voice determined everyone would hear.

'You know what they're doing of course, don't you? They're having sex in every position possible. Some of the female carvings are sucking on the men's...'

Nadine's descriptions of the lewd statutory spread from girl to giggling girl.

'*Miss Burton.*'

Judging by her flame-coloured expression, Miss Clark looked about to explode.

Nadine didn't care. Satchel tucked beneath her arm, she sauntered off, her hat swinging on a ribbon around her neck.

She half turned, smiled and waved back to those gathered at the school gates. 'Goodbye Miss Clark. I'm off to dance seductively in a Hindu temple.'

Dumbstruck, and perhaps too embarrassed to do anything more, Miss Clark only thundered, 'Girl! You'll get sunstroke!'

Nadine turned round and poked out her tongue. 'I don't bloody care!'

'*Miss* Burton!'

'*Miss* Clark!'

She snatched at the slides and ribbons that kept her hair in tightly braided plaits. Let loose, it fell like a black cloud around her bare arms.

'I'm going to get brown, even browner than I am now,' she shouted. 'And I'm going to flaunt my body and become a *nautch* dancer, Miss Clark. A *devadassi*. Just like my mother.'

Flinging her hat into the air gave her an immense sense of freedom; so did slinging her satchel to the ground and seeing its contents spill all over the road.

Miss Clark did not follow her. Neither did she shout in that bullhorn voice of hers. Disapproval creased her craggy face, but she looked smaller, less intimidating than she had ever been.

3

The day was fine, the heavy scent of rosebushes brought out from a garden in Surrey mixing with the tang of spices and the metallic weight of scorched air.

Wearing a tight bodice and a flame-coloured sari, Nadine kept close to the house, picking her way over the grass verge. She knew she would not be welcomed in the house dressed as she was, which was precisely why she was dressed this way. She had no wish to participate in morning coffees, afternoon teas, or evening soirees. Isolation gave her chance to think.

At this time of day, the path dissecting the lawn at the side of the house was scorched by sunlight. A veranda shaded the grass closer to the house. Although Akim, her father's gardener and man of all trades, disapproved, she walked on the grass in the deep, dark shade.

A car she recognised was parked at the front of the house; her father had visitors, and Mr and Mrs Grantley-James had a son. His name was Vincent. He was thickset, wore glasses, and was terribly self-opinionated for a young man of nineteen. His chin jutted forward like a square mug.

Sometimes she talked to him, though usually at a safe distance. Vincent had wandering hands and lips like fat, wet oysters.

On his last visit, he'd caught her unawares. She'd been dancing in the shade of the pergola, humming to herself as she carried out the well-practised movements Shanti had taught her.

'My,' he'd said, his lips making a disgusting smacking sound as he brought them together. 'You're absolutely ripe for it!'

He'd lunged at her, slipping one hand as far up her skirt as possible, his other groping her breast.

He'd found out just how ripe she was when she brought her knee up into his groin.

'Ow!'

Unfortunately he recovered quickly.

'You could have damaged me for life, you know. I might never have children. Look!' In a trice he'd undone his flies and flashed his member, pointing to the tip of it.

'And the world will probably be a better place for all that,' Nadine had snapped, determined not to blush. 'Now put it away. I'm not going to examine it any more closely. It's ugly. Like a tiny toadstool!'

She turned smartly away, grinning from ear to ear. Vincent shouted after her.

'You bitch. You bloody bitch!'

He was devastated. She smiled to herself. The day was suddenly brighter. She'd hurt Vincent's pride plus his manhood and thoroughly enjoyed doing so. However, no doubt he'd have his revenge.

She was right. He'd complained about her. He'd actually had the nerve to complain about her!

Her father ordered her to report to his study.

'Vincent said you attacked him in a very unladylike manner. I'm neglecting my guests because of you.'

She eyed her father disdainfully, noting the flesh of his face hung sparingly on his cheekbones. It gave him a jaded look, as though nothing much surprised him and life was sometimes tedious. At one time she'd respected him, never loved him. He'd been too distant for that. Since Shanti's death, she felt only a cold hollow contempt.

'I was merely protecting myself against his unwanted attention.'

'I don't think you should play so hard to get. He's a good catch and quite frankly, the sooner you're married off the better.'

'Vincent Grantley-James disgusts me.'

'He's a gentleman.'

'He was not being very gentlemanly at the time. He got his privates out in front of me. I found it quite disgusting.'

'Nadine!' His mouth dropped open but he quickly collected himself. 'Young women should not speak in that manner. Your mother...' He stopped himself. The truth flushed his face.

Nadine's eyes glittered. 'My mother...?'

Recalling that the truth was out, he changed tack immediately.

'All the same... under the circumstances, I think you should not condemn him out of hand.'

'Well I do.'

'He said you led him on.'

'I...? I would sooner swim in a cesspit!'

Speechless with anger, she turned her back.

'Nadine!'

The house shook when she slammed the door behind her.

Her father did not seek her out or have anything to do with her for the rest of the day. Perhaps he thought she would seek to make amends in her own good time, perhaps bump into Vincent again. He certainly had him visiting enough just lately.

It was late afternoon when she saw him heading around the back of the house. She guessed he'd gone to relieve himself in the old privy where wire was still secured over the drains and in the seat of the bowl to stop snakes coming up.

With revenge in mind, she waited what she judged to be a reasonable passage of time before following him.

She slid behind a rose covered trellis, the flowers still dripping moisture from the second soaking they'd had that day – not from natural rain of course, but by virtue of Akim, their dark-brown gardener who talked to the plants as he went about his work. Rarely acknowledging human contact, Akim tended the garden to his own timetable regardless of what her father ordered him to do.

Spying a discarded snakeskin in the shade at the side of the house, an amusing thought occurred to her.

The snakeskin was quite large; pity the poor snake she thought, how tight his old suit must have felt. The head was almost intact; no eyes or noticeable nose of course, and no flickering tongue. She formed a fork shape from dried grass. This she inserted into a small hole where the snake's top lip used to be. Gleefully imagining Vincent's surprise, she crept towards the privy.

As she neared it, she heard groaning and put it down to Vincent not having the benefit of a daily dose of laxative.

Just as she was about to thrust the crisp monster up into the drain, causing Vincent to spring from his seat, a rustle in the bushes to her left drew her attention.

A tiger?

She turned her head very, very slowly – barely an inch at a time.

Velvet brown eyes blinked back at her, and she blinked in

response. A slim girl slipped out from behind the bush and into view.

The girl was around her own age. Normally trades people and peddlers would stay outside the gate. The only way she could have entered the garden was through the hole in the wall.

This girl reminded Nadine of a stray mongoose, long and lean.

She wore heavy earrings, a stud, and an ornament dangling from her nose.

Nadine addressed her in Urdu. 'Who are you? Don't you know you're trespassing?'

She tried to sound superior – just like her father.

The trembling of the privy walls behind her distracted her attention. Vincent was groaning as though his relief was close at hand and the privy was rocking enough to send it crashing from its foundations.

The girl responded. She must have been about twelve years old.

'I am waiting for my sister.'

'Is she in there?' Keeping her voice low, Nadine gestured at the rotting wood of the privy.

The girl opened her mouth to answer but was interrupted by Vincent's voice.

'Who's out there? Go away whoever you are or it will be the worse for you, mark my words!'

He spoke in English, but faltering, spewed out along with a quick expelling of breath.

Nadine ignored him and addressed the girl again.

'What is your sister doing in there with Vincent? Surely she is not helping him pass a stool?'

The girl shook her head. 'Oh, most certainly, no!'

'No. I didn't think so.' Nadine grimaced as she imagined Vincent and the girl's sister doing something similar to Hindu temple carvings she'd seen – though not too vigorously. Not in that space.

Eyeing the flimsy structure, she said, 'Their vigour is such that this structure is likely to fall to pieces.' Nadine frowned as a very important thought occurred to her. 'Why is your sister doing this? This *sahib* is not the most handsome of men.'

The girl shrugged. 'He saw her dance. He wanted her and paid to have her. That is all.'

She said it as though it were the most natural business transaction in the world. She had the knowing look of a small adult, a worldly woman in a young girl's body. She was wearing thin silky garments of pale green edged with gold and pink. Her feet were hennaed. Her eyes were outlined in thick lines of black kohl.

'My name is Nadine.'

'Ah! Nadine. Yes. My name is Zakia.'

She bowed greetings in the acknowledged way. Nadine returned her greetings.

'You are dancers, Zakia?'

'That indeed is our caste, our lot in life decreed by the gods. My sister, Sureya and I are both *nautch* dancers and are very sought after, my sister more than I as you can see.'

Inspired by the entranced look on Nadine's face, Zakia warmed to her subject. 'We entertain the most important men in the city – even *maharajahs* – even *sahibs* though my sister says they would never admit it. We're banned you see. Taboo.'

'She is "entertaining"' Vincent Sahib?'

Zakia jerked her chin in that knowing way and held her head to one side. 'Vincent Sahib always asks for her – even if it is only to dance. But today he wishes relief. My sister does not sell her body, only her hand.'

Detecting ignorance obviously gave pleasure to the jangling, dancing girl. She laughed and explained further.

'You know?'

She made a backwards and forwards action with her clenched fist. 'He wishes her to pull on his snake until it spits milk, you know,' she added, noticing Nadine's confusion. 'The snake that crouches here.' She made a pouch with her hands and held it against her groin.

Nadine recalled the sight of Vincent's penis and laughed.

'This size,' she said, cupping her hands to make a much smaller pouch.

Understanding immediately, Zakia laughed too.

Nadine recalled that last day at school when she'd told Jennifer that she intended becoming a dancer, dancing the steps taught to her by her mother, her *ayah*, her darling Shanti.

One thought tumbled upon another and the rudiments of a plan formed in her mind, a plan that must be kept secret.

She was not aware that her mouth was hanging open until a particularly persistent insect perched on her bottom lip. She waved it away. Covetously, she scrutinised Zakia's pendulous earrings and the smudge of dust on one cheek.

'Did you crawl through the hole?'

The girl grinned, her teeth startlingly white against her gleaming brown skin. 'Yes. I wriggled through like a great python. Shall I show you how?'

She nodded. 'Yes.'

The girl proceeded to demonstrate, her sinuous body writhing in the manner of a cobra rising to the plaintive notes of a flute. The girl's hands made the shape of the flamingo's neck, the flying wings of the wild swan, the flapping of the limbs of a turtle.

Nadine's eyes misted over. If she narrowed them she could almost believe that Shanti was alive, whirling and twirling again, just as she used to, Nadine joining in. As dusk fell, unseen by her father, the two of them would dance until it was too dark to continue.

Nadine sighed. How well she remembered!

The right foot came to land in front of the left, knees bent, hands brought together and clasped above the head.

The dance was over.

Nadine turned and hammered on the side of the privy. Vincent shouted.

'Didn't you hear me? Go away. Go… a…'

The rest of his words were smothered in a groan of sheer ecstasy.

Nadine looked down at the discarded snakeskin then up to the croquet lawn, the hoops white and rigid in the fading sun. The flower-covered pergola where Shanti had first taught her how to dance stood at its narrowest point.

'Follow me,' she said to Zakia. 'We will dance.'

Nadine strode across the grass, reassured by the tinkling of ankle bells and jangling jewellery that Zakia was following on behind.

The pounded earth of the pergola was warm beneath their feet.

'Take off your shoes. You cannot dance like that,' said Zakia, pointing a hennaed, pink tipped finger at Nadine's feet.

Nadine did not contradict her and tell her just how well she knew these dances.

As she pointed, she twisted from the waist thrusting her abdomen to her right, her chest to the left. Her feet, Nadine noticed, did the same, one set of toes pointing right, one left and the heels tight together but at an uneven angle.

Taking off her shoes then her stockings, she pretended that she needed to practice at achieving the same position. Pretending wasn't easy when you knew a dance so well. In order to maintain the illusion, she toppled slightly.

'Look!' Zakia's voice was sharp staccato. She pointed at a row of bushes. 'There is your audience. They are rich handsome princes wearing diamonds and gleaming sapphires. They own many palaces, many elephants and even motorcars of many different colours. If you are lucky you might become a great favourite. If so he will give you many presents and perhaps take you with him each time he progresses from one palace to another. You will see many sights.'

The way her new friend spoke and the promise of seeing a wider world was far more attractive than jewels or a handsome face. With a liberal dose of imagination, the bushes became beings, handsome faces decked in colourful gems and finery.

'That is good,' cried Zakia, as Nadine executed a perfect imitation, thrusting the halves of her body in opposing directions, placing her feet and curling her toes, adding sensuality by positioning her hands in front of her face – just as Shanti had taught her.

'It would be better with music,' she remarked.

'You are a fussy woman!' Zakia frowned as she said it, but Nadine could tell it was only in fun. The frown disappeared, her smile widened, and she began to sing a wordless song, the sound imitating the insistent twang of a sitar.

Like mirror images, they danced, heads shifting from side to side, hands layered beneath chin, their bodies twirling and curving as though, like the cobra, they were mesmerised by music.

'Zakia!'

A slim figure clad in a full skirt of the richest red matched with a shiny green bodice called from the path leading towards the bougainvillea.

Zakia's dark eyes glittered with pride. 'That is my beautiful sister,' she said. 'Every man wants her. Her body is like elephant grass; it bends with the wind. I too am going to dance as well as her.'

She turned to go.

Nadine's heart leapt in panic. 'Do you have to go? Right now? When will I see you again?'

It could have been urgency or sincerity, but whatever it was, Zakia seemed to recognise the well of emotion in Nadine's voice.

'You are right. We must meet again. We dance so well and look so alike – just like sisters. You are only a little paler.'

'Zakia!' Her sister called more urgently.

Zakia's bright face shone. 'We dance again? Will you be able to leave your duties in the house? Will the *memsahib* scold you?'

She let Zakia believe she was only a servant. 'I can get away.'

Nadine surged with excitement. 'Tomorrow?'

'Tomorrow.'

Nadine watched breathlessly as the girls bundled their skirts around their waists and ducked beneath the bushes.

Despite the languorous heat of late afternoon, she stood there long after they'd gone, staring at the hedge.

4

Dancing in the pergola became a habit, their exploits undetected. The pergola was hidden behind a rhododendron with a trunk the size of an oak tree, its basic form obliterated by a variety of climbing plants. No one could see them from the house and no one cared where the Sahib's daughter might be. They had too many duties to do. The gardener was the only man they needed to fear, but he could be heard approaching, talking to the flowers or grumbling at the holes left by vermin and mongoose. Her father seemed to prefer that she kept out of his way. She was no longer required to attend the school for young ladies. Whatever plans her father had for her he was keeping to himself.

On the few occasions she did bump into him, he eyed her thoughtfully but said nothing. Until such time as he spelled out what her future would be, she spent her time dancing.

Zakia's sister never came after that first day when the Grantley-James's had been visiting. Nadine asked Zakia the reason why.

'She has to work.'

'What does she do?'

'Please men,' Zakia said matter of factly.

'And they pay her well?'

Zakia made a kind of scooping motion with her chin – yes with emphasis. 'My sister knows how to make a man pant for her,' Zakia explained. 'The missionaries did not like the *nautch* dancers – oh no they did not. Some scorn us where once they desired us. My sister said so. It is hard to make a living dancing now. That is why she does the other thing. But only sells her hand,' she said, wiggling her fingers.

'Does she like it?' Nadine asked as they sat in the shade drinking lime juice she'd taken from the kitchen. 'You know. Using her hand to make a man's snake spit milk.'

Zakia gulped back most of the jug. 'Unless she particularly likes the man. It is a very worthwhile job. Better than sweeping the street or living in a house with a baked mud floor with a husband who grumbles about his lot in life.'

'She has no husband?'

'Of course not. She is married to a tree.'

Nadine burst into laughter. 'Mr and Mrs Tree!'

Her laughter faded when she saw by Zakia's expression that she was quite serious. 'In the old days, *nautch* girls danced at the temple and were married to trees, but their favours were available to anyone who would resume the role of the god. It is not so common now, but still acceptable. Coupling with a woman married to a tree is like fornicating with a god. She is holy because the god is holy.'

Nadine had learned something of Hinduism from Shanti but couldn't remember any of this. It occurred to her that Zakia wasn't strictly accurate or perhaps was teasing her.

Afternoons with her new friend passed pleasantly. Her dancing improved enormously; submerged memories seeming to break out from a deep well within and run like fluid through her body.

She also learned that Sureya had three children and Zakia had one. They had no husbands. The news had shocked her. They were so young.

'You don't look old enough,' she'd said to Zakia. In her estimation, she couldn't be more than fourteen years old.

Zakia shrugged. 'I am old enough.'

Nadine wondered about the woman she now regarded as her mother. How old had Shanti been when she'd given birth, and how far away had she been from living a life like theirs?

The realisation that her father had at least claimed his daughter did nothing to mend the bridge between them. Zakia had awakened some sleeping spirit deep within. She'd even stopped smoking and drinking her father's Scotch. Dancing had become everything, like a tribute to her mother.

One day, Zakia brought her a dancer's outfit.

'Put it on.'

Nadine started to put it on over her underwear.

'Not with your drawers still on,' said Zakia looking bemused that Nadine could even consider it. 'Take this off.' She tugged at the button that fastened Nadine's drawers. 'And this,' she said, poking at one cup of her salmon-pink bra.

Once her British cotton underwear was removed and replaced with ankle length, silk pantaloons, Nadine slipped the bodice over her head and the silk skirt up over her hips. Her body shivered deliciously in response to the feel of cool silk against her skin. Her eyes shone as Zakia tied ribbons of tinkling bells around each ankle.

'And you need to paint your feet and your hands. Even your toe nails.'

'I will.'

'Now your ears and your nose.'

'My ears are already pierced – well they were – years ago of course.'

Of course. Shanti had taken her to have them done. Her father hadn't approved, but she'd kept them open with small gold hoops and only at night in bed, her last tribute to her beloved nurse.

'But not my nose,' she added, a knot of apprehension tightening her stomach.

Zakia drew in her chin. 'It is customary.'

Nadine groaned.

Smiling Zakia produced what looked like a large hatpin.

'Good grief!'

Zakia grinned. 'Do not worry. The point is very fine.'

Although she gritted her teeth, she almost screamed as Zakia pierced her right nostril and fixed a pendant from her left.

A trickle of blood flowed into her mouth. She used her knickers to wipe it off.

The hem of the purple skirt Zakia had brought her was encrusted with gold filigree thread and turquoise sequins. Bracelets, necklaces, and bangles were added. Her hair was gathered and plaited with gold thread.

Hands perched on hips Zakia stepped back to survey her work. 'You look splendid.'

Nadine drew in her breath. 'My ears hurt a little. My nose hurts a lot.'

Zakia threw up her hands in the manner of a woman five times her years. 'Do you wish to be a dancer or a street sweeper?'

'Of course not.' Nadine expressed a desire to see herself in a mirror.

Zakia shrugged. 'Trust me. You look like a gaudy peacock.'

Nadine protested. 'But I want to see for myself whether I look like a gaudy peacock or a moth-eaten old hen!'

The afternoon heat had emptied the garden of all sensible life forms including the servants. Seeing that the coast was clear, the two girls crept around to the back of the house, opened the shutters, and climbed into her bedroom.

A full-length mirror stood in one corner. Even before she'd fully straightened from climbing through the window, Nadine caught sight of herself and sucked in her breath.

Zakia peered out from behind her.

'See,' she hissed. 'You look like a much-loved and respected dancer, not servant to a *memsahib*.'

Her eyes grew round. She was no longer Nadine Burton, the girl who had seemed destined to do nothing more spectacular than becoming the wife of a merchant, an army officer, or government official. From glossy hair to painted toes, she was now a dancing girl.

'I want to dance,' she said simply.

'Keep your mouth open,' ordered Zakia. Using just the tip of her finger, she spread cochineal along Nadine's open lips.

'I want people to see me dance,' Nadine said once the task was complete. 'I want everyone to see what I look like.'

Her eyes shone with excitement.

'Men,' exclaimed Zakia. 'You want men to see you dance. You want to inflame them. You want them to dream of *houris* when they lie beside their wife. And when they open her fat thighs and she lies there like a basking elephant, they will think of you and pretend they are coupling with a goddess.'

Nadine laughed. Surely they were teasing. 'Is that what I will do?'

Zakia was adamant. 'Of course you will. Imagine a handsome man running his fingers over your body.' Nadine tingled as Zakia did exactly that, leaving goose pimples in the wake of her fingertips. 'I will prove this to you. You will dance with us tonight.'

Nadine could barely drag her gaze from her exotic reflection.

The scenes Zakia had described flicked through her mind. 'Tonight? You are dancing tonight?'

Zakia's jet black eyes shone gleefully. 'If you can get out just after sunset, you must meet us at the house of Haramuk the silk merchant. He has business guests. There were only two of us entertaining him and his guests, but now there will be three. The musicians are arranged.'

Nadine felt a fluttering in her chest. 'Dare I?'

'You will dare. I can see it in your eyes.'

'I will dare,' Nadine whispered. 'Yes. I will dare.'

* * *

The first time she danced in public with her new friends was the most difficult. Two or three times more made her more confident.

The steps first taught her by Shanti, her *ayah*, the nurse who was really her mother, became more skilful, more touched by the erotic awakening of a blossoming girl. Her body was lithe and there was no movement, no exaggerated stance her slim limbs and supple torso could not master. She was the enchantress, the diametric positioning of her body, the jingling of bells, combining to bewitch the soul of those who watched.

Reluctantly, even Sureya who considered herself superior to both Nadine and her younger sister grudgingly admitted she was a natural dancer.

Crawling out through the hole beneath the wall she met the sisters in the usual place: an alley not far from the great mosque of Aurangzeb cloaked in the shadow of its leaning minaret.

'You were fated to be a dancer,' said a breathless Zakia, flicking water over her face from a battered enamel bowl. 'Better than being a servant to the *memsahibs*.'

'I feel I am living.' Nadine cupped her hands, dipped them into the bowl and hid her face in the scooped water. Dark haired and her skin the colour of creamed coffee, it was easy to pass herself off as Indian.

'Your mother taught you well,' praise indeed from Sureya who regarded herself as the best of the crop.

No one questioned her absences. The world had become an exciting place.

The fates that Zakia most assuredly believed in were bound to intervene. The inevitable was bound to happen – and did.

It was a night of a thousand stars – or at least that was the way it seemed as she clambered into the gharry beside the two sisters. Sequins spangled like stars all over their costumes as though they had reached up and dragged down portions of sky.

Tonight was a most special night; they were to perform in the presence of the local *gaekor*, an official prince not dissimilar in rank to a British baron.

The wheels made a rushing sound over the dusty road, the horse's hooves muffled by the same dust. A full moon turned a black sky to one shade lighter than indigo.

'The *gaekor's* residence,' whispered Zakia.

Nadine eyed the castellated battlements towering from rose-red walls, like teeth biting chunks from the spangled sky.

Gharries, rickshaws, and many motorcars pulled into the arched gateway, dispensed guests, and withdrew, the dust from the wheels clouding the evening air. Light from a hundred windows threw arches, squares and oblongs of amber over chauffeured cars and spindle-legged Chinese pulling decorated rickshaws.

A group of men with slicked-back hair and pink complexions, bowties tight around flaccid throats, alighted from a chauffeur-driven car. They were speaking loudly and sounded drunk.

'*Sahibs*,' said Sureya, a wary look stiffening her sensuous features.

It was not the first time Zakia's sister had betrayed a wariness of their British rulers.

'*Nautch* girls used to sell their bodies in the precincts of sacred temples and shrines. The fees charged went to temple funds. And then the British stopped it. But never mind. We still dance. We still entertain. Now. Let me do your eyes. You have rubbed one. It looks like a bruise.'

Nadine found herself sympathising with her dancing sister. She'd heard people – white people say – that the natives were sensual and given over to indulging in much debauchment. She'd danced at enough events to know that the British and other Europeans were the most avid audience.

Sitting on a stone close to the back door of the wealthy man's kitchen, she stared up at the sky whilst Zakia outlined her eyes.

Thinking of British passions brought Vincent and the outdoor privy to mind. She smiled.

'Why do you smile?' asked Zakia.

'I was thinking of Sureya and her hand.'

'We have to live. We have to survive.'

A question came to Nadine's mind. Would I sell my body in order to survive?

The seeds that would lead her to a different part of the world and the answer to that question were sown that night.

The *sahibs* were drunk. Sweaty, laughing men tried to grab her ankles as she made her way to the dance floor. The musicians were already in place. The smell of all things Indian – food, spices, and tangy perfumes – mixed with the pomades, tobacco, and heavy linens of western men. No wives were present. This was a night for men only.

The Nadine of the day and the last sixteen years was supplanted by a lithesome figure who lost herself in the sound of the bells tinkling around her ankles, the plaintive twang of the sitar and the exhilaration of pleasing an awestruck audience.

She was the temple dancer declaring love for Vishnu, Siva, and the whole pantheon of Hindu gods; she was the wife of the tree and moved like one, her arms moving as branches in the wind, her face cupped on the backs of her hands, presenting her emotion and her love.

The faces of those watching dotted the palatial room of arched windows, hanging silks and whirring fans. They were without feature, except for the eyes, more details becoming obvious when she halted, contorted her body, passed her hands over her face and became the lovesick princess peering through the shutters at her unfaithful lover.

This part of the dance called for a pause when except for her eyes, she stood as though she'd been chipped from marble and not real at all. In that small segment of time she studied the faces of those in the audience, the fantasies of their minds shining in their eyes.

She saw the glossy faces of minor princes, the open-mouthed admiration of the British *sahibs*. And then she saw the white hair, the flaccid features. Her father was in the audience.

Her heart thudded. Her blood raced.

The dance called for her to hang her head, her eyes looking up from behind a curtain of semi-precious stones hanging on her forehead.

She would not flee. Let him see if he must. See what I can do. See for sure who my mother was! What I surely am.

Whirling more vigorously into the dance, and preoccupied with what *might* happen, she failed to see what was *about* to happen.

The man who reached for her wore a white suit and had a sweaty red face. The smell of whisky drifted into her nostrils.

'Show us your pretty titties, my dusty little beauty.'

Before she could whirl away, his fingers hooked over the neckline of her bodice, ripping it in half.

'There,' he shouted, his demand accomplished. 'Just look at these pretty little dumplings!'

An avalanche of sound tumbled around her, claps, yells, and shouts that he should remove her skirt.

His words were slurred but loud. She tried to tear herself free. Zakia and Sureya tried to help and called for assistance.

Sureya was shouting. 'Get him off her.'

A turbaned retainer with strong arms and a square jaw line reached out. Just as his hands were about to grip the man's shoulders, he hesitated.

Sureya screamed at him. 'Well, go on!'

He shook his head, fear in his eyes. 'I cannot. He is a very important man. I do not want any trouble.'

It wasn't the first time she'd danced before *sahibs*, but never as many as this. Even so, she could have coped with that. She could even have coped with the fact that he'd exposed her breasts. What she could not face was the look in her father's eyes. She heard his voice shouting at the man who held her.

'Martin! Let her go!'

At his word, the nervous servant and others like him dragged the white suited man off her.

Swiftly tying the ragged ends of her bodice between her breasts, she paused long enough to meet her father's gaze.

Zakia's sister Sureya shook her out of her terrified daze. 'Come. We will ask for our money and leave early.'

They ran, Nadine and Zakia waiting in an anteroom until Sureya came back, the coins jangling in the silk purse she wore at her waist.

Their anklets jangled as they rushed headlong towards the exit.

'Not that way! Not for such as you,' a servant shouted.

He was old, tall and had rounded shoulders, a slight hump immediately below the nape of his neck making him look like a tortoise leaning out of his shell.

'Out the back way,' he shouted waving his arms. 'Out, out, out!'

He ushered them to a narrow passage sloping downwards between lumpy walls down stone steps past the kitchens and storerooms. The smell of sweat and smoke from roasting mutton permeated the unventilated corridor.

Nadine felt a tickle at the back of her throat and began to cough in response to the smoke. By the time they'd gained the warm air of a moon drenched night, they were all gasping for breath.

Zakia shoved something beneath Nadine's nose that revived her instantly.

She clasped her throat with both hands, her eyes watering.

'What is that?'

Zakia grinned. 'Smelling salts.' She jerked her chin at her sister. 'Mr Vincent gave them as a present along with a few rupees for my sister's favours.'

The sound of men laughing drifted on the air ahead of them.

'They sound drunk,' said Sureya as the three girls made their way across the dark yard to the back gate that would lead them into the maze of alleys bounded by houses – and even palaces – hidden behind rich facades.

'Everyone is drunk,' said Nadine.

The smell of freshly butchered meat and the buzz of flies led to the rear gate. They were passing close to where animals were killed by those of lower caste – an area and people separated from the house.

The moon threw their shadows like black trees towards the gate. Sentries in red turbans stood to attention either side. Normally at this late hour they would be lounging, leaning against the wall in a fitful doze. Their alertness meant their British officers were present.

There was an art to keeping their heads down at the same time as keeping a look out, and Nadine was as flexible as her friends. She saw much whilst seeming to notice little.

Behind the sentries a square of light fell out from the guardhouse.

The door to the squat block building opened at the same time as the gate. A figure appeared silhouetted against the inner glow. Although they could not see his features, judging by the way he paused he could certainly see them.

A Scottish accent bawled out into the night. 'Hey fellas! Come and see what I've found.'

'Quickly,' murmured Sureya to her sister and Nadine.

Nadine drew her veil over her head, hiding her face, and quickened her footsteps, Zakia close behind her and Sureya in the rear.

Too late, thought Nadine, her heart beating a thundering tattoo.

A number of broad shouldered, barrel-chested men stepped out into the compound, their shadows straggly across the ground.

'Come on girls. Dance for us.

'Do a shimmy,' shouted another voice.

Nadine responded in heavily accented English. 'We do not understand.'

The girls hurried through the gate, sticking together like glue, elbow to elbow.

The gate closed behind them with a satisfying clunk, but their relief was short lived. The heavy thud of boots and the raw vulgarity of drunken men echoed between the high walls bordering the alley.

Although impeded by the weight of their skirts, they broke into a jog.

The boots tramping the night road also broke into a jog. The men were laughing, revelling in the chase.

'Come on girls. Dance for us.'

Nadine glanced over her shoulder. She counted four, though one was trailing behind, intermittently resting his hands on his sagging knees.

One of their pursuers also saw him. He shouted to his colleagues. 'Gordon's had enough. It's three all now lads. One for each of us.'

The girls quickened their pace, their chests tight with exertion. As they ran, they looked for some way out of the maze of alleys.

'This way,' gasped Nadine.

They ran to where a handsome dome of white marble shone like silver in the moonlight above the rooftops.

Nadine recognised it as being part of a Hindu shrine some way behind the Rajah Potia temple. Beyond that was the sacred River Ganges and far meaner alleys than the one they were running through. Once they'd reached these they would be safe – if they hurried.

Their pursuers thundered after them until they ran into a blind alley where rats scampered through the pungent foliage and snakes slithered into gaps in the wall.

Nadine was jerked off her feet as strong arms wrapped around her. She screamed and scratched at the man's bare arms.

He laughed. 'Oh, I do like a fighter!'

His laughing lips turned into a straight line as he threw her against the wall. 'Let's get to your thatch, my little wog girl,' he said through gritted teeth. His breath stunk.

Out of the corner of her eye she glimpsed Zakia running away.

'Damn!' one of the men shouted. 'Now we've only got two left.'

'Hold that bitch. We'll have this one first. Bring her over so that she can see what she's in for.'

The other two men were holding Sureya down. Her breasts were exposed and her skirt bundled around her waist. She was struggling and swearing in Urdu.

One of the men was holding Sureya's arms, the other her legs. At the same time he was unbuttoning his trousers, sliding them down until the crease of his buttocks shone like a haunch of hairless pork.

Sureya managed to bite him.

Suddenly he slapped her.

'Bite me would you.'

He slapped her again.

Whether it was too much drink, breathlessness, or the fact that he was mesmerised by what the others were doing, the man holding Nadine slackened his grip.

A minute ago, she could see the sweep of her captor's shoulder out of the corner of her eye. Now she couldn't. She flexed her muscles without moving her arms. She glanced towards the dark alleys that led to the river. Her path to escape.

She kicked backwards. Her heel connected with the softness between his legs and he howled as he crumpled to his knees.

Nadine ran. She didn't care that her breasts were bare and bouncing like tennis balls. She was scared but what about Sureya?

She stopped running and turned back. The soldiers looked surprised to see her, were about to grab her, but stopped when adopting the plumiest of voices, she said, 'Tomorrow I will report this to your commanding officer. I'm British and will not allow this to go unpunished. So let her go now, or you will face the consequences!'

Their jaws dropped and their grips lessened. Sureya took advantage and fled the scene.

Surprised and disappointed that Sureya had left her alone, Nadine stopped only long enough to tie her ragged bodice. Never would she forget this night; never would she forget how ugly men could get, how they could treat defenceless women so shamefully.

She ran until she was on the other side of the Rajah Potia Temple, but still a long way from home.

Gharries and rickshaws were lined up outside the shrine. Some of them never went home: The smell of fresh dung and homelessness hung listlessly in the drowsy air.

She roused a sleeping *gharry* driver, gave him her address, and told him to hurry.

He struggled to his feet, clenched fists rubbing the sleep from his eyes. As he stirred to a half-hearted wakefulness, he looked her up and down, saw her nipples peering from among tattered rags and grinned.

He pointed. 'Is that how you are paying me?'

She held her head haughtily and reverting to English, for the second time that evening adopted a cut glass accent.

'What are you grinning at? Hurry along there. Don't keep me waiting or it will be the worse for you!'

The grin vanished. Nobody grinned at the *memsahibs*. She didn't look like one, but... that tone!

He took the few rupees she gave him and roused his skinny nag with a flick of a whip.

The journey seemed to take twice as long as it should, the lean flanks of the thin horse rolling beneath the flea-bitten skin.

The tops of nearby trees swayed in the night breeze. Something scurried across the road in front of them, probably a rat or a mongoose. Someone somewhere was melting ghee over too high a heat, the sickly smell turning to equally sickly smoke.

Life was distracting, but not for Nadine. With every yard her nervousness mounted. What would her father say? Would he have got home before her?

When she got home she avoided the main gates, instead diving into the side alley.

Scrambling through the hole in the wall, scrabbling beneath the hedge, she caught her skirt on stray branches and the stony ground scratched her breasts.

By the time she'd climbed back through her bedroom window she was totally exhausted.

Quickly and quietly, she stripped away the gaudy clothes and pushed them back into their hiding place in a travelling trunk. After that, she poured water from pitcher to bowl, wetted a flannel and rubbed away the makeup and sweat until she felt refreshed and smelled of violets. Finally she crept into bed stark naked, glad of the coolness of fresh sheets against her skin.

Usually after dancing, her dreams were a whirling mist of colour, clanging jewellery, and the smell of strong spices. Tonight there was only a nightmare vision of the drunken British soldiers, a nightmare she knew would stay with her for a very long time. She also knew that she could never go dancing again, not now her father had seen her.

A draught, a sudden change in the atmosphere, the stillness of an empty room filling with presence disturbed her only slightly, but as is the way of instinctive people, even in her subconscious she knew someone was there.

The cool air caressed her body. The bedclothes seeming lighter than the finest Punjabi muslin – so light it seemed they did not exist at all. She realised she'd kicked them off.

Her eyes flickered open. What time was it?

She eased herself up onto her elbow, her sleepy eyes adjusting to the dim light.

The familiar sight of washstand, mirror, wardrobe, dressing table emerged into solid shapes, but they were not the only shape, the only solid figure.

Eyes blazing with anger, her father stood over her.

Suddenly aware that he had never seen her naked, she reached for the tangled bedclothes at the foot of the bed.

'Dancing for men! Just like your mother.'

He hissed the words just as her fingers touched the tangled sheet.

As she raised herself on one elbow, her hair cascaded over her shoulder, soft against her cheek.

'Disappointed, father? In me, my mother, or are you disappointed in your own weakness, the fact that you fell under the spell of a native woman!'

In the dim light she saw the shape of his jaw altering as he clenched and unclenched his teeth.

She heard a whistling sound as something long and fine sliced through the air before stinging her unprotected body. It hurt. It stung, but she gritted her teeth.

'Cry!' he shouted. 'Go on! Cry!'

Perhaps she might have if he hadn't asked. Sheer stubbornness and her determined loyalty to her mother's memory made her keep her mouth tightly shut.

Her flesh stung at the very first stroke. It hurt like hell. She would not give him the satisfaction of knowing how much it hurt, how much her life hurt, and how wretched she felt.

Again and again the riding crop left stinging stripes across her bare body. Beside herself with pain, she finally tried to flee but only succeeded in rolling across the bed and tangling herself against a mound of mosquito netting.

'You *will* be a dutiful daughter,' he said before leaving. 'You *will* obey.'

5

There was blood on the sheets in the morning and she tasted blood on her lip where she'd bitten it.

She looked out of the window towards the pergola. Beyond it two male servants were assisting the gardener, pushing stones and mud in a wheelbarrow, disappearing beneath the hedge against the wall. Her escape route was being filled in but escaping into the city was no longer enough. In the depths of her soul she knew she wished to escape her father, her life as it was, for anything, anything far away from the place where her mother had died.

A tray was brought to her room: juice, bread, butter, jam, and sweet-smelling tea.

'Take it away.' She buried her face in her pillow.

Servant and tray retreated.

Shortly afterwards a servant came to bring her the message that she was summoned to the drawing room.

She slid on a pair of cami-knickers with wide legs and a side button. Even so the feel of the soft silk against the raised wheals made her wince.

Strangely enough she felt no fear at what would happen next. The worse had already happened. She'd been found out and beaten. What worse could there be?

On her way to the drawing room she paused and listened to the sound of monkeys scampering over the roof.

Voices from within the room made a statement she wasn't supposed to hear.

'The girl has tainted blood.'

'It's not *that* noticeable. She's very brown, but still looks passably British.'

'But people *know*, Burton, they know my dear fellow...' The voice of the man speaking was unfamiliar. 'But I myself... well... I don't mind a bit of native blood, and she'll fit in at my place. We're miles from Singapore and I ain't never likely to go back to Brisbane. Malaya's my home now. No one will be any the wiser, but do you mind if I ask one more question?'

Her father responded. 'Of course.'

'Her mother. She's dead?'

'Yes. She killed herself a few months back. Nadine was too old for a nurse and I didn't consider it in Nadine's interest to discover her mother was Indian. I sent her away. She threatened to take her life. I'm afraid I called her bluff.'

Nadine stood rooted to the spot. It was as though time had stopped, as though she had entered a great void from which she would never find the way out. Her father had finally admitted that her *ayah*, her darling, beloved *ayah*, had also been her mother, and not only that; he was responsible for her death.

Feeling hollow inside, Nadine leaned against the wall for support and instead of listening to the scurrying on the roof, listened to the beat of her heart. The blood in her veins turned to ice, was replaced with molten lava. Whatever happened next, she knew that she could not continue to live under the same roof as the man responsible for her mother's death. Whatever fate had in store, she'd face it headlong.

Composing herself, she stepped into the drawing room.

The room had high ceilings, white walls, and a tiled floor scattered with patterned rugs of mottled reds.

She avoided looking at her father. Her eyes were drawn to the man standing there in a crumpled white suit. He held his hat in sturdy hands. His eyes were brown, and the thick moustache covering his upper lip was slivered with grey.

Her father smiled a tight, controlling smile that never made his eyes.

'Nadine!'

She gave him no chance to make excuses. 'I lit the flame beneath Shanti's funeral pyre. You knew that. Why didn't you tell me then that you'd killed her?'

'I did not...' He had the decency not to continue.

'So what have you planned?' Her tone was clipped and bitter.

Her father eyed her as though seeing her for the first time and perhaps seeing himself in her.

'Mr Martin McPherson has asked to marry you and take you to Malaya. He has a rubber plantation there. You'll be quite well off. You'll have your own servants.'

Her blood turned even colder. She felt no surge of rebellion, just a chill emptiness that she thought could never be filled.

'What a very good idea that I leave here for Singapore, father. I would not want my pedigree to embarrass you any further.'

His mouth, half-hidden by his moustache, moved wordlessly, as though he'd become incapable of finding his voice.

Their visitor, who had watched the interchange with interest, now spoke to her.

'If you'll have me as your husband, girl, I'll have you as my wife.'

He spoke English, though not as an Englishman. His Australian roots battered his words.

'Better than being here,' she said bluntly.

Her father dropped his eyes to the swirling contents of his brandy glass, the liquid heaving from side to side...

All through her childhood, her existence had been tolerated rather than cherished. She owed nothing to this man. Whatever it took to get her away from here, she would do.

She became vaguely aware that the man in the white suit was trying to hide a grin. It wasn't until she became aware of his intrigued expression that she recognised the drunken man who had bared her breasts as she danced the night before.

She swallowed any thought of protest. What did it matter?

***

The marriage took place in St Cuthbert's church, its stucco walls blindingly white. Its interior was cool and apart from the whirring of the ceiling fan could have been any place in England.

Her father and two of his cronies attended. There were no women or servants. Just enough people to ensure the ceremony was legal.

Once the ceremony was out of the way, the newlyweds made their way to the Royal York Hotel, a place frequented by box *wallahs* as British tradesmen were referred to.

The room was pale green and shady. The shutters were closed.

Nadine shivered. Martin was so much older than her. Although resigned to her fate, she wasn't looking forward to what might happen next.

'Might as well get it over with,' said Martin, flinging off his coat and tugging her towards the bed.

I'll remember this forever, she thought as the weight of him pinned her to the bed. She winced when he entered her. No words of love. No whispered assurances that he would be gentle. She almost screamed, but something held her back. She thought of the woman with the starving children. A woman had to do what was necessary to survive. It could be worse.

* * *

Her last memory of India was on a dry day when each lungful of air tasted of dust.

Piles of rubbish discarded on the street side of the sentry post heaved with thin, ragged people. She saw two British soldiers come out of the back gate, their uniforms crisp except for the sweat patches already seeping beneath their arms.

One of the women searching for food among the rubbish saw them. Gathering her skirts about her, she approached them cautiously her two children following close behind.

The children gripped their mother's skirt with scrawny hands; the woman touched the tattered veil fringing her face. Whatever she was going to ask was making her nervous.

The woman brought her skirt up to waist level exposing her naked loins and straggly pubic hair.

Eyes bleak with hunger, the two children peered from around their mother's skirt as she gesticulated that she would endure carnal intercourse in exchange for food for her children.

Nadine heard her words spoken in Urdu. 'Please. My husband is dead from smallpox. My children have eaten only sparingly these past days. Be merciful, *sahibs,* or take what I offer in exchange.'

One of the soldiers waved her away. 'Get lost! Go on. No whores around here.'

The other searched his pockets. 'Steady on, Fred. I've got a few coppers here...'

'Don't be so bleeding soft.' Fred waved and shouted at the woman. 'Go on. Clear off!'

The woman stepped back, her children cowering behind her.

'Wait!' Nadine dug into her purse. Her exclamation turned heads. She marched over.

'Here,' she said to the woman in Urdu. 'Take this.' She gave her almost everything she had in her purse, leaving herself just enough to take a *gharry* home.

'Thou art kind,' said the woman, gratitude glistening in her limpid brown eyes. 'May Vishnu's light shine on you.' A thin brown arm rearranged the ragged veil before she hustled her children close and hurried away.

The soldier who had shouted at the woman stood shaking his head.

Nadine met the contempt in his eyes. 'Her children are hungry.'

He sneered. 'No decent woman would do that though, no matter what.'

'Yes they would! If my children – if I had children and they were hungry, I would do the same.'

Controlling her anger was like trying to push down the lid on a boiling kettle. She snapped her handbag shut.

As she walked away she heard him snigger and comment to his friend.

'Well that figures, Bert. They all sticks to their own kind.'

Back in her schooldays she would have bristled at the implied insult that she was native. Her dancing friends had changed all that. Her anger melted in a ray of burning pride.

Her thoughts went back to the woman who had been so desperate that she was willing to sell the only thing of value she had. She felt pity but also pride. They were both women and knew the value of life. She hoped the hungry children would survive. She hoped the mother would too.

6

They arrived in Malaya as newlyweds at the end of November. Rumours abounded that the Japanese were about to declare war, but nobody in Malaya was taking the matter very seriously.

Two weeks later, on 7 December, they bombed Pearl Harbour and panic began to spread.

'Shouldn't be a problem, girl,' said Martin. He was sitting on the veranda sipping a large G and T and squinting at the white clouds that were scudding across an ocean of blue sky. 'The Malayan Peninsula is well defended and we can always run to Singapore if things get bad. It's an island and everybody knows that Japs don't like water.'

'I thought that Pearl Harbour is in Hawaii? Isn't that an island?'

He folded his arms across his broad, barrel chest, almost as though such a question didn't deserve an answer. 'Take it from me, them Yanks must have been doing something wrong to get taken unawares like that.'

She couldn't think what the Americans might have done wrong but took his confidence at face value. It wasn't that she respected his opinion; she didn't care much what he thought.

The plantation, some forty miles from the town of Sampajan on the east coast, was lucky enough to have a generator. The house was cool.

Nadine was lying on her back in the marital bed, eyeing the blades of the overhead fan. Shadows from its blades flitted across her face and Martin's naked back. Martin was indulging in his conjugal rights, and Nadine was watching the fan, noting that it made a whirling noise in time with his grunts of exertion.

The air moved and that was good. She thought of other things when he was doing it to her. Imagine if there was no generator to drive the fan, only a *punkah wallah*, a lowly oriental labourer, pulling for all he was worth just outside their bedroom door. Imagine how much stickier they would be, how many more flies there would be, how many more lizards clinging to the ceiling.

Shuddering at the prospect she closed her eyes and opened them to the sight of her husband's thrusting buttocks. They were pink, glistening and wobbling like an unset blancmange.

She lay there, accepting what he was doing but not really taking part. In her mind she was dancing, showing what her body could do, arousing passions in others that she had barely tasted herself.

Even after their first copulation she'd felt no compunction to meet his firm thrust with a likewise jerk of her own hips. She felt nothing except impatience to have it done with, to retrieve her body and realign it with her thoughts.

Martin never referred to her pedigree, though once following his drinking half a bottle of Johnnie Walker he had asked her to dance for him.

'As you did that night,' he said to her. 'And not too many clothes,' he'd added, his fat tongue licking his equally fat lips. 'Leave your breasts bare.'

She'd hit him over the head with a dinner plate and run out of the door, locking herself in an outhouse. She'd stayed there all night. Martin had staggered out, knelt outside the door and begged her to come out. She'd refused.

'Come on, girl. You know I don't like going to bed alone. That big old bed – without you in it – is no good at all.'

'Use your right hand.'

Martin was a man of the world. He'd known what she'd meant. She could imagine him using his right hand a lot before marrying her. Now it was her that he used, at least once a week, sometimes three.

That night he slept alone. In the morning he looked and acted contrite, and never mentioned dancing after that.

At last Martin made a kind of yelping sound against her ear, stiffened as though he'd just died and slid out of her like an oily, soft slug.

He neither kissed her before sex nor after. Foreplay was horseplay; attempting to tickle her whilst demanding she get her tits out.

'We've got to get out of here,' he said suddenly once he'd got his breath back.

She averted her eyes from his belly in case she might catch a glimpse of his dormant penis and the hairy loins beyond its gleaming swell. There was nothing she found enticing about Martin's body and thus made a great effort not to look at it.

'I thought you said the Japanese couldn't possibly get this far.'

He slapped her thigh before struggling into an upright position. 'Better to be safe than sorry, girl. Now get your knickers on. We're for Singapore.'

'How long will we stay?'

He fumbled for his socks on. 'Just until we get the all clear. Shouldn't be long before they're whipped. Them damned Japanese ain't much bigger than Snow White's bloody dwarfs.'

Nadine reached for her dressing gown. 'So are the Chinese.'

He shook his head as he pulled on his socks. 'The Chinks ain't no different. It won't be the same trying to knock our army about, especially the Australians. Big and professional, that's the British army.

Martin was Australian by birth, but colonial material through and through, from his broad shoulders and wide girth to his vulgar language. It was easy to imagine some convict ancestor. Martin had that look about him: sturdy, clever, though far from refined – especially now, she thought, his naked belly throwing a shadow over his socks, the only item of clothing he'd managed to put on.

'Do you think we'll ever come back here?' she asked him.

'Don't be stupid, girl. Of course we will. Everything will get sorted pretty damn quick, don't you worry.'

* * *

Things were not sorted. Even when the Japanese landed at Kuatan in the north of the peninsula, no one really believed that they would succeed in their objective.

'Look at it,' said Martin as they drove southwards from the plantation towards the relative safety of Fortress Singapore. 'You need an army of bloody supermen to get through this lot?'

As they travelled, Nadine eyed the trinity of jungle, tin mines, and rubber plantations, the latter offending the eye by the Prussian regularity of their planting, as though they too were soldiers, consistently under threat from the hot, damp jungle. The former was full of menaces and wonders, hotter and damper than any Turkish bath, heated and soaked by the radiant mists produced by a sea of emerald green.

She wondered why the labourers were still there, why they hadn't run away.

'They're paid and fed well,' said Martin when she'd asked him. 'And they're loyal.'

'They might not be when the shooting starts.'

'If they run I'll shoot them my bloody self,' said Martin.

Nadine believed him. They were just workers not soldiers, so why would they stay?

The British enclave in Singapore was acting as though their presence was ordained by God. Nothing could possibly happen to shake their complacency or casual indifference as they sipped their Singapore Slings in the saloon bar at Raffles, or played a *chukka* on the Officers Club polo field.

At Raffles they lived an assured life, the British waited on by white-clad servants with brown skins and courteous manners.

Even when clouds of Zero's dropped bombs from a humid sky, no one seemed to notice that Singapore had few aircraft to fall back on.

'Just a foray,' Martin said. 'Testing our defences and scurrying away.'

On a dreadful day in mid-December when Repulse and Prince of Wales were torpedoed, the first panic began. Hordes of Chinese took to the traditional water craft, *sampans*, junks, and fishing boats, anything that would float.

Despite Martin's reassurances, the planes came back and more bombs fell on a sunny day when Nadine was out shopping with her friends.

The British ran for cover and so did those of other races. The afternoon was a shambles. Professional mourners and the brass band following the lead-lined coffin of a Chinese funeral scattered in panic. The coffin was abandoned, the ornate blue and gold funeral cloth whipped away by a passing *havildar*.

Shading her eyes, Nadine watched the mass of humanity charging across Kavanagh Bridge; brown-faced men carrying chairs and carpets on their heads, plump native women with babies, bundles over their backs, children hanging onto their skirts. She wondered if Martin's workers were also running. It was more than likely.

The Singapore seafront, already bristling with barbed wire and gun emplacements, now bristled with people.

Nadine watched from a distance on a green lawn pierced with the kind of flowerbeds more usually found in an English park.

'Poor people,' she murmured.

'Who can blame them? They hate the Japanese, and with good reason.' Her friend, Lucy Lee van der Meer, daughter of a wealthy Chinese businessman, and wife to the owner of a Dutch mine, sounded unusually sombre.

Nadine sighed. 'I can't help thinking we should be leaving too.'

'You sound serious,' said Lucy.

'Of course I am. I don't want to be killed. There are too many things I want to do. We should leave. I'm sure we should leave.'

'We can't do that!'

Her second companion was Doreen Tracey. She was married to a police officer and although her husband had tried to persuade her to leave, Doreen, who had two children and was four months into expecting another, was having none of it.

'We're not like these cowardly natives. We have to stand our ground. Our troops will hold them back. You just see if they don't.'

Nadine and Lucy exchanged horrified looks. Nadine was moved to comment.

'Doreen, that's downright unfair. They are not cowards. They have families.'

Doreen was tall and had chestnut hair that curled around her ears. She always looked well scrubbed, as though both her and her clothes were freshly laundered and ironed just minutes before exiting the bungalow the family lived in. Today she wore a blue gingham dress with a wide white belt and matching white gloves. Doreen always wore gloves.

Lucy and Nadine both wore lemon. Lucy was wearing a traditional *cheong-sam*, the embroidered satin clinging to her body like a second skin. Nadine's dress was of cotton. They both had the same blue-black hair. Their bodies were the same shape, slim but curvy. From a distance they might have been mistaken as sisters except that Lucy had brown eyes and Nadine's eyes were grey.

'My father has urged me to leave,' said Lucy. 'Like yours, my husband thinks the war will pass us by. But my father thinks otherwise and is rarely wrong.'

'Nonsense!' Doreen snorted the word and turned to Nadine. 'What does Martin say?'

The corners of Nadine's mouth twitched because she didn't entirely believe what Martin had said.

'He says we have nothing to fear. We are staying in Singapore until things settle down. It's just a precaution.'

'Right! That's settled,' said Doreen. 'We're staying. We have to. I need all hands to help make decorations for Wendy's birthday. Wendy and William are counting on it, and there's only days to go until the big event.'

'When is it?' asked Nadine.

'The twelfth of February.'

The date hung in the air. Hopefully by then the war would have passed them by.

The sound of guns firing rumbled over the nearby buildings. Beyond the city, small puffs of smoke stained an otherwise perfect sky.

The afternoon simmered with heat as befits a city only one

degree north of the equator, though the nights were cooler at this time of year.

They made their way to Doreen's house for afternoon tea.

'Milk?

'Yes please.'

'Sugar?'

'No thank you.'

'Biscuit?'

'No... perhaps, yes...'

Their talk remained trivial, each woman shuttered inside her own thoughts, waiting for something to happen.

The sound of explosions sounded close at hand. Nadine exchanged a look with Lucy.

'The causeway?'

'They've blown it up!'

They all gasped. The causeway connected the Malay Peninsula to Singapore Island.

'Nonsense,' said Doreen with a confidence neither of the others felt. 'Just target practice I expect.'

The children were chatting excitedly, the women drinking tea when the telephone rang. They were not to know it would be the last telephone call any of them would receive for a very long time. They were also not to know that some of them would never hear a telephone ring again.

Nadine helped William cut out stars from red shiny paper but looked up when the tone of Doreen's voice changed for the worse.

'Geoff! You can't mean that, darling!'

The others trained unblinking eyes on her face, their expressions taut with anxiety.

The colour drained from Doreen's rustic complexion. She paused, her mouth hanging open. 'Get packed? Now? But how...'

No one moved. Sensing the gravity of the occasion, even the

children fell to silence, their attention trained rigidly on the drawings they were colouring in or the winding up of a toy train.

Nadine and Lucy held hands. Nadine wondered if her own hand felt as cold as the one she held. She couldn't bring herself to check; she couldn't bring herself to drag her attention away from Doreen.

'Martin's coming to fetch us in the car?' It was obvious that Doreen was repeating whatever her husband had said word for word for Nadine and Lucy's benefit. 'But what about you?' There was another pause as her husband said something else. Doreen was almost hysterical. 'You can't mean it!'

It was obvious from Doreen's expression that he did mean it, and whatever was being said was serious – very serious indeed.

Whether her husband had severed the connection at his end was unclear. Doreen's face lengthened like that of a wax doll left too close to the fire. Whatever Geoff had said had shocked her to the core. Her confidence was turning blurred and shapeless.

Feeling a need to take charge of the situation, Nadine got to her feet. 'Doreen?'

Doreen's mouth opened in a silent scream. Her fingers stiffened to either side of her face, the telephone receiver slithering down her arm and finally crashing to the floor.

Seeing their mother's uncharacteristic behaviour, the children began to cry.

Wendy's bottom lip quivered. 'Mummy?'

Seeing his sister disturbed, William howled like a puppy that has taken on its parent's terror.

Lucy Lee van der Meer put her arms around them and opened her mouth, meaning no doubt to say comforting words, but none came out.

Nadine concentrated on Doreen, grasping her arms and shaking her.

'Listen, Doreen. Listen to me. Pull yourself together and tell me what Geoff said. What must we do?'

For a moment it seemed as though Doreen was staring right through her, or perhaps feeling slightly insulted that such a young woman was demanding she pull herself together.

In a bid to calm her, Nadine lowered her voice. 'What did he say, Doreen? What must we do?'

'Pack,' she said, and licked at her lips. Small flecks of sweat sparkled like sequins on her brow. 'Martin is coming for us to take us to a ship. We have to leave. The Japanese are almost here.'

Lucy Lee got to her feet. 'I have to go. I have to find my husband.'

'What about your father?' Nadine asked.

Lucy Lee smiled sadly. 'My father is a very wise man. He has already left.' She reached for her handbag. 'I must go.'

Nadine grabbed her arm. She'd known Lucy Lee van der Meer for only a very short while, but in that time had become fond of the lovely Eurasian girl. She couldn't help being concerned.

'There may be no *gharries* or rickshaws to get you back into town.'

Lucy shrugged. 'Then I will walk.' She left alone.

The change in Doreen's demeanour was extremely worrying, brought on, understandably by her concern for her children.

Nadine waited and worried with her, trying as best she could to keep the children occupied.

It was an hour before Martin arrived. 'Quickly,' he ordered, throwing the children into the car with as much lack of care as he did the luggage. 'There's no time for niceties. We've got to get the hell out of here.'

Doreen shot him a disparaging look. 'Language, please! There are children present.'

'Bollocks, Mrs Tracey. They're going to have to put up with a lot bloody worse than bad language before we're through!'

The roads were crowded. Detours took them past locked shops once owned by Chinese and Punjabis, now fled in fear of their lives.

Pretty faces looked out from dark doorways in Bugis Street, frightened eyes searching for business from sailors who now had more important things to do. When they'd first come down this street, Martin had taken great delight in informing Nadine that the sinuous beauties were male, not female. Today he didn't give them a glance. Finding a ship about to leave was all that mattered.

Geoff, Doreen's husband, waved to them from amongst the crowd milling around the ship's gangway, forcing his way towards them as best he could.

Nadine helped the children from the car. Martin handed her the luggage he'd hastily packed on his way to the Traceys' house.

A surge of people carried them towards the boat.

'Hardly a ship,' said Nadine, remembering the shining white P and O liner on which they had spent their honeymoon on their way from Bombay to Singapore. The ship had carried a bristling armoury of extras on its decks. She remembered being impressed. This small vessel failed to impress her, carrying as it did just one solitary gun.

'It's very small,' she added, her eyes alighting on the high paddles straddling the ships' sides.

'Beggars can't be choosers,' said Martin, pushing her along in front of him. 'Get yer ass aboard.'

The boat lay heavy with the weight of passengers, no more than two feet between sea and deck. The gangway was slippery. So was the deck.

Once they were aboard, Martin looked over the side. 'Don't put your foot too far forward whatever you do. A slight roll and a shark's liable to bite it off.'

Somehow they managed to stick together, Doreen, themselves, and the kids all crammed like sardines along the railing, adults sitting on suitcases, children clamped against their parents' side.

Doreen continually scanned the shore. 'Where's Geoff? He'll miss the boat.'

'He'll join us when he can,' said Martin. 'Perhaps in Australia. There was something he had to do.'

Nadine nudged him. 'Is it true?'

He shrugged. 'He went off with some bloke who's looking for his daughter.'

'Can't we get the boat to wait?'

Martin shook his head. 'Forget it. The faster we get away from here, the better.'

'But he's your friend.'

Martin shrugged again. 'Every man for himself, girl. That's the way it's going to be from now on.'

Typical! It never ceased to amaze her how selfish Martin could be, and cynical too it seemed. She didn't dislike him all the time, just now and then, like now.

'You'd better not tell Doreen,' she warned, keeping her voice low.

'I won't go without him,' said Doreen, braving an attempt to push through the crowded deck, children in tow and heading for the lifting gangway.

'You're too late. We're moving,' said Martin. 'Better make the most of it.'

The fact that he wasn't used to handling women like Doreen and certainly not children was glaringly apparent.

Nadine took over.

'Doreen!'

Doreen lurched towards the gangway that was already being swung against the ship's side.

Nadine held her back. 'You can't go ashore. We're moving, and besides Geoff knows what he's doing. He is a policeman after all.'

'I can't leave him,' said Doreen, twin spots of redness bright as pennies on her cheeks. Lines of concern creased a brow that was usually so smooth, so shiny and sure of itself.

Nadine leaned closer. 'You must. He's depending on you to look after the children. You must think of them.' She jerked her chin downwards to Doreen's belly. 'All of them.'

The gap between the boat and the shore widened. A wash of churning water sprayed out from each paddle as those on board fell to silence, worried faces watching as powder puffs of cannon fire exploded a few miles inland.

Nadine watched too. *So here I am, leaving another country. What next?*

Was it her imagination or were the puffs of explosion closer now than they had been that morning.

Watching for too protracted a period was painful. Lowering her eyes to the rushing water, she wondered how long it would be before she saw Malaya again, or any land again for that matter.

Initially Martin laid his huge hand on her shoulder, his fingertips straying to the curve of her breast. Embarrassed, she took a step away.

Martin grinned. 'Don't you worry, girl. We'll get through this, you just see if we don't.' He leaned closer. 'Not very private here for man and wife is it. Shame. Never mind. I'll make it up for you some time.'

Strangely enough there was something very reassuring in having his bulk so close. It no longer mattered that he failed to arouse any desire in her and that he was coarse and crass. His body was strong. God help anyone who stole or injured anything of his, and that included his wife.

7

By morning, the sky in the direction of Singapore glowed red, the rays of the rising sun streaked by the grey smoke of burning buildings.

No one on the boat seemed keen to look for very long, just quick glances. No one wanted to dwell on what they'd been told couldn't possibly happen. The normal sound of people living went on all around, but muted as though they were afraid to make too much noise and be noticed. Routine acts were carried out, but rushed and quietly.

People washed and fed themselves as best they could. The ship's crew – mostly Malay and Chinese – shared out what provisions had been brought aboard.

Nadine rubbed at her eyes and neck. She'd slept standing up, her head resting on the ship's rail. Stretching, she looked around her at the host of fleeing civilians and the few servicemen aboard – mostly Australians.

She also looked for Martin but couldn't see him. She looked for Doreen and the children and couldn't see them either.

For a while her gaze rested on the sea but it made her feel sick.

She turned her attention to the horizon, the only part of the sea that was constant. The queasiness in her stomach dissipated. She tried to focus her mind in order to stop it coming back.

Feeling suddenly bereft and scared, she looked for Martin. He was forcing its way through the crowd, a bowl of something held high above his head.

'Breakfast,' he said as though he served her breakfast every day, when the truth was he'd never prepared any sort of meal since the day they were married.

'It's only fruit I'm afraid,' he said. 'A bit of mango, banana, pineapple and stuff, and before you guzzle the lot, this meal is for two.'

She looked into the dish and frowned. 'That's for two?'

He grinned. 'No. Only joking.'

'This is hardly the time for joking.'

In the period following that, she would remember the meal as being generous to the point of gluttony, but not then.

'Where are Doreen and the children?'

He pointed to the other side of the deck. 'Over there. I found them a bit of floor space, enough room for the kids to sleep and Mrs Tracey to sit down.'

Martin's consideration surprised her.

He caught her looking at him but misinterpreted the reason.

'Don't worry, girl. We'll get through this. You just see if we don't.'

Typical Australian optimism.

A shout went up that another ship was approaching, resulting in an instant buzz of excitement. They were not alone!

Swallowing the last of the fruit, Nadine turned her head in the same direction as everyone else.

'More evacuees?'

'Could be,' Martin answered.

'That's the *KL Princess*,' drawled an Australian soldier standing nearby. Tipping back his hat, he swiped at the sweat dribbling through his eyebrows. 'Yeah. That's her all right.'

The grey outline of the old launch shimmered in the glitzy haze of the Malayan dawn.

Nadine narrowed her eyes against the morning glare. She could see figures lined along the deck, standing in tiers around a funnel belching black smoke.

'I can see people,' she said, shading her eyes in an effort to make out more detail.

Martin said nothing but his expression said it all. Martin never looked afraid, but he did now.

A feeling like a tiny claw scratched at her heart.

What has he seen?

She looked at him at exactly the same moment as he looked at her, wanting to see a reassuring expression, but knowing instinctively that she would not.

His manner was abrupt. 'Get over to the other side of the boat.'

She tried to turn but was hampered by the press of bodies. They were packed too tightly.

'I can't...'

'Here!'

He stuck out his arm, enveloping her at the same time as pushing her behind him. Held flat against his back, she stumbled along unseeing, aware that he was using himself as a battering ram to get through the crowd.

Just at the moment she glimpsed Doreen and the children, the panic spread.

There were no shouts that the launch was full of Japanese soldiers, but she knew that it was so. A pushing, shoving, screaming tidal wave moved inexorably across the deck, the boat tilting in response to the sudden shift of weight.

Doreen struggled to her feet, held the children against her and screamed. 'Nadine!'

Nadine screamed back. 'Over here.'

Her voice barely carried above the noise of men, women and children shouting, screaming, and crying.

Doreen tried to move forward, but the rush of frightened souls held her back.

Martin pushed his way through, scooping the two children into his arms as though they weighed no more than bags of rice.

Doreen's face was contorted with fear.

Nadine reached out. 'Grab my hand.'

Their fingertips touched. Bit by bit, they inched closer together until their fingers intertwined and their palms met.

A huge plume of water coincided with a tremendous explosion. The air filled with screams of terror, crying children, shouting men.

Rivets popped and the ship creaked and groaned as she rolled further onto her side. All hell broke loose. Crew abandoned ship, men abandoned women, and those women without children took advantage of their encumbered sisters, violently shoving them aside.

A mass of humanity slid reluctantly or jumped into the water.

Nadine sank deeply into a turquoise haze, its touch as cool as silk. Not for one instant did she fear she might die. She would not!

You have not left India and your father's house to drown in the sea.

Suddenly the aqua ceiling above her head broke open and she burst through the surface, gasping for air. She was alive, afloat in a sea of struggling humanity. Her first thought was Doreen. She saw her not too far away and instantly looked for the children. They were nowhere in sight.

Kicking her legs and flailing at the water with one arm kept her afloat. With the other she jerked Doreen to the surface.

Doreen made a great whooping noise, water gushing from her nose and mouth as she fought to catch her breath.

Nadine attempted to get her bearings, the water ballooning her clothes as she kicked and turned, searching for land.

'The children are there,' she gasped between gulps of air and water, nodding to where spumes of surf surged and recoiled onto a sandy beach. 'There!'

Up until now Doreen had seemed disorientated, too shocked to do anything except tread water. Now she was like a sleeper awaking.

'Where's Wendy? Where's William?'

Clenching her jaw, Nadine tightened her grip and tugged her towards the shore.

'They're safe. Martin has them.'

Disbelieving, Doreen began to jerk her head around, searching for sight of her children.

Nadine tugged her again. 'Doreen! They're on the shore. Martin has got them to the shore! Look! See?'

She pointed in a vague manner, no more than a flippant flick of her wrist to a point where the strongest, mostly the soldiers, were dragging themselves ashore beneath a crop of straggly palms.

Martin chose that moment to pop up between them, blood trickling from a wound in his temple. He wrapped his arms around both of them.

A look of panic threatened Doreen's features.

'I told you,' Nadine said. 'The children are safe and now he's come back for us.'

'Kick and push with your hands,' he ordered.

Nadine obeyed. So did Doreen but to a lesser extent.

Sometimes she swallowed water. It tasted funny and didn't seem as blue as it had been.

Whether Doreen presumed he'd left the children on the beach and came back for them, Nadine did not know.

Her fears proved unfounded. Bare footed and ragged, Wendy and William came running through the white sand, finally throwing themselves into their mother's grateful arms.

Not everyone was so lucky. Bodies and bits of bodies floated on the water.

Those who had made the shore ran into the green mantle surrounding the silver sand, hiding in the dense undergrowth, hoping against hope they could survive – somehow.

A last explosion ripped apart the old boat, debris and surf joining in a huge waterspout. Seemingly pleased with a good day's work, the Japanese launch fired only a few more shots towards the shore before considering the shooting of civilians a waste of ammunition and turning away.

After warning Doreen and the children to stay down, Nadine crept out of a hollow beneath the roots of leaning coconut palms.

Martin shouted at her from an adjacent hole. 'Stay down you silly bitch!'

Taut with nerves, Nadine clenched her fists and glared at him. 'Stop giving me your bloody orders, Martin!'

He looked surprised. She didn't care about that. She was shivering, scared, and only seventeen for God's sake! Seventeen and married to a much older man and totally ignorant of the possibilities life had to offer. It wouldn't be fair if she should die now.

'I'll see if I can help anyone,' she said.

Once she'd got to her feet, she had a great urge to run, the natural urge to flee, she supposed. Unfortunately her legs were not of the same mind, tired after kicking their way ashore. She only managed a stiff march, the soft sand tumbling between her toes, her dress steaming as the sun dried it.

The beach that looked like Paradise had become Hell. The

wounded were being dragged ashore and into the shade. The wounds were terrible: limbs smashed, abdomens torn open by flying shrapnel, faces roasted in burning oil...

She looked towards the ocean. Small vessels peppered the far horizon. Judging by the fact that some of them were smoking like chimneys, they too had felt the accuracy of the enemy's guns.

The sea around the submerged ship was littered with debris, bodies, and pieces of bodies. The waves lapping the white sand were fringed with pink spume, pieces of flesh, spectacles and personal belongings. The blood mixed with spilt oil. The smell was terrible and had attracted seabirds and sharks. Things that had been whole littered the sea and the sand. Bits of flesh floated amongst bits of china, wood, metal and leather.

The sea breeze warmed Nadine's face and played with her hair and the sun baked her shoulders, yet she felt so very cold. It was as if nothing around her was really happening, not so much a dream as a moving mural painted on a blank wall.

Someone said something and brought her back to reality.

'Do you have clean underwear?'

She stared into the dirty face of a woman with bright blue eyes. She was wearing a uniform that might once have been smart but was now streaked with blood, dirt and sweat, drying to a crisp in the heat.

The woman's voice softened. 'I'm sorry my dear. I know you must be in shock, but there are others far worse off than you. We need your underwear for bandages.'

Nadine looked dumbly down at her lemon cotton dress as though expecting her petticoat to have travelled from the inside out and for her to be wearing it on top of her dress. Once she'd clarified her thoughts, she saw her dress again. Yesterday it had looked crisp and clean. Today it was crumpled but already dried.

'I'm wearing a white silk petticoat,' she said and began unbuttoning her dress, but stopped and looked around her, suddenly realising she was surrounded by people.

'What about my dress? Do you want that too?'

'If you don't mind. No point in being shy, dear' said the nurse with a wry smile, noticing her hesitation. 'There's worse things to worry about. You'll just be showing a bit more leg but be thankful; there are those totally lacking legs.'

Nadine couldn't place the woman's accent: somewhere in England.

On the shadiest part of the beach, a line of rocks formed a barrier between sand and undergrowth. This part had become a makeshift hospital. Nadine wondered at the resolve of the people who were already organising things and helping people out.

On the fringes of the hospital, women rummaged in vanity cases and peered into powder compacts – as though the sight of a red nose was going to shock anyone. Some could not abstain from familiar habits, dabbing powder or applying lipstick. Normality keeping people sane and inspiring hope, she thought.

Within the hospital area, women wearing only their underwear were tending the injured. Others nearby were stripping off their dresses, ripping them into bandages with knives, scissors, anything that came to hand.

There was a smell of oil, of burned flesh – and even of face powder.

'The wounded – they're so quiet,' Nadine remarked.

The nurse who had asked for her underwear was named Rose and it turned out she was from the East End of London.

'It gets like that,' she said as she tended the severed arm of a young woman who was whimpering with pain. 'The pain becomes commonplace and bearable. Just as well really. The morphine and other medical supplies went down with the ship. All we've managed to rustle up are a few jars of aspirin, a box of plasters, three pairs of scissors, and a *kukri* knife – you know – one of them knives the Gurkhas use.'

Nadine watched as Rose began cutting the petticoat into strips.

The nurse noticed her expression. 'Sorry about this. It's real pretty and a shame to rip it up.'

'I bought it for my honeymoon.'

'Oh well. Never mind the sentiment; think of its practical uses.'

'I won't miss it. Here,' she said handing her the lemon dress. She nodded in the direction of the men, women, and even children lying in rows along the beach. 'They need it more than I do.'

She stood there in nothing except a pink satin brassiere and a pair of French knickers, grateful for the breeze cooling her skin. Her feet were bare, her shoes now at the bottom of the ocean.

She went back to where she'd left Doreen, the children, and Martin, and stopped.

Looking down at her nakedness made her feel instantly vulnerable. She knew her husband well. The thought of Martin taking advantage of the situation was unbearable. She couldn't be sure of his reaction despite his protectiveness of late. Deep down she was still his wife, a chattel, something that he'd paid for. She'd found his constant demands tedious. If she refused he'd remind her that she was 'touched with the tar brush', as he put it.

'I put aside my prejudices and married you anyway,' he'd said.

She decided to follow the nurse. 'Do you need any help?'

'If you think you've got the stomach for it.'

Out of the corner of her eye she glimpsed Martin leaning against a palm tree.

She looked away. She wouldn't go to him but knew that if she was away long enough, it was certain he'd come looking for her.

8

The days turned into a week. Like everyone else, Nadine turned worried eyes seawards. The sinking had left them in this isolated place without much water, little food, without anything very much at all.

'Of course we'll be rescued. We're British subjects,' declared one resolute matron.

Nadine heard the words but wasn't sure she believed them. Silhouettes of unidentifiable vessels slid along the distant horizon.

Desperate to do anything to relieve their despair, tired men had erected a distress beacon on the beach.

None were close enough to warrant lighting the sturdy looking tepee of debris and dried logs. Hope still remained in the stoutest breasts. Spirits rose at the sight of some ships that seemed to send out a signal of their own. Inevitably, the sudden flash of red mushroomed into an explosion of fire and thick, black smoke: yet another ship sunk by an unseen submarine.

Others were more obviously destroyed by Japanese Zeros swarming like bees and diving on their targets.

Sometimes the aeroplanes came close. A low flying Zero sent

the bedraggled masses scattering into the thick foliage before it swooped low over the lines of injured left on the beach.

Prayers were muttered that it would not fire. It did not, flying away, perhaps to seek more worthwhile targets.

Rations were halved; a few dry biscuits spread with army-issue corned beef being the main meal of the day supplemented with coconuts and the odd fish they managed to catch. The greatest joy was when a shark got stranded on the beach. Greedy for the bits of flesh still floating on the water, it had swum too close. Martin killed it with a kukri knife and the flesh lasted three days.

Life was primitive and far from private. Nadine stayed close to Doreen and the children, but sensed Martin was getting restless.

'It's not only food that's rationed,' he remarked, his expression leaving her in no doubt of his meaning.

She knew it wouldn't be long before he caught up with her and in a strange way she longed for a moment when there was just the two of them again. Kissing, embracing, even indulging in what he regarded as making love, would help her forget – help him forget too – that death was all around them.

A reaffirmation of life, she thought. That's what sex is.

Circumstances came together on a day when she was assisting in an operation, holding a man down whilst a surgeon cut off a mangled leg with a pair of kitchen scissors. That was when Martin came looking for her.

As he spoke he stood with his hands resting on his hips, his eyes on the trembling hands of the tired young surgeon.

'I've been talking to a few navy types over there. They reckon we're at a place called Sinkop. Reckon we should try and get a ship – perhaps a junk or a *prauw*, anything – to Sumatra.'

Nadine recognised the names of the fragile craft that roamed the coastal waters and wondered whether they were sea going. She fixed her eyes on his face, anything rather than see the scissors digging into a man's flesh.

'Is it far?'

'They reckon not. A week at most.'

'What about the Japanese?'

'They're pretty sure they're not in Sumatra.' His eyes drifted from the bloody wound to her cleavage. All she was wearing was her underwear and a sarong tied loosely around her hips. The sarong had once been a table cloth which she'd found in a suitcase, one of the few not requisitioned for bandages. The owner had not stepped forward to claim it.

'You've lost a bit of weight, girl,' he said to her.

'This is hardly the time for comments like that, Martin,' she retorted sharply.

His expression darkened.

The man losing a leg was on the verge of convulsions. The stick he was biting on splintered beneath the pressure of his teeth and his agony. His body was soaked with sweat. He'd been given a small amount of morphine in a measure of whisky. Someone had found both items in the debris littering the shore.

Martin's presence was irritating. 'Finished now?'

'Yes.'

'Right. Come on. We've got things to plan.'

He put his arm around her, his fingers gripping her firmly.

'I don't like you looking like a bloody native,' he hissed.

He nodded at the sarong.

Would you prefer me to wander around in my underwear?'

'You should have kept your frock on. At least it made you look as though you were white even if you're not!'

The comment was meant to hurt and it did, though not in the way he'd intended. Exposure to strong sunlight had turned her as brown as the Malayan women and the *serangs*, the Malayan labour force who fetched and carried for the army and navy personnel. Turning brown reminded her of who her mother really was, how much it must have hurt to be sent away from her only daughter.

He led her forcibly to a group of men in torn and dirty shorts, their bodies varying in colour from clay pink to mahogany, crouched in a circle. One of them was using a stick to draw in the sand. He looked up at them, glanced at Nadine, then turned back to Martin.

He jerked his chin at a Malay deck *serang*. 'This chap here has some knowledge of navigation. He's not exactly Royal Navy experienced, but the best we can get.'

Beggars can't be choosers,' said Martin, hitched up what remained of his trousers, and crouched down.

Nadine couldn't help herself from asking the obvious. 'Do you have a boat? Only it strikes me that all the determination in the world isn't going to get us across the ocean without a boat.'

The man who had spoken heard the sarcasm in her voice. 'Your wife doesn't sound too confident.' He gave Martin a direct look, almost as though he were questioning whether he was beating her enough.

Nadine persisted. 'So where will you get one?'

He spit in the sand. 'Let's hope we're lucky and one comes sailing along. Now, Martin,' he said, purposely pushing her aside and crouching down beside her husband.

The man who'd pushed her out began explaining. 'Now this is what we've got planned...'

She took the opportunity to leave and make her way back to Doreen who was coping well enough with the children. The family were sitting surrounded by empty coconut shells. Wendy was making a din knocking two more together whilst singing to herself. William was grizzling, complaining that he was hungry.

Nadine addressed Doreen. 'Haven't you got anything else to give them?'

'A few biscuits and some corned beef, but I'm having to go careful. They say we're going to have to catch fish in the same way as the natives do.' Her eyes flickered as she took in Nadine's appearance. 'You're very brown. You look like a native.'

Doreen wasn't quite herself, so Nadine swallowed the perceived insult. 'Looking like a native doesn't mean I'm any good at fishing.'

Doreen's comparative good humour swiftly turned to contemplation. The corners of her mouth turned downwards.

Nadine guessed the reason. She touched her hand gently. 'You're thinking of Harry?'

She nodded at the same time as smoothing a sweaty strand of hair back behind her ear. 'I only hope he's still alive. Better to be a prisoner than dead.' She looked at the children. 'I wouldn't want them to grow up without a father.'

It was on the tip of Nadine's tongue to comment that as long as they grew up, it was all that mattered, but she couldn't say it. Doreen – strong, forthright Doreen – had turned terribly fragile.

Suddenly a skinny woman called Mrs Jeremiah Stevens dashed into their midst, waving her arms and shouting that there were Japanese hiding in the bushes around the burial ground. 'They're raping our girls and then they'll kill them, and then they'll kill us and eat all the babies!'

Nadine sprang to her feet and attempted to grab Mrs Stevens's flailing arms.

'Now calm down, Mrs Stevens.'

Mrs Stevens' husband had been a depot manager for a large American engineering firm but had retired some five years before and opted to stay on as a consultant. He'd died of malaria, swiftly picked up on landing here and just as swiftly killing him. He was one of those buried on a patch cleared of undergrowth that was steadily getting bigger as more people died.

'Back there, back there,' cried Mrs Stevens, waving one pure white arm in the direction of the sandy beach and undergrowth behind where the drowned and mutilated dead now lay in peace.

It was already accepted that Mrs Stevens had taken leave of her senses, sitting out in the sun all day, staring at the sky or the sea. She looked wild and unkempt, her hair as white as her tired flesh, her face as red as raw offal.

'Now, now,' said Martin, his voice dripping with confident bonhomie, as he held her bony shoulders. 'Don't you worry, now. Me and my missus will go in and take a look.'

Nadine frowned. 'Don't you think some of the men should go with you?' Martin shook his head, held a finger before his lips and whispered, 'Just humour the old girl.'

Smiling down into the lined, sunburned old face, he spoke clearly and loudly as though she were deaf. 'We'll go and take a look. OK?'

Eyes wild with approaching madness stared up into his face. 'You won't let them take Wilfrid, will you? They're savages. They'll eat him. Cut him up into little lumps and eat him!'

In the past the idea of eating a dead body would have made anyone sick, but these were different times. Already rumours were rife and imaginations were fertile.

'That's what natives do,' said Mrs Stevens.

'Along here.' She danced on ahead of them, her spidery arms held out in front of her like a water diviner without any sticks.

'Poor old sow,' muttered Martin.

They followed her to the nearly full burial ground. People had been dying since the first day they'd landed. The interior of the island was thick jungle, too difficult to dig without proper equipment. The sandy soil nearer the beach was softer and easier to get at. A few bits of driftwood used as spades were enough to dig a hole deep enough to avoid the crabs.

Mrs Stevens whirled on ahead, a blur of blue cotton against the velvet green of the jungle path. She led them around an outcrop of rock and onto the graveyard.

'There,' she shouted, pointing upwards into the trees. 'There!'

Above them a troupe of black gibbons leapt from bough to bough.

Nadine exchanged a look with Martin. He shook his head.

Nadine moved swiftly to stand beside the poor woman and put her arm around the bony shoulders.

'They're monkeys, not Japanese, Mrs Stevens. Do you see?'

She pointed at the gambolling figures screeching above them.

Mouth hanging open, Mrs Stevens fell to silence, eyeing the monkeys as though she weren't really sure what they were. Eventually her shoulders slumped as though all her energy had bled out through her toes. She shook her head mournfully. 'I didn't know Japanese climbed with the monkeys.' She shook her head again. 'I'm tired. I want to go to bed.'

'There,' Nadine said soothingly. At any other time she would have laughed out loud at Mrs Stevens' comments about Japanese climbing with monkeys, but not now. Now was too tiring and serious a time. 'We'll go back now.'

Just as they turned to go back along the path, Mrs Stevens' shoulders stiffened and she exploded with energy. 'I must get back! I must get back. The frying pan will be on fire!'

Following a big shove from her bony arms, Nadine fell into the bushes. Martin made a grab for the older woman, but she proved too quick for him. She ran off, her ragged dress flapping around her white thighs, her skinny figure slapping into thick leaves before disappearing.

Martin helped Nadine up from the ground. Even before she

looked up into his face, she knew what would happen next. The world spun around her and the sound of insects filled the air. The afternoon was drifting into evening.

'I think we've got a bit of catching up to do,' he said, a low guttural voice as though his tongue was cleaving to the roof of his mouth.

She tried holding her breath and pushing him away. 'Not now, Martin.'

'You're my wife. No matter what happens, you're my wife,' he said, his eyes glittering, fingers hooking at her bra strap, pulling it off her shoulder.

'Martin, I don't... someone will hear... or come...'

He ignored her.

'Over here,' he said, pushing her onto the edge of the beach where the sand was soft and away from the scampering of hermit crabs.

As usual she turned her head away. Closing her eyes she pretended it was happening to someone else.

He pushed his leg between hers and slid his hand up the leg of her knickers, groaning as his fingers touched her warm crotch.

She gasped as one finger slid inside her.

'Don't you like that?'

She didn't answer.

'Never mind. I've got something better for you.' He began fumbling with what was left of his fly buttons.

For some inextricable reason, her thoughts went to her knickers, the only barrier left between her and near nudity. Who was to say when she'd encounter decent underwear again?

'Wait,' she said, pushing her palms against his shoulders. 'Don't.'

He frowned, his expression turning angry. 'Don't?'

She managed a tight smile.

'These are the only pair of knickers I've got left. I don't want you ripping them. Who knows when I'll get another pair? Be patient, please. I know where the button is.'

His feathers were ruffled, but he begrudgingly allowed her to undo and take them off herself, though not once did he shift far enough to allow her to escape.

She slid them off along with her bra and the sarong, bundled them together and put them under her head to serve as a pillow.

Martin watched her. He looked a little puzzled.

'I don't know when I'm likely to come across a dress shop either,' she said and even managed to sound amused. Then she lay back, just as she had in their bed back on the plantation, gazing up at the sky whilst he entered her, ejaculated, and finally rolled off.

To Martin having sex was like drinking tea or eating rice every day; it was something he had to have. He rarely asked her whether she'd enjoyed it. She was left wondering whether it would always be like this. Yet somehow today it was totally acceptable. Life going on as it always had, as it always would – once they were out of this situation.

'You coming?' he asked once his loins were covered.

'In a minute.'

He shrugged and left her there.

Conflicting emotions stirred insider her. Ordinarily she could never love Martin, yet in these circumstances his earthiness was a bulwark against her fear and the probabilities of what might happen.

Immediately after retying her sarong, she looked dreamily seawards, gazing at a sky full of stars.

One star seemed larger and closer than all the rest. Narrowing her eyes, she considered whether it was merely a reflection of a star dancing on the water. It blinked again, a pinpoint of light not varying in size.

A wave of hope washed over her. A ship! It had to be a ship, and not too far away.

She took to her heels, yelling at the top of her voice as madly, if not more so, than poor Mrs Stevens had done just an hour or two earlier.

When she got back to the beach, everyone was gazing seaward; she was not the only one who had seen the vessel.

Martin and other men were running around finding dry matches and pieces of used, dried dressings in order to light the beacon fire they'd made.

Those strong enough gathered around the bonfire, the dancing flames making their haggard faces and half-naked bodies look more hideous than they already were.

Half a dozen soldiers who had kept themselves to themselves and done little to help anyone else, now rushed forward waving bits of rag that had once been army issue tropical kit, eyes fixed on the light coming towards them.

Nadine ran to fetch Doreen. 'There's a ship,' she said.

'Is it one of ours?'

'Of course. The Japanese are still miles to the north; everyone says so.'

'That doesn't mean to say they're right,' said Doreen, reaching out and gathering her children to her side.

She had a point. The Americans had not expected Pearl Harbour to be bombed in December 1941 and the British had not expected the Japanese to take Singapore in February 1942. Via her friend Lucy Lee, she'd heard about the rape of Nanking and the atrocities happening in other parts of China. She shivered. The enemy were not likely to treat them any differently.

'All right,' she said, sliding down with her back against a palm trunk until she was in a comfortable sitting position. 'I'll reserve judgement and stay with you.'

The palm tree was on a low ridge where tough grass grew between the tangled roots of dead mangroves. She turned her gaze seawards watching the light move closer. Men and women shielded their eyes against the light situated on the bow of the boat, its brightness preventing them from making out any detail.

The excitement that had run through the gathered crowd at the prospect of being rescued became a breathless hush, a vacuum of silence.

What at first looked like pieces of blackness fell off either side of the boat, and as it turned sidelong, they became men; soldiers bearing arms, someone shouting orders. The red and white flag of the rising sun fluttered at the stern.

9

The boat, some kind of larger launch of the type used for coastguard patrols, held off a few hundred yards until dawn. Those on the beach watched in grim fascination. Some suggested hiding among the vegetation covering the heart of the island until it was pointed out that the island was barely two miles by four and wouldn't take long to search.

Martin trod a constant track along the beach close to where the coconut palms divided sand from loamy soil, close to Nadine, Doreen and the children.

'Why don't they bloody come, take us prisoner or whatever?' He stared out at the black outline at the same time as he peed against a palm tree.

'They don't need to,' Nadine remarked.

Doreen's children were asleep, but their mother was not. Her face stiffened with disapproval. 'Martin, don't you think you could relieve yourself elsewhere?'

Martin buttoned up what was left of his shorts. 'Never mind being fussy. Won't be so bloody fussy in future when they take us prisoner.' He turned his nervous eyes back to the sea and the black shape bobbing gently in the surf. 'But why don't they come now. We're here – waiting – just waiting.'

'You're talking rubbish.'

'And you're too outspoken for your own good, woman!'

'That may be, but I always think before I open my mouth, which is more than can be said for you.'

Judging by the look on Martin's face, he wasn't sure whether she'd insulted him or not.

'So what do you mean?' he said, his discomfort hidden by speaking louder – his usual trick.

Smiling, she made herself comfortable against a pillow of fallen palm fronds. 'They can come any time they like.'

'I know that!' he snapped.

'Well,' she said, wriggling her back against the greenery and folding her arms behind her head, 'We're not going anywhere are we. They've got all the time in the world.' She closed her eyes, shutting him out.

Martin muttered something that sounded like 'Bollocks,' and, 'Stupid mare,' then stalked off.

His waiting finally paid off around dawn. The Japanese soldiers, short, stocky men with glinting eyes and square jaws, landed as swiftly and violently as a tropical storm, instantly separating the men from the women and children, and then the men into separate units; civilians to one side, servicemen to the other.

'Line up for *tenko*,' ordered a Japanese officer, the toes of his boots barely missing the tip of his lengthy sword.

A whisper went round. 'What's *tenko*?'

The word would haunt the dreams of some forever.

He interpreted swiftly. 'Roll call. Line up. Now, please. Japanese soldiers will not hurt you.'

The Australians overrode their fear by making light of the situation, purposely deriding the enemy's flat black hair, the sharp almond-shaped eyes, and their lack of height.

Unfortunately they were overheard and understood. The enemy went among them cracking rifle butts across bare flesh already red raw with sunburn.

Nadine watched with a sinking heart, sensing that she was witnessing a collision of cultures. What did she know about the Japanese? Only that their women wore kimonos.

The Japanese flag was raised on a hastily made pole cut from a tree branch.

'Bow. All men bow. All women bow. All children bow! All bow to conquering army. Like this.'

The small men in khaki showed them how to bow, head low, arms fixed to their sides.

Those injured but able to move were bludgeoned towards the makeshift flagpole.

'Bow!'

Some were more reluctant – and foolhardy – than others.

'Certainly not,' exclaimed the woman who had believed they would be rescued. 'I'm British.'

The force of a rifle slamming into the small of her back brought her to her knees.

'Bow! Obey!'

The rays of the rising sun beat on a wave of burned backs as heads were bowed towards the Japanese flag.

In the midst of bowing, Doreen continued to bleat her concern for her children.

'Nadine. Do you think you could ask the soldiers for some food? William and Wendy have had nothing to eat since noon yesterday.'

A Japanese heard her. 'Silence!'

'We'll get some later,' Nadine answered once he was out of earshot.

Next they were broken down into smaller units. Women with children, injured men and healthy men were segregated and counted by three soldiers. They compared numbers when they'd finished but appeared to disagree. Their findings were reported to an officer who ordered them to count again. The disagreements went on and on.

Standing in the scorching sun began to take its toll. Children whimpered, women sighed. The injured capable of standing sagged and swayed; some of the older women and the weaker fainted.

The soldiers counted again, their booted feet sinking into the soft sand, kicking those on the ground when they refused – or couldn't hear – the order to stand up.

Nadine felt as though her sweat had turned to ice.

Doreen appeared preoccupied.

'Nadine? The children...'

Nadine shook her head slowly – just three turns – left, right, left. She had to impress on Doreen just how serious the situation had become.

'But they're hungry...'

She repeated her action. Her mouth was too dry to speak.

The woman on the other side of Doreen told her to be quiet. 'They'll beat you if you keep talking,' she told her.

The men were ushered towards the waterline where the sea curved in ribbons of white surf. Over a hundred of them were ordered to stand in a line facing the sea. Those unable to stand were also included and laid out along the shoreline.

Five or six women were selected and given a pile of bandages torn from dresses, shirts, petticoats, and other items of clothing. With a series of shouted orders and rough handling, they were told to distribute one piece of cloth to each of the men standing at the water's edge.

'Not to injured,' shouted the Japanese major, standing like a fighting cock, hands behind back, feet apart.

Each man looked to his neighbour. Murmurings of disquiet were silenced by a rifle butt in the small of the back, or the tip of a bayonet in the back of the knee. Blood and sweat trickled onto the sand.

Nadine heard someone say, 'What's happening?' It wasn't Doreen who spoke. She was looking at the ground and telling her children to do the same. She had been cuddling them to her, but a soldier had insisted they part, the children forced to stand to attention just like the adults.

Now the soldiers were standing in a row behind the men, rifles poised waiting for orders.

The major barked something out in Japanese. The interpreter, a lieutenant judging by the way he adjourned to the major and the other men adjourned to him, translated.

'Blindfold your eyes.'

The men looked one to another.

Hearts rose in throats.

A hum of noise rose like a swarm of bees. The initial agitation of the men at the shoreline spread to those watching.

An Australian soldier with sandy hair and pink skin turned round and addressed the crowd, spreading his arms wide, his eyes and mouth swollen with terror.

'The bastards are going to shoot us!'

Reaction was instant. A soldier smashed the butt of his rifle into the man's mouth. He fell back spitting teeth and blood.

The condemned men, their faces streaked with terror, sprang into the surf, swimming for their lives.

Nothing, not even the threat of shooting, could stop the women screaming. The surf turned red.

Nadine opened her mouth, but no sound came out. Frantically, she tried to make out Martin. Was he there? Was he behind her? She couldn't remember. Her chest heaved, her breath choked in her throat. She heard Doreen crying, heard the children turning hysterical, but she couldn't move. She couldn't tear her eyes away from what was happening. Who was next?

Broken and bleeding, bodies were flung upwards on incoming waves. Those who avoided the hail of rifle bullets and managed to swim some distance were cut in two by the machine gun mounted on the bows of the patrol launch.

'Will they kill us too?' a woman murmured, her bottom lip trembling and trail of drool running from her mouth.

Nadine did not respond. Terror rooted her into the warm, soft sand. Terror caused her to whisper one solitary phrase that would stay in her mind for a long time to come. 'I am seventeen. *Seventeen*! I don't want to die. No matter what, I do *not* want to die!

What was it Shanti used to say? She instantly corrected herself. What was it my *mother* used to say? *Life is precious whatever it is.*

Something flapping drew her attention to the gathering of civilian men: old planters wearing battered panamas, still dignified despite the fact that their trousers were torn and flapping around their bony knees; bespectacled administrators, no hopers at home in suburban Surrey, who had come out east to serve both empire and themselves. A selfish thought crept into her mind. If anyone else were to die, surely it would be them: Not the women. Not the children. It would be them!

Please God!

'They won't kill us, will they? Not women? Not children?'

A ginger-haired woman with a blistered face was asking her, her who had just asked herself.

'I hope not,' she replied. 'Just be brave. We'll get through this.'

'I wish I had your courage,' the woman murmured.

Courage? Nadine almost shouted out, *I'm terrified. Absolutely terrified!*

'They'll kill the other men first.' Though her voice trembled, the woman sounded almost hopeful.

Nadine swallowed. *Is this what it will come to? Hoping it will happen to someone else, but not me, please God not me?*

At one time she would have been ashamed to think such selfish thoughts, but not now. Now there was only numb fear where shame used to live.

Doreen drew her attention with high-pitched whining noises. Her features were contorted, an ugly caricature of how they usually were.

Nadine looked away and clenched her jaw. She could offer no words of comfort. Her mind, even her body had become hollow.

The male civilians stood in straight rows, as did the women. She saw a tall man standing head and shoulders above everyone else and assured herself that it must be Martin.

Around her women retched or cried uncontrollably as they crumpled to their knees, whispering the name of the husband or lover they feared never to see again. Some, like her, had turned to stone.

A woman was loudly exclaiming that the corpses floating in the surf should be buried.

The Japanese did not respond.

The woman, a tough Australian type, everyone's ideal of the archetype hospital matron, stepped forward and shouted. 'You're all bloody savages. But you wait. You'll reap what you sow, you just see if you don't.'

At an order from an officer, three soldiers dragged her out to the front. Two of them held her arms, tugging them to either side until it seemed they would be pulled from their sockets.

The shock of those watching spread: a rushing sound like the sound of the surf meeting the shore and sucked into silence by the sand. No one was left in any doubt that protest – or even comment – would not be tolerated.

The bloody corpses ebbed and flowed on the surf, the redness finally dissipating to a dull pink and then grey.

The lifeless corpse of the shot woman was left half in, half out of the water.

The Japanese, their expressions showing no sign of emotion, turned their attention elsewhere. Their first task was to collect all valuables. Nadine took off her wedding ring and a thin gold chain her father had given her as a wedding present. Everything was gathered into a stiff canvas bag.

An officer walked up and down the lines of women. A common soldier accompanied him, a paintbrush in one hand and a pot of ink or paint in the other. Every so often, at the officer's behest, he made a black tick on a woman's forehead.

Nadine stared at the ground. She didn't know whether a black tick was a good thing or a bad thing.

To her dismay, he stopped in front of her. She trembled when he lifted her chin. For a moment – just the smallest moment, her eyelids flickered. She saw his face, black eyes above prominent cheekbones, a thin-lipped mouth.

She received a tick from the sentry, shivering as the brush wetted her forehead.

They passed on, formed a huddle, discussed what they had done, and with curt nods agreed a course of action. She thought she saw money change hands. That in itself seemed surreal. Money? For dead people?

'You!'

The shouted command made her jump. A soldier slammed the butt of his rifle across her back, herding her ahead of him like she'd seen the natives herding livestock in India.

'There! You! Go there!'

She found herself in the company of two Eurasian girls, two Chinese, one Indian who still wore the remnants of her nurse's uniform, two Australians and two young British women.

The commanding officer strutted along the row, looking them up and down, stopping occasionally to make some comment to a lesser officer who turned out to be an interpreter.

Still presuming they were next to be shot, she stood on tiptoe, searching for sight of her husband. Her husband! There had been no love lost between them, and yet if anyone could save her, he could. A fragile hope, a false hope but the only one she had.

Seemingly satisfied with those chosen, the commanding officer said something in Japanese to the interpreter.

The interpreter, taller than most of his colleagues, saluted his superior before stepping forward to speak. He addressed those selected with a black tick.

'Ladies. Major Yamamuichi declares that Japan does not make war on women. Your men turned and fled the battle. They are cowards. They left their women behind. So sorry. Japanese soldiers are honourable men. We would not do this to our women. We would protect them and we will now do our best to protect you. We will give you the opportunity of working in very good conditions. You will do laundry and other things for Japanese officers. However, you will not be forced to do this. It is your decision.'

Nadine's gaze drifted beyond the uniformed figures to where the dead littered the shoreline.

If she refused this work, how long before she too was lying face down in the water?

'What other services are they talking about,' muttered an Australian nurse, a pretty girl with dark hair and blue eyes.

'The proverbial fate worse than death?' added an English girl of similar colouring.

The interpreter's eyes followed each sentence of conversation, interpreting it for the officer's benefit.

The major nodded and said something. The interpreter gave a respectful bow of the head and faced the women.

'You will not be forced. Those who do not wish to work for their food may re-join the others and be taken to a women's camp. We will give you a moment to consider your options.'

'I'm frightened,' said one of the Eurasian girls. Her name was Rosa.

Nadine crouched down, picked up a stick and made lines in the sand. 'We're all frightened.'

An Australian girl spat into the sand. 'Laundry! My aunt Fanny! Who's crazy enough to go with them believing that? Who really wants to make that kind of choice?'

Nadine drew a gallows in the soft wetness of the sand. Out of the corner of her eye she could see clouds of flies colonising the bare backs of the dead as though they were islands.

She jerked her chin at the floating bodies. 'They might have liked that choice. Will we live if we stay here?'

There was instant reaction.

'You don't think...?'

Nadine said nothing but concentrated on completing the gallows, digging the rope and noose more deeply than its supporting structure. She raised her eyes to where the Japanese waited, the major inspecting some kind of roster passed to him by someone on the boat.

He nodded as though something had been agreed.

Suddenly a woman appeared on the boat. Nadine shielded her

eyes. The woman took deep breaths as she walked up and down the narrow side deck escorted by an armed soldier.

The sun was immediately behind the boat. The sea glittered. For a moment it seemed that the woman stopped and gazed straight at her. Although the glare obscured the woman's features, there was something familiar about her shape, the way she held herself, the blue-black hair, the yellow dress...

After completing one circuit of the boat, the woman disappeared. Even after she'd gone, Nadine stared, unsure to trust her sight, but hoping, hoping desperately, that she had just seen Lucy.

No one else had been killed; in fact, a bucket of milky rice and one flavoured with dried fish had been handed to those left on the beach. They fell on it ravenously. Even the remaining injured were being tended.

Nadine assured herself that Doreen and the children would be fine and would probably end up in a family camp. One of the Dutch women had assured them such places existed. She hoped it was true.

Martin was dead. She was pretty sure of that, and although she surveyed the bobbing bodies at the water's edge, one sunburned corpse was much like another.

The officer in charge said something to the interpreter. After saluting smartly, he trudged through the blindingly white sand.

'He wants an answer,' whispered one of the girls.

Nadine watched him approach, waited until he was just a few feet away, then bowed. 'I will accept your offer.'

His round face broke into a beneficial smile, like a priest, she thought, about to baptise a willing supplicant.

Her stomach crawled with fear. Like the others, she wasn't sure of what she'd really agreed to, but Lucy was on that boat. For that reason alone, she was drawn to it.

The interpreter, lieutenant so someone said, addressed the others. 'All of you?'

To Nadine's surprise, they bowed in unison, gathered around but slightly behind her.

'Looks like you're our leader,' said one of the Australian nurses.

This was a responsibility she could well do without. 'You don't have to do as I do.'

'I will if it means staying alive.'

The Japanese officer was beaming. 'You have made good decision. You board boat now. Do not be afraid. You will not be harmed. Japanese are kind to those who serve army.'

Nadine studied her companions and saw the fear in their eyes. It occurred to her that all of them were young, all pretty. Fear coiled like a tight rope in her stomach.

They were waved forward with shouted commands and violent gestures.

'What about the women and children staying behind?' whispered Betty.

Nadine whispered back. 'They'll be all right. They don't shoot women and children.'

She realised the hollowness of her words when her gaze rested on the woman who'd been shot was slowly being sucked out in the undertow. They chose not to mention her. Holding onto hope. It was all they had left.

The urge to look was too overwhelming to ignore.

Glancing over her shoulder, Nadine studied the beach, looking for Doreen, William and Wendy. Would they ever meet again?

They were herded through the water to the base of a ladder at the side of the boat. The ladder stopped short of the surface by a few inches. The weight of the water and their weakness as a result of hunger made it difficult to clamber aboard.

An order was snapped out in Japanese which resulted in a

body being wedged at the bottom of the ladder to make clambering aboard that much easier. She forced herself not to mind, not to feel anything, even trepidation. She only glimpsed the back on which she stepped as it sank beneath her weight. It was broad. Red. She retched, but nothing came up. For once she was glad that there was so little in her stomach.

Once she'd been helped up onto the deck she took one last glance towards Doreen and her children. Overcome by revulsion and fear, she closed her eyes. What she had seen today must be stored to memory. There were no rules in love and war, but surely no human being should be allowed to treat others like this.

Summoning up a bucketful of courage, she looked over the side of the boat to the blood-stained water. No longer needed as a platform, the body floated away from the side of the boat. She fixed the scene in her mind. That was when she realised whose broad back she had stepped on. Her stomach retched as the truth hit her. She was not just seventeen; she was also a widow.

10

Sickened and numb with fear, she allowed herself to be herded with the others into a tiny cabin. In the dim light she saw two other women already occupied it; one was a pretty Malay with oval eyes and a perfect mouth. The other had blue-black hair and a familiar face.

'Lucy!'

'Nadine!'

Nadine fought down the terror that threatened to overwhelm her. 'How did you get here?' She forced herself to sound confident.

'We were on a Malayan *prouw* – it was owned by someone who owes loyalty and money to my father. Unfortunately he wished to relinquish his debt without settlement but with interest and so sold me to the Japanese.'

The door slammed shut as the girls squeezed themselves into what little space there was, Nadine sitting tightly against Lucy's side.

'Doreen's still on the beach with the children. I think they've left some soldiers there. I hope they'll be all right.'

She wrapped her arms around her bent knees, staring at them so Lucy could not see the fear in her eyes.

'I heard the gunshots,' murmured Lucy.

'Martin's dead. They shot all the men.'

Lucy sighed. 'I think my husband is still alive, but I don't know where.'

One of the Malay women who appeared to have understood addressed Nadine. 'They will not shoot your friends. They have left guards until a prison ship arrives. That is why they shot the soldiers and very fit men so they would not overpower the Japanese soldiers.'

Nadine jerked her chin, the only sign that she understood.

'And what about us?' she asked Lucy. 'They say we are going to work for our food. Is this true?'

Lucy looked away. 'Yes,' she said. 'I am afraid it is.'

* * *

That first night at sea they were fed rice mixed with a little fish, but they ate little, their appetites suppressed by a state of fear and nausea as a consequence of the steady drumming of the engines, the rolling of the ship, and the stench of fuel.

The room they were in was unbearably hot. Sweat glistened on their faces, trickled between their breasts, and seeped into their clothes.

Two of the women threw up in a bucket supplied for them in the corner. Nadine tried not to look in their direction.

The smell was dreadful: vomit, urine, faeces and oil plus the steady increase in stale sweat. The bucket had to be used for everything and the hold they were stowed in was dark and airless, the bulkheads running with condensation.

The guard who brought the food lingered, his gaze moving slowly over the eight girls crouched in the small space.

He made comment to his colleague as he eyed each girl in turn. Both laughed before closing the door.

Not one of the girls ate a mouthful of food until the door was firmly shut.

'A charming pair,' muttered Nadine.

'What did they say?' asked the Indian girl, her eyes black with fear. 'Can you tell me in English?'

Nadine shrugged. 'I would if I could. The tone of their voices was enough for me.'

Lucy remained silent, her eyes lowered to her untouched rice.

Nadine frowned. She could tell from Lucy's face that she knew what had been said. 'What is it, Lucy?'

One of the Australian nurses had also noticed her expression. 'Well? You look as though you might know some Japanese. What did they say?'

'Lucy isn't Japanese. She's half Chinese and half Dutch,' Nadine remarked defensively.

'No need to get touchy. I only wanted to know what was said, not where she's from. My name's Peggy Bennett.' She offered her hand. Nadine took it. 'Pleased to meet you.'

Betty rolled her eyes over their dismal surroundings, 'Raffles Hotel would have suited me better. Yep! A nice cool pink gin would have done the job.'

'And I'm Betty. We're nurses – or at least we were nurses.'

Again a shaking of hands. 'Nadine Burton.'

'You all alone?'

Nadine nodded. 'I am now.'

Wanting to change the subject, Nadine turned to Lucy. 'What did the soldiers say?'

'Wait,' whispered Lucy, her porcelain features frozen with tension. 'Wait and you will see.'

The guards returned about an hour later led by the officer, the interpreter trailing respectfully in his wake. One of the guards placed a bowl of water on the floor.

'For washing bodies and food dishes,' explained the interpreter.

'Which first?' whispered Nadine. In the past, despite having seen all manner of ablutions carried out in the River Ganges, she would have been appalled at washing dishes and bodies in the same bowl. During the Robinson Crusoe existence of the last few weeks, she'd got used to it.

She glanced at Lucy, saw her head was bowed, her flickering eyes fixed on the floor, her glossy hair curtaining her face.

Major Yamamuichi stepped into the cramped cabin carrying a bamboo cane topped with a silver handle. He used the tip of this to lift Lucy's trembling chin. Wisely she kept her eyes lowered.

He said something in Japanese.

The interpreter translated, though with a sour look on his face. 'The major says you are pretty.'

The major let her chin drop, turned to the other Chinese girls and lifted their chins too.

The two girls were pleasant looking but comparing them with Lucy was like comparing reeds to roses.

The major said something to the interpreter.

Nadine tried desperately to understand.

The interpreter's eyelids fluttered nervously as though he was loath to repeat what had been said. Nadine shivered and although her stomach was almost empty, she felt sick at the thought of food.

The major snapped an order and departed. She'd heard enough Chinese to know that the two girls had been ordered to follow the interpreter. Reluctantly they rose to their feet, keeping so closely together that they appeared joined at the hip.

The door closed behind them. Silence reigned yet Nadine was convinced that every heart was thundering in each frightened breast.

'I suppose we should wash up,' she said, desperate to occupy herself rather than think.

Lucy nodded silently, started to rise but sank immediately back onto her haunches, her face buried in her hands.

'Lucy? What is it?'

Lucy's hands dropped from her face. She shook her head. 'Nothing. Not now.'

The Australian girls were nothing if not persistent.

'So where are we going? What will it be like? Do you know?'

Lucy answered. 'I'm not sure. I think Sumatra.'

Pamela, one of the English girls, looked worried. 'What do you think is happening to those Chinese girls? Surely they aren't doing laundry at this time of night. Do Chinese do laundry at this time of night? I know their laundries are very good...'

Betty interjected. 'Don't be so bloody ignorant!'

Nadine asked the same question but more quietly. 'And what will this place be like? Will we be expected to beat clothes on stones in the river?'

'I will tell you later,' whispered Lucy.

'Tell me,' whispered Nadine. 'Tell me where they're taking us.'

She heard Lucy sigh.

'They call them comfort houses: I heard they had them in Manchuria along with all the other horrors they instigated.'

'Is that a place where geishas entertain?'

Lucy stifled an anguished cry of laughter. 'Hardly. Geishas sing, dance, and write and recite poetry.'

'Like *nautch* girls?' asked Nadine.

'What does that mean?'

She went on to explain. 'Dancing girls in India. Temple dancers mostly.'

A beam of moonlight gilded Lucy's face with silver. Nadine saw her raised eyebrows. 'And what would a well brought up *memsahib* know about girls like that?'

Nadine curbed her tongue. Now was not the time for confessions but she couldn't help wondering how Zakia, Sureya and even her mother would handle this.

'Nothing – not really. Go on. Tell me more.'

'Why do I get the impression that you know more than you're letting on?'

'Because you know me so well?'

'That is so.'

'Never mind that now. Tell me more.'

Lucy sighed heavily before continuing. 'We are to be *ianfu*, comfort women, selected women installed in an *ianjo*, a comfort house, to attend to the physical needs of Japanese officers. They are what we would call prostitutes, or better still actors and dancers, to entertain as well as provide... well... you know. It seems we have been purchased by a private contractor who provides girls for men of a more cultured nature – not for the ordinary solider. For that alone we have to be grateful.'

'I heard that.' The voice was Betty's.

The other girls had heard too and raised themselves onto their elbows.

'If I had known I would not have agreed to come,' said an English girl. 'I must protest. I really must.'

'Who to?' asked Nadine, feeling as though her brain had turned to jelly.

'Well I don't know! All I know is that I've changed my mind.' She hissed at Lucy. 'Why didn't you tell us this earlier?'

Nadine sprang to Lucy's defence. 'Leave her alone. You made your decision. No one forced you. Besides, Lucy was already on the boat at the time. She couldn't tell us.'

'But I didn't want to stay! I might be dead by now! Those back on the beach might all be dead by now!'

'If you're really keen to go back, you can leap over the side and swim there,' said Betty.

'As long as you don't mind sharks,' said Nadine. 'Besides, those left back there on the beach were being fed and watered. You don't do that if you're about to shoot them. It's a waste of rice for a start.'

'Damn and double damn,' said Betty who appeared to have resigned herself to the fact that there was nothing she could do and now lay flat on her back in the limited space. 'I could have stayed back there and made myself a little grass skirt if I'd really put my mind to it. Can you imagine how pretty that would have been?'

'Over your salmon pink thighs? Give us a break, Betty,' chuckled Peggy.

'I'm tired,' said Nadine, 'and I really think we should all conserve our energy.'

'In case of emergency? Do you think we are likely to sink?' asked the Indian girl.

'No. Just because we've got the option to enjoy our sleep. We've only left an island and lost a battle. There are a lot of people who have left this world and lost their lives. We have to get through this.'

'Too true, Little Miss Wisdom.' Betty sighed and turned over.

Silence reigned, but only until the return of the Chinese girls.

Both were flung in by soldiers who laughed before closing the door. The girls huddled close to each other, their faces turned to the wall. They made no sound, but their pain was tangible.

It was almost daybreak, and the grey light of an early dawn replaced that of the moon.

Nadine sat up first and saw the huddled figures, bent like twin foetuses against each other.

Lucy brought the bowl of water in which they'd washed their rice bowls and their bodies. She spoke to the two girls in Cantonese, the language of Hong Kong and Malaya.

Their faces were bloated. The right eye of one girl was almost closed. Blood ran from the other girl's nose and into her mouth. They were both trembling, their few remaining clothes torn and clutched against their bellies.

Nadine prised a piece of material from one of the girls and proceeded to bathe her wounds. One of the girls moaned and clutched at her stomach. A trickle of blood ran down the inside of her thigh.

The others were horrified.

'Will this be our fate too?' Nadine asked Lucy. 'I thought our new owner caters for cultured clients, not brutes like this?'

Lucy did not answer.

The same thing happened at regular intervals on the journey; the same two girls taken, raped consistently, and returned in much the same state.

They screamed and held onto their colleagues. The guards came armed with staves that they used to beat the women back.

'I can still hear them screaming,' said Betty whilst rubbing at the bruises left by the staves.

'That's impossible. We're surrounded by steel.'

Nadine fixed her eyes on the central point of the floor. 'It's in our heads. It always will be.'

'How long can they last?' she whispered.

It was Lucy the two girls confided in, speaking in subdued voices, their eyes becoming more glazed, more hopeless. In the quiet of the night, Lucy repeated to Nadine what they had told her.

'Besides the major and the interpreter, there are fifty military personnel on this boat, mostly ordinary privates, a sergeant, and a corporal. Each pays two yen and is expected to spend no more than five minutes, three for preference. Some take longer and although not everyone spends the same each night, there is always a queue.'

Nadine was stunned to silence.

Lucy too remained silent, her head bowed. Then she said. 'They are only thirteen years old.'

Nadine closed her eyes and remembered Zakia and Sureya, mothers at thirteen.

Swallowing did not take away the taste of revulsion. Neither did closing her eyes or placing her hands over her ears form a barrier to what was happening. The sight, the stink, the sound would be with her till the day she died – whenever that might be.

She looked at Lucy who seemed much thinner than she had been, but then, they all were.

'What about us? When will it be our turn?' she asked softly, fearing the answer, but needing confirmation.

Lucy sighed.

'The Chinese girls have been bought for the common soldiers' house. We have been bought for a special house. A lot of these places are run by civilians.'

'But the major – surely he's an officer. The interpreter too; why have they left us alone?'

Although it was dark, Nadine sensed Lucy was smiling.

'The men have told Hang Choi and Chan Moy, the two Chinese girls, that the officers prefer each other. That is why they have been given this mission. It is felt they can be trusted to deliver the women unmolested.'

The other girls had listened in silence, heads bowed, eyes half closed. One or two sobbed. Some bit their knuckles. The Indian girl was sick. Once her stomach was emptied, she stared up into Nadine's face with fear-filled eyes.

'What do we do? What do we do?' she wailed.

Although just as scared, Nadine showed outward calm. 'We survive,' she said. 'We survive to live on – no matter what.'

* * *

The ship's engines shuddered to a halt. One of the more friendly guards told them they were not far from Palambang in Sumatra.

Because they had been shut in the cabin for so long, the strong sunlight blinded them, the heat as thick and heavy as a damp blanket so it was difficult to take in their surroundings.

Nadine took a deep breath, delighting in the taste of fresh air as opposed to the stink of diesel oil by virtue of their close proximity to the engine room.

Blinking in the strong sunlight, she surveyed where she was just in case she should ever pass this way again, but the light was blinding. It was so hard to see. They had docked at a quayside, which bustled with brown-skinned people and Japanese soldiers. Junks, *sampans* and Malayan *prouws* jostled for space between military shipping and inter-island traders. The common gibbons that the Malays called *siamangs* screeched in the trees surrounding grass-roofed houses, and water buffalo dropped steaming piles of manure between army lorries and men riding bicycles.

The two Chinese girls were siphoned off to a truck carrying other women and a detachment of soldiers. Their faces were blank as though all trace of hope, along with their very souls, were gone forever.

No one waved goodbye, wished good luck, or even cried. They were too numb.

Lucy saw the woman first. Elegantly dressed, she was leaning against the bonnet of an equally elegant car. She wore black gloves, a dark-red suit, plus hat and shoes that matched the gloves. An extraordinary sight in such an out of the way place, she was smoking a cigarette held in an extra-long holder. She looked oriental, and yet her clothes were distinctly European.

In the manner of a merchant sizing up bolts of cloth, her gaze flitted over each of them, a sardonic smile fixed on her bright-red lips.

'Pinch me,' said Peggy. 'Are we in Paris, and have I seen that woman in a magazine?'

Even at this distance, Nadine imagined she could smell expensive perfume.

'I think that mannequin is our new owner,' she whispered.

Major Yamamuichi saluted the woman. She smiled in response and handed over a package.

Nadine and Lucy exchanged glances. It had to be money!

'She is from French Indo-China,' said a voice at their side. The interpreter had advanced on them silently. 'You are to go with her. She is Madame Cherry, your *ianfu*.'

Nadine bowed and said, 'I do not know this word, *ianfu*. What does it mean? Can you explain, please?'

'Yes.' He folded his gloved hands behind his back and cleared his throat. 'Your owner. She it is you will work for. She it is who keeps the Bamboo Bridge House. You are very fortunate. It is for officers only, but special. Colonies of British Empire are now Japanese. Colonel Yamoto wishes to learn more about British women for when he is posted to London. You will be happy. Very much food. Very easy life.'

As he led them forward, the girls whispered amongst themselves.

Peggy was beside herself. 'They haven't taken Australia have they? Please say they haven't taken Australia.'

'And India? No. I don't believe it.'

'Propaganda,' said Nadine. 'Whatever they tell us isn't necessarily true. Conquered peoples are obedient people.'

'That's what they believe, is it?' whispered Peggy. 'Well, are they in for a surprise.'

Nadine bowed her head to hide her amusement which seemed out of place in their grim predicament. Despite everything, Peggy and Betty were still defiant and she welcomed that. Bravery was going to be needed in big portions in the coming months. So was resilience. So was cunning.

As they lined up in front of the sleekly gorgeous woman and her car, the interpreter repeated his mantra.

'Very easy life.'

Nadine doubted it but pretended subservience all the while glancing around her in case at some point she had the chance to escape.

11

At first glance it resembled Paradise. In the distance, the blue of the sky melded with that of the sea and the beach was a ring of gold dividing one from the other. Palm trees grew straight and stark around the perimeter of the stockade-like stakes dug in the sand to keep the jungle at bay. Beneath the trees, buildings built from wood and woven matting with palm frond roofs clustered defensively together.

The temperature was another matter. It was hot and humid because they were surrounded by jungle and it was hard to concentrate. Sweat dripped into their eyes, sapped their strength. All anyone wanted to do was move as little as possible. Nadine did her best to take in the details, but her heart sank. She had contemplated escape and was determined to note specific landmarks. There were none, just miles and miles of dense tropical forest, moisture and greenery going on forever.

There were two British, Caroline and Roslyn, Betty and Peggy, the two Australians, Lucy and Nadine, plus two Dutch girls. The Chinese girls had gone elsewhere. Hopefully they were still alive.

All of them were taken by truck through a barbed wire gate

into a compound ringed with huts. For the most part the huts were flimsy, built for short-term occupation; it was becoming common knowledge that the Japanese were contemplating a swift victory.

The cone-shaped hats of the labouring Chinese bobbed about over various tasks. Tired eyes glanced as stonily as a bullock or mule, without emotion, their wills broken, backs bent to the task.

At the end of the compound, a bamboo bridge had been built, linked to a small island set by itself in the water. On the island was another hut, larger than the others and seemingly newly built.

The day was hot, the journey had been long, and they were stinking, stiff and glad to tumble down from the truck.

Appearing unscathed from her car, the woman in the red suit urged them to be quick.

Once their feet were on solid ground, she introduced herself.

'I am Madam Cherry.' The name raised a few titters. Madam Cherry clapped her hands. 'Quiet please. Line up, please. Line up.'

Lucy's icy fingers reached for Nadine's hand.

'Your hand is so cold,' Nadine whispered.

'So is yours. Like ice.'

Flanked by two Japanese soldiers, the small woman with the huge presence clapped her hands. 'No talking please.'

There was a sound of swishing silk as Madam Cherry lit up a cigarette, her lips staining the holder bright red and perfectly matching her dress.

Once she'd taken a puff, she walked up and down, inspecting their hair, their features, and even their fingernails.

She smiled all the time as she tweaked necklines or tidied hair.

'You will all be happy,' said the smiling woman, cupping Nadine's cheek. 'You will work hard for the Japanese army. In time you will work off what I have paid for you, and then you may go home – if the war is over.'

Nadine's smile fell from her face. She sensed the apprehension in the other girls, but kept her eyes fixed on the Indo-Chinese woman. Two yen. That was what Lucy had said. Two yen for every soldier: Did officers pay more? And how much had Madam Cherry paid for her? She had to know for sure that Lucy was right.

She braved asking a question. 'What work are we to do? Laundry was mentioned.'

Madam Cherry spun round on three-inch heels. The lips that had smiled so easily became a straight line. Now when she cupped her face, the tips of the long red fingernails dug sharply into her cheek.

'You are to be of service to the Japanese army, but only to officers. There is another place for ordinary soldiers. Rejoice that you have been especially chosen.'

Despite the sharp nails digging into her cheek, Nadine persisted.

'How much have you paid for us? How much have I to work off?'

Features of Indo-Chinese women resembled fine porcelain. Madam Cherry's features hardened to glass. She narrowed her eyes as though marking her for close observation.

'I will tell you when you have worked it off.' She spoke with a slight French accent and her tone was more than worrying.

Her fingernails dug deeper. Nadine winced.

Madam Cherry's face came close to her own. 'In future you will bow and ask permission to speak before addressing me. You will also bow at sunrise to the rising sun and at sunset to the setting sun. You will also bow to all soldiers and officers of the Imperial Japanese Army. Is that clear?'

The sharp nails were removed. Nadine ached to rub at the soreness on her face, but wouldn't. Madam Cherry, she realised, was far from being a smiling friend, but to show fear or even pain would be a mistake. There would be no pleading to her better nature. In all likelihood she didn't have one.

The cut glass voice continued. 'There are some here who speak French. Some speak English. Few of the Japanese speak French, but some do speak English. Colonel Yamoto, the commandant, wishes that we speak English. This is to prepare everyone for the time when all the British Empire is under Japanese control. Is that clear?'

No one answered at first, everyone unsure of what to do. If they had thought Madam Cherry was just a porcelain doll, their opinions changed very quickly when she grabbed the hair of the girl closest to her, dragging her to her knees.

The tendons of the girl's neck pulsated as she fought the urge to scream, her head bent unbearably backwards.

'Now,' she said, a self-satisfied smile on her face. 'This is what you do. Bow!' She jerked the girl's head forward with such force Nadine thought she heard a bone crack. 'Bow,' said Madam Cherry, her face stiff with intent.

The girls left standing bowed their heads.

'Lower!'

They bowed from the waist, arms held against their sides just as they were taught back on the beach.

A trio of officers descended steps from a building immediately behind Madam Cherry and sauntered across the yard, smiling and making jokes, smoking and staining the air.

'Bow,' barked Madam Cherry. 'Bow to the officers.'

All the women, including the woman who was to be the bane of their lives for some time to come, knew the importance of kowtowing to the victorious enemy.

Like reeds before a breeze, they bowed.

An officer appeared and addressed Madam Cherry in Japanese. 'Good. They are respectful.'

'I will ensure that they always are,' replied Madam Cherry.

Still bowed, she hurriedly assured him that he would be pleased with the women she'd chosen.

Her voice barely a whisper, Lucy interpreted as much as she could. Nadine felt her shiver.

The officers brushed their new owner aside. 'Now I will inspect,' said one who carried two swords in his belt.

Madam Cherry ordered everyone to stand straight.

'No slouching. And smile. Smile for the officers.'

'Are you kidding,' muttered Betty in a disbelieving New South Wales twang.

'With your mouth, not your eyes,' whispered Nadine.

Peggy winked and immediately stepped forward. 'Madam! May I ask a question.'

Elegant French made shoes stopped in their tracks. Madam Cherry's simpering expression snapped swiftly to hostile.

'What question?'

Her voice flew straight as an arrow.

Peggy winced, but kept her nerve.

'One or two of us are suffering from malaria. Will there be medical supplies available? Quinine for instance?'

Madam Cherry's smile was as tight as her skirt. 'Yes. You will be charged three dollars per tablet and the amount will be put against the sum I paid for you.'

Peggy looked horrified. 'But that's exorbitant!'

Face like thunder, Madam Cherry, retraced her steps and looked up into Peggy's face. Peggy was quite a bit taller. It gave those watching great satisfaction to see the 'Madam' having to crick her neck.

'You will pay. You will pay for everything and only when you have paid off the debt you owe me will release be considered. Now. You will stand straight.'

The sun beat on their backs as the three officers inspected each woman, Madam Cherry following discreetly behind, explaining who each one was, where she was from, and why she had been chosen. They stopped in front of Kochi, the Indian nurse. A faint smile trembled on her lips as Madam Cherry looked her up and down.

'You are Indian?'

Kochi nodded.

'Good. Then as a woman from a conquered nation you will be willing to serve the mighty Japanese Empire who have pledged to free her country from its British masters.'

Kochi stared at the ground. She had earlier told Nadine that she was marrying a doctor, a pilot in the RAF.

They moved on. One of them stopped to touch Peggy's hair. It was blonde, curly and framed her heart-shaped face. She wore a sarong like the rest of them and had ample hips; one leg was bare to mid thigh. Like most of them, she had lost most of her possessions to the sea.

The officer glanced down at her exposed flesh. There was no need to guess what was on his mind.

Madam Cherry caressed the redness from Nadine's cheek. 'She has lovely eyes. See their colour? So unusual. And she is so young, perhaps even a virgin? Where were you born?'

'India.'

'Occupation?'

Nadine thought swiftly. They'd been brought here to entertain. Perhaps she could emphasise her credentials and thus protect herself in some way – if possible.

'Dancer.'

Madam Cherry raised her eyebrows. 'A British *memsahib* dancer?'

'My father was British. My mother was Indian and a professional dancer.'

The officers smiled, nodded and exchanged comments.

Nadine looked beyond them, seemingly mesmerised by the staunch tree trunks skimming the boundary fence.

The party moved on stopping in front of Lucy.

The elegantly dressed woman spoke and indicated the lovely Lucy Lee Van der Meer.

'And you?'

'Chinese mother, Dutch father.'

Nadine saw the look that passed between the three officers. On the boat they had all seen how the Japanese had viewed and treated the people of China. This might be a special place, but Lucy was still partly Chinese. The two nations had been enemies for centuries. Hate was imbued in every vein of the Japanese body.

Lucy was dragged from the line up.

Madam Cherry addressed her. 'You are to go with the officers once they have finished their inspection. They wish to speak to you alone'

The smell of damp, thick forest was muted by the smell of fear. Lucy's porcelain complexion bleached deathly white. Her lips pouted into a silent plea, 'help me'. Nothing could save her. She was led away.

No one was in any doubt of what would happen.

Nadine stepped forward. 'May I ask a question?'

Madam Cherry's smile had stagnated on her face. 'Yes?' She spoke through clenched teeth.

'As prisoners of war, we should be treated as such.'

'No you are not. You were given an option. You decided to come here. You are now under contract to me.'

'But surely Japan...'

'Nothing to do with Japan. You are under contract to me.' Madam Cherry's eyes blazed with anger.

It occurred to Nadine that to push the matter would be suicide. Instead, she bowed, every fibre in her body wanting to hit the woman, kill the Japs, and set Lucy free. But she was helpless. Totally helpless.

Nadine had been fully expected a beating but got away with her questions, perhaps because Madam Cherry was in a good mood calculating how much money she would make from her new investment.

'Come now!' she laughed and clapped her hands. The sound was like a thunderclap to break their fear. 'There is no need to be afraid. Disobedience will be punished. You will do as you are told. Now. You will wait here while officers make inspection.' Her tone was as sickly and sweet as syrup. 'This way.'

They followed where she led, all afraid, all feeling an emptiness inside that had nothing to do with hunger.

The small party passed towards where a sentry and a tree stood sentinel each side of a bamboo bridge.

The beautifully dressed woman from French Indo-China was supplied with a chair, a cool drink and a Chinese labourer with a palm leaf fan whilst they waited. Everything was placed on a shady veranda.

'Sit,' she cried, waving one perfectly manicured set of fingers.

The guards gestured with their rifle butts. The women sat on the dusty ground. The sun was hot. Their throats were dry.

An hour passed. The flies buzzed. Scorpions and centipedes scurried between them, pausing in the shadows they threw on the scorched dust. No sound came from the other side of the bridge. Each woman averted her eyes from the place, preferring to stare at the ground. It was as though a spell had been cast, as if looking in that direction might tempt fate.

'I'd murder for a sip of water,' said Peggy. She was perhaps the most audacious member of their troupe. On the transport coming here she had declared she was from Melbourne and had six brothers all serving in the forces. 'I've got a seventh, but he's still in short pants. Hope this bloody war's over before he's old enough to get killed.'

'I'd murder that bloody woman,' said one of the English girls. Her name was Caroline and she'd fancied herself as a bit of a Florence Nightingale so joined up. 'It was the uniform,' she'd explained on the journey here.

'The one you wore or the one that came with a bloke inside it,' said Betty, the girl from Brisbane.

Peggy nudged her arm. 'Ssshh! She's listening.' She jerked her chin towards the shade.

'No she's not.' Nadine had not entered the conversation. Instead she had scrutinised Madam sipping her drink between writing something on a pad resting on her lap. 'She's counting,' said Nadine.

'Counting what?' asked Caroline.

'Her money.'

'I can't see any money.'

'That's what I mean,' said Nadine. 'We work. She earns.'

Kochi whispered. 'Is that what your friend Lucy is doing? Earning her money?'

Nadine stared at the trees.

Kochi hid her face against her folded arms. Nadine didn't need to answer.

12

The hot day did not lose its heavy sense of foreboding; the feeling that hell was on earth and no one was going anywhere else.

Nadine closed her eyes and sucked at her dry lips. No matter that they were women, they had entered a battle zone. No matter that Lucy was going through hell, she must not dwell on it. If she – and others – were to survive this place, her mind must be clear.

The Australian girls were muttering.

'Wonder who's next.'

'Any chance mine might look like Clark Gable?'

'Any chance I can join a nunnery?'

Someone laughed derisively. 'It's too late for that.'

'I just want to get in the shade. What do they think we are? Chinese labourers?'

Their questions and answers were going round and around in circles and getting on Nadine's nerves.

Nadine kept her gaze fixed on Madam Cherry. Her voice was calm and low. 'Do you realise how close we came to being shot? It's thanks to Lucy that we're still here. I bet she wishes that being thirsty was her only problem.'

Even the Australians fell to silence. It was a few minutes before anyone said anything.

'Wouldn't mind one of their hats,' groaned the irascible Peggy.

Where Peggy went, Betty followed. 'Then get one.'

'Oh yeah. How?'

Nadine intervened. 'By shamming.'

'Shaming?'

'No. Shamming. The beggars in India were past masters at getting what they wanted.'

'Including hats?'

'Yes. Including hats.'

Ensuring no one saw her, she rubbed dust over already parched lips and then slowly, feeling the earth hot beneath her palms, she got onto all fours.

'Water,' she said, barely audible, a rehearsal for the act to come. Tottering like a drunken man, she staggered to her feet.

A guard shouted and raised his rifle.

Hearing the commotion, Madam Cherry looked up, frowned and got to her feet. 'What are you doing? You have been told to sit down.'

Nadine was as one in a dream. Tottering from side to side and holding her hand against her forehead, eyelids fluttering.

'Water,' she whispered, tottered a little more and then fell to the ground.

Caroline attempted to get to her feet and go to her.

Betty stopped her. 'Don't rock the applecart,' she whispered. 'We've been told to sit, so sit. Let's see what she's up to.'

Madam Cherry sprang from her chair and shouted orders to a gang of nearby labourers who were attempting to erect yet another hut.

The language was foreign to her, yet Nadine was sure she knew what would happen next.

She kept her eyes tightly closed as they rolled her over onto her back. Instructed by Madam Cherry, one of the labourers forced water into her mouth, washing away the dust from her lips and the dryness from her throat.

The barked order was obviously not obeyed quickly enough. She heard a sharp thud but kept her eyes tightly shut. Cool air wafted across her face. She made the relevant murmurs of appreciation before slowly, very slowly, opening her eyes.

'Was I dancing?' she asked innocently.

'Dancing?' Madam Cherry looked puzzled.

A Chinese labourer was using his hat to fan her. He was also rubbing the side of his head. A tin ladle – no doubt the one from which she had drunk water and clouted the man with – hung from Madam Cherry's hand. She snapped an order. Reluctantly, the labourer placed his hat lopsidedly on Nadine's head.

The two guards were requisitioned to assist her onto the cool veranda.

A hint of French perfume escaped from the silk suit as Madam Cherry sat down. Her slender fingers reached for a silver cigarette case and a lighter. 'You will sit with me in the shade.'

Her voice was enticing. Like a snake, thought Nadine. She glanced briefly at the others, the sun baking their backs.

The hat was on her head, not theirs. She was the picture of submissive innocence. Defiance did not get you what you wanted. It only got you killed.

She dared to speak. 'Madam, I have seen pictures of geishas and other Japanese ladies and they are very pale indeed. Am I not correct in assuming that their men folk prefer clear white complexions? Therefore, do you think it would make sense if the skins of your investment be preserved from the sun?'

Madam Cherry narrowed her eyes. Nadine read distrust in her

expression but also something else. The suggestion was being digested, the options weighed.

Nadine reeled from a sudden slap on her face.

'That's for your insolence!' Springing to her feet, the elegantly attired woman barked an order that was immediately obeyed. The prospect of greater profits had won the day. The others were moved into the shade, their owner inspecting each one in turn to assess what damage had been done.

Whilst she was gone, Nadine glanced at the sheaf of paper she'd left lying on the table. Thanks to her friendship with Lucy and the need to barter with Chinese merchants in Singapore, she understood some of what was written there.

The top page listed the women and how much had been paid for them. A breeze lifted the page, flipping the details out of sight. She recognised a few words on the second page: medical supplies, each priced at exorbitantly high figures.

The shadow of Madam fell over her. A drink was offered.

'You said you are a dancer?'

Nadine nodded. 'I was training to be a dancer back in India. I was very young. I still am.'

Madam Cherry narrowed her eyes. 'You are indeed. That was one of the reasons you were chosen. Officers prefer girls who are like green sticks – unbroken. Why did you leave India?' asked Madam Cherry, the smoke from yet another cigarette trailing out of the side of her mouth.

'I was sent to school in Malaya. My father disapproved of my dancing.' She made no mention of Martin.

One lie fell upon another. The Japanese, who had plucked her from the beach, had confiscated all valuables, including her wedding ring.

Some inner instinct urged her to emphasise her youth.

'And this dancing... you danced in public? For money?' The fascination in Madam Cherry's voice was repeated in her face.

Nadine nodded. 'I did indeed. I was much admired. Much copied too.'

She was telling half-truths, gradually weaving a web of lies and determined to keep doing so. *If it keeps me alive...*

Madam's eyes were sparkling. 'I too have danced... I danced in a theatre in Hanoi and also in Bangkok, Tokyo and even Hong Kong. Did you dance in a theatre too?'

Nadine shook her head. 'I danced at private parties in the palaces of Maharajahs.'

Madam Cherry's eyes arched high into her forehead. 'Princes! Real princes?'

'Yes.'

She lied, but did so purposely. This was a woman impressed by power and she had intimated that they had common ground. Inadvertently, she had exposed weakness.

'Hmmm!' Smoke curled from flared nostrils and almond eyes narrowed as the woman gazed into the distance. 'I think we need to talk some more. I have intimated to Commandant Yamoto that the officers might wish to be entertained with dance and music.'

Nadine kept her gaze fixed on the women sitting in the shade beneath a tamarind tree. Dancing would be much preferable to other duties.

'You show no concern for your friend. I find that surprising.'

Swallowing the words she really wanted to say was incredibly difficult, but they had to be swallowed. To utter them would get her nowhere – nowhere at all.

Instead she said, 'Is there anything I could have done to stop it?'

Madam Cherry tossed her head. 'Nothing!'

The next question was even harder. 'Is there anything I can do to stop it happening to me?'

She made a so-so noise. Nadine imagined that her head swam from side to side as she said it – like a puppet pulled by a master's hand.

'You will be proud to entertain Japanese officers.'

'You could charge them more money if I were to dance for them. I guarantee my dancing will fascinate, intrigue, and arouse them.'

Nadine felt the almond-shaped eyes fall on her. There was no warmth in them. Nothing except cold calculation.

'You are very clever for one so young. Yes. Very clever.'

They both fell to silence. Nadine's heart stopped fluttering. She had sowed a seed. Hopefully it would take root and produce a flower.

The sound of raucous laughter drifted from the direction of the bamboo bridge. The officers reappeared.

'Ah! We are finished.' Madam Cherry rose from her chair. 'Now you may go back with your friends.'

She clapped her hands. 'Line up. All line up. Bow,' she said sharply. 'Remember to bow to all members of Japanese army.'

Dutifully they bowed in the direction of the officers until the door of the main building had swung noisily behind them.

Two guards positioned themselves slightly behind and on either side of the elegantly dressed woman.

She clapped her hands again. 'Now you will go to your quarters. You will be happy there. There is much comfort. Clean clothes, even soap.'

She sounded elated, as though she had gone out and bought the items herself: A woman of contradictions, thought Nadine, her mind buzzing with possibilities.

Madam Cherry's voice suddenly sprang from sharpness to a

deceiving smoothness. 'Wash yourselves. Wash your clothes. Eat, drink and rest. Prepare yourselves for the officers. Prepare yourselves to be good *karayuki*.'

The Englishwoman named Rosalyn had hazel eyes, red hair, and a small, receding chin. Nadine hardly noticed her falling into step until the woman's fist punched against her thigh.

'You want to watch out making friends with the enemy like that.'

Nadine punched her back. 'You should be grateful. I got you shifted into the shade.'

Rosalyn looked offended and far too superior for her own good. Her small eyes narrowed further. 'That's as may be, but I've lived in Bombay. I know what you natives are like. Treacherous. Ungrateful and not to be trusted. I'm going to be watching you!'

The tirade took Nadine totally by surprise.

'Come on, girls, cut that out.' Peggy pushed in between them.

Rosalyn swung aside muttering something about bloody wogs.

'Take no notice of her. Bloody cow!'

'I won't.'

Peggy frowned. 'You look worried.'

Nadine had already decided which women she could trust. Besides Lucy, Peggy was top of the list. 'From what that woman said, it seems we will never buy our way out of this place.'

Peggy slumped down beside her. 'Hmmm. You could be right.'

'How many of us are likely to get malaria?'

'All of us probably.'

Nadine looked into Peggy's face. Her expression was usually as breezy as her personality, but not at the moment.

'And with quinine at three dollars a time?'

Peggy threw her head back and closed her eyes. 'Ah!'

'Ah, indeed. Madam has no intention of letting us go.'

Other women had gathered round to listen. 'Hey,' said one of the Dutch women from Macao, 'how about the Geneva Convention?'

Nadine remembered Martin and his politicising about the threatening situation before the fall of Singapore. 'I don't think they agreed to it.'

'Great!'

A terrible silence descended. Some girls cried openly. Others pretended to be sniffing or clearing their throats. The mood was dark and worrying.

'She'll charge us for everything,' said Nadine thoughtfully. 'Everything has a price and she has everything for sale.'

'Something will turn up,' said Peggy, slapping her thighs as she got to her feet. 'Something always does.'

'I'll pray it does,' said Betty. 'And I'm not in the habit of praying much.'

Nadine narrowed her eyes and watched a native trader pushing his cart towards the guardhouse steps. The eyes of off duty guards looked up with interest.

As Nadine watched, her mood lightened. 'Unless we find things to sell too.'

'Including sexual favours?' said Peggy with a raising of eyebrows.

'If need be.'

13

The Australian nurses, Nadine and Kochi, the Indian girl, took a corner of the mat Lucy was lying on and carried her through to the back of the hut.

They looked down at her, all grateful that they had not been picked out, even more grateful that they were not Chinese.

'She'll be fine here,' said Betty who was doing her best with the few medical supplies Madam Cherry had given her – though *given* was the wrong word. The cost would be set against Lucy's earnings.

A brooding silence persisted, a dull ache because they all knew what was to come. If they were treated better than Lucy they'd be lucky – extremely lucky.

Kochi broke down completely. 'I'm so frightened.'

Nadine hugged her though she felt scared herself. 'We're safe for now. I've suggested to Madam Cherry that we entertain the men just like Japanese geishas. The colonel has agreed this should be so. Apparently he wishes to learn more about English-speaking women so he can take full advantage when the Japanese army march into London or New York.'

Peggy looked astounded. 'Is he serious?'

Nadine shrugged. 'Apparently so.'

Their moment of reckoning delayed, at least for the time being; their spirits and the atmosphere became less strained.

Madam Cherry showed them how to make tea – served without milk in tiny cups without handles and bitter tasting.

'More of such supplies will be here soon,' they were told.

She showed them how to serve sake in the same tiny cups they used for tea. 'First you warm it.' She also encouraged them to sing – one at a time. 'Your officers wish for entertainment. Music is good and helps them relax and they will value you more.'

'I'd sooner die,' muttered Rosalyn, her hazel eyes hard as walnuts. 'Music. This is ridiculous.'

Madam Cherry heard her. 'What was that you said?'

All eyes turned in Rosalyn's direction. She kept her head down, her eyes staring at the floor.

'You!' shouted Madam Cherry and pointed.

'She said it makes sense,' said Nadine, her desire to take advantage of the occasion outweighing her dislike of Rosalyn. 'The British have a saying – music soothes the savage beast – exactly as you said, Madam. It helps even the most ferocious beast relax and become almost civilised.'

For a fraction of a second, Madam's black pupils turned denser as she considered whether Nadine's reference to beasts was meant as an insult. She decided it was not. 'Such a young head holding such wisdom; and as a dancer, you would know this?' Smiling she patted her on the head as though she were a beloved child.

To those watching it seemed that way. Nadine controlled her shiver and the feeling that one day it could just as easily be patted by a very sharp sword.

'Yes, Madam.'

'Then dance for us.'

Nadine was taken by surprise. 'There is no music.'

A red fingernail rested against Madam's equally red lips as she thought about it. 'Hum!' she said at last. Her eyes swept over the assembled women. 'Hum,' she commanded. 'Go on. Hum a tune.'

The women exchanged puzzled glances.

Rosalyn's voice carried. 'What tune?'

Peggy began humming the Death March.

Nadine's whispered comment carried along the line. 'This is getting us nowhere. We have to entertain these men. That is why we have been brought here. Let's not make things more difficult for ourselves. Dancing and music could hold off the dreaded day...'

'I'm not listening to a mere child – and a native one at that,' muttered Rosalyn.

Peggy, typical of her countrymen, spoke louder and less discrete. 'Well she's a kid that talks good sense!'

'Stop this!' Madam Cherry signalled one of the guards who up until now had watched the proceedings. Peggy fell forward as a male hand swiped the back of her head. She dared to mutter, 'Ouch. That hurt.' And earned herself another one.

Nadine admired the Australian girl's defiance. She saw Rosalyn look up at her with outright malice in her eyes – as though it had been her fault.

'Right,' said Madam Cherry, a fixed smile on her glossy lips. 'Now we will sing a song so Nadine can dance for us. I will choose. Nadine, step out here.' She pointed to a clear spot in the centre of the longhouse.

Nadine waited.

Madam Cherry came to a decision. '*La Vie en Rose*!'

The sharp delivery made everyone sit suddenly upright.

Seeing puzzlement on a lot of faces, Nadine made a suggestion. 'Couldn't we have something simpler?'

'"Oranges and Lemons!" Just a thought,' said Betty with a shrug of her shoulders.

Madam Cherry clapped her hands. 'So! "Oranges and Lemons!"'

The familiar words of the old nursery rhyme stirred the air and their hearts, reminding them of times and people long gone.

Nadine danced, her arms waving like the reeds by the river, her heels digging into the floor, her toes pointing. As is the way of traditional Indian dance, she used her hands, her arms and her eyes to express emotion.

Lucy was never far from her thoughts; every so often her gaze strayed to the dropped reed curtain behind which Lucy lay battered and bleeding. How many of us will end up like that? She determined to do whatever she could to make their ordeal more bearable.

Thoughts and emotions were dangerous. Through sheer willpower, she curbed them showing on her face. She must dance, smile and be pleasant. They all had to be pleasant. It may just keep her alive.

* * *

Some days later, the imminent arrival of the officers made the air tremble.

Madam Cherry had given the women a pep talk, though a warning harangue would be a better description.

'This is not a common establishment. The colonel and his officers expect more for their money. They want clean girls, good looking girls of different cultures who can help them adjust to the new order when Japan and her allies win the war.'

A strange sense of relief ran through the girls, though they were hardly in a good predicament themselves. Rumours on the ship had been rife of terrible places in which girls were forced to submit to twenty, thirty or more men a day.

There were fourteen of them now, new arrivals having been brought in from other islands and Burma. Fear made them all edgy and quarrels broke out over the slightest thing.

'Some girls will slit their wrists,' said Peggy to Nadine.

Nadine didn't ask whether she was being serious.

They'd been given time enough before the officers' arrival to wash and change into silky sarongs and tightly fitting tops. There were also some pieces of jewellery and sandals. Some were stained with the blood of their previous owner. Arguments ensued over who was having what.

'Listen to us. We sound like bloody schoolgirls about to go out on their first date,' said one of the Australians.

There was muted laughter. Deep fear lingered beneath the apprehensive expressions.

'At least we can get clean,' said Bunty, a round-faced girl with a turned-up nose who Nadine couldn't quite take to.

Their initial pleasure in sharing a bar of violet perfumed soap and changing into clean clothes had been neutralised by Madam Cherry's version of reality on the very first day.

'The cost of your new clothes will be charged against your earnings.'

'A fat profit for stolen clothes,' remarked Nadine.

Rosalyn had decided that as a general's daughter, she should be leader of their little clan, totally oblivious to the fact that Nadine was already respected as leader.

'I insist we should keep the same protocol as we do in the services; senior officers' wives take precedence over those married to lesser officers. I'm used to chairing committees.'

The British girls shrugged their acceptance. The Australians were less convivial about it. The newly arrived Malay girls agreed out of ignorance. Holding ballots and creating management committees was not part of their culture.

'Right! That's it,' declared Rosalyn licking the tip of a pencil and opening a notebook. 'Now for some rules and regulations.'

'Can I ask something?' asked Peggy.

'Certainly.'

'Am I right in thinking your father is attached to the military police?'

'Yes,' responded Rosalyn with a proud uplifting of her chin. 'He was.'

'Not a bad guess,' muttered Betty, Peggy's fellow Australian nurse.

Later they all gathered around Rosalyn's list of rules that she'd hung on a handy nail.

'Loss of privileges, blah de blah de blah,' said the Australians.

'What privileges?' asked Nadine.

No one knew.

'I understand the crimes though,' said Peggy.

A breathless hush settled on them as they read the main reason why one of them might end up imprisoned in one of the three huts made of corrugated tin standing close to the latrines at the edge of the camp.

'Black marketing, smuggling and undue fraternisation,' Rosa read out loud.

The Australians raised their eyebrows in disbelief. 'Undue fraternisation? What the hell are we here for if it isn't to fraternise?'

'Congratulations, Peg.'

Peggy turned to her fellow Australian. 'For what?'

'For using the polite "f" word.'

The girls laughed, all except Rosalyn who was taking this all very seriously. Rosalyn was well built – something between voluptuous and formidable. She puffed herself up to what seemed her full size.

'We betray our bodies but not our minds. That is what I mean. In other words, we don't get emotionally involved.'

The women erupted.

'Of course we won't!'

'Kill them if we have to.'

'Fight them. Yes! Fight them!'

'And die!' said Nadine.

Nadine never shouted, but her voice had a certain gravitas that was hard to resist. The single word hung in the air.

Peggy thought she sounded like a female James Mason.

'Go on, Nadine. Tell us what's on your mind.'

Nadine got to her feet. 'I want to survive this and I'd prefer that none of you go killing our captors. That way we're all dead meat.'

'So, Miss Clever, tell us *your* little plan.'

Rosalyn smirked in her superior way, as though no one could be quite as brilliant as the daughter of a general.

Nadine found it easy to ignore her. 'This is a business and with a bit of forethought we might be able to buy things with the money we earn. We know there are traders who come to the camp. We can bide our time and wait to be rescued. And...'

She waited until she had their full attention.

'We can buy our freedom.'

Betty frowned. 'Won't she try and load up the amount we owe to her?'

'As I've said, mark the tradesmen that come in here. Bribe them to get us out as soon as we can, or wait until we're liberated – whenever that's likely to be.'

Even the outspoken Australians didn't question when that was likely to be. No one wanted to face the fact that they might be forced to 'be nice' to the enemy for a long time to come.

Bunty and Caroline asked the same question in unison. 'So how do we do that?'

Nadine smiled. 'There are ways, but don't expect other people to do it for you. You have to watch, you have to listen. Eventually the right opportunity will present itself.'

Nadine saw Peggy smile and presumed it was because she'd trounced the dreaded Rosalyn.

Peggy was sharper than most. Though Nadine didn't know it, a life of isolation in India had left its mark. Believing her cunning was common to everyone, she failed to see that others had not been blessed with such sharpness.

'How about if we refuse to do this and ask to be transferred into a proper POW camp?' she said.

Nadine rested her chin on her hugged knees. 'We've all heard what they're like. We've all heard how little there is to eat, how many are dying. What price life? What price survival? If you can't manage a fate worse than death, then go over there. Your choice. I want life. At any price, except,' she said, looking up, 'betraying my friends.'

* * *

On that first night they were open for business, everyone washed and dressed silently, their despair hidden behind masks of resignation. In a last-ditch attempt to put off the dreaded moment, Peggy had refused to comb her hair.

'If I look ugly, no one will want me.'

Nadine, who was tying some tiny bells around her ankles, corrected her. 'Not necessarily. If you look like an old sack they may treat you like one.'

Peggy looked disbelieving.

'Or worse... like a Chinese,' Nadine added.

Peggy, and a few others who'd followed her lead, fought over the hairbrush.

Conversation always returned to the same subject.

'I want to get out of here. Regardless of this paying off business, I think I'll ask to be interned properly with the other prisoners when the stockade is finally built,' said Caroline. It was whispered she was the daughter of a barrister and hailed from Cheyne Walk, Chelsea. She certainly spoke like that and her clothes had quality. 'I don't think it's going to be terribly easy.'

Nadine raised her eyebrows. 'That is an understatement!'

Lucy worried her. She lay on her bed staring into the distance. She refused to talk about her ordeals and refused to return the pitying looks of the other women.

Nadine searched the women's expressions. Some hid their fear very well indeed. Others did not. Kochi's thin, brown arms shivered and set her earrings jangling. They were large and long, taken from a box containing similar. Nadine touched her hand and said, 'We must be brave.'

Kochi bit her lip so hard that it turned bright red as the blood rushed to the surface. Her eyelids fluttered. Her voice trembled.

'I have to tell you something. I have never been with a man. You know – naked.'

There was little privacy in rooms where the walls were made of woven matting. Rosalyn had overheard. Her voice carried through like water through reeds. 'Well you have to do your duty. Like the rest of us,'

'Shut up, Rosalyn!' Nadine's smile for the poor girl was feeble, but all she had. 'Take no notice,' she said with a little shake of her head.

It did no good of course. It was an attempt to salve to ease Kochi's nerves; she could see by the way her dangling earrings trembled that she hadn't been successful.

Rosalyn wasn't giving up easily. 'I won't be responsible for your non-compliance.'

Nadine, who had been mixing a concoction of coconut milk and rice, was getting angry. 'Rosalyn, if you don't shut up and I'm going to come in there and cut out your tongue – with a...' She paused and stopped stirring. '...With a spoon!'

Rosalyn tossed her head. 'Hmm! Well I wash my hands of you natives. Get into trouble and you're on your own.'

'And us whiteys?' asked a bemused Peggy, puffing on the tail end of a cigarette that four of the girls were sharing between them.

Rosalyn sniffed. 'That's different!'

'And I'm different,' said Nadine. 'Isn't that what you're saying?'

'You're not European.'

'My father was British.'

'So you're half caste.'

'Oh for goodness sake!' Caroline, the girl from Chelsea interrupted. 'Come on, Rosalyn, old girl. Give it a rest. We're all in the same boat together.'

Rosalyn looked deflated. Caroline, being from an upper-class background, was the only girl she sucked up to. She obviously hadn't expected to be put down by her own kind.

Caroline was a law unto herself. 'Take no notice,' she said, walking over to Nadine whilst inhaling the smoke from the very last of her cache of expensive cigarettes. 'She's a cow, darling. An utter bloody cow.'

Nadine smiled as Caroline sat down on the floor beside her. Caroline had such a wonderfully upper-class way of swearing, almost as though she were delivering the dictate from the pulpit.

'Common at heart,' she added. 'Just tries to put it on. Take no notice.'

'We'll get through this.' Nadine eyed Kochi as she said it. The girl was wringing her hands together, almost to the point of tying them in knots.

'That's right,' Caroline added. 'You'll get over this. You just see if you don't. You're both so young,' she said. 'Especially you, Nadine. Surely you're not long out of school.'

'Not long.' Nadine's attention drifted out towards the bamboo bridge. In the distance she could see boxes being unloaded from an army truck and taken into Madam's quarters. Other things went in too: the brocade covering of an ornate chair flashed in the sunlight. Another Japanese was carrying a carpet; yet another was staggering beneath the weight of an elaborate and very large candelabra. Narrowing her eyes, she remembered something Martin had said about people making fortunes during war and telling lies merely to survive.

An idea occurred to her. Yes, she did look young. She was after all barely seventeen and suddenly very scared. Rosalyn would never be on her side. It was up to her to do what she could to protect herself. Was it possible her youth could save her – if handled properly?

The setting sun was fingering the velvet sky with tongues of orange.

A few curious eyes glanced her way as she got up and headed for the door. Her face was a mask, impervious even to those who bothered to look; fear had made islands of them all.

She watched her bare toes making marks in the dust on the floor. On the outside she appeared calm. Inside she was terrified.

Caroline, of course, was the exception to the rule. The others might be experiencing first night nerves, but Caroline was made of sterner stuff. 'Get a grip, girls,' like the head girl at school.

Nadine made a sudden decision.

'Hey. Where are you going?' Caroline shouted after her.

'To see the She Dragon.' Using the name the girls had decided suited their 'benefactress' rather well.

'She'll bite your head off.'

Nadine fixed her gaze on the bridge and beyond to the closed door of Madam Cherry's abode.

'Which could save you the bother of presenting it to her on a plate.'

Caroline frowned. 'What do you mean?'

Nadine kept her gaze fixed on the bridge. 'We don't know for sure whether the Japanese are winning or whether we are. Who knows? In a few days we might be liberated. It wouldn't hurt to buy a little time in the hope that we will be rescued.'

Rosalyn sniffed. 'Oh, really! And how, might I ask, does our innocent little schoolgirl intend doing that?'

Nadine looked at her in such a forthright manner that the older girl was forced to look away.

'By offering something of great value to the She Dragon. Something only I can give.'

14

Nadine heard the laughter of officers nearby as she made her way from the Bamboo Bridge House. Perhaps they were coming for her.

'Not yet,' she whispered. If she could only hold off the eventuality of her situation for a short while longer, it might be long enough for rescuers to find them, for the war to end, for her to be free of both her captors and her husband.

Although she knew she was treading a dangerous path, she bowed low to the guards and asked to be taken to Madam Cherry.

The She Dragon appeared in the doorway and her face expressed displeasure. 'You should not be here! What is it you want?'

Nadine bowed respectfully. 'I have something very precious and sought after to sell.'

A deep frown registered between the finely plucked eyebrows. The little red mouth pursed. 'What is it? I see nothing in your hands.'

Nadine smiled in a cunning manner, the sort of smile that would intrigue the avaricious woman.

'I have brought you an unblemished rosebud. I am sixteen years old and not long out of school. Surely that is of some value even here in this place? If I spent some time dancing, my price would be even more than it is now for the first man to take my virginity. Is that not so? Would I not be worth more?'

'Sixteen? A virgin?'

The imagined tinkling of coins falling into a cash register was like music to Madam's ears. The door opened wider.

It had been a last-minute decision to reduce her age to sixteen, a good decision.

'Come in. And shut the door behind you. I warn you, you had better be telling the truth.'

The floor of the room was warm to Nadine's bare feet. There were shoes and native-style sandals to wear, but she'd decided to go barefoot. It hardened the soles, and besides, she could run faster in bare feet.

Madam Cherry's accommodation had atmosphere. It also had movement. Moths battered their fragile wings against a lighted oil lamp. Two empty glasses sat on the table waiting to be filled.

Madam Cherry's calculating eyes narrowed as she folded her graceful hands. 'So! You are untouched?'

Nadine lowered her eyes almost bashfully and nodded. 'Yes. Is that not of value?' Tonight was the first night the Bamboo Bridge House was open for business. If she could just put unwanted intimacy off for one month, one week, one day... until rescue came... hopefully.

Madam Cherry eyed the slender girl standing before her.

'Well,' she said slowly, her enthusiasm hidden behind a mask of casual indifference. 'So how much do you think you are worth?'

Nadine was not fooled. Madam Cherry's greed was like lava bubbling unseen in the heart of a volcano.

'Quite a lot if handled properly. I thought perhaps I could be offered at some special event. I could dance first. I could dance at many events – even outside the compound, and thus my fame would spread. You could make much money.'

If it occurred to Madam Cherry that dancing outside the compound might also provide an opportunity to escape, she did not mention it, though doubtless it did cross her mind. She wasn't stupid.

The woman's pencil-thin eyebrows rose along with her interest. 'And then auction you to the highest bidder?'

'For the whole night.' Naturally the idea was abhorrent, but just one man, thought Nadine, hopefully no more. It was some consolation, though little enough. Ultimately she still hoped to escape or be rescued. If she had money, in time she might be able to bribe the guards or the Chinese labourers.

Madam clapped her hands. 'And make even more money! Yes.' Her laughter exposed her uneven teeth, a number of which had gold fillings.

Nadine pushed the suggestion a little bit further. 'Until then perhaps I should remain out of reach and live here with you? Otherwise the men might be tempted and our efforts ruined.'

She imagined the effect this orchestrated arrangement would have on some of her colleagues, but this was no time to worry about petty jealousies. She'd told the Australians about her plan; she'd even told Lucy, though wasn't sure that she'd taken it in. She didn't speak. She didn't seem to hear.

Seeing Lucy like that had made her determined. What she proposed was about survival and having access to inside information that might result in all of them regaining their freedom. More importantly, she might gain access to medicine and they were certainly going to need that.

Madam Cherry held her head to one side as she considered the proposal. 'Yes.' She nodded with guarded enthusiasm. 'Yes.

There must be no suspicion that you have been undone. You will stay here with me until the time is ripe.'

'And I think I deserve ten percent of whatever I earn from my deflowering, but for me directly, not to pay off my debt to you. Yes?'

'Ten percent?' Madam Cherry looked quite shocked at such a brazen comment. 'That is quite out of the question. Five percent.'

Nadine thought quickly. No matter how little the amount, she sorely needed money to buy things that were needed, things that would soar in price as the war continued.

Freedom also would come at a price. Five percent was better than nothing.

'Five percent of whatever you get for me. I won't ask for a cut of what you will make for putting on entertainment, drink and food. After all, it is I who own this much valued pearl.'

Madam Cherry tilted her head from side to side and back again as she considered this.

'Yes. I agree to this, but I will have to charge you for the items needed to fully exploit your potential.'

She could see from the deep black eyes that there was no room for negotiation.

Head bowed to show her subservience, she smiled as though she truly believed the woman. 'I agree. I will get my things.' Nadine bowed herself out.

The path back to the Bamboo Bridge House was black with shadows thrown by a silver moon. Her heart was light – or lighter than it had been, but there was no room for complacency, but still... if she'd been sure of not drawing attention to herself, she would have ran all the way, skipping and shouting *Hallelujah*!

If escape or rescue was impossible but she used her cunning, she might become the privileged whore of whoever bought her virginity. Whore! Virgin! Neither word suited her. She did not wish to be the former and she certainly wasn't the latter. If the latter was found out – as ultimately it would be – she would be in even deeper trouble. Something had to happen before then.

A queue had formed on the landfall side of the bridge: officers only, of course, and all with lust in their eyes. The fact that the opening of the establishment had been awaited with politeness and great self-control on the part of the men amazed her. That didn't mean their patience would last.

Her steps slowed, her nerves tightened. She had to pass them. Would they fall on her as they had on Lucy despite the guards to either side of her?

Her mind worked quickly. *Show them you are human and they will show respect.* She bowed as she came level with them. Not in the Japanese style, but in the manner of the Hindu, hands together.

They exchanged what sounded like ribald remarks before bowing and returning the same greeting. She would have left things at that and bid a hasty retreat, but a group of three men were blocking her escape. Her heart began to beat rapidly.

Suddenly the lonely sound of a flute drifted into the night, faintly and almost magical. Blessing its gentle intrusion, she began to dance. The men fell to silence and gazed, enraptured.

She danced as she'd never danced before, weaving her arms around her face and over her head, tracing lines in the empty air with her fingers, moving her feet and body at different angles.

Smile, smile, smile... make them feel you only wish to please them. She wished she was wearing bells around her ankles, bangles on her arms.

It is just a case of keeping your nerve. Sureya had said that.

Spreading her arms and deftly crossing one foot over the other, she bowed low.

They clapped enthusiastically giving her time to dart over the bridge.

Peggy was waiting for her, smoking nervously. 'Well that was some show!'

Closing her eyes, Nadine leaned against the hut, unable to control her trembling.

Peggy looked anxious. 'They didn't touch you, did they?'

Nadine shook her head. 'No.'

'So what did the She Dragon say? Did you get what you wanted?'

Nadine nodded. 'Yes. I'm moving out.'

Peggy's jaw dropped. 'Tell me more. I might want to come with you.

Nadine told her what she had done.

'My, my, but aren't you the dark one. You've certainly drawn yourself a cushy number, but if you could get your hands on some quinine – a few of us are already showing signs of malaria. Do you think you can?'

'That's my intention. But I don't want everyone to know. One whisper and I'll get the same treatment as Lucy got.'

'OK.' Peggy nodded then indicated the inside of the hut. 'Her majesty Queen Rosalyn's going to have something to say about that, you know. *Fraternisation, darling.*' That's what she'll say.

'I know. But think about it, Peggy. What are our needs, and I don't just mean medicine? A few luxury goods would keep our spirits up, wouldn't they?'

Peggy pursed her lips around the dwindling cigarette – the first of the last packet she owned. 'Food, soap – various sanitary items that all girlies need – oh, and cigarettes.'

Nadine's eyes shone. 'Everything. Everything and anything can be bartered to get things we want. And aren't things going to get scarcer as the war goes on?'

'You bet.'

'I'm hoping it might be over by the time my virginity is sold off.'

Peggy narrowed her eyes. 'I thought your husband got killed back on the island.'

Nadine nodded. 'That's right.'

Peggy's eyebrows shot up. 'Sorry to disappoint you, sweetheart, but I don't think the war is likely to be over before you're required to hand over the goods. Then what? It's not too easy to reinvent your virginity and not delivering the goods as described could land you in very deep water.'

'I'll cross that bridge when I come to it.' Her eyes shone with excitement. 'Think of it, Peggy. I'll be *inside* the She Dragon's lair. Did you see the boxes going in there today? Can you imagine how much she's making from all that stuff?'

Peggy blinked. 'You're a crafty little cow for your age, aren't ya?'

It almost felt treacherous to laugh in such dire circumstances, but she'd achieved something. However, there were concerns.

'Peggy, I don't want you to mention what I'm up to. Some of us can't keep our mouths shut. It's a bargaining chip. Yes?'

'Yeah, and some of our colleagues would do anything for a few things to make their lives more comfortable.'

'Exactly. She's dealing on the black market with anything and everything she can get her hands on. We'll need some of that stuff, Peggy. And there's sure to be more medicines besides quinine in there, don't you think?'

Peggy's eyes lit up at the mention of medicines. 'Crikey, Christmas comes all at once, don't it?'

'You could say that.'

Peggy flicked the stub of her cigarette into the water. 'That could be bloody dangerous.'

'I know, but think of the benefits.'

Her nervousness diminished, Peggy shook her head and smiled. 'We can use a bit and sell a bit. Marvellous idea!' She slammed her hands down on the railings.

'We're desperate women, Peggy.'

'You do realise you're going to leave yourself open to accusation. Hope you've got a broad back.'

'I have.'

15

That night Nadine slept on a mat in a small alcove leading off from the main room of Madam Cherry's quarters, considering the likely repercussions of what she had done. Her sleep was fitful and full of troubled dreams. Something woke her. Rolling over onto her side, she lifted the screen between her and the main room.

The noise she had heard was the grating of a chair and the rush of paper money and coins onto a table. Madam was counting her money, saw her looking and reached for a bamboo cane lying next to the money.

Nadine curled herself into a tight ball whilst three raps from the cane landed on her shoulder.

'Go back to sleep. In the morning you will prepare my breakfast. Get rice from the kitchen and fruit. Make coffee. I like plenty of sugar. It is all there in that cupboard.'

Morning came and Nadine was up early, sweeping the veranda outside with a flimsy brush, occupying herself until called for.

'You may prepare breakfast. Everything you need is on the small table inside the store room. Here is the key.'

The key was warm in her hand. Nadine unlocked the door.

Madam's private stash was something to behold. The storeroom was like an Aladdin's cave, and there were things in her private cupboard that were already fetching high prices on the black market: coffee, sugar, tea. There was even a tin of shortbread biscuits.

Normally Nadine would have salivated.

'You may pour yourself a small cup of coffee and take a piece of fruit with your rice. There is also a tin of sardines in oil – so much nicer than Japanese dried, don't you think?'

Whilst Nadine devoured her breakfast on the floor inside the hut, Madam ate out on the veranda where she nodded and made polite conversation with passing Japanese officers. To native tradesmen she nodded imperiously, as if marking them for future investment.

Making the excuse to Madam Cherry that she had left a particularly pretty sarong behind at the Bamboo Bridge House, Nadine crossed the trickle of water separating the house of women from the rest of the camp.

Her whole body turned numb with each faltering step. This was the morning for facing what the women had done and what she herself had done. She kept telling herself that her purpose in becoming resident with Madam Cherry was twofold – to obtain medicine and things they could use to barter plus her own survival, but not everyone might see it that way.

She took a deep breath before entering.

The smell of men pervaded the hut: the stew of sweat, polished leather, sex and cigarettes. The girls had rolled up the bamboo blinds that formed the walls of the hut. Their future was mapped out. They would repeat the action for many mornings to come until they were worn out or dead.

Fearful eyes stared from strained expressions and they were silent – so terribly silent. A few trembled and rocked backwards and forwards, arms hugging their bellies. Some had serviced more than one man. There was no refusing even the most ugly of conquerors, though no one, it seemed had been beaten.

'They lapped it up,' whispered Peggy. 'The music, the dancing, the playing of cards – so even those who indulged in sex didn't turn violent – thank God!'

Nadine refrained from asking her how she'd fared. The question was too painful and she wasn't sure she could cope with her answer. The niceties of their world had changed and would not be easy to deal with.

Caroline looked up from rummaging in her sea chest. 'Nadine. We wondered where you got to. Are you all right? Where have you been?'

The usual voice of confidence was strangely staccato – coping but only just.

She stood in the middle of the room looking around her. 'I've got something to tell you. I am to lodge with Madam Cherry for the time being until...'

She was the consummate actor, leaving the last part of the sentence unsaid in order to add affect.

'There, didn't I tell you?' shouted Rosalyn. 'Typical native! Traitors, the lot of them.'

'Hold on there, Rosalyn...'

Rosalyn appeared not to hear. 'Never darken our door again. You understand me? Never again! Collaborator!'

'All right for some,' grumbled Betty.

Peggy threw her countryman a warning look. 'Give the girl a chance. You don't know what you're talking about. You don't know what's going on.'

One of the Malay girls threw a sandal at her. A row of dark eyes regarded her with something close to hatred, but also fear.

Nadine wasn't surprised by their reaction. That was what fear did to people, but it was obvious that she would have to watch her back. She hung her head, took a deep breath and told them the basics. 'I'm being auctioned off to the highest bidder. She insists on chaperoning me until it happens – or until we are rescued. In the meantime I will do whatever I can to make your lives more comfortable.'

She was the subject of disbelieving stares, the girls not sure whether to pity or envy her predicament.

Rosalyn was outraged.. 'More comfortable! I don't believe a word of it. She's a collaborator. I swear it. I know her sort. Blood will tell. Always does, always will,' she said, and stalked off in the direction of the latrines.

Peggy watched her go. 'Not quite the comment I'd expect from a general's daughter.'

Nadine gave her a grateful smile and joined Peggy as she went to see how Kochi was doing. The girl had been a virgin but wasn't one any longer. The officer who'd taken her had drunk a few bowls of sake beforehand so hadn't noticed. Kochi was still in pain, curled up in a corner, her brown eyes staring vacantly above her thin, brown knees.

'The pain will pass,' Peggy said, kneeling down beside her. 'Here.' She passed her a sanitary towel. 'Last one in the camp. You'll have to wash it and reuse it, but it's better than nothing.'

* * *

Items looted from the Red Cross, captured British military supplies, contents from the homes of displaced persons and empty plantation houses were being carried into the storeroom when Nadine got back.

'I have a task for you,' Madam Cherry said, her gaze following the burdened natives carrying a variety of merchandise into the already packed storeroom. 'I need to keep a careful record of my transactions.' One fine black eyebrow rose quizzically. The dark iris of an ultra-dark eye measured her from top to toe; *because I too am a commodity*, thought Nadine.

'I am expanding,' said Madam Cherry. 'I have no clerk to record my stock. I believe you know some Chinese. You will do this I think.'

She handed Nadine a notebook and pencil.

'Write these down for me. One box of silk stockings. Twelve in box.' She passed a box to a waiting native and told him where to store it. 'Not there! There! Come on, I haven't got all day.' As she cussed him in Chinese she cuffed his head so hard, his neck sprang like a bedspring. 'One piano,' she said. Lifting up the cover, she poked at one the keys. There was a muffled, dead sound, certainly not the sweet note she'd been expecting.

She shouted at two young natives. In response they lifted the lid and her expression dropped.

Nadine too saw that the piano was no more than a fancy wooden case, the guts of the thing mangled beyond repair.

Madam was livid. 'Robbers! That native headman robbed me! All we can do is use it for storage.'

Besides medicines identified by a red cross on the side of the box, there were also luxury goods, wines, food, clothes, antiques and furniture. Nadine listed everything, including the broken piano.

Once everything was stored, the key to the store room was hung on a nail above Nadine's sleeping mat.

'They are your responsibility,' said Madam Cherry.

'Of course, madam.'

Nadine bowed gratefully, and why shouldn't she? She was trusted.

Madam Cherry had a bathtub, running water and a mirror.

She also had a whole box of soap tablets. The following day, Nadine took one. Now to get it along to the Bamboo Bridge House. God knows they would need it.

She pushed it into the knot that held her sarong.

Sentries guarding the overworked natives busily building the prison stockade opposite their compound followed the roll of her hips as she made her way along the lean road between huts, palms and heaped supplies.

When she arrived, the girls were washing and squabbling over the only soap they had.

Betty snatched it from one of the Malay girls. 'Hey, go steady with that. We've only got one bar.' She passed it to Caroline.

Caroline swirled it in a bowl of water, took it out and placed it to one side.

'It won't last long,' Caroline sighed before dipping a cloth in the water and gingerly dabbing between her legs.

Nadine looked for Peggy and saw her crumpled in a corner, her head resting on her knees.

One eye peered out over the crook of her elbow, then disappeared again.

'She had a hard night last night.' It was Peggy's friend, Betty. 'It's the blonde hair, I suppose. Something different that they had to try.'

Nadine sighed. 'I'm sorry. Here,' she thrust the tablet of soap at her. 'I stole it.'

'Wow!' Betty took it, sniffed it and lovingly fingered its smooth, rounded surface. 'Can't believe I feel like billing and cooing over a piece of bloody soap. My, but we have sunk low!' She looked up suddenly. 'I suppose you and the She Dragon have got plenty.'

'Too much. I thought a little redistribution might be in order.' Lowering her voice, she moved closer. 'I thought it best that I steal a few small items we can trade for other things. She's got loads of stuff: jewellery, clothes, food and goodness knows what else. We might even be able to pay someone to get us out of here.'

Betty squinted as though she could see right through her. 'Don't think I can't guess what you're up to. Peggy and me have been best mates for years. Not that she told on you, but then she didn't need to. I can read her well enough. Bin cobbers for ages!'

'Cobbers?'

'Friends.'

It worried her that too many might find out what she was up to, but she decided Betty was trustworthy.

'How's Lucy?'

Nadine saw a look in her eyes she couldn't quite read.

'What is it?'

'They would have had her again if Peggy hadn't intervened.'

She looked to the corner where Peggy had been.

'Where's she gone?'

Betty nodded to a place in the wall where the woven panel had come adrift. 'Her favourite place.'

Ducking under the matting, she sat down beside Peggy. The floor at the back of the Bamboo Bridge House stuck out like a balcony high above tangled vegetation and a stream that seemed to bubble up from nowhere.

Penny was dangling her legs over the side, her eyes fixed on the trickle of water flowing beneath their feet. She noticed a bruise on the side of Peggy's face.

Nadine flexed her legs and studied her toes. There were no right words. She waited for Peggy to speak. Eventually she did.

'I'm a tough old bird really – at least I thought I was, but in there...' she jerked her head back at the wall. 'I felt... invaded. But I won't let it kill me. I'm blowed if I will!'

Despite Peggy's air of defiance, her thigh muscles tightened as though she were subconsciously drawing her legs together.

'Did you fight?'

Peggy smiled as she fingered the bruise. She shook her head. 'No. Does that surprise you?'

Nadine shook her head. 'No. They expect obedience as theirs by right. That's what I think anyway.'

Peggy nodded. 'I think you're right. Do the other and you're a gonner!'

Nadine looked at the water. 'I'm sorry I wasn't here.'

'And suffer as well? No worries,' said Peggy, looking at her. 'You're going to be living dangerously enough along with that slit-eyed bitch. Get caught pilfering her stuff and you get...'

She didn't finish the sentence. There was no need to. Both women knew what would happen once things – really important things – went missing from Madam's cache.

Nadine gave Peggy a hug then got to her feet.

'I think I'll keep Lucy company for a while.'

She left Peggy sitting there.

Back inside the hut, the little woman who looked after the till when Madam wasn't around was calling for Peggy.

Nadine passed back through the communal room that served as the girls' daytime quarters. A young lieutenant was preening himself at the front door, taking off his hat and smoothing his jacket as though he were out on a date. She guessed he had come for Peggy.

Betty had just finished washing herself. She was stripped naked but seemed totally unreserved, as though she walked around naked all of the time.

Once she'd finished with the bowl, Nadine took the same scented water to bathe Lucy's bruised flesh. She also managed to force a little coconut milk mixed with mashed rice between Lucy's lips.

Lucy managed to speak. 'I'm not a dog. Nor a slut.'

'Of course you're not!' Nadine spoke softly as she smoothed Lucy's hair back from her forehead. 'None of us are.'

Lucy's lips trembled. 'The Japanese have always been envious of the Chinese. It's traditional.' She spoke defiantly – proudly even.

Nadine put down the rice. 'Let me make you feel better.'

Pulling back the sheet, Nadine bathed the bruising on Lucy's belly and between her legs. She gritted her teeth, determined that neither her horror nor her fear would show.

'Let me help you turn over.'

Painfully and with Nadine's help, Lucy did as she was told.

Nadine paused. There were bruises; there were even teeth marks. Worst of all, dried blood crusted the cleft between her buttocks.

'Tell me if I hurt you,' said Nadine. She barely succeeded in controlling the trembling in her voice, bathing Lucy's soreness through a veil of tears.

Once she'd finished, she pulled the sheet back over her and pasted on a brave smile. 'Does that feel better?'

Lucy smiled back. 'Yes.'

The sound of a flute being played sounded from outside.

Nadine squeezed out the cloth and threw the contents of the bowl out of the window.

At the sound of the water splashing onto the foliage, the flute player paused and looked up. He was an officer. Their eyes met and for a moment the world seemed to fall to silence.

'Who's playing?' asked Lucy.

Nadine gritted her teeth. 'Just another Nip.'

There was a faraway look in Lucy's eyes, as though she wasn't really listening. 'When they abused me, I pretended I was not here. I imagined I was back in Singapore. What a different world that was.'

Nadine clutched at her throat. If she hadn't she would have

sobbed out loud. But she mustn't do that. Giving into despair would help no one.

'We'll be back there before very long.'

Lucy appeared not to have heard what she'd said. In her thoughts at least she was still in Singapore.

'The parties, the nights of stars, the smell of the sea, and all those beautiful people...'

'None of them were as beautiful as you.'

She could have bit her tongue after she'd said it. 'And you still are,' she added, regretting that she'd used the past tense.

Lucy smiled. 'Here's to Singapore,' she said, raising her hand and cupping her fingers as though she were holding a glass.

Nadine copied her. 'Here's to Singapore.'

The truth hurt and clutched at her chest. The battered, bruised woman had once dressed in the latest fashions and had been married to a handsome Dutch planter. Lucy had been the epitome of a westernised Chinese girl. Her perfume, like her body, had been elegant, refined.

Small cries of entreaty came from one of the small rooms adjacent to the one Lucy was lying in.

Through a gap Nadine saw a man sandwiched between two Malay girls over in the corner, switching from one to another as the fancy took him. His voice was low and guttural; she had no idea what he was saying.

In the next cubicle, the young lieutenant she'd seen earlier was examining Peggy's pubic hair. He looked totally entranced by the fact that it was a little more reddish than that of her head.

Peggy was good at smiling and snarling at one and the same time.

'Do you realise how much I hate you,' she was saying sweetly, her words barely sliding through a clenched smile. 'Yes, you're the conquerors now, but you know that old saying, he who sows the wind will reap the whirlwind. I hope you get sucked up in the worst of it, sucked up into a bloody great fiery tornado, you nasty little bugger!'

Being here was difficult. Death or dishonour. A fate worse than death. All those trite sayings trailed through her mind. Words Shanti had once spoken to her overshadowed them all: *life is precious no matter what.*

The man who'd been with the two Malayan girls came out from behind the bamboo curtain. He was naked and made no effort to put his clothes back on. Like most Japanese, he was fastidious about bathing, preferring to swim before visiting the women and swim or bathe again afterwards.

A bathhouse was provided adjacent to the Bamboo Bridge House for the use of officers. Sometimes the women were taken there to scrub their backs and help them bathe, the custom in Japan.

The officer padded on bare feet the length of the room to where the old Korean woman sat behind a cash register. The cash register was extremely ornate and silver in colour. Rumour had it that it had come from a haberdasher's shop in Singapore.

The officer paid, the old woman stabbed at a key – not always the right one, but any would do in order to open the drawer.

Nadine lingered, her eyes feasting on the amount of money going into that till. *Think what you could do with it.* Only a little so it wouldn't be noticed; enough to buy medicines and extra food and, best of all, pay someone to take us out of here. But how? Madam Cherry didn't let the cash register out of her sight. Nobody else was trusted to sit there except the old woman, and when the old woman wasn't there, she took the money herself, two guards groaning beneath the weight of a silk brocade armchair brought from her private quarters.

The naked man went outside to pee over the front veranda before returning to put on his uniform.

Rosalyn, along with her sidekick, Bunty, a new arrival, were waiting outside as Nadine left.

'The prodigal returns,' sneered Rosalyn. 'Are you back to suffer like the rest of us, Nadine, or still intent on saving your own skin?'

After seeing Lucy, nothing Rosalyn could do or say could upset her. Her voice was as chilly as the look in her eyes. 'Leave me alone, Rosalyn. I don't like you and you don't like me. Let's leave it at that!'

'Just you watch your step,' Bunty snarled at her.

Rosalyn interrupted. 'Shut up, Bunty.' She turned back to Nadine. 'I've spoken to Madam about laying down certain rules in this house. She agrees that we should be self-governing and will be mentioning it to the colonel. She's sure he'll agree.'

Nadine gritted her teeth. 'Oh I'm sure he will. Divide and conquer, and you're handing him victory on a plate!'

Before crossing the bridge she saw a bruised and battered native being manhandled by two guards and shut in a box made of corrugated iron. She shivered. If Rosalyn had her way, she'd be in there too.

16

Madam Cherry set the auction of Nadine's non-existent virginity for one month hence. Nadine was told this as she helped check the stock piled ceiling high in the small room behind the main living quarters. She'd been hoping for longer, enough time to plan her escape, but she had learned to flatter. 'How very wise. Leaving it so long will generate the optimum interest. Do you think I should put myself on display a little more? You remember, I did say if I gave dancing displays outside the camp, to rich merchants perhaps? Or I could go back to the Bamboo Bridge House and dance there. More men, more bids.'

Madam rocked her head from side to side on her slim little neck as she thought about it. 'It could indeed be financially rewarding, but...'

Nadine waited in a sweat, praying she'd say exactly what she hoped she would say.

'But,' said Madam, holding up her customary warning finger, 'the men may see you and take advantage. With good reason: All girls in the Bamboo House are there for one reason.'

Nadine wanted to say, to make you money. But she didn't.

'So,' said Madam, looking as though the idea was all hers. 'You will not go there.'

'Yes Madam.' She paused, apparently concentrating on folding some fine white table linen stolen from those fleeing the Japanese. She imagined it had once graced the table of a very fine house. It seemed an odd thing to pack when an invasion was imminent, but people have affection for different things. Now she was unpacking it. Goodness knows whom Madam intended selling it to.

'I hear the old Korean woman who oversees the cash register is not well at present.'

'She has bad feet and is not Korean. She married a Korean. She is Chinese. Did you not see her feet? The toe was broken as a very small child – little more than a baby. Her feet were then bound, the toe gradually rotting into the soles of her feet. That is why she has such trouble walking.'

Nadine pretended the catches on the brown suitcase she was struggling to open were stiffer than they actually were. The woman with the bound feet was bad tempered, ate fruit all day and spat the pips and stones all over the floor. Some of it stuck to the sides of the cash register.

Madam crouched down beside her, her black eyes glinting like polished jet.

'When Anku, the old woman is not there to take the money, you will take her place. That way you are seen but unavailable.'

It had worked! She would have access to the till. A thrill of triumph shot through her, but she was careful not to let it show. 'Of course, madam.' Less words meant less chance of elation seeping into her voice.

Peggy, Betty and one or two others were amazed to see her replace the old lady with the bound feet.

'Saves us having missiles spat at us,' said Peggy. 'She must think you're a good honest Asian at heart.'

Nadine grinned. 'Think of it as a shop window and me as a box of chocolates. Highest bidder gets to taste.'

The population of the Bamboo Bridge House had grown to twenty. Madam selected a number of girls to move to the comfort house used by the common soldiers. Fear spread like wildfire. Rumours had reached them of girls servicing more than twenty officers a day in such places

One of the girls selected to go escaped into the forest where she devoured poisonous fruit. She died in agony. The rest were closely guarded until it was time to leave.

'These girls leave,' said Colonel Yamoto cheerfully, proud that he had managed three words of English.

There were no cheerful goodbyes.

'No point in worrying about them; we have to worry about ourselves.'

Rosalyn had spoken.

Nobody argued. The ringing cash register was the happiest note in the whole place. The officers who called were a little subdued. They'd been quite happy to be outnumbered.

'How far are we to paying off Madam for our purchase price?' Betty asked Nadine.

Nadine had access to the accounts. She grimaced. 'The closer you get to paying it, off, the more expensive your needs become.'

Betty nodded. 'That's what I thought.'

Everything had doubled, and that included food, clothes and other essentials like medicines. Even if they were still fairly reasonable on the black market, Madam upped the prices a bit.

The days went past, the auction loomed. At night, Nadine awoke in a cold sweat, wishing she hadn't taken this option. Sometimes in the night she saw Martin's features bloated and fish eaten, open eyes staring up at her through the water. And then it was blue again.

The following morning, Madam Cherry was smiling like a cat satisfied that the mouse was not able to escape her sharp claws. She was explaining why she'd scheduled the auction for the end of the month.

'The paymaster arrives at the end of the month. That is when the officers are paid. Their pockets will be bulging, they will get drunk on saki and by the end of the night, their pockets will be empty.'

The slight perspiration caused by the consistent humidity froze on Nadine's skin. She hadn't prayed much since childhood except when Martin was partaking of his conjugal rights and she'd prayed for him to hurry up and finish. She now prayed for courage.

'You must show me that dance again,' demanded her benefactress breaking into her thoughts.

Nadine slid the pencil inside the leather-bound notebook in which were written details of stock kept and up to date transactions. Teaching Madam to dance in the Indian way had become a daily duty.

'Like this.'

Bending her knees, toes pointing outwards, Nadine showed her how to position her feet, how to move her hips and how high to raise her arms, the hands bent from the wrists and the fingers held straight. She brought them across her face, palms turned inwards, her grey eyes peering over them. 'This is the screen through which the princess observes the man she loves...'

The older woman copied, though her limbs were stiffer, the effect less fluid.

'She aches for him,' Nadine added, twisting from the waist so that one hip formed a voluptuous curve. She crossed and uncrossed her feet in a series of intricate steps that symbolised indecision. 'But she does not know whether she should run away with him or obey her father and marry the man he has chosen.'

Madam Cherry followed every movement, toppling slightly when she whirled like a top. Back in India, the skirts of the *nautch* dancers would be spinning round at waist height, the dancers' limbs hidden in silken jodhpurs. Here their movements were restricted by slimmer skirts that barely skimmed their thighs.

'You dance well,' Nadine remarked, careful to pitch her voice between flattery and outright condescension.

The nut-brown eyes glowed with pleasure. 'I think one day when it is free of the British that I would like to visit India.'

Nadine bowed her head and hid her smile, thinking that if Madam had been a peacock she would have displayed her tail in a dazzling fan.

'Such a pity we do not have music,' said Nadine. Her willowy body moved in time with a silent tune. Her tiny head tilted on its slender neck. She had a beady-eyed look, like a snake before it strikes.

Suddenly Madam Cherry stopped dancing. 'I have an idea. Major Genda Shamida has a flute. We will ask him to play for us so we can practice better. I am sure the commandant will allow it.'

Major Shamida! So that was the name of the flute player. She'd heard the flute many times but had not known the players identity up until now. He'd never frequented the Bamboo Bridge House. On the few occasions she'd seen him go past, he'd never once looked in that direction. Out of all the officers, he was the most intriguing.

Nadine maintained her tone of gilded sincerity. 'That seems a very good idea, Madam. How clever of you to think of it.'

'Of course we will have musicians when we entertain beyond the barbed wire fence and on the night of your auction. Major

Shamida will do for practice. Did you have many musicians when you danced for a maharajah?'

'Indeed we did, Madam. The palace used to ring with the sound of many instruments and with the bells that tinkled around our ankles, and the sound of rattling bracelets around our arms and wrists. There was much sound.'

'And the palace was beautiful?'

'Indeed.' Nadine twirled on the spot. Madam Cherry followed suit. 'It was built by a great Moghul emperor. The floors were of pink marble, the walls white ran through with rose coloured threads – like veins, I used to think. And there were the gold and jewels, rubies, emeralds and sapphires, glorious statues of marble, gold and silver all encrusted with stones. I remember a life-sized elephant made entirely of silver with sapphires for eyes and rubies in his ears.'

Madam Cherry's eyes grew round as saucers. 'Was this so?'

'Indeed it was.' One arm curved over her head, the other across her belly, she turned on the spot, carefully placing her feet and flexing from the waist. Again, she was copied and surmised from Madam's dreamy expression she was inflamed with descriptions of a place that only existed in Nadine's fertile imagination.

'You must tell me more about the palace.'

'What do you wish me to tell you?' asked Nadine, seemingly concentrating on placing one foot behind the other, her torso above her waist held at an angle to her hips.

The woman who now managed her life – and those of the other women – looked thoughtful.

'Tell me about the city you lived in.'

'Benares? It is ancient. It sits on the banks of the holy river Ganges.'

'Is that all?'

Nadine stepped sideways, one foot behind, one in front... one behind... one in front. Shanti came into her mind. Forcing herself to concentrate on increasing the tempo helped her endure the pain that never really went away. She spoke eloquently.

'It is a city of Moslem minarets and Hindu shrines, of richly ornate palaces, bustling bazaars and holy men. There is also much gold, beautiful gardens with tinkling fountains and many elephants adorned with richly decorated caparisons, their tusks studded with jewels.' Not that I've ever seen one decorated so richly, thought Nadine, but Madam loved ostentation and rich descriptions of rich worlds.

Madam's eyes sparkled. 'The Japanese say that soon they will be India. That India will be freed from British rule. This will make you happy?' she asked, a little breathless as she tried to keep up.

Nadine literally thought on her feet before answering. She felt a surge of patriotism for British sovereignty and fear and hostility for the invading Japanese.

She was succinct. 'India will be happy to be free.'

As she slid into the last movements of the tuneless dance, she sensed Madam's quizzical regard.

'I find it hard to believe you never knew a man. You cannot fool me. I know dancers do more than that. They arouse the sleeping snake. Do you not admit this?'

Sureya came to mind. Nadine kept her voice light. 'Of course. But we have very pretty hands. Do you not think so?'

Smiling she waved her right hand to emphasise the point.

Madam Cherry, having knowledge herself of the dancer's life and even more for that of the *houri*, the prostitute, smiled in an equally knowing fashion.

'Ah yes. That is indeed true.'

* * *

After tucking her mosquito net securely around her sleeping mat Nadine lay in the darkness, listening to the night sounds drifting through the glassless window.

Sleep would not come as she wrestled with her conscience. It was like climbing a very high mountain that grew taller the higher she climbed. Her cunning had got her comfort; it had also got her the envy of the other girls. Even those that weren't as outspoken as Rosalyn showed it in their eyes. *Taking care of number one.* The thing was, they were all doing it. The girls argued over trivialities such as not taking turns 'entertaining' the troops or observations that whoever was in charge of doling out the rice portion that day was keeping the biggest portion for herself. Even the pillow Lucy was laying on had been taken; somehow it had been deduced that everyone should take it in turn to use a pillow.

Nadine sighed. To some extent, they were all taking care of number one, generous spirits swiftly turning mean. And all over such simple, everyday things.

The keys to the locked storeroom glinted in the darkness.

Madam had been at the bottle again and the sound of her snoring was enough to stun the crickets into silence.

Nadine rose naked from her bed, her bare toes gripping the rough floor.

Taking the key into the palm of her hand, she slid out from behind a screen of woven matting and made her way to the locked door.

Earlier that day, she had recorded the latest arrival of stock. She particularly remembered a crocodile skin vanity case full of quality makeup. There had also been a box containing tins of tobacco; another held tins of toothpaste. A torn mosquito net that madam had considered too shabby to fetch good money had been thrown to one side and when Nadine asked if it could go to the Bamboo House, the She Dragon had agreed.

Tip-toeing her way, she went back in carrying the net and unlocked the cupboard. Just as before, she remembered the location of the bottle and found it by touch.

She felt her way to the items she wanted, remembering where they were situated, feeling the shapes with her fingers.

She pilfered a few small items from the vanity case and the boxes, then softly closed the door behind her. She knew where the quinine was kept. The small key nestling next to the door key opened a wooden, wall-mounted cupboard.

Something behind her rustled. Expecting to see an angry figure in the doorway, she turned round. A mongoose ran over her feet and out of the door.

Heart thudding, she moved quickly, relocked the cupboard and then the door. Everything was wrapped in the mosquito net

The next morning, with the mosquito net bundled beneath her arm, she made her way to the bamboo bridge.

She exchanged a swift look with Peggy. 'I've brought things,' she said quietly. Even at this hour, one or two officers were still there, sleeping off the excess of the night before.

'Come,' whispered Peggy.

Nadine followed Peggy into Lucy's cubicle. She was sitting up and looking better. Kochi, on the other hand, was clinging to a bamboo upright, her eyes big and staring into space.

Lucy was trying to tempt her with breakfast, just rice and fruit.

'Kochi is their favourite now,' Peggy explained, her voice as pinched as her once full cheeks. 'Do you know how many she had last night?'

Before Nadine had chance to guess, Peggy told her. 'Five! Five!'

Nadine sat on the floor in native style, her bangles tinkling as they filed down her arm, her painted toes poking out from beneath the hem of her sarong. Kochi pulled away when she tried to pat her arm.

'Perhaps if I suggest to Madam that girls take rest periods to help them get over excess use?'

'Would she wear that?' Peggy looked doubtful.

'It's a risk I have to take. That poor girl can't take any more. I can advise madam that she'd be protecting her investment. The officers pay five times what the soldiers pay at their establishment in the town. I've seen the accounts.'

'You'll try?'

Nadine, feeling sick to her stomach but very determined, nodded. 'I'll try.'

Before she had time to unwind the mosquito net, Rosalyn poked her head in.

'Ah!' said Rosalyn, folding her arms and stepping into the already crowded cubicle. 'I detect a foul smell in here. Please get rid of it so we can all breathe less contaminated air.'

Nadine glanced at Peggy before directing her comments at Rosalyn. 'Yes, I know that, Rosalyn, and I've been thinking about this place all night. Whatever I decide to do will have an effect on everybody. I believe I have two choices. The first is that I move back in here and take what comes like the rest of you do.'

Rosalyn's face lit up light a Christmas tree. 'That's right! That's what any patriotic woman would do.'

'But you will have to forgo the little extras I can get you. Peggy and I agreed...'

Rosalyn interrupted. 'We've had a meeting. Can you imagine what it's like having them paw you with their grimy little hands? You've got it made and I... we... took a vote.'

You took a vote, thought Nadine eyeing the long nose and dark brows. Hearing raised voices, the other girls – those not entertaining an officer – had crowded round outside.

'What is the second option, please?' Roslyn asked.

Nadine took a deep breath. This was a gamble that might work to both their advantage.

Carefully, so as not to smash the quinine, she unrolled the mosquito net. Those that could see what she'd brought gasped with delight. Others behind her that couldn't see were asking so many questions that Peggy had to order them to be quiet, go away, and not attract enemy attention.

'It's little enough,' said Nadine, shooing an insect from her face. 'But better than nothing. In time, I might be able to steal more. It's getting here that's the problem. But...' she exchanged a swift look with Peggy.

'I've got a medicine bag and Nadine's got a back window. She pops things out and I pick them up and bring them here.'

A tremor of excitement ran through the girls like a breathless breeze.

Peggy shushed them again.

Nadine explained further. 'We can take advantage of the situation and the storeroom keys that dangle so close to my head. Steal a little, trade a little and perhaps accumulate enough money to buy our way out of here. Remember what Madam Cherry said? Make enough money to cover her costs and we become free – or at least get a transfer into a proper prisoner of war camp – if that's what we want.'

In her heart of hearts, she prayed for rescue to come before things deteriorated, before she was faced with a scenario based on a lie. The lie about being a virgin might kill her.

Stomachs that had already digested a small bowl of boiled rice mixed with a little papaya grumbled a response.

'We'd end up in an internment camp? Like the one they're building across the way?'

'It might be better than here, and anyway by then we might have set up a good circle of trading contracts,' said Nadine, finding solace in the plans that whirled around and around in her mind. She frowned. 'They're taking their time building that camp.'

'Prisoners are on the way, so I hear,' said Betty. She grimaced. 'An officer told me.'

'Is what you are doing not dangerous?' asked one of the Malay girls.

'As dangerous as can be! I could be shot if I get caught.'

A hum of noise erupted around her as words were said and translated and decisions made.

'We'll take a vote,' said Rosalyn, folding her arms across her bosom.

Peggy intervened. 'Sod the vote. We'll give you a list.' She glared at Rosalyn. 'I'm all for getting out of this place as soon as possible.'

'As the senior mistress here...'

Betty and Peggy burst into laughter. 'That's what we all bloody are! Mistresses by nature and whores by circumstance!'

* * *

It was Nadine's day to man the cash register. The little old woman, though recovered from her illness, had hobbled off to the soldiers' comfort house to help with their laundry.

Although under strict orders not to leave the till unattended, Nadine went to see Lucy in the small cubicle at the back of the long house.

'I come bearing gifts,' she said, 'though most have already been requisitioned,' she added, indicating the girls out in the common room.

'Were they grateful?'

'So so.'

Lucy's face clouded. 'A tube of lipstick and a bar of soap won't lessen their jealousy. They say you have feathered your own nest.'

Nadine set down the fruit, the fresh bandages and the healing balm she'd purloined from Madam Cherry's locked cache. Lucy was building up quite a little cache of her own inside her new pillow.

Nadine was less cynical. 'They'll stand it. They want to live and they want to escape.'

She began to cut up a mango.

'So,' said Lucy, her eyes keeping to Nadine's face, 'when is this auction?'

'That depends on how long I can string the She Dragon along.' She shivered. 'Hopefully forever.'

'Might I ask a question?'

'Of course.'

'You let them believe you're fresh out from school.'

'I lied. You didn't tell them?'

'Of course not. But any Asian man will want proof of your virginity: a red splash on a white cloth so he can boast of what he has done.'

Nadine sighed, the mango juice running from one corner of her mouth.

'I was hoping he'd be drunk.'

'Think carefully, Nadine.' Lucy's lovely face, now healed nicely, took on a worried frown.

Nadine leaned against the wall behind her and looked out at the platform that jutted out over the water. Major Shamida's flute playing floated in the air.

'I was brought up between two cultures; my father was British, my mother Indian. There was good and bad in both races; it has to be the same here. All we can do is survive; I'm not going to stop thinking on my feet. The longer I hold things off, the longer I'm likely to survive – until the end of this damned war if possible.'

'Have you heard how the war is going?'

Nadine shook her head. 'Judging by the way the Japanese are strutting about, I would say that no news is good news. I don't think things are going well for us, that's for sure. But we're not beaten yet.'

'The Americans are bound to retaliate over Pearl Harbour.'

'I should think so.'

'I wonder what they will do.'

'Something the world isn't likely to forget in a hurry,' murmured Nadine.

* * *

Close to dawn in the Bamboo Bridge House, everyone lay sleeping with the exception of one person.

Kochi rocked backwards and forwards, her arms wound tightly around her folded legs. She was sitting on the platform protruding over the water at the back of the house just beyond where Lucy slept, and she was talking to herself.

'You know I wanted a white wedding, David, and that I want six bridesmaids. I think they will look lovely in turquoise. What do you think? Pink? No. It should be turquoise. I insist. You think it unfair? No. No, it is not unfair. I became a Christian for you and now I will have the colours I want for my Christian wedding.'

She burst into tiny high-pitched sounds.

Lucy heard and lifted her head.

The muttering went on. 'It will be all right. I think it was a spear. I saw his face. Or was it more than one? Never mind. The faces all became one. And it doesn't matter really. Christ forgives sinners doesn't he? Doesn't he, David?'

Her body heaved with sobs, the sound catching in her throat. She fixed her gaze on the vaporous steam rising from a grey mirror of water, the colour of everything just before dawn.

Tears streamed down Kochi's face. There would be no white dress, no bridesmaids and no David.

She dangled her legs over the edge of the platform. The stream was deep and muddy. Someone had seen a crocodile or alligator swimming there. Nobody quite knew which.

'I am so very sorry.'

Lucy pushed aside the bamboo screen in time to see Kochi hit the water, a flurry of boiling water and then nothing. Calm. Emptiness.

* * *

Madam Cherry had informed Nadine of business with a rich German planter who had supplanted a Dutchman on his own plantation. He was having a birthday party and wanted entertainment. This would be Nadine's first outside performance. With a bit of ingenuity and a lot of begging, stealing and borrowing, she had made a costume from silk scarves, strands of tinsel and Japanese jewellery.

Rosalyn was reluctant to hand over a particularly fine sarong with a gold hem.

'Parading yourself like that,' she spat.

'Doing a reccy is more like it,' said Nadine as she fastened it around her waist. 'The more dancing I do outside the camp, the more I learn about our surroundings. There's a lot of jungle to get through. A lot of sea too.'

'Better views than round here then.'

Nadine grimaced. 'Never mind a view. We need a boat.'

Her heart was racing. Time was ticking away and although she tried not to think of what was to come, it was there hanging over her. At least travelling to the party she might have the chance to better survey her surroundings. She needed to escape – she *had* to escape before the auction, before the truth was found out.

It was just after breakfast and Madam Cherry was off to collect the fee for this evening's performance – Nadine's first performance.

'Practice, you must practice your *sringara*,' said Madam before leaving. She used the Hindi word as though *she* were the knowledgeable one. Nadine smiled to herself. If she remembered rightly, the word embodied the erotic longings of the dancer for the gods. She'd told the wily woman that it applied to a particular movement, the folding of limbs as a dancer sinks to the floor, the toes pointed, the arms and head still moving.

Ah well, she thought, rubbing her hands down over her hips: to work.

As the sound of the car receded, she took the keys from the hook and headed for the storeroom. Unlike the Bamboo Bridge House and the labourers' huts and the others being built, Madam Cherry's quarters were as substantial as those occupied by the Japanese army.

She smiled at the keys lying in the palm of her hand: the keys to an Aladdin's cave of stolen, bartered and exchanged supplies.

The floor of the storeroom was of hard-packed earth. Boxes marked with the international sign of the Red Cross jostled for space alongside bolts of cloth, bicycles, boxes of chocolate, soap and tins of food and bottles of medicine.

She selected the things she thought the girls in the comfort house needed most: quinine, oil of cloves, something that smelled like witch hazel, bandages, plasters and scissors. One or two of the girls were coming down with malaria. Others had sores, insect bites and private parts that had never been so sorely used and despoiled. Health before beauty: a few tins of food were added, plus a reasonable piece of terry towelling. The latter would be ripped up and used for their periods, washed and used again, passed from hand to hand depending whose time of the month it was; such simple things, but sorely missed.

Considering Madam was out, it didn't seem much of a risk to wrap the stuff in a square of silk and sling it over her shoulder. Smiling sweetly enough and keeping an air of confidence would get her past the guards.

No one challenged her. The guards seemed preoccupied with beating the hell out of the Chinese labourers who were thin and skull faced, their work of building the barbed wire fences stretching along the road now nearing completion. The rumour was that enemy civilians would be interned there. Word came via an officer keen to improve his English and wanting to impress the girl he was lying with. Peggy was best at this.

Nadine grinned. 'Funny that men think blondes are dumb.'

'They speak to you more slowly,' Peggy had told her. 'And a clever girl takes advantage of that.'

A basket of earth wobbled at the ends of poles carried by the labourers. Whilst two held corner posts of yet more huts, the others stamped the earth around its base so it remained standing upright.

The huts were increasing in quantity. She'd counted six on arrival; now there were twenty. Woven matting fixed to rough planks formed the flimsy walls. Palm leaves – termed *atap* – sat multi-layered on the roof. In time, they would rot in the high humidity and become home to colonies of insects. The occupants of the new huts would be tormented night and day.

A lone figure watched from the veranda outside the officer's quarters, the smoke from a lighted cigarette drifting upwards before his face.

She glanced only briefly but thought she recognised the flute player, Major Genda Shamida.

Would he stop her? Search her? Ask what was in the bundle tucked beneath her arm.

Reasoning that a leisurely pace would not arouse suspicion, she sauntered along, not chancing to glance in his direction. Her shoulders tensed in anticipation and relaxed again once she'd passed him by and was approaching the bridge.

Unburdened of tension, she imagined the pleased expressions when she arrived. She smiled. This would work. She was doing something useful.

Silence greeted her as she slipped her sandals off at the entrance. She had stopped going barefoot following an incident when a hookworm over a yard long had been pulled from Rosa's foot.

The other women were all sitting around the walls of the communal room, their expressions blank as though their features had been wiped from their faces.

A breakfast of rice, dried fish and slices of papaya sat barely touched in tin trays. They were all thinner than when they'd arrived here, but nobody was starving. The officers did not appreciate skinny girls and the little sweetmeats were usually eaten ravenously.

With a pang of guilt she swallowed the residual juice of her own breakfast from the back of her tongue. She had eaten a piece of cooked pork, its skin smoked to dark tan over a charcoal fire. Madam Cherry lived well. So did those who pleased her.

The blank faces did not respond to her beaming smile. She assured herself that they would once they saw what she'd brought them.

'Surprise, surprise!' She set down the offerings.

Their expressions remained untouched by her exuberance.

Before she had chance to ask why, Lucy slid through the opening at the end of the room. She looked gaunt and unsteady.

'What is it? Are you feeling bad?'

'Kochi threw herself from the balcony and got chewed up by a passing crocodile. Or leopard. She's gone.'

Nadine sank to the floor. 'Why?'

Betty rounded on her. 'Why? Because she'd been shagged half to death and whatever ate her was bloody hungry? That's a stupid question, Nadine.'

Her breath caught in her throat. Her chest heaved as she wrestled with the overwhelming shock. They were blaming her – because she hadn't taken her turn. Even the eyes of the Malay girls had hardened with resentment. She was one of them, but not one of them. By her own hand, she had contrived to ease her situation. She'd only half won them round by promises of trading their way out of here.

It was Lucy – dear, graceful and philosophical Lucy – who poured the necessary oil on the threatening troubled waters.

'It's not Nadine's fault. The blame lies with the Japanese.'

'And Madam bloody Cherry,' snarled Peggy.

One of the British girls, Caroline, was half-heartedly eyeing her complexion in the small mirror of a powder compact. She was chewing one end of her lip. 'I would like some lipstick. And something oily to eat. My skin's getting dry.'

Peggy turned and regarded her open mouthed.

Lucy stepped in. 'And Nadine can get it for us. I thought we all agreed on this. We have to make life bearable whilst we are here, otherwise we will all be throwing ourselves off of the balcony.'

The harsh looks and rigid features turned into frowns. Whispered comments passed from one woman to another.

'Don't you see?' said Lucy. 'We are being given twice the rations of the Chinese labourers, but even that is only half of what we've been used to. Madam Cherry is a trader of some renown – I think we're all aware of that. She has plenty of everything locked in that store room of hers. And it's all stolen. We steal from her. She's stolen from us – she's stolen our lives. That woman has everything.'

'Except heart,' grumbled Peggy. 'I doubt she's got much of that.'

'Precisely,' said Lucy. She was dressed in a turquoise kimono, a rope wound around and around her waist and ending in heavy gold tassels. She knelt next to Nadine, her hands resting in her lap.

Caroline poked at the blood spot she'd raised on her lip. 'That's not the point. Nadine should be here doing what we have to do.'

Nadine heaved with resignation. 'If that's what you want, then so be it. This auction for my virginity is bloody nonsense anyway. The Japanese shot my husband not long after we escaped from Singapore.'

Those that understood eyed her with disbelief. Those that didn't have much command of English waited with interest for their compatriots' interpretation.

The Australians burst out laughing.

Lucy shook her head, her eyes sweeping over each woman reproachfully. 'Nadine has Madam Cherry's ear. She also has access to the keys to the storeroom. Do you not think it wise that she remains in this favoured position? Do you not think it to be of benefit to us if she does? We did agree on this. It is a good idea.'

Rosa, the Burmese girl, leaned forward, her eyes wide with interest, her arched brows raised even higher. 'It is hope. A slight hope, but the only one we have.'

Betty clutched the coffee-brown shoulder and tugged her back, her attention directed at Nadine.

'Can you get some laxatives? And liquid paraffin. Anything that causes loose motions.'

Nadine frowned. 'I suppose so.' Luxury items she'd expected. They could be used or bartered for useful things like quinine, mosquito nets, clothes and things to eat. But laxatives?

Something between a grin and a grimace lifted one side of Betty's wide mouth. 'Gin would be good too.'

Before Nadine could question her choices, Betty explained. 'Soft options for getting rid of unwanted puddings.'

Everyone except Caroline knew what Betty was getting at.

'Close your mouth before a fly makes its home in there,' said Peggy. 'When was your last period?'

Caroline shrugged her pale, thin shoulders.

'Has it occurred to you that you might have a turnip in the field?'

There were puzzled frowns.

Peggy continued. 'In case one of the *Law Pak Tau* gets you pregnant.' She turned to Lucy. 'Is that the right word, Lucy?'

Understanding Chinese, the Malay girls and Rosa burst out laughing.

Lucy grinned and explained to the others. 'It means turnip heads,' she said, her grin turning into a delightfully elegant chuckle. 'In China we call the Japanese turnip heads.'

It was finally agreed. Nadine would do what she could for as long as she could. What she'd do when the truth was found out was a mystery, but she'd cross that particular bridge when she came to it.

In the meantime, she rang money into the till. Although a magnificent piece of machinery, polished daily on the express orders of the She Dragon, it did not record how much went in.

Nadine was careful. Just a few dollars a day. Over a period of time it would grow into quite a nest egg, and then...

That was where the plan came undone. How could she buy her freedom? Madam would want to know where the money came from. It would be necessary to keep it hidden until it could be spent wisely. Her heart was leaning more and more towards escape. Could it be done?

The takings were counted first thing in the morning. Madam would arrive to oversee the count, her tongue licking a wet thumb as she leaved through the notes, her mouth moving with numbers.

Sometimes she'd frown.

'You have stolen from me. You have kept some for yourself.'

Then she would lay the cane across Nadine's shoulders, though only lightly, her price as an unblemished commodity always foremost in Madam Cherry's mind.

The routine was always the same and Nadine realised the She Dragon never knew for sure whether she'd taken money. The cash register did not record transactions. She realised it was a warning that if she did she would be beaten, especially once she had made Madam Cherry much money. Once that happened and she did get caught, her life would be forfeit.

17

Though life in the camp was bleak, Nadine's efforts to sneak small luxuries and necessities were gratefully received – even by Rosalyn, who continued to make her resentment of Nadine abundantly clear.

On occasion, it felt as though even Madam Cherry herself tried to make life more bearable for those in the Bamboo House. Such as the day she announced that she had acquired twenty chickens. It was presumed they had come from a local farmer via her lover, Commandant Yamoto.

'Eggs,' said Madam Cherry as she surveyed the new arrivals clucking and scratching in the dust.

'At a price,' muttered Peggy.

The hens were housed in wire-covered runs constructed by the army of Chinese labourers still on site.

'That is what I have them for. Eggs. And meat of course when they have finished laying.'

Nadine closed her eyes. Rice, rice, and more rice was the order of the day. What wouldn't we all give for a slice of roast chicken dripping with juices?

Nadine was given the job of feeding them. Sumatran chickens were not particularly fussy about food. Initially it was a case of fencing off a suitable piece of vegetation. From then on they were like locusts pecking until the earth was bare of anything green.

Once the land was cleared – a matter of days as it transpired – their greedy little eyes turned to the vegetation outside their fenced domain.

It occurred to Nadine that the women at Bamboo Bridge House were just like the chickens; thoughts of freedom were never far away. Unlike the chickens, they were more aware of their mortality or the market price of their eggs or their flesh. Nadine shivered at the prospect of her own flesh being sold off, though in a different way to the chickens. The date of the auction was fast approaching.

It was on a languid morning, when the humidity in the air soaked them with sweat, that their minds became focused on what could happen if they jumped the fences.

Water dripped from branches, the star like leaves of bamboo, and the eaves of the hut. It saturated clothes, spangled on hair and hung like pearls from the tip of the nose.

'Come!' ordered a stony-faced Madam Cherry.

Wondering what was up, Nadine followed her to the Bamboo Bridge House. The girls were being hustled over the bridge by guards with fixed bayonets.

Madam Cherry eyed them the same way she did chickens loath to produce eggs. 'You will follow me.'

Madam Cherry led the girls to the Commandant's office. 'Line up! Line up for *tenko*.'

The word for roll call was becoming a byword for lectures on how the Japanese army was destined to rule the world – or at least that part of Asia.

Nadine tacked herself onto the end of a row, her nerves

tingling and her mouth dry. Colonel Yamoto came out, flanked by two other officers. She recognised one as being the flute player Madam was organising to accompany their dancing. So far he'd proved unusually reluctant.

'Bow,' barked Madam Cherry.

'Wow,' muttered Peggy which raised a slight titter amongst those closest to her.

Colonel Yamoto spoke in Japanese, immediately turning to Madam Cherry to interpret.

She lifted her head that bit higher, her soft hands clasped against a shantung skirt that changed colour when she moved. 'Colonel Yamoto *san* says...'

The words of the commandant were not revealed as a common soldier chose that moment to come running. He addressed the colonel, but his news obviously had something to do with Madam Cherry. He bowed woodenly to his senior officer, but his eyes slid sidelong to her.

'The chickens have escaped,' muttered Lucy.

After offering a hasty bow, Madam Cherry rushed off with the private and after a quick shout and a rigid pointing of the commandant's stubby finger, two more joined them.

The line-up fractured a moment, rushed glances passing from one woman to another.

The commandant was still barking orders, this time to the flute-playing major. A conversation ensued. The commandant looked to have lost patience and when he received a message from yet another officer, this one lowlier than those gathered, the junior man received a clout around the ear for interrupting. The colonel stormed off, followed by the subdued soldier. Only the flute player was left.

Madam Cherry came rushing back in hot pursuit of an

escaped chicken. The major bent swiftly, scooping it up by its scrawny neck.

He said something to Madam Cherry to which she smiled, bowed and said something back. She looked apologetic.

When she turned to face them, her features were stiff, perhaps with indignation. It was difficult to tell.

'It has been reported that some of you have been less respectful to Japanese officers than you should be.'

No one moved. The sun was hot, heavy on their shoulders.

'This will not happen again. You will be respectful to Japanese officer at all times. You will fulfil his every need and be honoured that he has chosen you.'

Her eyes slid sidelong to Major Shamida. He stood with shoulders back, legs slightly apart, the squawking chicken hanging from the hands he clasped behind his back. She smiled and bowed respectfully, a sign that she was inviting him to pronounce punishment.

'You will not do this again,' said the major.

The women's attention was transfixed. It was the first time they'd heard him speak English which he did so with a hint of an American accent.

Madam Cherry gestured to the remaining guards. Two of them stepped forward and dragged Peggy from the line up. The culprit surprised nobody and looked almost proud to be chosen.

'You will be beaten,' hissed Madam.

A loud squawking came from behind the major's back. He winced and brought the chicken around to the front of him, holding it up before his amazed eyes.

Raising his arm, Genda Shamida stared at the blood pouring from his thumb. Surprise replaced the anger he'd been supposed to direct at the women. His features stiffened as he held the bird out in front of him, the legs dangling and the beak slightly open. He seemed to come to a decision. Both hands closed around the chicken's throat and there was the grating sound of one vertebra crunching against another.

Satisfaction lit his face. He pointed to each woman in turn whilst they stood, unblinking and quaking inside. More than one trembling hand stretched protectively over a neck already scrawny, each one imagining his hands screwing their necks like that.

'Be warned,' he said. 'Your necks are no stronger than that of this chicken. No more insulting Japanese officers.' He flung the bird to the ground. 'Behave. Like ladies.'

* * *

Peggy escaped worse punishment thanks to the major's symbolic warning and some well-chosen advice.

'Ten strokes only,' she said, rubbing at her backside. 'I won't be able to sit down for a week. Not that Cherry is worried. She still wants her money. Still wants me to earn some. I think Shamida pointed those particular facts out to her. If he hadn't, I would have got twenty strokes I think.'

Shamida had become something of a talking point. First off was his very distinctive English. Secondly, he was distant. And, though they argued about this, they agreed that there was something unusual about him.

'Like a tiger's different than a lion, though still just as likely to tear your head off,' commented Peggy.

Having learned a little of the local dialect, Peggy assisted the doctor examining Saint Soppy, the name they'd given to a Malay girl brought up by missionaries. Her predicament was becoming pretty obvious.

The girl was pretty but regarded as a bit below par. 'I'm not really having a baby,' she exclaimed. She was the only one who believed it. Her belly was already the size of a football.

Peggy smiled and stroked her hair. 'I'm afraid you are.'

'No. I don't think so. God wouldn't allow it.'

'Have it your way,' said Peggy, her legs still weak from all the punishment she had received.

The doctor looked over a few other girls whilst he was there, giving them cream for the various itchiness and infections with which they were plagued. Only one was injected for venereal disease. He looked surprised and inferred that the girl must have brought it with her.

Lucy interpreted. 'I do not think so. She was pure before she came here.'

His jaw hardened. He slapped her face. 'Officers do not have such disgusting diseases.' The girl was never seen again.

* * *

Nadine feared the march of time striding ever onwards. At times, she wished she had never passed herself off as a virgin, but she'd been driven by fear and driven to survive at any price.

It was less than two weeks away now. Only in dancing was some of her fear kept at bay. When she danced, the bells tinkling around her ankles helped her to imagine that she was back in India, dancing in the pergola with Zakia and Sureya, not here in this awful place.

'I think I prefer these slower dances,' said Madam Cherry as they practiced in her quarters, twisting from the waist and wafting her hands before her eyes. She finished the routine then declared she must attend to business elsewhere, though Nadine knew it was because her energy was spent. Madame Cherry was too proud to admit that.

There had been a number of outside events where Nadine had been required to dance and sometimes the She Dragon joined her on stage. When she did so, Nadine purposely chose the most exuberant dances, those that left Madam Cherry breathless and begging for water – with a dash of whisky. Sweet revenge, or at least that's what she'd thought at first.

After breakfast and a brief check of the accounts, Madame Cherry stated she had to go out. 'I have business with the local headman. You will dance alone but first feed the chickens.'

Nadine did as she was bid. The ground was warming, the monkeys chattering in the trees and she felt hot and dusty when she returned to Madame's quarters.

The shutters at the front of the house faced east and kept out the worst of the heat and the glare of the sun. The shutters at the back of the house were rolled up. The interior was cool.

Having set down the rattan basket used to hold corn for the chickens, she mopped her brow with the front of her sarong. For a moment, she saw nothing. On dropping the shimmering blue silk, she saw she was not alone.

Major Genda Shamida was standing in front of the window with his back to her, blue smoke curling up from an unfinished cigarette. His flute rested against the crook of his elbow.

The light from the window outlined his features and form. He didn't turn round. She chanced studying what some of the girls in the Bamboo Bridge House had called a chiselled profile. It had surprised her to hear them talking so charitably about an enemy officer. Just recently he had visited there for the first time, but only to play the flute. He had shunned the girls' interest and took only one or two glasses of saki with fellow officers, never overindulging, never losing control. His aloofness was interpreted as arrogance. To Nadine's eyes, he seemed entirely different from his comrades. It was hard to describe. Just something about his demeanour, as though he didn't see things the way they did and had experienced things they couldn't possibly understand.

She bowed and whispered his name. 'Major Shamida. I was not expecting you.'

'Are you ready?'

The sound of his voice surprised her.

'Yes, Major Shamida.' She bowed again, feeling a mix of fear and anticipation. What did he want her to be ready for? Her death? Did he know she sometimes took an extra hen's egg?.

'You are not concentrating.'

His sudden comment scared her so much she flattened herself against the wall and stared at him wide eyed.

Shamida sighed and rubbed at his eyes. 'Honey, I'm playing a flute, not aiming a gun at your head. I play the flute. You dance.'

'Dance?'

'I accompanied your dancing along the road there. Madame requested me to play for you.'

'Oh!'

He sighed and flicked his cigarette stub out of the window.

'OK. Let's get started.'

'You made me jump.'

'Nadine. That's your name, isn't it? Nadine?'

She nodded, wanting to comment on his accent which was so much more pronounced now she was close to him here in this shaded room. She'd heard American accents before in Singapore where sailors from the US Pacific Fleet had perused the bars and clubs and eyed the local girls.

'Try and forget that I'm Japanese. Pretend I'm just a regular guy who's doing his best in difficult circumstances. Now who is it you see?'

'The enemy.'

She thought she sounded foolish. Certainly not brave.

He looked down at his fingers spread the length of the instrument.

'You're Indian. Am I right?'

'Half Indian. My father was British.'

She hadn't meant to speak the truth. She flushed, thinking to cover her mistake. 'That is...'

'It's all right. I won't tell anyone.' His gaze fixed on his flute. 'I see. Born between two cultures. Difficult, isn't it?'

Without hesitation, she nodded. 'Yes. Sometimes.' And suddenly she knew. It was there in his words and the tone of his voice. Genda Shamida had also been born between two cultures.

He fingered the flute and blew a few notes, not tunefully, but purely as though he was considering what to say next. Although he was trying hard not to show it, she knew he was feeling nervous.

'I know how that feels,' he said. 'Being born between two cultures.'

'Your accent... were you born in America?' She feared she might have overstepped the mark asking him such a question, but he didn't seem to mind.

He nodded, raised his eyes slowly and looked into her face.

'So why...'

'None of your business!'

'I'm sorry.' Fearing the thunderous look on his face, she bowed and stayed in that position, watching his thudding feet raising the dust from the floor.

She shook so much that the knot at the front of her sarong shivered like a buffeted flower. He must have noticed. Was it bad manners? Her questions might have been.

Purposefully, he sat in a chair beside the window. Her heart stopped fluttering and she dared raise her eyes.

He nodded in a casual way, as though he really saw no point in telling her. 'Let's just say I got caught up in things.'

It was instilled in her, in all of them, to despise the enemy and to maintain a barrier between them. Major Shamida had caused hers to slip. There was something about him that invited trust, despite the uniform he wore. She eyed him curiously but not without apprehension, watching as he passed the flute from one hand to the other as if trying to guess its weight.

'I'm to be interpreter between you and the colonel when you are alone together.'

Nadine's mouth dropped open. Alone with the colonel? 'I don't understand.'

'Madam couldn't bring herself to tell you that you will not be auctioned off.'

'I won't?'

Setting the flute aside, he shook his head, stubbed his cigarette out on the windowsill and threw it out of the window. 'No. Colonel Yamoto's orders. You should be very happy he has chosen you. Unfortunately, Madam Cherry is not.'

She licked the dryness from her lips. The She Dragon had been in a bad temper this morning. Her considerable income depended on her relationship with Yamoto. His interest was wandering in Nadine's direction and Madam Cherry had been forced to make a deal! Nadine was terrified.

'What if I refuse?'

She detected a tensing of jaw that he tried very hard to hide – without success. Face empty of emotion – suspicious in itself, he straightened and reached for his flute.

'You are honoured. Be thankful.' Now there was warning in his tone. He turned away. 'We'd better get some practice in. A fast tune or a slow one? Which would you prefer?'

The lonely notes drifted like smoke, spiralling up and down, around and about. Slowly, she raised her slender arms, fixed her eyes on his face silhouetted against the window, and began to dance.

The news he'd brought her regarding the colonel was not welcome. What would he do when he realised he'd been duped and that she was far from being a virgin? Would he laugh and think it a huge joke? Not likely. He would be furious. Would Madam give him his money back? Not likely. She recalled hearing a phrase: *hell hath no fury like a woman scorned.* Madam was business-like but also jealous. Whose fury would be greatest? she wondered and shuddered. There was little to choose between them.

The major's eyes were closed, as lost in his music as she usually was in dance. The air was filled with tension and when he suddenly opened his eyes, it took Nadine's breath away, such was the intensity of his gaze.

A flapping of wings heralded the arrival of a chicken, breaking the log-jammed atmosphere. Feathers flew everywhere as it crashed into the major's shoulder, causing him to drop his flute.

'Damn!'

The startled bird fled to the window ledge. The major clouted it.

In a flurry of feathers, the bird flapped away.

The major reached for his flute which was now in two halves.

'Would you look at that? Hell. If it's broken, I'll wring the necks of the whole scrawny lot! That bloody woman too!'

Nadine clapped both hands over her mouth to smother her laughter.

It wasn't until he'd put the two halves back together that Major Shamida realised what he'd said and, more to the point, how he'd said it.

Smiling shyly, he rubbed one palm on his trousers.

Nadine eyed him quizzically, weighed him up and threw in a question. 'How did you feel about Pearl Harbour?'

His face clouded over. He looked away. 'That is my business. You are a prisoner. I am a Japanese officer. Bow when you speak to me.'

He spoke sharply.

Nadine jumped to attention and bowed quickly and deeply.

'No! I didn't mean that. Don't bow!' He groaned, shaking his head.

Holding the flute in both hands, he stood with his back against the window and eyed her as though he were as wary of her response as she was of his.

'God damn it! Don't look at me like that. I'm not going to eat you,' he said.

Nadine almost laughed out loud. He'd sounded less like a Japanese officer, more like an American in a pre-war film.

She uncurled her bare toes. The bells around her ankles tinkled slightly as the tension left her body.

'Thank you.' Without being asked to, she bowed again. She could no longer think of him as a turnip head. Major Genda Shamida didn't fit into that category and she understood why. He was American educated but of Japanese extraction, a man between worlds – just as she was.

He was taller than most Japanese. She glanced at his legs. They were muscular, straight and strong.

She felt embarrassed and almost guilty. She should not have glanced at his legs. He was the enemy, and yet that accent, that instantaneous outburst, made her curious to know more about him. She bowed her head aware he was studying her, and watched a cockroach skit into a slit in the floor.

'Hold your head up.'

He sounded angry. Her father used to turn angry when

wishing to hide his shortcomings.

His thumb dug into her chin as he lifted it. She let him do it and boldly looked up into his eyes which for a moment smouldered with warning.

'You will not tell anyone that I spoke like that,' his voice softer now. 'Do you understand?'

'Yes, Shamida *san*.'

His sharpness persisted. Pointing his finger at her forehead, he said, 'I will shoot you if you do.'

She imagined the finger replaced by a gun barrel and closed her eyes. 'Yes, Major Shamida.'

Slowly, very slowly, he dropped his arm. 'That's good.'

His chest expanded and contracted with each deep breath until the familiar aloofness returned. He nodded silently before raising the flute to his lips.

The nod was his signal for her to resume dancing. The tune was mournful and slow. She immersed herself in the erotic symbolism of the ancient dance of India. It wasn't easy. If it wasn't for the fact that she had to concentrate so hard, her legs would give way.

In the final steps she sunk into a heap on the ground, hands seductively posed, head bowed, eyes lifted.

The music stopped. When she looked up, the major was staring at her, an entranced look in his eyes. For a moment he was a man chipped from marble. Without saying another word, he sprang away from the window, his flute tucked beneath his arm.

Nadine got to her feet. 'Are you going now?'

'I have to.'

'I wish...' She paused, not sure she should say what she so wanted to say. 'I wish you could stay longer. I have many steps to practise.'

His eyelids flickered. 'I wish I could. I have other duties.'

'Today you have other duties.'

'I always have other duties.'

'Will you play for me again?'

He paused at the door, turned and looked at her.

'Yes. Yes I will.'

The look in his eyes and the tone of his voice said it all. Something had shifted between them, something that neither of them had planned to happen.

18

Escape! The word haunted her dreams and she could taste it in her mouth. She'd seen the commandant's eyes following her in the relative safety of Madam Cherry's company. But it couldn't last. Money and jealousy fought for dominance in the She Dragon's eyes.

Nadine knew she had to escape before her lie was discovered – before she died.

Death was all around. An elegant Eurasian girl who was rumoured to have been the mistress of royalty had been caught with her fingers in the till. They were all summoned to witness her punishment. A gasp had gone up as the colonel had taken out his sword and cut off the small finger of her right hand. That night, although in terrible pain, she was still forced to give her body to whoever wanted her. By morning she had killed herself. As with Kochi's death, it cast a shadow of depression over those in the Bamboo House.

Nadine sighed, turned over and tried to sleep. Sheera's fate, as well as her own impending encounter, were occupying her thoughts. Little over a week remained until Madam Cherry was to sell her finest prize.

The auction had been postponed, but it was only a matter of time before Yamamoto claimed his prize.

By day, she occupied herself in an effort to keep her fears at bay. At night, she had difficulty sleeping, staring into the night and wondering how many more such nights she would see.

Through the window she could see a crescent moon pinned like a paper cut out against an ink-black sky. Shanti, her sadly neglected mother, had once told her that wishes made upon a crescent moon always came true.

'I wish I knew how to get out of this,' she whispered.

At dusk the next night, she saw Major Shamida playing his flute on the veranda in front of the officer's quarters.

The women in the Bamboo Bridge House were also apprehensive. Their fears that a whole army was about to arrive and occupy the many huts erected on the other side of the high fence were proved unfounded with the arrival of women and children – prisoners of war.

Talk about the new arrivals and what would happen next bounced backwards and forwards between the residents of the Bamboo Bridge House.

Up until then, Nadine had been sipping quietly at a cup of weak tea. There was no milk and little sugar to be had, but Rosalyn and one of the Malay girls had concocted some kind of rice cake that they'd flavoured with treacle Nadine had purloined from the She Dragon's store.

Nadine refused a cake.

Peggy noticed and eyed Nadine quizzically. 'You OK?'

'I've got a problem,' whispered Nadine.

'Well you don't really need it do you,' said Rosalyn, snapping the tin shut before anyone could argue and grab an extra portion.

Nadine ignored Rosalyn and confided in Peggy. 'A big problem. Yamoto's got his eye on me. He's expecting a virgin.'

Peggy's chin dropped to her chest. 'Oh! Is that a problem?'

Nadine locked eyes with Lucy, who explained the situation in an equally soft voice. 'It is if you're not one.'

Perhaps he will not notice if you cry out a good deal,' said Peggy, her face pinched with concern.

Lucy shook her head. 'Some men like to wave a bloodied sheet like a flag, evidence of their undoubted prowess.' The women fell to silence.

The two Australian nurses whispered something. Betty got up and went over to their few belongings that they kept in a battered brown suitcase, whispering as though they were about to unveil a very big secret.

'Ok!' said Peggy sitting down close to Nadine. 'We're going to come clean.'

A smug faced Betty sat down beside her. Lucy leaned closer so she could take in all that was being said without everyone knowing.

She sang what resembled a fanfare. 'Da, da! May I present...'

'We, Betty and me, may *we* present... It belongs to both of us.'

Peggy dug her elbow into Betty's side. 'Well go on you silly cow. Show them.'

Betty unclenched her fist to reveal a single red balloon.

Lucy eyed it blankly. 'Are you going to have a party?'

Nadine frowned. 'It's a little perished?'

Peggy smiled. 'It is indeed. Left over from our Christmas party. Something the Japanese didn't bother to steal from us. Just a party balloon.' Her eyes misted dreamily. 'My, but we had such bloody good parties on our ward. Dancing and drinking from dawn till dusk. Parties to be remembered.'

'This is no time for a party,' Lucy pointed out.

Peggy touched Nadine's shoulder. 'You're a pretty astute girl, Nadine. I think you've guessed the plan. Fill it with blood, slide it carefully up inside you and when he... well... you know... the balloon bursts and you run with blood. He's satisfied, the She Dragon's kept him sweet and kept his money, and you get to keep your life. Seems all square to me!'

'Peggy, if it works, I could kiss you.'

Peggy pretended disdain. 'No need to get physical!'

Lucy was sat facing the door. 'An officer's arrived. He looks as though he's looking for a girl.'

Those sitting opposite scrambled to their feet in readiness to bow.

Peggy smiled. 'It's only Shamida, the flute player.' She straightened and spoke in a pleasant tone. 'Hi there, you miserable young sod. How the devil are you?' She said it with an ingratiating smile before lining up with the others and bowing low. 'Don't look so worried,' she whispered to Nadine. 'Even if he did hear, he don't speak much English so can't have understood much either.'

Nadine didn't answer, but saw just a hint of a smile. She wondered how long he'd been there.

'Women making too much noise,' he said entering into the charade by speaking halting English. 'Women be quiet now. Be obedient to Japanese masters. Bow. All bow.'

Feet shuffled into position and the women bowed.

Nadine only half bowed. Her eyes followed him to the door where he paused, turned round and winked. 'I will see you tomorrow. Same time, same place.'

* * *

Major Shamida was already at Madam Cherry's house when Nadine returned to her quarters.

As usual, he was staring out of the window and smoking, the repaired flute cradled against his arm.

'Major Shamida *san*.' She bowed low.

He didn't turn round.

'Colonel Yamoto is going to be very busy pretty soon. More of the huts you see across the way are going to be occupied. The first prisoners have arrived. There's going to be a lot more women here, children too.'

Perhaps he had sensed her concern and therefore restrained a detailed depiction of what he truly meant. Perhaps it was just the Japanese way; seed the mind with a few words from which greater detail would grow. Whatever the reason, she knew what he was trying to say. He would not have so much time to play the flute when she danced.

The balloon she'd poked into the waist of her sarong sucked damp and limp against her skin, an uncomfortable reminder of what was to come.

She managed to slide it out and hide it among the vivid silks and chunky jewellery she used in her dance. Tying the rope of tiny bells around one ankle, another rope of bells around her other ankle, gave her time to think about what to say next. Shamida pre-empted her.

'The colonel is determined. Some guys will do anything for a taste of juicy tail.' He sounded so American.

'What you mean is, the She Dragon is furious?'

He fixed her with a very direct look. 'The She Dragon? Is that what you all call her?'

Nadine smiled. 'She breathes fire – sometimes.'

She's jealous as hell,' he said solemnly. 'She cannot deny Yamoto what he wants, but beware. She'll smile at you as long as it pleases him, but as soon as he loses interest – bang! She'll get rid of you pretty damn quick.'

Nadine stood looking at him, trying not to tremble. She was sure she could hear her knees knocking.

'Good! I'd like to be out of here.'

He scratched nonchalantly at the back of his neck where the black hair was coarse and cut close to the skin.

'You could be out a lot quicker than that if this business with the balloon fails to work.'

Nadine opened her eyes wide. 'You were listening.' Her fear intensified. Shamida was charming, but he was still a major in the Japanese army.

He shrugged.

'Why were you there?'

He grinned. 'Why is any man there?'

She shook her head. 'Not you. The girls say you never do. So why?'

He looked at the floor, out of the window, then back at her. 'For you?'

'You're asking me, not telling me.'

'OK. For you. I went there to see you. I like watching you dance. I like playing the flute. It takes me out of myself – away from this awful place.'

'I'm flattered.' She bowed. 'I bow respectfully to Japanese officer.'

Her sarcasm was obvious.

'Cut it out.'

She frowned. This was not the speech expected from a Japanese officer and somehow she was sure an opening had occurred between them.

'Where are you from?'

The disarming smile faded. 'Here and there.'

'Japan *and* America?'

He sighed, rested a foot on a pretty little table with brass inlay, his arm resting on his knee.

'I lived in California since I was three years old and was educated there, grew up there. The All-American Boy!' He spread his arms to emphasise the point.

'So why are you in the Japanese army?'

'I was over visiting my grandparents. I got caught up in events. My grandfather was taken ill. I overstayed my visit and ended up getting called up.' He paused and looked at the ground. 'That was back in 1939. I did well in the army, got promotion.' He shrugged again as though the memory was painful. 'First I went to China. Two years later there was Pearl Harbour. I found myself on standby close to the Malay Peninsula; it was obvious what was going to happen.'

'You were caught between two worlds.'

He nodded.

She wanted to say that she knew very well what he meant, but she held back. He was still wearing the uniform of the Japanese Army, the army that had killed her husband. She hadn't loved Martin but her husband and many others had met a brutal death.

'You won't tell anyone – you know – about the balloon plan.'

He shook his head and smiled. 'Yamoto will swallow it. You look like a virgin.' His smile faded and a more worried look entered his eyes. 'But be careful. He's a dangerous man.'

'All Japanese are dangerous.'

He didn't retaliate or offer to be her friend.

'You were married?' he asked.

'Yes. I was married. Now I'm a widow.' She didn't give details, but sensed he guessed that Japanese soldiers had killed her husband.

He narrowed his eyes against the smoke from a freshly lit cigarette and looked out of the window.

Nadine dared to join him. Even though he had promised to say nothing of her plan to hoodwink the commandant, she reminded herself again that he was Japanese.

'What's so interesting?' she asked, looking in the same direction as he was.

The question seemed to amuse him: just one note of laughter.

'Sad. Not interesting. You and I and millions like us are caught up in this war. No one asked us whether we were in favour of it. No one really explained the reasons why.'

'Japan attacked Pearl Harbour.'

He nodded. 'Sure. We are told to fight, to give our lives in the name of the emperor.'

'So you disagree?'

He smiled. 'I think I am like most people. All I want is to deal with the small stuff of life. The rest of it – politicians, wars and all – can go to hell!'

* * *

As Nadine and Shamida continued to meet for her dancing, he revealed more insight into the situation between Yamoto and Madam.

It had been eighteen months since her arrival here. Singapore had fallen in February 1942. They were now halfway through 1944.

'The colonel has been called back to headquarters so you have respite until he gets back. I understand he has paid Madam Cherry a deposit so she does not offer you to anyone else.'

'He seems to be away quite a lot.'

'Orders from his superiors. He's not much of a soldier, ideal in fact for being a camp commandant.'

Nadine sighed. 'So I've been lucky. I certainly didn't foresee this. Somebody up there loves me.'

She dashed to the window, rested her hands on the rough edging of palm leaves and breathed a deep sigh of relief.

'Or somebody down here.'

There was something about the major's voice that made her turn her head and seek his expression. Her eyes met his.

'I have influence. Or rather my grandfather, the general, has influence.'

Amazed at what she was hearing, Nadine stared at him open mouthed.

'Don't ask how I did it,' he said, pressing his finger to her lips. 'Let us just hope that a particularly poisonous snake bites him and he never comes back.'

Nadine could hardly believe what he was saying. He had pulled strings in order to keep her safe. However, he'd forgotten one thing.

'Even if the colonel never comes back, Madame Cherry will still want a return on her investment. I'll be on the auction block again.'

The major touched her shoulder at the same gazing out into the thick jungle beyond the fence.

'Then I would have to act, and if I did that we could both endanger our lives.'

The weight and warmth of his hand on her shoulder made her blood race. She told herself she shouldn't be responding like this, but she couldn't help it. Neither had yet stated the obvious; they were kindred spirits and couldn't help being drawn to each other.

* * *

The rest of the day passed in something of a haze. She couldn't get Major Shamida out of her mind. He was Japanese, the enemy, and yet something more human had reached out and touched both of them in this awful place.

She was humming happily to herself as she picked out a few items of medicine, another tablet of sweetly scented soap and even a canister of lilac-perfumed talcum powder when the sound of car tyres scrunching on gravel sounded from outside. Madam Cherry was back.

Nadine secreted the stolen things beneath her mattress. Madam Cherry was shouting for her.

'I have news!'

She sounded exuberant, but there was a tight-lipped set to her mouth and her jaw gave the impression that she was in two minds about what she was about to say.

Nadine went out to greet her, bowing deeply.

'Madam.'

'The Colonel has directed me to have you ready for him two days hence. He is back.'

19

Two days hence, at late morning, the two Australian nurses, Betty and Peggy, were attempting to fulfil their promise to help hoodwink the colonel. Tonight he would finally claim her non-existent virginity. They were Nadine's only hope.

'Relax. I'll be as gentle as I can. Betty? Put a bit more of that Vaseline on my fingers. And relax. This won't hurt a bit.'

Nadine was lying with her knees bent and her legs apart on a makeshift table made from a few wooden planks and two oil drums. The top of Peggy's blonde head was just visible between her legs. Betty assisted. 'Peggy Parker, you said the same to them soldiers we gave jabs to before coming away.'

Peggy laughed. 'Wrong! I said it won't hurt me like it's going to hurt you, sport.'

Despite the seriousness of the occasion, Nadine giggled. Betty peered at her from between her legs. 'This is serious stuff, you know.'

'I can't help it. A party balloon, chicken blood, three hags and not a cauldron between us.'

'What?'

'Like the three witches in Macbeth,' said Lucy who was guarding the door.

Typically, the Australian nurses kept up the light-hearted banter.

Nadine steeled herself. It had to be done. The banter continued.

'The rice rations have been cut. Do you think you can get us some eggs to mix in with it?' said Peggy

Nadine swallowed and managed to nod. 'I suppose so. I'll sneak out when it's dark. When this is over.'

'Well you wouldn't want to pinch them when it's light,' laughed Betty.

Nadine managed a grin.

Slowly and carefully, Peggy pushed the greased balloon and her equally greased fingers into Nadine's vagina. Nadine herself had crept round to the chicken house and took an eggcup full of chicken blood which Peggy had syringed into the neck of the balloon.

'Getting back to important stuff, why's the rice ration been cut?' asked Peggy. She said it casually as she might over afternoon tea complete with jam tarts and fruitcake, certainly not whilst shoving a blood-filled balloon up a young woman's vagina.

'I expect their supply ship was torpedoed.' Nadine gritted her teeth in response to the tightening across her groin.

'Sorry, sweetheart, just hit the lower pelvis,' Betty explained having seen her wince. 'That's the top end of the vagina where your hymen used to be.'

Nadine felt the pressure of Lucy's hand on hers. 'Nearly over,' she heard her say.

She opened her eyes long enough to focus on Lucy's face. She looked concerned. Nadine wanted to say to her that she should save her concern for herself. She was looking thinner, her complexion pale and her skin stretched too tightly over her cheekbones. A little rest would do her good. Perhaps she might persuade Madam Cherry to let her recuperate.

Peggy's voice interrupted her thoughts. 'You've got good reason to smile.'

Nadine opened her eyes to see Peggy wiping her hands over her hips.

'Operation Spring Chicken is over!'

They all laughed at the joke and the interior of the comfort house became lighter despite the seriousness of the event.

After that, there was silence, the women looking at each other and looking away when eyes met eyes. Nadine sat up, brought her legs together and pulled her sarong down over her knees. 'It won't fall out?'

Peggy shook her head, sighed and sat back on her haunches. 'Not for some time; I'd say it should stay in place for roughly twenty-four hours.'

Nadine calculated how long it was likely to take from initial greeting to final thrust. 'That should be enough.'

Her heart was thudding. In a way it was like getting married all over again. She didn't know whether the penetration would be rough or gentle and whether she would bleed very much or nothing noticeable. Only it wouldn't be her blood; it would be that of a chicken.

Peggy read her mind.

'Don't worry. There should be enough of a show for him to think he's achieved something.'

'Would be better if you spent all day lying down,' Betty advised.

Nadine looked down at her feet, half expecting to see a Vaseline smeared balloon fall between them. 'I can't. Madam wants me to help her with some new stock she's got hold of.'

Of late the She Dragon had insisted on having things recorded in English as well as Chinese, never in Japanese.

Lucy suggested she didn't want the colonel to see exactly how much she was worth and how much stock she was carrying.

Some of Madam's new stock had been looted from the civilians newly arrived at the internment camp, though God knows the new arrivals didn't look to have much. They were ragged and thin, their feet sore from forced marching, their skin blistered and raw.

The ragged women on one side and the better dressed and fed on the other, stared through the criss-cross of wire and guard posts. The girls chosen for the Bamboo Bridge House lived within a compound and were guarded. But not like chickens; not restricted to an acre of dusty, bare ground and dressed in rags. The expected insults came thick and fast.

'Whore!'

Nadine hung her head as she made her way back to Madam Cherry. If only they knew, she thought to herself. She'd ate less than usual over the last two days. Her skin had an icy clamminess and her nerves felt like fine wires running through her flesh.

A newly arrived column of women and children were being shepherded into the camp. Nadine raised her head and slowed down. Perhaps she might see somebody she knew.

'Nadine.'

She heard his voice and knew Shamida was behind her. Snatched moments dancing to the sound of his flute usually raised her spirits, but not today.

'Look at those women! Have you seen the state they're in? You should be ashamed of yourself!' She couldn't bear to turn round and look at him.

Flute tucked beneath his arm, he followed her to the cool

room where he would play and she would dance. Madam Cherry was nowhere in sight.

Nadine clenched her fists and went to the window, dropping the blind against the glaring light.

Shamida came and stood beside her. He blew a few mournful notes.

Nadine hit the flute away with a backward swipe of her hand.

'I don't care about your music. I saw those women. They looked worn out.'

He gave a curt nod of his head. 'They had to walk from their last camp. It was bombed.'

'Good,' she said, her eyes glowing fiercely. 'I hope more bombs fall and blast every Japanese soldier to hell.'

He looked hurt then angry. A chill passed over her as she remembered him wringing the chicken's neck. She told herself to tread carefully.

They glared at each other like beetles with locked horns until Genda seemed suddenly to come to a decision.

Lovingly, almost reverently, he placed the flute on a small, japanned cupboard inlaid with mother of pearl birds and flowers, a beautiful object that had only appeared a few days ago.

She tensed expecting him a slap or a punch. Nothing happened except that a mix of emotions crossed his face.

His voice was soft and sad. 'We should all be ashamed. We are all doing what we can to survive against overwhelming odds. Even you, Nadine.' He paused, his expression tensing as he fought to remind her of the night ahead. 'I hear you will give yourself to the colonel tonight.'

His comment sent the blood rushing to her cheeks.

'I have to. I don't want to. I have to!'

He nodded. 'War makes monsters of us all. We are no longer the people we were. We do what we have to do to survive.'

Nadine hung her head and for the first time in a long time, her tears flowed freely.

Her head rested on his shoulder. His arms were around her.

'I want to kill him. One day I will. I know I will.'

Nadine could say nothing, but instinctively knew that he meant it.

20

The tropical night was alive with the sound of insects and long-tailed monkeys chattering in the trees. Nadine's mind was closed to these sounds and despite the humid heat of early evening, she felt as though she was covered in snow.

Two guards came to escort her to the Bamboo Bridge House where a room at the far end of the building had been reserved for this momentous night.

Inside the Bamboo Bridge House, the atmosphere was smoky and warm, the air heavy with spices and perfume. She noticed little of this and she was still chilled to the bone.

All eyes were upon her as she walked through the open area of the house into the curtained off area at the far end of the building. It was pleasant enough, with a balcony overlooking the thick greenery outside.

There was a mirror in one corner. Naked beneath the soft silk of a loosely fitting kimono, she eyed her reflection and saw not the Nadine of India or of Britain. The reflection was Japanese in style, an odd covering for someone and something she couldn't possibly be. She let the kimono fall to the floor and viewed her nakedness.

A battle raged inside her; a respectable white woman would kill herself rather than submit to such an ordeal, a shame that would stay with her forever. The voices in her head were those of the *memsahib*'s back in colonial India. She reminded herself that she was only half British. Was her Indian half telling her to depend on her wits and even her body to survive?

Madam Cherry's dark shadow fell over her. She'd glided in silently like a preying tiger on padded paws. 'Drink this.'

She did as ordered. Whatever it was it made her light headed. 'I'm not sure I can go through with this.'

'Too late.' She spat the words like shooting bullets. Her hard expression came close, almost touching Nadine's shoulder and reflected in the mirror. 'The colonel has paid me half of what I demanded. I hope for your sake you have not lied to him. He will kill you. If you refuse, he will kill you. In fact if you do anything to upset him, he will kill you.'

Madam's hand pushed her downwards until she was kneeling on a woven bed mat. Her hair was bundled up into an elaborate design that Madam Cherry had teased over padding and fixed into place with bone and tortoiseshell ornaments.

She sat like a stone; her hands were folded in her lap and her face very white, her eyes outlined with charcoal, and her top lip bright red, her bottom lip as pale as the rest of her face.

Her reflection was that of a biscuit thin china doll, a fragile cover of the true person beneath.

The cloying stink of cooking and bat dung drifted through the open shutters.

She was sitting on a white cloth; that too was as requested, a trophy for Yamoto to boast about once it was stained with her blood. Her blood? The truth could get her killed.

'Lay down.'

Nadine lay with her eyes closed clenching her pelvic muscles against the threatening slip of the blood-filled balloon. Whatever it was that Madam had given her was doing the trick.

'You are afraid?' asked Madam Cherry.

'A little.' Whatever she had given her caused the room to spin, making her unsure of what was real and what was imagined. In her mind, she danced and the palace was pink and a man with dark, secretive eyes was playing the flute. As she danced around and around the floor, she saw his eyes following her.

'I will help you relax.' In reality it was Madam Cherry's voice but for some strange reason she was reminded of Shamida about to play his flute.

She felt a soft tickling between her legs. Madam Cherry was smiling at her.

'This is pleasure. This is a man.'

The sensation continued and moved higher, eliciting a response she tried hard to resist.

All the pressure of the past few months seemed to burst out of her in a single nerve tingling explosion. People were sick, hungry and dying all around her; there was a chance she wouldn't last too long herself. In the receiving of pleasure, her body was telling her that she was still alive. Among all this ugliness, there was still life.

When she opened her eyes Madam Cherry was smiling. 'Good. Good.'

Her head was still swimming after the She Dragon had left. Her thoughts were hazy and the room spun around her.

Sounds came from beyond the bamboo screen: loud laughter and Japanese words interspersed with comments from the girls.

There was ribald laughter, shouts of protest and the bamboo screen bulged as someone fell against it. A drunken young officer thrust through the gap brandishing a bottle of sake. With his other hand he was yanking hard on Lucy's glorious hair so tightly, that she was bent double, one side of her face flat against his hip.

One side of her mouth drooped with pain; one eye pleaded for help.

As his eyes feasted on Nadine's nakedness, his grip on Lucy's hair loosened. She gasped and sobbed, crumpled to the floor, falling forward onto her hands. For a moment she was indecisive. It passed. She disappeared, glad to escape her tormentor – at least for the moment.

The man stood in the gap, his eyes glassy and his mouth hanging open. A drool of spit trickled like that of a man about to take a bite of the best meal he'd ever had.

* * *

A tropical sky on a moonlit night has a certain glow: not quite indigo, not quite purple and softening to a silvery mauve where it meets the sea and the tops of the jungle trees.

Major Genda Shamida saw only blackness. Even the notes rising from his flute did not satisfy his tortured mind. Escaping into music helped him recover from the horrors he'd seen: not just battles, but the beasts released in ordinary men, men he might once have viewed as honourable.

Tonight Yamoto was claiming his prize. Nadine would be waiting for him. The thought of it made him feel sick.

He'd seen him beat raw recruits who had not responded quickly enough to orders, shivering young men, no more than boys; wetting themselves when Yamoto's cruel eyes fell on them. There was only one thing the man loved better than power and that was money. Madam Cherry, although she might not admit it, satisfied his greed rather than his lust. What she could not know was how much he enjoyed torturing and debasing all that was good. But Genda Shamida knew and wished with all his heart that he had not taken that visit to Japan to see his family back before the attack on Pearl Harbour. He had satisfied family obligations in the land of his fathers, but America was the land of his birth and his heart.

Wishing to lose himself in music, he touched the flute to his lips, fingered the notes and heard them rise, but they did not please him. There was no purity left in the sound. Not tonight. Not on this very dark night.

The flute lived in a very smart leather case bought as a present by his mother back in California. His parents were of the old school, tolerated his playing, but as a descendant of samurai, the old man had been keen that his son return to Japan, join the army and study modern techniques of battle under old masters. Out of a traditional respect for both parents, he had obeyed and had reached the rank of major by the time of Pearl Harbour.

He felt a pang of regret closing the case that in itself was like a bridge between his past and the present, modern America and Japanese tradition.

He found himself walking towards the Bamboo Bridge House like a man in a dream, his hand resting on his sword. He was off duty. He did not need to wear it.

The smell of roasting meat lay lightly on the air. A private had caught a wild pig earlier and it was being roasted on a spit at the back of their hut.

He looked over to the wire surrounding the internment camp. A group of women and children were standing on the other side of the fence looking out. The children were sniffing the air.

'How about us having some of that instead of that swill you gave us earlier,' one of the women shouted.

He saw a guard slam his rifle against her so hard that she fell backwards. He saw him raise the rifle.

'Soldier!'

The soldier snapped to attention.

Genda faced him, fists clenched behind his back, itching to smash his knuckles into the private's peasant jaw. 'What are you doing?'

Keen to impress, the private poured out his story in rapid Japanese. 'The woman shouted abuse at me.'

'So! You understand English?'

The man faltered. 'No, Major Shamida *san*, but her tone...'

'Have you eaten yet?'

'No sir. I am on duty until...'

'But you smell it.' Shamida sniffed the air. 'It smells delicious, does it not? Are your colleagues saving some for you?'

'I have told them to, Shamida *san*.'

'Then be glad you are not as these women. It is punishment enough that you will be devouring what they can only smell!'

There was something of a joke in his comment. Inside he didn't feel amused at all, but the man understood, his stupid face cracking into an equally stupid grin.

'Continue your patrol, soldier; leave the woman to her torment.'

He knew as he proceeded that the woman he had saved from a beating had spat in his direction, but he gave it no regard. Already his mind was on saving another woman, though this time he was far from sure of success.

He was jeopardising his own safety; he had taken such care to prune the Americanisms he'd grown up with, to convince himself that he was following an honourable tradition. He kicked at a stone. Who are you kidding? There it was again. He was thinking in English. The truth was always there. Like a painted actor on a cardboard stage, he was playing a part, strutting around in an imperial uniform to which he felt no affinity.

Inside the Bamboo Bridge House, women in various stages of undress were serving saki and small rice cakes mixed with fruit and sticky with sugar. A brazier smouldering with sweet-smelling leaves stood next to it, going some way to keeping the cockroaches at bay.

Low tables were set at regular intervals around the room. The men were sweating, the talk and saki flowing thick and strong. The women's pleasant expressions and tiny smiles were like masks held tightly as though they were wary they might slip and betray their distaste. Their stoic acceptance of their circumstances amazed him. The hungry women in the camp chose how best to survive. These women had no choice. Both sets were doing what they had to do.

'Chinese dog bitch!'

The shout came from a young lieutenant who was dragging Nadine's friend Lucy by her hair at the far end of the hut. Her face was contorted because her hair was straining at the roots and she couldn't help rising from her knees. With each attempt he brought his clenched fist down on her head.

A few of the other men glanced in his direction. One or two frowned; others shook their heads and turned away, philosophically deciding that he'd paid for the woman so could as he wished.

The lieutenant began dragging Lucy to where a bamboo screen shielded the private cubicles from the rest of the house. Genda followed, saw him tense and with a surge of sudden temper, knew what he was seeing. Feeling his grip loosen, Lucy escaped. Genda grabbed the man's arm, pulling him back. 'She's not for you,' he said in Japanese, his voice steady despite the churning in his guts. He could see her out of the corner of his eye, sitting there, naked and waiting for a man he knew was a butcher of men, women and children.

Unsteady on his legs, the lieutenant swayed slightly and attempted to focus his eyes on Genda's face.

'Huh! Is she yours?' He grinned. 'I thought you only made love to your flute. How about we swap girls. I know. I'll fight you for her!' He began undoing his jacket.

Genda pretended to be amused. He covered the man's hands with his own and felt the man's weakness. 'I tell you what, how about you fight the man she belongs to.'

The lieutenant tried to recommence unbuttoning his jacket. 'I will. Who is he?'

Genda clung to his hands. 'Our honourable colonel.'

Resting on one elbow, Nadine's eyes flitted between the two of them. Major Shamida's voice was firm but not severe.

The lieutenant bowed albeit a little shakily. 'Honourable Major Shamida. My apologies.'

Genda returned the salute. 'Be on your way.'

Once the man was gone, Genda filled the gap quite adequately by himself. He knew it was wrong to observe Nadine as she was; if Yamoto arrived now, he would be furious. Yet he could not take his eyes off her. There was much he wanted to say, but what would be the point? He turned and walked away, back into the dark night.

* * *

Nadine's mind was hazy thanks to the drink Madam Cherry had given her. For a moment had thought Shamida about to say something, but changed his mind. His eyes dropped away before letting the curtain go and she had the greatest urge to call him back and beg him to stay.

Her eyes strayed in the other direction beyond the wooden platform and the trees. There was a village beyond those trees, a headland and a jetty. Madam had taken her to dance for the crews of local patrol boats. Low, single storey houses clustered around a rough wooden wharf at the edge of the lagoon where fishing boats were moored.

The boats and their location had stayed in her mind. They hadn't been very big, certainly not ocean going, but escape was going to be about compromise. They're just around that bend, she thought, just out of sight.

The idea was to sail south. Eventually she and whoever escaped with her would reach Australia – at least that was the plan.

Concentrating on what seemed an impossible plan helped her control the ball of apprehension knotting like barbed wire in her stomach. She was aware of the sudden lull among the women and officers on the other side of the screen and knew what it meant. Yamoto had arrived.

The effect of the drink was wearing off. Reality thudded behind her eyes. She attempted to focus, attempted to reason. This will be no different than lying with Martin who had always taken her without as much as a kiss. She'd survived one older man. She'd most certainly survive another.

The screen made a clattering sound and there he was, Colonel Yamoto escorted by Genda Shamida.

She arose unsteadily and leaned forward from her haunches, bowing until her head almost touched her knees.

'Welcome, Yamoto *san*.' Madam had coached her in the Japanese form of address. She hoped her voice did not tremble.

The sound the bamboo made as he let it fall was as if someone had dropped a bundle of stair rods, or a bucketful of hard-shelled beetles or the ever-present cockroaches.

Yamoto stood with his legs' slightly apart, his fists perched on his narrow hips. He lifted her chin with the tip of a silver-handled cane. He always carried the cane. She'd seen him beating people with it. She dared raise her eyes to meet his. She even dared smile. A smile was disarming and also alluring; Zakia had taught her that.

Look beyond them. See the audience, a hundred strong, watching you as you take the stage, aching to see you move, to dance, to be as the cobra, weaving and circling, lithe as a river. It will give you courage.

'*Hai*,' said the major, and translated accordingly. The colonel responded.

Major Shamida looked embarrassed at whatever had been said.

'He says everything has been done to his satisfaction. You appear an adequate purchase.'

The colonel said something else.

'He asks if you are frightened,' said Shamida.

She asked herself the same question. There was indeed a trembling in her legs. She wasn't sure whether it was fear or the drink she'd been given.

'I feel like a bride on her wedding night,' she said.

Shamida interpreted it for the benefit of the colonel. The colonel responded.

'He says that he has a wife.'

'What would she say if she found out about me?'

Shamida's eyelids fluttered. She sensed he did not want to put the question to the colonel, though he seemed to do so.

Again he translated the colonel's response.

'He says that even in the unlikely event that she protested at this, what she says is of no consequence. Wives are for making a family. Courtesans and concubines are for pleasure. Japanese women understand that. He also wishes you to speak English. He thinks he will learn that way.'

'That's nonsense.'

'I will tell him you are pleased to comply.'

Looking pleased but arrogant in the extreme, the colonel dismissed the major. Shamida gave a final, unreadable glance at Nadine as he left the room.

Nadine bowed her head, her gaze following his exiting feet with a feeling of dread.

The fluttering of wings diverted her attention. By day, every hut was full of flies; by night giant moths fluttered around the small kerosene lamps, their only form of lighting. Some were huge and brightly coloured. A thought occurred to her: Perform – dance for him as best you can.

Trembling with apprehension, he picked up the lamp and took it to where he had set down his drink. A droplet of spilled whisky shivered on the table. Colonel Yamoto was pouring whisky, the bottle poised over the glass. His eyes were on her.

She knew the light was flattering and had turned her skin golden. The look in his eyes was almost frightening. One moment he looked self-satisfied; the next he looked awestruck. She wondered what was in his mind.

A soft fanning of air against her cheeks gave her the answer; the moths, their wings a blur of violet, blue and yellow followed the lamp, their wings a wreath of colour around her head and shoulders.

A breath of wind stirred the coconut trees that ringed the crescent of sand between the compound and the cool, green sea.

Yamoto cocked his head as though he had heard something else – or perhaps it was merely a welcome excuse to break the spell at the sight of her.

She waited, the fear she'd tried so hard to control tingling in her muscles, urging her to flee. But where to? Thousands of miles of sea lay to one side of the camp, acres of tangled jungle to the other. She thought of Kochi and tried to slow her pumping heart and curb the weakness in her legs. She asked herself what price was survival? Her attention was drawn to the lust rising in Yamoto's eyes and knew there was only one answer.

One of the men in the main room beyond the bamboo screen

began to sing. Nadine turned to the sound. The song was Japanese and although the music was alien to her ears, she began to dance, adjusting the vibrancy of the Indian temple dancers to the slower tempo of the Japanese.

Yamoto sat down, glass in hand, his eyes following her every move, the placing of one foot slowly before the other, the twisting and contorting of her limbs, her body, the feathery lightness of her hands fluttering across her eyes... *bare your soul with your eyes...* Zakia's words again.

Zakia! Her and Sureya, Benares and the hole beneath the garden wall seemed a lifetime away.

This is to their memory, she told herself her arms waving like the willow, her eyes shifting with the movement of her body. She was *Kali*, the terrible one, dancing as though she had many arms, her movements worshiping death as well as life. The smell of men, the flies, the snakes, the mosquitoes and the vermin that ate their food melted away. Tears came to her eyes as she imagined herself back in her father's garden, dancing with her mother. Her mother: that loving woman who had never been allowed to declare herself to her own daughter.

Eventually, the song ended. It felt as though her whole body had turned to water. The moment had come.

Yamoto got to his feet and slid off his belt.

Her eyes opened wide with fear. He was going to beat her?

'Yamoto *san*! No!' She dropped to her knees wishing she'd never thought of the virgin idea.

The leaves of the coconut palms rustled around the fringe of the hut. Something scuttled beneath the house: Perhaps a rat or even a snake.

With one brawny hand he dragged her to her feet. Silly, but she couldn't help noticing that his fingers were short and square ended. Their strength was apparent when he wound them around her neck four fingers high, his thumb against her throat.

His gaze dropped to her breasts. He grinned and said something in Japanese. His teeth were yellow; his breath smelled of whisky. He said the same thing again and jerked his chin, indicating that her gaze should follow his to the mirror.

The sight of her hardening nipples filled her with shame. They looked lascivious. Decadent. But she felt no arousal, only fear.

A sinking feeling dropped like a lead weight within her stomach. She attempted to collect herself. 'Do you wish me to dance for you again?' A foolish question! A last-ditch attempt to allay what had to happen.

Fool. He speaks little English.

She pulled herself together, worrying in case the blood-filled balloon chose that moment to leave her body.

Again he spoke in Japanese. She did not understand.

She turned her puzzled expression to face him.

He spattered words of exasperation.

She shook her head. 'I don't under…'

He swung her around until she could feel the dampness of his uniform mix with the perspiration on her back. The flat of his hand thudded between her shoulder blades. She fell forward onto her hands and knees.

This was a place where anger must never be hot, but controlled to seep out at a later date like droplets of venom.

The mirror was directly opposite her. She saw her made-up face, the dark sootiness outlining her eyes, the dark hair pulled back into a cushioned design that framed her face.

He brought the light from the table and placed it on the floor. Her breasts and face took on its amber light. The moths formed a cloud of colour around the lamp, her face and her body.

Moths basked in the warm glow, their fluttering wings

brushing her breasts. She saw herself in the mirror and saw what he was seeing.

She tensed. She'd never felt so sick. There was lust, malice and sheer glee on his sweaty, hot face, but also something else, something that became clearer as her breasts reddened from the heat of the lamp.

Forcing her legs apart, he thrust himself into her without pause or consideration. Her thighs strained, her shoulders tensed and her breasts scorched in the heat of the lamp. And all the while the brightly coloured moths fluttered around her, their presence duplicated in her shadowy reflection.

One of them landed on her back. Yamoto caught it and crushed it in his hand. And the same could happen to me, she thought to herself.

* * *

Genda listened in the semi-darkness beneath the house. There was not enough height to stand upright so he settled for standing slightly stooped, one hand resting on his knee, the other on the handle of his sword. Despite the likely presence of snakes, scorpions and rats, he would endure the stench of mildew, stagnant water and hordes of angry ants. No danger, no monster could compare to the man in the room above him.

Spears of light and clouds of movement pierced the gaps in the rough floor bursting onto his face. He heard the singer lamenting about lost love and his sadness at being far from home. He heard Yamoto's voice but his words were indistinct. He thought he detected a strangled gasp, but couldn't be sure.

Perspiration ran into his eyes. He took his hand off his sword and rubbed more sweat onto his trouser leg before returning it to the reassuring steel. Crafted by a master sword maker, the weapon had been in his family for generations. He wondered what his ancestors would think if they knew his intention should Yamoto turn into the beast he knew him to be and kill her. Perhaps not yet. Yamoto liked to play with his prey before killing them.

He heard another sound from above – just a gasp – no more, but enough to tell him what was going on. He thought he heard her voice. Jeez, he wished he'd never left America. And for what? Loyalty to a land he'd never known first hand, traditions passed from one generation to another like an antique clock.

He shut his eyes. He didn't want to think of what Yamoto was doing to the beautiful dancer. The time he spent watching her and playing for her were the closest he had come to happiness for a long time. When talking to her he could almost forget they were on opposing sides of a hellish war, so entranced was he by the subtle steps of the dance and even the way she walked. Her eyes were filled with fire and for some inexplicable reason he felt empathy with her.

If Yamoto's mood changed, he would kill her. Shamida tried not to visualise what he was doing to her at that moment.

Eventually, the floor above his head vibrated with the sound of Yamoto's departing boots.

He listened for weeping but heard none. There was only silence, and then there was one long wail of anguish – an odd sound that slowly turned into hysterical laughter.

The overhang at the back of the room jutted over dry land. He got a foothold, swore at his scabbard for getting in the way, but managed to clamber up the wooden stilt and onto the platform. He found the naked Nadine on the other side of the sliding screen, her head buried in her hands.

'Did he hurt you?'

She started. Her eyes were very round, her cheeks pink and there was a red mark around her neck.

'Are you all right?' He dropped to his knees, his disgust for Yamoto burning a hole in his guts.

The dancer's skin looked luminescent in the amber light. He offered the discarded kimono to cover her nakedness; she took it, and as she did so his eyes took in the fact that her thighs were smeared with blood. The bloodstained cloth that would prove Yamoto had taken her virginity was gone.

She shivered when he touched her shoulder. 'You feel so cold.'

Her jaw trembled, but she held her head high and defiant. 'I survived.'

He winced when she looked into his eyes. He'd expected terror, but saw only triumph. What had happened to cause that look?

'Did he hurt you?' he asked again.

She rubbed at the redness around her neck and spoke through gritted teeth. 'Do you want to know the details?'

Her voice was defiant and made him ashamed.

'No! No, of course not. I was merely enquiring... because I...'

He couldn't go on. He felt as tongue-tied as a high school kid on his first date. He tried again. 'Look. I'm only trying to help.'

She nodded. 'Yes.'

What was it about that look in her eyes? If he wasn't mistaken, she was almost smiling.

'I can't believe how calm you are. Most women are nervous wrecks by the time he's finished with them.'

'I'm not most women! And stop staring. I wish to wash myself and get dressed. Do you mind turning your back, please?'

He looked out over the ledge he'd climbed up. His eyes skimmed the trees of the jungle, a border of blackness against an ink black sky.

Wincing, Nadine reached up inside herself and found the knotted end of the balloon. It slid out easily enough, now disposal.

She pushed it between the woven fronds of the reed walls. It went straight through, falling out the other side.

'I'm dressed now. You can have this back.'

Genda turned. He couldn't help the flush that spread up from his neck when he looked at her. No girl or woman had ever intrigued him like she did.

'You look very nice,' he said.

She now wore a short blouse and a silky sarong tied in a knot at the side. The edge of one did not meet the other; her midriff remained bare.

'Nice?' She looked surprised at first, and then angry. 'Oh, I see! The colonel's at the head of the queue and you've got permission to be second!'

Taken aback, Genda shook his head vehemently. 'No! Not at all. I really do think... from the time I first saw you dancing...'

The sound of soldiers laughing and women shrieking sounded from the communal room interrupted his concentration.

'Damn them all,' he muttered, his eyes darkening as he sought the right words.

She covered her eyes with her hands. 'I need to get out of here. A little fresh air – just for a moment.'

A crashing sounded in his ears; the rules he'd made for himself about not getting too close to internees smashed to pieces.

'I know a place,' he said, hardly believing that he could be so foolish, but unable to stop himself. 'Just trust me. OK?'

She nodded silently and swayed as though the colonel had left her weak and helpless. On the contrary, the vision of the beautiful moth squashed to nothingness was still in her mind. In time the colonel would tire of her, she would earn her money, perhaps finally escape. Escape! The word would haunt her dreams.

* * *

The Bamboo Bridge House was very busy. Rather than be seen by those in the outer room, Shamida helped Nadine climb down the same way as he'd climbed in.

Ducking down, they traversed the area beneath the hut, totally hidden by darkness.

Genda zigzagged around clumps of rock and bushes. At one point, he froze. She could see nothing herself, not until the light from a vehicle pulling up outside the guardhouse fell over a passing snake. The major swore a heartfelt oath. She sensed snakes were not his favourite animals.

The moon was hidden behind ragged clouds. He led her through a small opening to the rear of the guardhouse, not visible from the front of the building. The sound of loud voices came out through the open windows.

Nadine studied the route they took and also noted the position of the secret gate. Nothing, no opportunity or knowledge of this camp and its occupants, must be wasted.

A narrow path through an apron of jungle led to a small beach.

The salt smell of the sea! She took great gulps of night air as though it were a new and unforgettable experience. Like freedom. Freedom! Of a kind. She had survived her encounter with the most feared man at the camp. Despite her shaking legs, she was elated by the thought that her ill-conceived plan had worked.

They sat with their backs leaning against a rock, their feet digging into the soft sand, both gazing at a moon-speckled sea.

'Did he hurt you?' he asked again.

She took deep gulps of air. Her lips curved in a flickering smile. 'Not as much as he would have liked to. I'm a widow, not a virgin.'

'If he ever finds out he will kill you.'

'I realised just how dangerous he is,' she said, thinking of the way he crushed the particularly beautiful moth. 'He enjoyed hurting me.'

'I've seen what he can do. Somehow you must keep away from him.'

'The only way I can do that is to escape – and that's difficult.'

She waited for him to respond and could almost hear his thoughts ticking over, accompanied only by the surf rolling into the sand.

The bay became flooded with moonlight. For a while they both studied it. No words could express its beauty – or the fear she was feeling.

'Are you in danger from him, Genda Shamida?'

He shrugged. 'I think he would have me killed as a spy if he could. The only thing that stops him is the fact that he'd like a command – a proper command with a proper army. He doesn't consider being commandant of a brothel and a women's prison camp an honourable position. In China it didn't matter to him so much. He didn't regard the Chinese as a worthy enemy. His attitude has changed since Pearl Harbour. He wishes for glory, both for himself and his family. I could recommend him to my grandfather, the general, if I'd a mind to.'

'But you won't.'

'I most certainly will not!' He said it with great conviction. She sensed he took great delight in standing in the way of the colonel's ambition.

'Wouldn't it be best if he left? Perhaps he'd even get killed.'

'But that would bring honour on his family. Oh no!' He shook his head. 'I will not allow him the satisfaction of bringing honour on his family, even by his death.' He saw the look of horror on her face. 'Yes, I mean it. His death would honour them. Japanese do not think like Europeans or Americans. This is *bushido*. Tradition.'

'So you wish you'd never returned to Japan.'

'Most of the time. I feel so guilty.'

'About Pearl Harbour?'

'About a lot of things. About not getting out of Japan fast enough. I saw the way things were going when my uncle burned his collection of western literature. Classic stories and poetry.' He curved his head towards his bended knees, hugging them closer to him at the same time as his eyes skimmed the moonlight shining on water.

The softness of his voice made her want to touch the nape of his neck. It seemed so exposed, almost as though he were inviting attention.

'So,' she said, gathering her words as diligently as she might the pebbles on the beach, 'why did he burn his books?'

He lifted a finger from among his clasped hands and traced the path of moonlight as though it were daubed in oil on cardboard.

'America and other powers had chastised Japan for their behaviour in China. There was a lot of anti-western feeling. He thought he might be singled out and punished. So he did what he thought was a patriotic thing; he burned his most precious possessions.' He hung his head. 'I was saddened. I loved those books, especially the poetry. I tried to save one, but he tore it from my hand so all I saved was one single page, one single poem.'

His earlier anger and concern for her was replaced by what sounded like melancholy.

Her curiosity was aroused. 'What poem was it?'

He raised his head and looked at her. She knew immediately that he was about to share a treasured secret. Without a word, he delved into his uniform and brought out a single piece of paper.

His face lit up with boyish enthusiasm. 'Call me stupid and sentimental if you like, but I kept it. I felt it signified something at the time. I still do, though for the life of me I can't put it into words myself. I suppose that's what makes a good poet so great.'

She felt herself relaxing and desperate to know what poem he had saved. What would a man like him, a hybrid man who was both East and West and also a soldier, what would he keep?

The paper was singed at the edges and crackled as he unfolded it. For a moment he seemed about to read it out loud, but he changed his mind.

'You read it.' He passed her the piece of paper.

There was just enough moonlight. She saw the title, saw the familiar words. It was totally unexpected. She began to read it out loud.

'How do I love thee? Let me count the ways.
I love thee to the depth and breadth and height
My soul can reach, when feeling out of sight
For the ends of Being and ideal Grace.

'I love thee to the level of every day's
Most quiet need, by sun and candlelight.
I love thee freely, as men strive for Right;
I love thee purely, as they turn from Praise.

'I love thee with the passion put to use
In my old friends and with my childhood's faith.
I love thee with a love I seemed to lose
With my lost saints, I love thee with the breath,
Smiles, tears, of all my life! And, if God choose,
I shall but love thee better after death.'

Reading a love poem in the midst of starvation, deprivation and brutality, seemed so out of place, so surreal. But there was something else.

She looked at the sea, the emptiness of it all, the dark sky, the moon wreathed in scrap of cloud, as thin and fibrous as lace. 'What are we doing here?'

'Trying to survive.'

All the anguish, the fear and self-loathing welled up inside her. She pounded her knees with her fists. 'When will it end?'

'When the great powers make it so.'

'Until then?'

'We are just pawns caught up in bigger things. We survive as best we can.'

She looked back at the sea. 'We are alike. You know that, don't you?'

He nodded. 'Our feelings are alike.'

'A bit of British, a bit of Indian; I was always aware that I was different.'

'You have a British name.'

She threw back her head so that her hair tickled the hollow of her back. Moonlight silvered her features. 'I wanted to be *more* British. I wanted to be *the Honourable* Miss Nadine Burton.'

He laughed and shook his head. 'The Honourable...'

'No one would notice anything else if I was called that.'

Genda continued to laugh and shake his head.

She slapped his shoulder. 'Stop it.'

He didn't stop so she repeated the action, but at the minute he turned and her hand landed on his face. Suddenly, she remembered he was a Japanese officer and froze.

Her fear vanished when he caught her hand and showed no anger. 'I wasn't being rude. I was just remembering. At college in the states I wished my name were Joseph Smith Junior the Third. Now is that stupid, or is that stupid?'

'Joe Smith?'

'Not just Joe Smith,' he said indignantly. 'Joseph Smith Junior the Third. The Americans set a lot of store about being a "junior" and a "the third".'

Relieved and genuinely amused, Nadine fell back against the rock and began to laugh. 'What a silly pair we are; I want to be an "honourable" and you want to be a "junior, the third".'

The amusement persisted until it struck Nadine that here they were, supposed enemies, laughing and sharing childhood secrets. The uniform and the circumstances suddenly became unimportant. They really were two people with a great deal in common.

'You're staring at me.'

'Yes,' he answered.

'We're supposed to be enemies.'

'But we're not. We can't be when we understand each other so well.'

For a moment she stared down at her clasped hands and attempted to evaluate her mixed emotions. 'I am afraid of the colonel. I am afraid of what he might do.' The brittle exterior behind which she'd hidden her fear fell away. She shivered.

'I'll try to protect you,' Genda said.

He looked so determined, so sincere. She knew he meant what he said.

Closing her eyes, she rested her head on his shoulder. 'Comfort me.' She closed her eyes.

Genda's voice trembled. 'I heard everything. I wanted to kill him.'

Nadine rolled out of his arms and stared up at the trees fringing the sandy beach. 'You were listening?'

'Underneath the house. I was afraid for you.'

Her thoughts were complex and disturbing. She needed to get them into some order. The secret gate leading to this beach loomed large in her mind.

Genda stared thoughtfully at the sea, his chin resting on her shoulder.

Nadine sat as though her head was empty of thoughts and stared at the sea. It couldn't have been further from the truth. She was thinking that Genda Shamida might prove a useful ally and might aid her survival. He might even help her get out of here. She would use him, but that was all. I feel nothing, absolutely nothing, she thought, but deep down she was unnerved that she felt more than she should; they had touched in so many ways.

'Do you care for me?' he asked.

The suddenness of his question coming at this particular moment when her head was full of intrigue surprised her. 'Yes. Very much.' She told herself she was exaggerating only to win his protection, but knew that there was more to her complex feelings.

He stroked her back. Much as she tried, she couldn't find any hatred in her heart for Genda Shamida. Despite everything, she could not deny that he was different, and that she wanted him near.

A sudden feeling of desolation threatened to destroy her.

'Hold me,' she said to him.

Slowly and gently he slid his arms around her and held her close.

'I need someone to care.'

'I care,' he said in a choking voice. 'Please, I do not wish to offend...'

'I need this to happen. I need to believe in something good and normal. I need to be loved.'

That night was the first time she lay with him. His lovemaking was gentle and considered, as though she were a china doll that might shatter at any moment. Yet it was also passionate and sensual, touching her more deeply than any other sexual act she had ever encountered.

And so it began. Illicit meetings snatched at opportune moments, mutual support between two people trapped in a situation neither of them had any control over.

* * *

Genda Shamida gave her hope. She carried him in her thoughts as she might a shield against the horror that was happening around her.

Madam Cherry had coldly informed her of some unwelcome developments. 'Colonel Yamoto *san* has decided to keep you for his exclusive use. You will remain here under my protection until such time as he tires of you. You have become his favourite. And get rid of this.'

The white cloth that had caught the chicken blood landed on her shoulder.

Nadine bowed respectfully. And you, she thought, have become my enemy.

The following morning she made her way across the bamboo bridge to take a little stolen quinine for her friends and to take some solace from their aggrieved but welcome companionship.

The humidity clung to her like a second skin and yet she shivered. The women had a decent breakfast this morning: rice and slivers of raw fish, char and sliced mangoes for breakfast – just enough to stave off the constant hunger they were becoming used to.

Peggy offered her a selection in a wooden bowl.

Nadine shook her head.

Peggy was persistent. 'You've got something on your mind. A problem shared and all that, though we've all got plenty of problems of our own. Still, you can tell me, old sport.'

Nadine had decided not to tell her about Genda Shamida. 'I

was just thinking about the native workers that disappeared overnight.'

Silence dropped like a fog. No one took up the subject. Everyone knew what had happened.

One moment they had been swarming over the camp like busy ants. Then they were gone.

No transport had been heard taking them elsewhere. There'd been no gunfire, but one of the girls had looked out and seen Yamoto's batman carrying the colonel's fine, Samurai sabre and guards wielding fixed bayonets, herding them forward.

In the morning, the ground to the west of the boundary fence was newly dug. Fresh green shoots would grow there soon, feeding on blood-rich compost.

'We're still alive,' said Peggy and patted her arm. 'We'll survive this. We have to.'

21

It was on an evening three weeks later that Nadine was dancing in the Bamboo Bridge House, glad of the company, happy to be away from Madam Cherry and her sullen looks and angry slaps.

Yamoto, who had been away at headquarters, came crashing in, saw her at once and pointed to the screen dividing the main room from the small room at the rear. It was obvious he'd been drinking.

The screen clattered shut. Trembling with fear she backed into the furthest corner. There was no escape. Yamoto pressed against her.

At first he caressed her hair, her breasts, and her face. As if suddenly ashamed he might be showing emotional weakness, his mood changed in an instant. Yanking her onto her feet, he spun her round, flung her to the floor and pressed his boot on her neck.

'I kill you, I think,' he said. 'I fuck you now I kill you.'

'No! Please.'

He laughed, dragged her to her feet and seemed to think it a huge joke.

She thought of jumping off the balcony into the thick foliage twenty feet below the balcony and running off into the jungle; running and being shot in the back would be better than doing nothing.

Muttering to himself and breathing whisky breath all over her, he pushed her towards the door and called for Major Shamida.

Genda Shamida appeared very quickly from out of the darkness. He glanced briefly at her. His face was taut, expressionless, a barrier between the world and his feelings, yet she saw through the façade, knew he had been close by, waiting to be needed.

'Is this that moment after which I may love thee better?' she whispered.

She could tell by his eyes that he understood. She had referred him to the poem, asking him if this was her time to die.

The colonel rattled off his requirements. Shamida translated.

'The colonel says he wishes to show you something.'

'Something pretty dreadful, no doubt.'

The colonel asked him what had been said.

'She asked me where we were going, Colonel Yamoto *san*. I told her I didn't know.'

The colonel grunted approvingly. 'Good. I want to feel her fear.'

Shamida sensed Nadine awaited translation but didn't give it.

Two guards carrying shovels as well as their rifles were ordered ahead of them. The major was given a lantern.

The night breeze ruffled her hair and a troop of monkeys awoke from their sleep and mocked from the trees.

Nadine's blood ran cold. Her legs felt as though they were filled with wet sand. Was this her time to die?

She noticed that Major Shamida's fingers were curled over the hilt of his sword. Would he be ordered to sever her head from her body? She grew numb at the thought of it.

Dying was something she saw and heard of more frequently

these days. Every night she wondered how her ending would be. Like skeletal fingers, death reached out from the darkness. In readiness for the event she drank in all the details of her surroundings: the drone of a mosquito was her death knell, the sweat trickling down her arms her lifeblood ebbing away.

They turned away from the centre of the camp and through the gate to a cleared area a few hundred yards away to the left.

The smell of turned earth and the sweetness of decaying fruit attracted hordes of flies during the day. Even at night the sound of insects thrummed on the air.

The earth and vegetation were soft beneath her feet. They stopped and Shamida held up the lantern.

Nadine's breath caught in her throat. She'd had nothing to drink but her bladder tingled with nerves.

The colonel barked an order. The two guards began to dig.

Yamoto's teeth were a rancid yellow in the muted glow of the lantern.

Nadine licked at her lips. Her mouth was as dry as dust, her fear of death covering her like a damp shroud.

She wanted to ask Genda if this was her grave, but no words came. Her eyes remained fixed on the rise and fall of the shovels. If this were to be her grave then she would relish every minute of life – whatever and wherever it might be. Her heart hammered against her rib cage.

The sound of earth being dug out and heaped up split the night. Suddenly the sound changed: a grating sound.

The colonel barked an order. The shovels were tossed aside. Both guards stooped down into the grave and brought out a round, gourd like shape smothered in mud and roots.

The light from the lantern picked out the features of two Chinese civilian labourers. Their flesh was swiftly decomposing.

Nadine retched.

The colonel laughed and spoke to the major.

He translated as ordered. 'The colonel likes to test his sword. Once drawn it must taste blood. To sheath it without doing so would be dishonourable.'

As if to prove the point, the colonel pulled the shining weapon from its leather scabbard and laid the blade on her shoulder, its sharp edge against her neck.

This was it! Less than twenty years of age and her life about to end!

Out of the corner of her eyes, she saw Shamida's hand tighten over his sword hilt. He was willing to fight his own colonel, but what about the guards? She could see their grinning faces as they knocked the rotting heads together in some gruesome game.

Three against one. That's how it would be.

Crazy! So be crazy yourself!

'Would the colonel like me to dance for him?'

Shamida looked at her. She dug her elbow into the major's side. 'He's a man of changing moods. Ask him. Go on.'

Although he looked dubious, Genda Shamida did as asked.

The colonel eyed his major. 'What would you do if I spare her life?'

'Ask him if he wishes me to dance for him – like the Scottish over crossed swords.'

Genda stared. 'What?'

'Go on.'

He translated.

Yamoto repeated what his major had said with slow deliberation. He was about to slice her head off and she was asking him if he wished her to dance? The idea was totally preposterous – and totally unexpected, so much so that he burst out laughing. His sword dropped to his side.

'Look at this place,' he said to Shamida, indicating the encircling greenery and the mounds of earth. 'We are in the middle of a cemetery and she asks to dance?' He burst out laughing again. 'Well, why not?'

To Shamida's surprise, he lay his sword down on the damp earth and indicated that his major do the same. Nadine crossed one over the other.

Looking amazed at what was going on, the guards threw the severed heads back into the yawning hole.

'I need a rhythm,' Nadine said to Shamida. 'Clap. Clap for all you are worth.'

She sprang into the steps she'd seen Scottish soldiers dance back in India, her arms raised above her head, her bare feet skipping lightly at the gaps between the blades.

Genda clapped just as she'd asked him. Laughing and red faced with glee, the guards joined in.

The ludicrousness of the whole scene was not wasted on Yamoto. Between slurps of whisky from a silver hip flask, he too began clapping.

Nadine didn't know how long she danced. She only stopped when one of the guards who'd been dancing around the grave, slipped in the soft earth and fell in. Eyes shining like a madman, the colonel immediately began shovelling earth in on him. It was left to Genda to stop him before the man was suffocated. At last Yamoto passed out, his whisky breath staining the night. Genda heaved him across his shoulders, ordering the two guards to carry the swords.

'Go,' he whispered harshly, labouring beneath the heavy load, for Yamoto was far from being a lightweight. 'And don't look back. Just go.'

Nadine had no intention of looking back. This was a place she would prefer to forget.

* * *

Two more days passed. Living in this terrible place took its toll. Sometimes Nadine was unable to stop her hands shaking, interrupting the normalcy of everyday tasks. This place was not normal. It was evil and death was a daily occurrence.

Genda visited whenever he could, though was careful not to attract too much attention. He always brought his flute or carried an official looking piece of paper in his hand.

On one particular day, he looked far grimmer than he usually did. She could see in his eyes that something distasteful had or was about to occur.

'The colonel has ordered that your quarters be extended. He will visit you and expect you to act as a Class One courtesan should. You will thank him for this and ensure that everything he desires is available to him. Food, whisky and cigarettes will be required. You will also dance for him. I will accompany your dancing on my flute.'

'What if I should refuse?'

The major flashed a warning look. 'That is not a good question.'

'I suppose not.'

Work began just a week later. The taking down of a wall between the original space and a cupboard extended her small room. Yamoto ordered that she be supplied with more furniture and visited regularly to check on progress, strolling around the room, hands clasped behind his back. As his shadow fell over them, the men making the alterations lowered their heads their gaze fixed on the floor. Even Madam Cherry was keeping her distance.

'A comfortable place to sleep, even if it is of the western style: You will like this,' ordered Yamoto.

Items taken from the abandoned home of a Dutch planter duly arrived. Nadine's attention was drawn to one particular item: a solid piece of Dutch craftsmanship with cupboards, drawers and a mirror. It was inlaid with ebony fashioned into inky black vinery and flowers. Alone in her own space she ran her fingers thoughtfully along the twisting pattern. Her heart thudded as she considered what was happening to her. She had attracted Yamoto's interest. Besides the obvious fact that he was a dangerous man, there was another price to pay. She could see it stamped in Madam Cherry's tight-lipped tolerance. She could also see it in the wary hostility of the women in the Bamboo Bridge House.

She had been favoured but this new room was for his convenience more so than her comfort.

'If it were me, I would refuse to leave my pals,' said Betty, and then smarted before Peggy's baleful look. 'Don't be so bloody stupid. If she does that, she's dead.'

'I have to make the best of it,' Nadine said, mostly to herself than to the others. 'At least for now. I need to buy a boat.'

Lucy sighed deeply and shook her head. 'That would take a lot of money. A lot of organising too.'

Nadine put her arm around her old friend's skinny shoulders, noting the dark circles beneath her eyes.

'I'll get the money – somehow. I would also like to get some food over the fence. There are children there. I know we've managed to get some over there, but it's not enough.'

Betty shook her head. 'It's difficult. I take in what I can when I go to check their health – such as it is – but it isn't easy. In fact, it's darn right dangerous.'

Nadine pondered about getting more food into the camp across the way, specifically for Doreen and the children. She had seen them several times but been unable to approach or even call out to them because of the guards.

Back in her quarters she trailed her fingers around the outer edges of an open drawer that ran full length beneath the mirror of a Dutch sideboard. It shot forward, taking her unawares, a rough edge pricking her finger.

As she sucked the blood from her finger a thought occurred to her. Planters were cautious people, always wary of the conquered peoples in the countries they'd occupied. Martin had told her that they often hid valuables instead of trusting banks.

It was a long shot, but worth taking a closer look. With an air of determination, she attempted to push it back in. It jammed so she reached inside. Her fingers closed around what felt like a box. She drew it out, opened it and gasped. Rings, a necklace, a pair of earrings: Were they real diamonds? Possibly.

This was bargaining power, things that could be sold for hard dollars, medicines, bribes and favours; perhaps even her most cherished dream: a boat.

Quickly, she stuffed the bracelets, necklaces, rings and earrings back into their hiding place. It occurred to her that the furniture might have more secret compartments. She poked and pried and found what she was looking for. There were two more compartments hidden behind smaller drawers to either side of the mirror.

Suddenly, she had wealth. For days she'd felt her spirits declining; now they soared. Here she had hope in her hands.

Trading, she decided, required immediacy. With that in mind, she reopened her stash – she'd learned the word from Peggy. She took the smallest ring and slid it onto her finger. Her finger was thinner than in India or Singapore, so the ring was a loose fit and too visible. She pulled a thread from around the hem of her sarong. It was shiny and thick, strong enough to hang around her neck: But not now. Tonight, it would stay out of sight. Tomorrow was soon enough.

***

That night, Nadine felt more hopeful than she'd felt in a very long time. The room that had stifled her was now very pleasant. She had chairs, furniture and a decent bed placed close to the coolness of the open shutters.

Lying down she listened to the sounds of apes – the orang-utans and gibbons – rustling and snapping the highest branches in their search for food, comrades and copulation.

She touched her stomach. Yamoto had left her body bruised, but her spirit was intact. Major Genda Shamida had made her feel whole again – and loved.

She closed her eyes. Things would not always be this way. Time would pass, things would change and she would survive. It was just a case of taking advantage of opportunities when and where they came.

***

Nadine had begun trading within hours of acquiring her new quarters, though now with more verve and less nervousness. One of the Korean guards bought a tiny box containing three silver edged lace handkerchiefs; a young Japanese guard, homesick to the point of suicide, bought a pretty brooch in the shape of a clog for his sweetheart.

She counted the money before putting it away. More than ever, she wished to escape. Closing her eyes, she wrapped her hand over her stomach, then opened her eyes and regarded her reflection in the handsome cheval mirror standing in the corner. Yamoto's visits were infrequent and therefore bearable. But her midriff was swelling and she hadn't had a monthly show. How would the colonel react when he found out that she was pregnant? Of greater importance to her was how Genda Shamida would react. It was his child. That's what she kept telling herself.

She'd put off the moment of telling Peggy and Lucy the news. They were nurses and in the absence of a doctor, they were all she had.

Earlier, she'd seen them with Lucy making their way into the women's camp. The two nurses were allowed to minister to the sick and Lucy went along as interpreter.

Nadine felt a nervous churning in her stomach. She'd counted her pregnancy since the night with the poetry and the full moon in the company of Genda. They would suggest to her that it might be Yamoto's; that was the reason she'd put this off; that, and the fear of facing up to the fact.

Usually she averted her eyes from the camp; the women had not ceased to hurl snide remarks or spit as she passed, but it was her friends she was looking for.

Normally the women in the camp beyond the fence gazed out with dull disinterest or the odd offensive remark. Today it sounded as though every woman in the camp had exploded with anger.

Shielding her eyes with one hand, she looked through the barrier to the hard-packed earth of the compound. All hell had broken loose. The women were rioting, running around and shouting and screaming. The guards looked unsure of how to calm things down, shouting and prodding the air with their bayonets.

A Chinese trader pushing a handcart was running under an avalanche of missiles. Cabbage stalks, stones, and meat bones boiled to whiteness hit him as he raced for the main gate.

Peggy, Betty and Lucy were also on their way back, though did not appear to be the recipients of the flying missiles.

'What's that about?' Nadine asked, once they were through the gate.

'Food,' said Peggy with a sardonic grin.

'It's always about food,' Betty added.

Lucy, who was mopping her brow and looking deadbeat, explained further.

'He's got fish and is charging double what he was charging before. The women are angry.'

Peggy threw the scene a knowing grin and slapped her hips. 'Even cabbage stumps make a reasonable soup. They don't usually waste them.'

Nadine nodded. Peggy had told her before that every morsel of food was used. No stalk, no peeling, not even a sliver of onionskin was wasted. The horniest bone of the toughest fish was boiled to distraction until all the flavour was gone. If they were lucky enough to get a few buffalo or horse bones, they were boiled with equal deliberation until the marrow had totally liquidised and nourished the soup.

The Chinaman, glad to have escaped the women, was muttering under his breath. The stench of stale fish and a spiral of predatory flies preceded him.

Nadine fingered the small ring nestling on the thread between her breasts. 'Ask him how much for the lot,' she said to Lucy.

Lucy asked him in Cantonese.

The Chinese stopped muttering, brought his cart to a halt and named his price. Lucy passed on the information.

Nadine glanced around her to make sure she was not being observed. The guards were rushing into the women's camp in a bid to help their colleagues calm the riot. She pulled out the ring.

'This is gold. It is worth a lot of money.'

Shrewd eyes narrowed in a face of shrivelled skin and warts. He made an affable sound. Spidery fingers reached out to take it. Nadine snatched it back.

The ring was worth more than a load of fish. She recalled the markets back in Benares. Shanti had told her that the real price was never the first one mentioned and long-term associations were always welcome.

She clutched the ring tightly in her palm out of sight of the covetous eyes.

'Tell him I will pay him what he asks, but not just today. I want him to bring us other things too. I will make him a list.'

Lucy looked at her, open mouthed. The two Australians looked puzzled.

'Go on,' she urged Lucy.

Lucy did so.

The trader rattled off a series of questions, his chin jerking forward with each one.

Lucy interpreted. 'He asks how you can do this. He says the women of the comfort house owe their good fortune and their income to Madam Cherry and that she drives a hard bargain. He says he knows this well and thus cannot understand why you still have valuables. Madam Cherry is usually very thorough.'

'So opening our legs for these yellow devils he calls good fortune?' Peggy almost exploded.

Betty grinned sourly. 'Is that what it is?'

Despite her friends' desperate outburst, Nadine kept her attention fixed on the Chinaman. 'Tell him once the value of this ring is all done with, I will pay him with another item of value, and secretly so the madam does not see. He will provide extras for the women and children of the camp, and both he and they will benefit from the transaction. Tell him that.'

Still looking puzzled, Lucy did as ordered. The Chinaman's face creased into deep trenches of delight.

'He says he will be pleased to do business with the sleek lady as long as the ring is of true value and that the turnip heads do not find out. He would not like to lose his own head, no matter how lucrative the transaction.'

Nadine nodded, patted her chest and glanced at each of her friends. 'Is the coast clear?'

Keeping a lookout had become second nature. No one did anything slightly suspect without checking whether they were being watched. The eyes of all four women swept over the huts, the guards and officers. Quelling the riot appeared to be demanding all their attention.

'Here.' Nadine handed the ring to the Chinaman. 'It's still warm.'

'Don't think he cares about that,' said Peggy.

Teeth stained by betel juice bit into the shank.

Eventually he uttered a sound of acquiescence, nodded his aging head at Nadine and fixed the deal with Lucy.

'Now,' said Nadine. 'Can you tell him to take the fish back to the camp?'

Lucy looked unsure. 'I don't think he's going to want to return there, Nadine. The women were angry with him.'

'With good reason,' added Betty. 'He was lucky to get out of there alive.'

Nadine realised she was probably right. 'Tell him if he doesn't mind us borrowing his cart, we will take the fish back ourselves. The ring easily covers the value of his cart.'

Lucy explained.

The man's face lit up. He said something to Lucy.

'He said you are welcome. He said he will not go back until they are women again, not she dragons.'

Peggy grinned. 'Tell him there's only one She Dragon in this place.'

The others laughed. So did the Chinaman once Lucy had interpreted that they were referring to Madam Cherry.

The ring was small and might once have belonged to a child. He tucked it into one of the many pockets of his grubby tunic over which he wore a western style suit jacket.

Nadine surveyed her friends. 'Anyone coming with me?'

Lucy nodded. 'I will.'

'I'd rather not go with you if you don't mind,' said Peggy with a tired sigh.

'She's not feeling so well,' blurted Betty.

Peggy shot her a warning look. 'It's nothing, Betty. Just a bit of inflammation. My guts have never been quite right since I got here. Bloody country! Bloody jungle!'

There was no anger in the set of Peggy's shoulders as she shuffled tiredly towards the bamboo bridge and the house beyond. Betty followed on.

With Lucy helping her, Nadine bent her back to the task in hand. She tried not to think of who might have owned the ring or whether they were alive or dead. It would help the starving survive and that was all that mattered.

Entering the women's camp was never without incident. First there were questions from the guards at the gate. This was followed by the silent antagonism of the inmates: deep-set eyes in haunted faces, like barely disguised skulls set on amorphous bodies.

The smell of dirt and depravation hung in the air. Stalks and the yellowed leaves of Chinese cabbage were scattered all around, but already these were being gathered up.

The cartwheels squealed from lack of lubrication; getting it to roll forward took a tremendous amount of effort. Their backs and calves were throbbing in protest by the time they reached the cookhouse.

The women inside were stirring huge cauldrons of steaming rice, the staple basic for every meal. Sometimes there was a little dried fish or meat, sometimes eggs plus a few vegetables from the patches of garden they'd carved from the encroaching jungle.

Their chatter was no different to that of any other gathering of women coming together to achieve a certain task. There were sarcastic comments about their miserable cuisine, remarks about other inmates and rude comments about individual guards and officers.

Most of the chatter fell away once Lucy and Nadine were spotted. Only one voice still rang out.

'I will not have that woman back in *my* kitchen. I know it's her that's stealing food and redirecting to her own people. Missionaries! They're all the same...'

Suddenly realising that she was not alone, the woman laying down the law turned to face them.

'Well! We have visitors!'

'We've brought food,' said Nadine before anyone had chance to criticise, call them whores and all the other nasty names. A host of flies surged in an angry cloud as she pulled back the mix of sacking and leaves covering the food.

Despite the stink, the women surged forward. Other interested faces gathered around the entrance.

'I hear his prices have doubled,' said Nadine.

'They have indeed,' said the woman, her voice as superior as her height. Bony elbows fixed at a sharp angle, fists on hips, she gave them the once over. 'If I was still on the bench, I'd give him thirty days! I used to be a magistrate. So,' she said, poking at the fish. 'You paid his price. You must have more personal valuables left than we have.'

'Not much, but enough; if we can help, we will. We have a little more scope than you do,' said Nadine.

The woman eyed Nadine's clear skin and glossy hair. 'I suppose you have a reason for doing what you do.'

Nadine gritted her teeth. 'Yes. Survival. But the price is high. Unlike you, we were bought and paid for by a civilian. So far the Japanese are ignoring our pleas to be transferred here because the madam insists we pay off our debt to her first.'

'Ah! We did wonder. Sleeping with the enemy and all that.'

'We do far from sleep! We are abused! We are abased. But we're still alive! Like everyone else, we have adapted as best we can. Haven't you?'

There were mutterings all round in response to her raised voice and the challenge it carried.

The big woman nodded and shook Nadine's hand vigorously. 'Point taken, my dear, and your provisions are most welcome. A feast indeed. Almost like high tea.' She indicated her tattered dress with a casual wave of her hands. 'I do apologise for not changing into something more presentable. I'm Marjorie Ford-Patterson. How do you do?'

After that, she turned away and barked out orders. 'Right! Get this fish unloaded. I also think we also have cabbage and coconuts! Now there's a delight for us all.'

The other women jumped to it.

'Have we any tea?' Marjorie shouted over her shoulder.

'It's very weak. About the seventh brew for the same leaves,' said a woman with pebble glasses and bandaged legs. Presumably the bandages were to absorb the pus from suppurating leg sores, a common complaint among the prisoners according to Peggy.

'We have to get back,' said Nadine. 'The man is waiting for his cart.'

Before leaving the kitchen, she turned round. 'We'll get whatever we can to help you out.'

'That's very good of you.' Marjorie turned her attention to the job in hand, handing out orders as though they were dinner plates.

'Cut all the fish up, *now*! No, no, we cannot save some for tomorrow,' she answered in response to questions about making it last. 'Cook up the lot! Skin, bones and flesh – even its eyes and tail; we have a great many mouths to feed. Edith! Show our guests and their cart to the gate. I want no incidents.'

The woman with the bad legs hobbled along with them, leaning on the cart for extra support. She responded quickly to those who favoured punishing women they viewed as collaborators.

'Lady Marjorie has vouched for them, dearie. They're here to help.'

Nadine wondered whether she'd heard right. 'Lady Marjorie?'

The blue eyes behind the pebble glasses twinkled with mischief. 'Yes. Lady Marjorie. She doesn't like being called that. All muck in together and all that, you know, just like at boarding school. She doesn't let on, but she does like people to know. It maintains something of her status, you see. Keeps her sane, I suppose. We all need something to help us do that, don't we dearie?'

Nadine left the women's internment camp feeling a degree of satisfaction. The fish would help alleviate their hunger. A regular supply of food would aid their survival.

As they pushed the handcart, she sensed Lucy looking at her, but kept her eyes straight ahead.

'You've put on weight,' said Lucy.

Nadine bit her bottom lip. She had been so determined to tell Peggy and Betty about her condition. If she didn't mention it now, she would bottle it up all over again. When the time came, she would need help, but they had to be warned. They had the right.

'I think I'm expecting a baby.' Nadine dropped her head. Suddenly she found herself blushing. 'You're the first person I've told.'

Lucy eyed her silently then said, 'Are you going to ask Betty and Peggy to help you get rid of it?'

'No.' Nadine shook her head emphatically. 'No. I can't do that. I want to keep it.'

Silence fell between them. When Nadine glanced in Lucy's direction, she blushed even more.

'It's Genda's child.'

A further moment of silence passed before Lucy responded.

'It doesn't matter whose child it is. It'll be sheer luck if the little mite survives for the first year.'

Nadine sucked in her breath and pushed her belly hard against the rim of the cart. Lucy was right.

'Then I have to get him out of here. I have to get him out of here even if it kills me.'

'It might very well do,' Lucy murmured. 'It might very well do.'

22

The man with whom Nadine had done a deal was true to his word and brought more ongoing provisions in exchange for the ring. Because of this, the women in the camp were not quite as hostile as they had been, though Nadine and Lucy usually accompanied him. Peggy and Betty were too busy giving medical attention where needed.

Today, he had not accompanied them but insisted on staying in the shade. Although he seemed to be alone, his mouth was opening and closing as though he were in conversation with somebody just out of sight.

Lucy was privy to the secret of her pregnancy.

'I haven't told a soul. When will you tell Peggy and Betty? You're going to need them.'

'Yes. I am.'

'So when will you tell them?'

Nadine shrugged. Her muscles ached. Her legs ached. Only the fact that she had access to a more voluminous sarong helped hide her condition.

She felt Lucy's searching look. 'Have you told the major?'

Nadine shook her head.

'I take it you will not tell Yamoto.'

'Certainly not. It can't be his. I heard Madam Cherry say that he is on his second wife and still has no children.'

'So you could be right,' said Lucy with wide-eyed surprise. 'A far better alternative even though he is Japanese.'

'He's American. That's where he was born.'

'Yes. I know. But there's no need to be defensive on his behalf. Most of us are agreed that he's the best man here.' She paused. 'If Yamoto ever finds out about you two...'

'I know. I'll be dead.'

The wheels of the cart screeched like an injured cat as they pushed it back to its owner. The Chinaman appeared to be talking animatedly to somebody standing in the shadows between two huts.

Nadine nudged Lucy and jerked her chin in the direction of the Chinese merchant. 'What do you think he's up to?'

Lucy shrugged.

'He might be talking to himself.'

'I don't think so. He looks too concerned to be talking to himself.'

Their attention strayed to Genda who was striding towards them wearing a serious expression. To their surprise, he helped with the cart.

'I need to speak to you,' he whispered.

The cart was far from heavy for a man of his physique, but heavy enough for two slender girls.

The fish trader noticed his presence, returned and thanked him swiftly and repeatedly. His short legs pumped like pistons as he shot off towards the main gate pushing his cart in front of him.

'What is it?' Nadine asked.

She glanced into the shade between the huts. Whoever had been there was gone.

'I came to tell you that it will not be long until you are transferred to the women's camp.'

Lucy's face lit up. 'In the women's camp? We're going to the women's camp?'

Genda nodded. 'Yes. Japanese women are arriving, women dedicated to serving the needs of our army.'

'We will starve,' said Nadine, folding her arms and eyeing him accusingly.

'I don't care,' said Lucy. 'Anything so I don't have to be a dog any longer! I'm going to tell the others. They won't believe me, but I don't care. I have to tell them.'

With that, she was gone.

Nadine felt ashamed for sorely underestimating the extent of Lucy's suffering.

She began to tremble. Now was the time. She had to tell Genda how things were. She had to stress an increased need to escape.

'Genda.' Her dark lashes whipped swiftly in a series of nervous blinks. 'I have to tell you something.'

So she told him.

His jaw dropped. He looked shocked but also awestruck, as though he couldn't quite believe her.

'Yamoto is on his second wife. He has no children.'

As the meaning sunk in, his eyes widened with wonder.

He looked away and shook his head.

'I need to think.'

She eyed him enquiringly. 'I can't help this. I'm merely stating things as I think they are.'

Genda took off his cap and rubbed his cropped hair even flatter. 'You have to get away. I will help you get away.'

Nadine hung her head. He understood that her confident exterior hid her fears, but they were there all the same. She was treading where angels feared to tread. Around here, there was only one way to buy safety.

She raised her eyes to meet his. 'You will help me escape?'

He nodded.

She saw his eyes follow her fingers. The ring had done its job. Since trading it she had secreted a single diamond earring between her breasts. She handed it to him.

'I think they're diamonds.'

'I don't need bribing,' he said, taking immediate offence.

She closed her hand over his. 'I know you don't. But the guards will need bribing. I've made many plans, but now it's up to you to make a plan. I don't think I can think straight any more.'

He nodded. 'And nothing can be arranged overnight. Escape has a high price. Anyone involved is likely to forfeit their life.'

Nadine swallowed the fear that sat like a stone in her throat. 'We both know what Yamoto is like. He's a cruel man and I am but a toy. I dance for him and he…'

'I have to do this – or die in the effort.'

Their eyes locked. They had made a pact. There was no going back.

***

When Lucy took the news that they were finally to be transferred to Peggy and the others, the hut erupted with noise.

'Are you sure?' Caroline, Betty and the rest of the women were agog with excitement. Only Rosalyn, who worryingly seemed to be enjoying the lifestyle, expressed reservations.

'We'll be terribly hungry. And we'll have no clothes, no soap, and certainly no makeup.'

'And nobody to dress up for,' said Peggy with a caustic sneer.

'It can't come soon enough.'

'And what about the money Madam Cherry owes us?'

'Don't count on getting anything. But it wouldn't hurt to ask.'

Peggy got to her feet. The high humidity and direct sunlight outside the shady hut brought her out into an immediate sweat. Feeling a little light-headed, she leaned on one of the uprights holding up the roof. After a few deep breaths, she felt better, though the pain in her stomach did not go away. Neither did the one in her head.

She marked Madam Cherry walking the camp and decided the time was ripe.

'Madam,' she called, running after her then dropping into a deferential bow once they were face to face.

'Madam,' she bowed again. 'I hear we are to go to the women's camp. Is this true?'

There was hesitance on the heart-shaped face and bad temper lurked around the little red mouth. Her response was sharp. 'You do go there. Very shortly. The colonel is a good man. He has arranged this.'

Peggy adopted as subservient a demeanour as she could. 'Yes, Madam, but perhaps it is thanks to you that the nurses visit the camp and do what we can for the women there. I thank you most sincerely for allowing this.' It was a downright lie. Nothing happened without the colonel's permission but Peggy knew when to suck up.

'I am glad to see you appreciate it,' said Madam Cherry.

Peggy pretended she did. In her mind, she wanted to slap the woman on both cheeks. Perhaps one day she would, and by God would she enjoy doing that! But for now, she took large bites of humble pie. 'I do. We all do.'

'So you should. You should be grateful.'

Peggy judged the humble pie had gone far enough. 'The

money you earned from us is rightfully ours. We should have been in that camp ages ago as prisoners of war. I understand it is our right under the terms of the Geneva Convention.' Her knees shook. It took guts to mention the Geneva Convention.

Madam looked at her, aghast. 'Japan does not recognise the Geneva Convention.'

* * *

Nadine called out to Peggy from around the back of Genda's private quarters where the chickens were pecking at rice grains and grass stalks. Genda was with her. 'Great news,' whispered Nadine. 'Genda tells me the Japanese Imperial army are being beaten back. It's only a matter of time...'

Peggy grimaced. 'Hope they get here before we're all dead. We might be over in the internment camp. Still. I'm glad to be going. They don't molest the prisoners there.'

Nadine felt herself heaving with relief. 'When?'

'Soon. She said she'll speak to old iron pants. It is he who will make the final decision as to the actual time and date.'

Nadine grinned at Peggy's disrespectful name for Yamoto. No one would dare call him anything like that to his face. 'I can't wait. She's made money from my dancing. But she wants Yamoto to herself.'

Peggy's blue eyes sparkled with disbelief. 'Christ, don't say the bitch is in love with that bastard.'

'And jealous with it.'

'Christ.'

Nadine exchanged a worried look with Genda. 'The sooner I get into that camp, the better. If he doesn't kill me, she certainly might.'

Genda handed out cigarettes, the three of them sitting in the shade beneath the hutch, the chickens clucking and scratching above them. It was the only place they were truly alone.

Peggy snapped a cigarette in half, passed one half over and stuck the other between Vaseline coated lips. Vaseline was their mainstay beauty treatment. Adding a little of a tangy herb used by the Malay girls helped keep the mosquitoes at bay.

Peggy inhaled deeply, exhaling the smoke with a sigh of relief. 'She's got you doing everything for these chickens.'

'I don't mind. I collect the eggs.'

She felt Peggy's eyes on her. She smiled. 'Once it's dark I pass the guard a few Kooas.' She pulled three cigarettes out from her bodice. 'He sneaks off for a smoke and whilst he's away I pass a few eggs beneath the fence.'

Peggy's eyebrows rose in surprise. 'Beneath?' How and when did you dig that?'

Nadine smiled. 'I didn't. The kids on the other side of the fence build little castles and forts in the dirt. The guards smile at them, but don't interfere.'

Peggy had a rich laugh, the sort that turned heads and influenced people. 'My, but you're a sharp one, Nadine Burton.'

'Steady,' said Nadine. She held a finger to her lips. 'We are in the dragon's lair.'

Peggy slid sidelong looks at Genda. In her heart of hearts, he still represented the enemy, and yet she could see there was a strong bond between the American/Japanese man and the Anglo/Indian girl. Every so often as they sat there enjoying their smoke, she eyed the young girl beside her with undisguised curiosity.

'You've got a wise head on your shoulders for a girl not yet twenty years of age.'

Nadine shook her head. 'I haven't been nineteen for a long

time.' She glanced at Genda. 'Sometimes I feel as I've lived a lifetime.'

'Peggy, I have to tell you something. I've got a little problem...'

'It's not little. I was waiting for you to tell me about it, but you've been taking your time. I was a midwife, you know.'

The smell of nicotine effectively masked the cloying reek of chicken dung and dusty feathers.

The major got to his feet. 'I have to go.' With great affection, he touched the top of Nadine's head, gently ruffling her hair as though she were a much-loved child.

Once he'd left, Peggy spoke again.

'Major Shamida seems a good sort; well, as far as you can regard any Japanese as a good sort. You know, the only good Jap is a dead Jap...'

'He got caught up in this like the rest of us. I think he's frightened.'

'Of Yamoto?'

She nodded. 'And he hates him. It's all to do with what happened in China.'

They'd all heard about China. They'd all heard about the outrages there.

'I'm frightened of him too,' Nadine added.

Peggy remained silent as they finished the cigarettes. 'If Yamoto finds out I'm pregnant, he'll kill me. I have to escape.'

'But you're pregnant! You need to be with us – me and Betty.'

Nadine shook her head. 'You know that I can't. I have to escape. So does the major.'

Peggy's blue eyes narrowed questioningly.

'Both of you?'

'Both of us.'

Peggy sighed. She felt sick but wasn't sure it was physical or apprehension that Nadine and Major Shamida were entering dangerous territory. Attempted escape was punishable by death. Even the major was not immune if it was found he'd aided her effort – worse still that he was escaping with her.

'How?'

Nadine lowered her voice despite the fact that only the chickens were likely to overhear her. 'There's a gate behind the guardhouse.'

'How do you know that?'

'Genda... Major Shamida showed it to me.'

'Why didn't you say before?'

'Someone might have done something stupid.'

'You bet they would.' Peggy sounded angry. She frowned. 'Why haven't you used it?'

'Sometimes it's guarded. It's behind the guardhouse so don't expect it to be easy. And if we don't get transferred into the internment camp, I intend to use it.'

Peggy slapped the dust from her behind as she too got to her feet.

A languid breeze swept the dust of the chicken run into dancing swirls before letting it resettle. Storm clouds brooded in the east, but still the sweat seeped into uniforms, sarongs and rags and down the spines of men and women alike.

* * *

Unseen by the two women, Madam Cherry watched with glowering expression. She could not hear what had been said and did not care. Jealousy burned greener than the jungle, hotter than the torturous glare of the midday sun. The one thing about conceding some of the women transferring to the internment camp was that Nadine might be one of them. Away from Yamoto. She hoped it would be so. She was jealous. She couldn't help it.

A centipede chose that moment to scuttle close to her foot. The creature was harmless but had chosen the wrong time to make his presence felt. Clenching her jaw she maimed it with the toe of her shoe, just enough to leave it writhing in soundless agony, just as she was.

23

Lights out was approaching and there wasn't much time. There was a tension in the sultry air falling on the camp from a moonless sky. The darkness was good. Not so good was the sheet lightening so desperately promising rain but failing to deliver.

Yamoto had left the camp for a meeting with a general somewhere. Madam Cherry had gone with him.

Lucy and Peggy sneaked in to see Nadine. Nadine found a little saki at the bottom of a clay bottle. The three of them took it in turns to sip before passing it on. There were also rice cakes smeared with honey. It was frugal but still something of a treat.

Lucy sighed. 'I hear the Japanese courtesans are coming at the end of the week. I can't wait to join the other women.'

'I agree,' said Peggy. 'Not that it's any great shakes. Beriberi is rife and there's not enough nutrients in watery rice and rancid vegetables, I'm afraid. The poor sods need protein. It's the kids I'm most worried about...'

Nadine looked up at the mention of children.

'They need eggs,' she exclaimed.

Peggy agreed with her. 'Yes. Any form of protein for that matter. There's the fish of course, but not enough and as for meat... well... I think they've forgotten what it tastes like though I'm told rat or snake flesh tastes a little like chicken.'

'Madam Cherry is out,' Nadine said suddenly.

'So?'

Nadine got to her feet. 'Then I'd better work fast.'

'You've got some eggs left from this morning?'

'A few, but a night time raid on the nesting boxes should add a few more.'

'What if you get caught?'

'I won't.' She didn't explain that a quiet soldier named Corporal Suzuki and trusted by Genda, eternally grateful for selling him bits of jewellery for his beloved, did the stealing on her behalf. 'I marry her after the war,' he'd explained to her in halting English. 'I go home to Nagasaki. We marry there in Catholic Church.'

'I bought some more food from the Chinaman. I've got some here but he's bringing more tomorrow.'

'How did you manage that?' asked Lucy. Everyone knew the man only came in once a week unless by special request.

'One of the guards likes shortbread.'

'Shortbread?' cried Lucy and Peggy in unison.

'I found a single tin of it amongst Madam's loot. Some poor mother had sent it out from England with her Malaya-bound son. The shortbread must have made it. Not sure about him, though.'

'You can't help everyone, Nadine,' said Lucy, frowning and wondering just how many people Nadine was bribing and how soon she might get found out.

'I know that, but helping just one mother and her children...' She stopped herself before putting her feelings into words, telling

Peggy about the pain her mother had suffered. 'A mother's heart bleeds for her children.'

'You've never been a mother.'

'No. But I had one.'

Lucy turned away. She'd so wanted children but now wondered if she ever would. None of them would ever be the same again.

Nadine noticed Lucy retreating into herself more and more. She'd hoped this evening might have lifted her spirits. Perhaps she'd be less insular once they were in the internment camp.

'How are you paying for these extra eggs?'

'With a ring.'

'Another ring?'

Nadine nodded. 'Yes.'

Peggy shook her head. 'Now come on, Nadine. You didn't have any rings on your fingers when you came here.'

'Of course not. I hid them.'

'I don't believe you. How are you doing this? Are you stealing valuables from the She Dragon? Because if you are, you could end up in bloody hot water.'

Nadine looked at Peggy and grinned. 'I could show you, but you must keep it secret.'

'Cross my heart.'

Nadine glanced at Lucy who had heard and looked interested. 'Let me show you.'

They slipped through the back door of the solid building that housed the storeroom and Nadine's own quarters.

'This,' said Nadine, placing her hand on the smooth surface of the highly polished credenza. She opened the drawer, slid it out and then reached in.

'This,' she said holding up the small casket, 'is my newly

acquired wealth.' She rolled the rings and other jewellery into the palm of her hand. 'Imagine how much fish and eggs we can buy with this.'

Peggy puffed out her cheeks and made a whooshing noise. 'Think how much quinine, salts and other medicines!'

Nadine dangled the sparkling gems before Lucy's eyes.

'They're pretty,' said Lucy.

'I don't care how pretty they are as long as they keep us alive. All of us,' she said, her hand moving protectively over her stomach. There was no sign of her condition as yet, but it was another thing to worry about.

Lucy noticed and made comment.

'I thought you would have had a termination.'

Peggy shook her head. 'They're determined to have this baby.'

Lucy's eyebrows arched quizzically. 'They?' She nodded as the penny dropped. 'Ah! The major.' Then she frowned. 'There are perilous times ahead.'

Nadine's eyes met hers. 'I don't... *we* don't want our baby born here.'

Lucy gazed at the credenza as though it was the high altar in a richly decorated cathedral though her thoughts were not of it, of what it contained, but of the possibility of both Nadine and her child perishing before the poor child had had a chance to live.

* * *

The hens had laid well. Two fresh eggs and Nadine had a Korean guard as lookout.

She added one dozen eggs to the half dozen remaining in the bucket. The others had already been distributed to Madam's business associates both inside and outside the camp. Under cover of darkness, she packed the remaining eggs into an empty tin, gathered up a few items from the storeroom and slid the whole lot into a half-filled rice sack. The rice would cushion their journey over the rough scrub to a spot where the wire fence of the internment camp was not so heavily guarded as elsewhere.

The wind was more vigorous and the first droplets of rain fell like pennies on the parched earth. Tree branches beyond the fence heaved like a huge black sea.

The women on the other side of the fence were taking advantage of the cooler air and the sprinkling of rain, milling around whilst their children slept inside their cramped huts. Their muted conversation was accompanied by the sound of rain falling into improvised containers. There was never enough water for both drinking and washing.

Gaunt and ragged, the inmates ambled about, staring at the sky or merely sobbing in a dark, secret corner.

She'd studied Doreen's habits from afar and knew where to find her.

There was six feet of wire and guards between them, and yet it might as well have been six miles.

Frequent flashes from a thunderous sky threw light upon their features. Hostility disfigured the old Doreen just as badly as the scabs on her face and the lice crawling through her hair.

A guard approached, apprehensively looking around him to check if anyone was watching.

Nadine passed him a packet of cigarettes; they were French and stolen from Madam's personal supply.

'Go!' He gestured with the muzzle of his rifle.

Nadine slid down the shallow bank and across the gully to the barbed wire fence.

'I've brought this for you.'

Doreen's tense figure turned round at the sound of her voice and sidled nervously closer.

For a moment Doreen stared, frowned and looked angry, not seeming to hear what Nadine was saying and offering her.

'Doreen! Take these. Quickly!' Nadine passed the sack of rice, eggs, sugar and tinned peaches into Doreen's snatching hands. 'And this.' At great risk, she added a box containing a Dundee fruitcake. Goodness knows how long it had been in the storeroom wedged at the bottom of an army kitbag, like many other things sent out from Britain by a loving mother to her soldier son. The rice remained in the bottom of the sack to cushion future smuggled items.

'It's so little,' said Doreen, staring disconsolately at the items Nadine had passed to her.

Nadine bit back the words she wanted to say, about the risk she was running. 'I wish I could get more, but it isn't easy. How are the children?'

Doreen's eyes flickered nervously. 'Wendy's bearing up. She always was the strongest. It's William I'm worried about. He doesn't like it here.'

'None of us do.'

Doreen's manner changed abruptly. 'Well you seem to be doing all right for yourself! Look at you! You're a fat little pig and that's for sure.'

Nadine knew it was far from being the truth. Their rations were adequate though not generous. And there were other things. She nervously touched the blue silk scarf adorning her neck. It hid the redness where Yamoto's buckle had bit in. The large shirt she was wearing covered her growing belly.

'I've been lucky.'

'You've certainly been that!' Doreen's voice heaved with malice.

'No respectable woman would ever consider sleeping with the enemy, not if they had any self respect that is!'

She turned away, leaving Nadine feeling devastated and dirty. She consoled herself that Doreen was worried about her children and that it was only natural she should lash out at someone.

'I'll bring more stuff tomorrow – same place, same time.'

Doreen did not acknowledge her. She didn't need to. Doreen would be there. She knew she would.

* * *

A week of frenzied activity finally resulted in the arrival of chattering, simpering Japanese women, courtesans who considered it patriotic to entertain and lie with the officer class.

The women who were to enter the prison camp were already packed and ready to go.

For whatever reason, the colonel had chosen to prolong their suspense and they found out his reasons

Forms for signature were handed out. Few of them read Japanese but those that did gladly interpreted.

'All we have to do is sign this form to say we offered our services of our own free will.'

'What if we don't sign?' Lucy queried.

Peggy made a slitting gesture across her throat.

Betty nodded. 'That's what I thought. Pass me the pencil.'

Peggy winced as though stretching that far was a great strain. As always Peggy determined to have the last laugh. 'Once you write your names on this list there's no more lying on your back and thinking of England – or Australia, Holland or America for that matter.'

There was more strained laughter, though deep down each woman would harbour memories that could never be forgotten.

Nadine became aware that Peggy was trying to catch her eye. 'Can I have a word?' she mouthed silently.

Nadine followed her out onto the front balcony of the long house. Two sentries chatted amiably on the landward side of the bamboo bridge. Below them, something slid into the water from beneath the house. The air vibrated with the sound of insects.

Peggy looked pensive. She took a cigarette from her cleavage and offered half to Nadine.

Nadine declined, fixing her attention on Peggy's face. She had lines at the side of her mouth, lines at the side of her nose, and lines across her forehead. When had those arrived? She was only twenty-four years old.

Some considered the Australian girls a bit brash and vulgar. Nadine found them refreshing.

'Not that it's going to be a picnic over there,' Lucy said, nodding towards where thin women were queuing for the evening meal. It would be followed by a wash – if the water wasn't rationed – drinking purposes only. Rumour had it that two hundred women and children shared just four latrines – basically buckets with lids and only to be used for solids. The place to pee was behind one solitary hut close to the trees, a channel dug, taking it away to the sea. The contents of the buckets were taken daily to be buried in a hollow amongst the trees. The stink was disgusting and, depending on the wind, unavoidable.

'We'll all get a lot thinner over there,' Nadine added. 'If it ever happens. Still, at least we'll be among friends.'

'We live in hope,' said Peggy. 'Though nobody seems to know for sure whether we're going over there or not. I hope we do.'

Peggy was less exuberant than she usually was, worn down by what they were going through and also her concern for the women and children. 'I've been over there more than you, Nadine. I've seen the condition of the kids. The adults are bad enough –

but the kids!' She shook her head. 'Without the little bit of medicine you pass through the wire there'd be a lot more dead. That jewellery you found is a lifeline. It buys us extra time as well as food. More will survive thanks to that.'

She folded her arms and blew the smoke into the humid, tropical air.

Nadine guessed what was coming and it frightened her. She chose to be calm. 'I know it's not much.'

'We need to keep those supplies coming.'

'Are you saying what I think you're saying?'

A shadow passed like a ripped sail over the moon. The coconut palms and the silver sea turned to black.

'We're going to miss you.'

Peggy's face also passed into darkness, her features barely discernible. The sound of the distant surf breaking on the reef seemed louder than usual.

Peggy's cigarette end glowed in the dark. 'We're going to lose a lot of the little blighters even with the few bits of medicine you can pass to us, but God Almighty, we'll lose a damn sight more if you're not around.'

The night was warm, but Nadine shivered. 'You're asking me to stay.'

Peggy hung her head over her folded arms.

Lucy broke the brittle silence. 'You can't stay. Your pregnancy is becoming too obvious. You have to get transferred to the other side of the wire with the rest of us. After that... well that's up to you.'

'This is a two-edged sword. It's useful for me to move in and out of both camps, but I have to think of my baby.'

Lucy nodded vigorously. 'You're right. Never mind about smuggling supplies, you have to come with us.'

Peggy shrugged. 'Those supplies are important. They're

keeping some of them over there alive. It's a lot to ask, but if you can continue to work for the She Dragon – as long as you can...'

'I can't do it,' Nadine blurted, hot tears running down her cheeks. 'I've got a baby to think about. I have to think of my baby.'

She sprang to her feet and walked away. The exultation she had shared at the prospect of joining the other women was gone. They'd made her feel guilty about smuggling supplies. Everyone was depending on her – including the baby she was carrying.

* * *

That night Genda played his flute whilst she danced for Yamoto. The latter had found Madam's secret stash of whisky so by the time the dance was over, the colonel was snoring loudly. Everyone else had transferred into the internment camp. Only Nadine remained. The burden of keeping medicines and food crossing the line was a heavy one. Perhaps there was still time she thought to carry on for another few weeks until she could no longer hide her condition. It came as a great relief that the colonel watched her dance but nothing else. His interest now lay with a Japanese courtesan.

Madam Cherry stopped her on the way out. 'You are getting very fat.'

'That is why the colonel is no longer so interested in me,' she retorted. 'The heat is getting to me. My feet are swollen in fact my whole body is swollen.'

It seemed a feasible excuse. Madam made no comment.

Genda followed Madam out.

Softly, without her feet making the slightest noise, Nadine slid over to Major Shamida and followed him to his quarters.

A single kerosene lamp lit the dark room. A host of moths fluttered around it.

He kissed her gently, almost reverently.

'You shouldn't be here. You should be on the other side of the wire fence. And I've arranged it.'

Nadine took a deep breath.

'Thank you, but I can't go – not yet. I'd be letting everyone down.'

'You have no choice. Not if you wish to live,' he said, shaking his head in exasperation

'Any number of children could die in there without the supplies I can give.'

She saw his eyes widen, the pupils like chips of coal.

'You must know that is madness.'

'I have to do what I can.'

He took hold of her arm, his fingers digging into her scant flesh which did not hang so loosely on her bones as some others with less access to food.

'Listen to yourself! It's as if there is nobody else but you who can smuggle food and medicines into the camp. Do you think yourself the only one who cares for the ill-used and starving?'

'So who will help them? You?'

Against all logic, in defiance of her natural will to live, she made her mind up.

'I have to stay. I have to do what I can. Just a little more time. That's all I need.'

She heard his deep sigh of exasperation. 'You are brave.'

'I don't think so.'

'You are also a fool.'

'Very possibly.'

His hand was soft upon her shoulder. 'I'm afraid for you.' In one way, being brave didn't come easy. In another way, it did. Doing what was right was making her brave, but underneath she was scared. This was one of those moments when she couldn't keep it down. It bubbled to the surface.

In a fit of despair, she allowed her head to fall, her forehead resting on his shoulder. 'You're right. I'm a fool. I shouldn't be doing any of this; but I can only live to survive and help others to survive.'

'You will,' he said, his voice breathing into her ear. 'You cannot stop yourself.'

24

Women and children lined up for roll call on the other side of the wire fence.

Nadine watched from beneath the shade of a coconut palm and wished she was with them, but Madam Cherry still required her services.

The women had taken little with them Madam Cherry had made sure they'd repaid the sums she'd paid to the boat major who'd brought them here.

Today Yamoto himself was overseeing the roll call – the *tenko* accompanied by Major Shamida.

Her old friends were standing together: Peggy, Betty, Lucy Lee, Rosalyn and Caroline. Rosa, the Burmese girl, was there too, yet she'd been told she did not need to transfer. Burma was conquered, though rumour had it the enemy were on the run.

Silver spurs acquired by Madam Cherry from the luggage of an imprisoned or dead American jangled at his heels as he paced the hard-packed earth. His sword was drawn, the glistening blade nestling on his right shoulder.

He walked slowly up and down the line, scrutinising each girl. Eventually, he turned abruptly and stopped. He looked puzzled.

'There are five women transferred today. I see six.'

He said it in Japanese. Shamida saluted and faced the women.

'Colonel Yamoto was told there were only five of you eligible to transfer to the camp today. He has counted six. Why is this?'

The women stood motionless, heads hanging and eyes studying the ground.

Nadine prayed no one would offer an explanation that could not be proved. Her breath caught in her throat as Peggy stepped forward and bowed.

'Colonel Yamoto *san*. If I could have permission to speak?'

Shamida opened his mouth with the intention of translating her request into English. Yamoto raised one hand to silence him.

'I know some English. I know what she says,' he barked.

There was a flash of light on steel as he swung the sword. A collective gasp ran through the women. The blade ended up only resting on Peggy's shoulder.

The rose and citrus yellow of Peggy's sarong fluttered around her trembling hips. A trickle of urine spattered the dirt between her feet.

Seconds seemed like minutes. Nadine tried to swallow but her mouth was too dry, her lips too cracked A lizard ran over her foot. The heat trembled, the midday humidity swelling with the promise of rain. She stood rooted to the spot, unable to tear her eyes away from the developing scene.

Yamoto's wide mouth spread into a grin, and then he laughed.

Peggy, who had been convinced her time was up, swelled with relief.

Nadine could almost smell the threat left hanging in the air. Bringing the sword down had been a great joke for Yamoto.

The guards laughed out of loyalty to their superior. Shamida nodded but remained expressionless when Yamoto turned and shared the joke with him. Once Yamoto's back was turned, his expression froze into a mask of concern.

Spurs jangling, the bad man in charge of these badlands, Yamoto went straight for Rosa. He asked her in Japanese why she was in the line up. Shamida interpreted.

Rosa's voice shivered. 'I want to stay with my friends.'

The colonel's voice boomed out like cannon fire. 'These women are not your friends. They are your enemies. Japanese are your friends now!'

Shamida murmured a warning in English. 'Do not give the colonel cause to be angry. It is best to go back to where you were.'

Nadine knew he was sticking his neck out and feared for him. Rosa appeared not to notice the increase in tension. 'I want to go with my friends,' she repeated with a childish resoluteness, her face contorted with fear and her body shaking.

Nadine saw consternation on Genda Shamida's face and guessed he was searching for some way of presenting her request in a favourable light. Not for the first time she wondered at the torment he must feel being part of two opposing cultures.

Yamoto's face turned puce. The sword scythed through the air as he barked orders at the two guards.

Rosa screamed and struggled as they hauled her out, forcing her onto her knees until her forehead hit the ground.

The other women covered their faces. Some sobbed. Peggy opened her mouth and stepped forward, but Shamida placed himself between her and Yamoto so that her action went unnoticed. He hissed at her to get back into line.

The guards moved away. Yamoto, both hands wrapped around the hilt of his sword, rested the blade on Rosa's neck.

The steel flashed. The women gasped. The sword swept down.

Rosa gurgled and gagged on blood until a second blow ended

her suffering. The women were shaking, wanting to hug each other but not daring to move.

Yamoto wiped his blade on the pretty sarong covering Rosa's backside, held it aloft and shouted exuberantly.

The guards and other officers echoed his cry of triumph – all except Major Genda Shamida, who looked as if he could kill him.

25

Cooled by a tropical downpour, Nadine danced in the fleeting coolness beneath the dripping eaves at the back of the hut. A jet-black cockerel fixed her with an orange eye. She pretended he was her audience, a rich man for whom she'd been paid to dance. For a blessed moment the jungle that dripped mist, rain and humidity was only a blur. In her mind she was dancing in a palace of green marble pillars topped with a sapphire roof. The rain running down her face mingled with her tears. She'd seen too much cruelty in this place. Seeing Rosa executed tore her to pieces.

Her dance was tottery and uncoordinated, her feet slipping and sliding in the oozing earth, the mud slopping around her ankles, splashing onto the hem of her sarong. Her sobs were louder than the sound of rain falling on the roof.

'I guessed I would find you here.'

She stopped in mid-movement.

'Genda.'

Although he smiled, there was sadness in his eyes.

'I've brought you a coconut.' He handed her the smooth

skinned fruit with as much pleasure as a man might give his wife a bunch of flowers. 'I've already made a hole.'

Eyes flashing with tears and anger, she lifted it aloft meaning to throw it as far as she could.

'No.' His hand caught her wrist. 'It isn't just for you. The child within craves sustenance.'

She dropped her arms and hung her head. One sip followed another. The milk was sweet.

He fingered the salty vestige of a tear. 'You saw what happened.'

She nodded. She drank again, wiping her mouth with the back of her hand. 'I thought I was used to seeing death close by. I was wrong. Has Rosa been buried?'

His face clouded. 'I understand so. But I did not see it. Yamoto didn't want any witnesses. Certainly not me. He doesn't trust me.'

Nadine felt sick to her stomach. Genda hung his head, too sickened and too aware that his disgust showed in his eyes. 'A good sword should only be touched by blood and silk and must be used regularly. That is his creed. That is samurai.'

'Aren't you samurai too?'

He avoided looking into her eyes. 'By descent, not inclination.'

'It's so difficult to be born between two cultures.'

He nodded. 'You would know that.'

'Yes.'

She looked up at him imploringly. 'So where do we belong? Where will we end up?'

Hugging her close to his side, he kissed her forehead. 'You have to get out of here, Nadine,' he whispered.

'Soon, but not yet. I need more time.'

Sometimes, she tried to remember at what point in her life she'd learned to adapt so swiftly to change. Perhaps back in India.

'I need your help.' She fingered his chest, her hair shining like a yard of silk around her shoulders.

He smiled. 'You sure know how to get under a man's skin. Now, what's this favour?'

'I want to visit my friends in the camp tonight.'

'That's no problem.'

'I want to stay there until morning.'

'Why?'

'There's an old friend there from Singapore. I'm worried about her.'

She had tried to make contact with Doreen, but for the most part, her old friend tossed her head and looked away, a definite sign of disapproval.

She would also smuggle in some supplies, but counselled that Genda didn't need to know that.

'I will see what I can do.'

'I heard that another Burmese girl tried to escape.'

Genda's nod was grim and barely perceptible.

'She approached a Malayan fisherman. He handed her over to a Japanese patrol.'

Genda bowed his head. 'I am ashamed.'

Genda's voice was low and intense when he spoke again.

'Helping you means I will be a traitor to my country. But I have to do it. I must take you out of here.' He paused, collecting his thoughts. 'We're both between worlds, you and me, a mix of east and west. We're stuck somewhere in the middle.'

His words and the resultant emotion tightening his jaw were almost painful to witness.

Nadine traced the tension with her fingers. 'You're a good man, Genda Shamida.'

She said it with absolute sincerity then kissed his cheek.

'You wish to visit your friends tonight?'

She nodded.

There was a powerful intensity to the way they looked into each other's eyes. Nadine wondered how things would have been if they'd met in a different situation, a different country, a different time. *Different* was the optimum word.

'I will do what I can,' he said after their lips had parted. His arms remained wrapped around her, his chin resting on her head.

* * *

If she hadn't given in to the lure of one more shot of whisky and looked out into the night, Madam Cherry would not have seen them embracing beneath a glistening moon. She smiled to herself. This was what she'd been waiting for. Watch the girl a little more closely, know where and when the two of them were meeting and have Yamoto there to witness it for himself. She could find somebody else to list her stock, somebody who didn't inflame her jealousy.

It was simple and predictable. She congratulated herself and to celebrate, poured another shot of whisky, followed by another and another.

* * *

Major Genda Shamida was true to his word. Peggy was waiting on the other side of the barbed wire. Nadine slipped her the supplies she'd smuggled in with her. Deep lines of concern creased her forehead as Nadine approached. 'Where's Lucy?'

Peggy frowned. 'Funny you should ask. She got permission to visit you. Haven't you seen her?'

Nadine shook her head. 'Perhaps she changed her mind or has been sent out on a work party.'

Either reason was feasible. Some of the women had been requisitioned to help out in the rice fields of the nearby village. The produce was destined for the camp – the guards rather than the inmates.

Mrs Yates stopped her on her way back to the gate. Considering she was partially crippled, she was faring pretty well for herself. Loss of weight had made her more mobile, though lack of calcium was causing the bones in her bad leg to bend most alarmingly. She'd also lost a number of teeth.

'Can I have a word?' she asked. The top of her head barely reached Nadine's shoulder. 'It's about your friend. You know she's going round the bend, don't you?'

For some reason Nadine took offence at the comment and presumed she meant Lucy. 'What do you expect? This place is enough to send anyone mad.'

If the woman noticed her sharpness, she gave no sign of being injured by it.

'She reckons her husband visits her in the middle of the night.'

Mrs Yates meant Doreen, not Lucy.

'You mean she's imagining things.'

'Yes. I mean we all do it to some extent. Pretending you're somewhere else or seeing people you were fond of all helps, doesn't it? At least I think so,' she said, pausing only long enough to pull at the tail of tapeworm hanging from her nose.

Nadine swallowed her revulsion.

'It's like this,' said Mrs Yates, wiping her fingers down an already filthy dress, 'Her youngster's likely to be hauled off to the men's camp before very long. He's tall for his age, almost as tall as some of the Japanese. The fact is, the poor woman's likely to lose her mind completely if that happens. I wonder... do you think you might have a word with your colonel? Do you think something could be done? I fear for the poor woman otherwise. She'll do herself in. I know she will.'

Nadine cringed. The knowledge that she was the camp commandant's favourite had spread around the camp. As a result of this, fewer insults were thrown at her. The advantage of such a relationship was becoming clear. All the same, it still came as something of a surprise to be asked outright to use her influence.

'I'm afraid I don't have the influence you seem to think I have. Not any more.'

'Shame. Perhaps you'd like a word? She's over there,' said Mrs Yates. She had eyes that protruded too far from their sockets. Nadine avoided looking into them, half fearing they might fall out onto her cheeks. She was hardly the most forlorn-looking woman on the camp, but at the outset had started from a more unfortunate position.

Doreen was lying down, her son hugged close to her body. It was obvious that William wanted to be off playing. He was squirming against her. The more he squirmed, the tighter she held him.

'She cuddles him,' said Mrs Yates. 'She cuddles him all the time.'

The more she thought about what Mrs Yates had asked, the more despairing she became. What could she do? Like the brightly coloured moths, she was already flying too close to the flame. So far she'd been lucky, but her luck might not hold out.

26

Madam Cherry came bursting into her quarters the next morning.

'Outside.' She dragged her out of her bed so forcefully that the mosquito net came too, wrapping around her until she resembled a parcel.

'Outside. Outside now.'

The generous bosom of the woman termed the She Dragon by the prisoners heaved with what Nadine could only interpret as excited anticipation. Her eyes glittered and one side of her mouth tilted upwards in a parody of a smile.

Fear knotted her stomach, but still she dared ask. 'What is the matter, Madam?'

'Dress!'

Obediently, she slipped a dark-red robe over her head and slid her bare feet into a pair of silk slippers.

Madam Cherry shoved her out of the door.

The burning rays of a merciless sun speared the ground, but the dusty, bloodied and bowed figure of Lucy Lee Van der Meer stung her more.

'Your friend tried to escape,' Madam Cherry hissed into her ear. 'She will be punished. She will be very much punished.'

The burning sun threatened her eyes yet it felt as though a door to an ice world had opened behind her. 'You will now be called upon to witness her punishment. You need only observe her miserable person before she is executed. This I tell you to observe very well should you tempt the same fate yourself.'

Nadine's mouth was dry, her eyes unblinking.

Lucy's knees made a furrow in the dusty ground as she was dragged off between two guards, Yamoto following on behind.

Lucy was screaming. 'Please. Spare me. Spare me!' Alarmed birds fled screeching from the trees.

Nadine fell to her knees, pleading in her voice and her eyes. Madam Cherry kicked her away.

The colonel stood rigidly, his eyes as hard and brown as the stones at his feet. His spurs glinted in the sun. His two Samurai swords, one short, one long, flashed each time the gleaming hilts were caught by sunlight.

Yamoto took the longest sword from its scabbard. He held it this way and that, examining its condition and polishing small smudges, whether imagined or otherwise.

Madam Cherry's voice slithered like a tape worm into her ear. At the same time, her talon-like fingernails dug into her arm, holding Nadine in place, ensuring she had to watch.

'Be thankful. It will be swift.'

The women in the camp were called to witness what was about to happen. Nadine could see them through the wire, standing in silent rows beneath a scorching sun. Another woman was about to die. Nothing out of the ordinary in that; many had already died, most from starvation and disease, but this was different. This was execution.

Unfortunately, as with other escapees, Lucy had sought

assistance in the wrong quarter and been handed back to her captors.

'You should not watch.'

She heard Genda's voice in her head, smelled his presence but knew he was out hunting rebels. It was just as well. This was not a day to be nice to Japanese. Today was hate day.

Glamorous as a Hollywood film star in pale, cream skirt and a checked jacket, Madam Cherry let go of her arm and bowed to the colonel.

An order was given. Lucy was crying and sobbing, her bladder and bowels opening simultaneously.

Nadine felt sick to her stomach. She wanted to scream, she wanted to lash out. Her mind refused to believe that Lucy would die. It wasn't fair. They'd been through so much together.

One fact suddenly sprang into her head. Somebody had betrayed Lucy. Nobody could really be trusted.

The little Chinese trader sprang to mind. He had been talking to someone hiding in the shadows on the day she and Lucy had wheeled the fish and other supplies into the camp. It could only be Madam! Her stomach churned with further fear, though this time for herself and her unborn child. Had he also told her about the valuables she regularly traded with him for food?

She turned her face into the cool breeze blowing off the sea. A sickness stirred inside her and made her dizzy. The breeze helped a little but did not entirely quell her nervousness.

Lucy was bent double between the guards, her forehead almost touching the ground. The Samurai sword made a rushing sound like a strong wind as it whistled through the air.

Nadine closed her eyes. When she opened them again, it was all over. The camp was hushed, the only sound that of buzzing flies.

The colonel's spurs jangled as he mounted the steps to his

quarters. Madam's heels hit like hammers, echoing in the space beneath the boarded floor until it seemed as though the whole building was shaking, the dust disturbed, the shutters rattling in their frames.

She'd been betrayed. She was sure of it. And Genda was away. Her beloved Major was away.

Yamoto shouted orders. Two guards responded, flattening Nadine against the wall, turning in the direction of her room and the storeroom beyond.

Behind her was the sound of destruction, of furniture being turned over, glass smashed. She knew it was the Dutch credenza. Even so, she hid her fear.

She was dragged inside Madame's quarters.

'Those are valuable antiques. I trust they will not scratch them,' she said glibly.

In actuality, her heart was in her mouth. Bits of wood splintered and cracked like bullets as they tore the framework apart. The mirror cracked into several pieces.

With a triumphant shout, a private found the first of the secret compartments. He held the box aloft, the money and jewellery spilling out and dripping from his fingers.

Nadine stood as though made from marble.

Madam Cherry bowed solicitously at the colonel before turning and slapping Nadine on both sides of her face. 'That is for stealing!'

Nadine tasted blood from a cut lip.

Madam Cherry threw her a look of pure malevolence before turning to the colonel. She spoke in Japanese. Nadine heard a reference to Major Genda Shamida.

A cold chill clenched at her stomach. Jealousy and greed burned in the blackness of Madam's eyes.

Her arms were grabbed and wrenched behind her back. The

two guards dragged her out into the yard and at Yamoto's command, turned towards the graveyard.

She felt her bowels loosen at the prospect of ending up headless with all the other corpses, the ones Yamoto had taken such delight in showing her.

Just before the alley between huts leading to the graveyard, they swerved towards the main gate of the women's camp.

Eyes that had once viewed her with envy and contempt now showed fear and pity as they sensed what was to come.

She was marched to the furthest corner of the compound where the tin lid of the punishment bin was being lifted

The punishment bin was positioned in a place without shade, embedded in hot sand.

A whisper went round.

'How long will she be in there?'

Women swiped tears from their eyes and children were told to look down at their feet.

'Three days,' somebody said. 'That's the usual.'

'She'll roast like a Christmas turkey,' muttered somebody else.

'Silence!'

The lid was closed and Nadine found herself in total darkness, the heat rising as the day progressed.

Her eyes closed as she retreated into her mind, controlling her breathing, her vital signs of life, hypnotising herself that she wasn't really here at all, that she was back in India and she was waiting for the coolness of evening when she would dance with Shanti, her *ayah*, her nurse, her mother.

27

Just days after being released from the punishment bin, Nadine found herself in the women's camp on the other side of the wire. Her baby was born small and premature, her fingers as fine as the veins running through the leaf of a tree, her skin wrinkled and red.

Despite her ordeal, Nadine still had enough fight left in her to ask after the health of her child.

'She's very sick,' they said to Nadine.

Neither mentioned the likely reasons, but both knew that diet, disease and brutality had all played a part. Nadine had barely survived her spell in the box. It was all Peggy could do to keep her taking some nourishment. She hadn't expected either Nadine or the baby to live, but they had.

Genda brought milk and what little else he could. Lady Marjorie tore a pretty sarong in two to use as swaddling for the tiny baby.

'The little soul needs it more than I do,' she said, wrapping the baby in the flimsy fabric.

Genda managed to purchase a goat so the little girl would have milk.

Nadine traced her daughter's dark eyebrows with her finger. 'I wish I could give her more, but unfortunately...'

The diet of rice and little else was taking its toll and Nadine had little milk in her breasts. Not that the baby seemed to be taking much.

Peggy also looked to be doing worse. Nadine was alarmed. Peggy had always been the biggest, bounciest of characters. She was now a shadow of her former self and even when she spoke, the prospect of death was frequently touched upon.

'I think my blood's turned to orange,' she said forlornly. 'That's due to lack of iron. Lack of everything in this place: And look! See the size of my arms?'

She managed to encircle her upper arm with one hand.

Nadine looked at her, trying to remember what she had looked like when they'd first met.

'It's not just malnutrition,' she said in response to Nadine's worried expression. 'Something inside is giving up – and I don't mean my soul. More like my spleen, my liver and my kidneys. It's been coming on for a while.'

'Don't say that Peggy. You'll get over it. You have to get over it. We all depend on you.'

'I'll do my best, Nadine. One thing I will promise is that I'll be around for the little one's christening. Thought of a name yet?'

'Yes.'

One week later, Sister Agatha, an Irish nun and the nearest thing they had to a priest or a minister of any sort, baptised the child as Shanti Lucy Burton.

Shortly after the ceremony, Peggy's condition worsened and she was confined to bed.

In the six weeks since she was born, Shanti Lucy Burton never once opened her eyes, never cried and only stirred long enough to be fed. Nadine was worried, not just for the child but also for Peggy. In her dreams, she saw Lucy, the pretty young woman whose life was now over. She determined that Shanti would not die. Shanti would live.

With the child tucked beneath her arm, she picked up a palm leaf and began to fan Peggy's face.

Peggy was still sleeping but feeling the draught and sensing that someone was there, she opened her eyes.

'Sod it! I'm going to die.' She sounded quite churlish about it.

Nadine attempted a wan smile. 'You're Peggy. You'll win through. You always do.'

A spasm of pain crossed Peggy's face.

Blood trickled from the corner of her mouth. Automatically Nadine mopped it up with a piece of daisy-patterned rag; proper bandages were a thing of the past. Anything would do.

Peggy regained control of her breathing. 'You've got that wrong, girl. *You're* the brave one. Oh, yes, I've got plenty to say for myself – that comes of being a girl growing up with a host of brothers. Keeping army and navy patients in order came easy after that, but this situation here with these Nips calls for cunning, Nadine. Cleverness that I just ain't got. I'm just mouthy; open my big gob before using my brain.'

Nadine shook her head and cuddled her child closer. 'Clever, am I? That isn't what some of the others call me.' She forced herself to sound bemused. But she wasn't bemused. She was sad.

Peggy's bruised lips strained into a smile. 'I know the truth. So do a lot of others. And you know the truth. You know how valuable those supplies are. Some of these women and children wouldn't be alive now if it wasn't for you.'

Nadine dipped the cloth into a bowl of water and began

dabbing at the open sores on Peggy's throat. 'Madam Cherry also knows their value,' she said grimly. 'She gets top price for them.'

Peggy's look was full of compassion. 'I know. Tell the major to be careful, Nadine. We didn't name her the She Dragon for nothing.'

Nadine was pleasantly surprised by Peggy's sudden concern for Genda Shamida. Like most of the other women, she found it hard to trust or like someone whose looks were so obviously Japanese.

'How's the baby?' Peggy asked. Too weak even to turn her head, her eyes slid sidelong.

'Fine,' Nadine said. 'She smiled at me today and kicked her legs.'

Peggy believed her, smiled and closed her eyes. Again, she slept.

Cupping her child's head in her hand, Nadine looked into the tiny face. Shanti was too quiet. Other babies in the camp cried lustily for food, for attention or just for the sheer hell of it.

Just then Shanti took her totally by surprise and began to cry for the very first time.

'Listen,' she cried loud enough for the whole hut to hear. 'She's crying.'

Marjorie was sipping a cup of weak tea a bed or two away. Their eyes met.

'Did you hear her?'

Marjorie smiled. 'Yes I did, my dear. So glad for you. So very glad.'

From then on, Shanti cried a lot: Weak and hungry, somehow her mother still managed to sleep, irritation outweighed by exhaustion.

Shamida had built up quite a nest egg of trusted guards. For now the goods flowed freely. He couldn't help thinking they'd been lucky. 'But our luck could always change,' he said to Nadine.

With gritty determination, she forced the likelihood to the back of her mind. 'Then we'll keep going until it does.'

* * *

Their luck ran out on a sunlit morning. A troupe of gibbons had gathered in the trees, their screeches and squabbles drowning out Sister Agnes's combination of Sunday prayers and a burial service for the latest batch of fatalities.

Women and children of every denomination attended, and even those who could count their church attendance on one hand stood with head bowed. Everyone in the camp needed to believe in something.

The sun was warm upon their backs as Nadine stood rocking her baby backwards and forwards.

Nadine watched as Betty shuffled down the hut towards Peggy's bed. When they'd first met, Betty had been wearing white pumps, a crisp nurse's uniform and silk stockings. Now her legs were blistered with insect bites and tropical sores. She also had a fungal infection of the foot. Caring for Peggy seemed to help Betty cope.

Another woman had sustained a cut to the bottom of her foot but offered to look after the baby whilst Nadine attended to the smuggling.

Nadine sighed. Following the birth of the baby, she wasn't as strong as she had been. She needed somebody to go with her. An American girl named Dianne offered.

Dianne wore trousers and a patched shirt.

'Thanks for stepping in at such short notice,' Nadine said to her.

'No bother, lady. Pleased to be of service.'

Dianne was from California and sauntered around in scraps of material that used to be men's clothes as though she were really at home in them.

'The truth is that trousers make me feel safe,' she said to Nadine. 'I wouldn't want to be raped by a Nip, nor get dragged off to one of their brothels. No siree!'

It was enough that the girl was willing. 'Just help me get the stuff through.'

Dianne's face lit up like a moonbeam. 'This is real exciting.'

'You make it sound like a great adventure.'

'Isn't it?'

Nadine grimaced. 'It's downright bloody dangerous.'

Dianne's bravado reminded her of Peggy and amused her, but her humour did not last for long. The moon was too bright for receiving contraband but they had to risk it.

They moved against the shadow of the barbed wire fence, matte black silhouettes against strings of wire and posts. A hunched figure made itself known on the other side. He gave a signal. The two women waited until they were sure that the look-outs in the wooden towers had swung away from them.

They had roughly ten minutes before they swung back.

* * *

The jungle night throbbed with the sound of insects, monkeys and the leathery wings of the flying fox.

Moonlight battered the treetops but failed to pierce the matte blackness among the trunks of teak, banyan and ground-hugging bushes.

Genda sniffed the air as he moved cautiously and slowly along the jungle path. He smelled men, rotting leaves, dung and stagnant water. After a while, he also smelled the sea. They were getting close to their destination.

His orders were to apprehend insurrectionists believed to be operating from a fishing village nestled between the jungle and the sea.

The sound of breaking surf told him they were nearly there.

Genda's concentration shifted between the job in hand and Nadine and the baby. Conditions in the camp were appalling. Would the child survive? Would Nadine?

He had done his bit, purchasing medicines from traders, smuggled in his flute case. Tonight he was out on patrol and in his absence had bribed Kikushu, a Korean guard, to hand over the medicines and food. Those Japanese he trusted most were with him on this mission. One of his own men had vouched for the Korean.

A whispered report came back from the men he'd sent up front to check the village.

'All is quiet. They sleep.'

The outlines of palm-roofed huts came into view against a dark-blue sea. A number of small fishing boats heaved gently on the swell, their prows tied to the stilts supporting the huts.

The silence was total, unbroken even by the barking of dogs or the cackling of chickens.

Genda frowned.

'A trap, major,' his sergeant whispered.

'Perhaps,' said Genda and his frown deepened. He was alert to all possibilities.

'So,' he said thoughtfully. 'If you have prepared an ambush, how do you keep the animals quiet?'

Even in the subdued light, he could see the consternation on his sergeant's face. An ambush would only be an ambush if it surprised those who were ambushed. But a village without the usual sounds was not normal.

He led them forwards.

Not even the smell of cooking fires disturbed the night. There were no dogs, no chickens and no plump children squatting on the sandy earth.

'They're not here,' he said, his feet sinking into the soft, white sand. 'They're gone. Someone warned them.'

His judgement turned out to be right. The huts were searched, but everything – including cooking utensils, animals and even their fishing nets – had disappeared.

It was surmised that the rebels were getting inside information, possibly from the traders who regularly visited the camp and the local girls who fraternised with some of the younger Japanese soldiers.

With a sinking heart, Genda surveyed the empty huts. He was certain they'd been betrayed and had no doubt Yamoto would root out whoever had betrayed their mission. And whoever it was would suffer, but so would the innocent, hostages taken from other villages beheaded as a warning to those who dared deny Japanese superiority.

Unconsciously, he allowed his gaze to wander along the path of moonlight to the far horizon. Diamonds of brightness danced on the water. His attention returned to the waiting boats, noting their position – *just in case*, he told himself. *Just in case.*

Time was running out. As long as his grandfather was favoured by the military high command, he was safe from the colonel who still sought advancement. But things could change. Opinions and strategic thinking were like the pieces on a chess board, always shifting. Favourites could become expendable overnight. If his grandfather did fall from favour then his life might then be forfeit.

28

Every fibre, every bone, and every nerve ending in Nadine's body screamed for release. Her arms were tied behind her but closer to the post than her legs so that her back was arched as tautly as a bow, her hips thrust forward. A bamboo stake had been wedged against the upright pole to which she was bound, the tip of its sharpened point stabbing at the small of her back. If she dared fall asleep, or even relax, the spike would sever her spine and exit through her stomach.

Her weariness was such that falling asleep would have been terribly easy, but Shanti was crying. Out of the corner of her eye she had seen Kia, the baby nestling in the crook of her arm. Kia's face had been tight with terror. Betty and Rosalyn were with her, their trembling hands hovering like hummingbirds about their faces.

They'd begged the guards to have mercy; she'd heard them. Butts of rifles and the threat of sharp bayonets had herded them back inside the huts. The start of curfew was long past and the moon was hiding its light behind ragged clouds.

The Korean guard they'd met had quibbled about handing

over the goods and argued for more money. Nadine had been aware that to give in would create a precedent for other occasions and refused.

'Then thee and thy own will go without,' he had said testily, pulling the goods back from her waiting hands.

Nadine had made a mental note to tell Genda that this man could not be trusted. But thoughts of those lying sick and dying were not far from her mind. She told Dianne to go to Betty.

'Betty will give you some money...'

Dianne had not gone three steps before the shout went up, lights were lit and they'd found themselves surrounded.

Flashlights brightened the darkness.

Dianne screamed.

Nadine cried out. 'It's nothing to do with her. I take full responsibility.'

Yamoto's breath fell on her face. 'Yes. This is indeed your responsibility.'

With one swift, dramatic movement he swung his sword above his head.

For one horrific moment Dianne's body stood headless. Then she crumpled.

Now it was Nadine's turn. She held her breath. As the tip of the sword tickled her throat, her daughter's crumpled face flashed into her mind. She closed her eyes. Any minute I'll be dead, she thought. Any minute.

But the colonel had other plans. He was angry with her, but also angry with Major Shamida, a man who by accident of birth alone he'd never trusted. But he'd heard rumours from far off Tokyo. The major's grandfather was advising the Mikado to sue for peace. Unfortunately for him, the hawks of the Japanese Imperial Army were in the ascendant and advised the opposite. His days were numbered. It was just a matter of time.

* * *

How long will I take to die?

Nadine's eyes flickered. What a stupid question.

Pain and fatigue fought for supremacy in her emaciated body. Neither won. They were too well matched.

By dawn her limbs were trembling, her blood pooling in her muscles. As the sun began its merciless climb into the sky, she sucked at dry lips. It had been over twelve hours since she'd had a drop of water or some food. Food she could do without; it was water was what she craved. Cool water. She imagined it on her tongue and, hearing the sound of the sea, imagined its coolness washing over her.

She heard scuffling, shouting and cries of anguish. Someone had tried to bring her water but had been chased away.

And all the time Shanti's crying gave her the strength to go on, to stay awake, but in staying awake she remembered what had happened to Dianne, the girl who had wanted adventure. The vision was painful. She was in danger of breaking so forced herself to concentrate on pleasant things and sweet moments. Shamida reciting his poem sprang into her mind.

How do I love thee... A few beautiful words printed on a ragged scrap of paper.

Genda! Where was Genda?

* * *

Madam Cherry couldn't stop laughing, rolling around on the tumbled bedding, her dragon-patterned dressing gown falling open to reveal her nakedness. 'You fool! You stupid fool!'

The colonel with whom she had shared a short but equitable relationship was a blur of shapes within a whisky fuelled haze. He had a long face and a very square chin, like a jar, she'd always thought.

'Like a jar,' she chuckled, her sense of self-preservation addled by half a bottle of whisky.

Yamoto's angry eyes were jet beads above his ginger jar chin and made her chuckle even more. He hated being reminded that the dancing girl had been dallying with the American-born major.

'She was your toy but Major Shamida was her bullock. It was his pistle that brought forth the golden egg! Not that the fruit is very healthy. It squalls all the time so I'm told.'

Yamoto fetched her a heavy back hander that sent her sprawling. Too late she sobered up enough to realise what she had said and what she had done. Yamoto's face was turning as red as the dress she wore. Virility was important to all men, but more so to Yamoto. Mocking it was dangerous. Telling him how frequently the major had met the dancing girl had intensified the insult and fuelled his anger, but Madam Cherry was drunk, her mind befogged by whisky.

The colonel's eyes narrowed to wafer thin slits as he took off his belt.

Realising her mistake, Madam reverted to the ways that had made the colonel her own, crouching submissively, simpering in a trembling voice. 'Whatever Yamoto *san* wants, I want too. He knows that, does he not? He knows I am his servant and that his prosperity and joy are mine also.'

She endured him ripping off her clothes, the digging of the buckle into her throat.

Her bleary vision worsened as the buckle pressed against her windpipe. Opening and shutting her mouth like a fish out of water, she fought for air.

With each thrust of his loins, Yamoto shouted curses on Nadine, the Anglo-Indian dancer, calling her a 'third-rate whore', calling Shamida a treacherous son of a *ronin*, a rogue samurai of no account.

He did not notice Madam Cherry's distress. He did not care that she was clawing at the belt, her fingernails breaking as she tried to get her breath.

He hardly noticed that the body into which he spilled his seed was now lifeless.

* * *

It was late when the patrol got back following a thorough search of the jungle and paddies surrounding the fishing village. Genda mused about the situation. Nothing had been found. It was obvious that someone had tipped them off, someone from inside the camp. The vision of the village stayed with him: the silence, the lack of either Japanese or rebels or ordinary villagers. Above all else he recalled the position of the fishing boats.

Shadows flitted through the undergrowth as they made their way back along the jungle track. Rebels swearing death to the emperor and all his cohorts leapt onto their gunfire. Superior weapons and tenacious fighting beat them off. By the time they got back to the camp they were tired and footsore. All were looking forward to a decent meal and some sleep. Some would not eat until they had bathed in the warm waves lapping the nearby beach.

On arrival, a young lieutenant that Genda had befriended stood with two guards.

The lieutenant saluted. 'Major. I need to speak to you.'

He looked nervous. The two guards with him looked uncertain. He barked an order as he waved them away. 'I will send for you when I need you.'

Genda frowned. As the senior officer present it should have been his order. He immediately sensed that something was wrong.

The lieutenant confirmed this and explained what had happened.

'I am speaking as a friend,' he began.

As the tale unfolded, the tiredness that was always present at the end of a patrol left Genda's body.

'Bastard! I'll kill him with my bare hands.'

Although spoken in English, the expletive was understood.

The lieutenant continued. 'He's posted guards at the gates. If you attempt to pass into the women's camp you will give them reason to shoot you. Those on guard there are those he trusts the most.'

'But I can see her?'

The lieutenant answered. 'Oh yes. Those are his orders and her punishment for dealing in contraband. He took great delight in stating that you may see her through the wire, you may even talk to her if you shout loud enough, but you may not go to her. It is your punishment to see her suffering from a distance.'

Every fibre of Genda's being was stretched to breaking point. The moment he had meditated on had finally come. He trembled inside as his lieutenant and his loyal sergeant followed him to the gate. Guards stood with bayonets fixed on the other side. He knew by their faces where their loyalty lay.

Beyond them he saw her figure, strained over the spike of sharpened bamboo and thought he could hear a baby crying. He stopped himself from shouting out. It took much effort for her to keep taut and not be speared. If he had to beg the colonel to let her live he would do so. If he had to die in order to have her released, he would do that too.

Too long he'd been unsure of where his loyalties lay: with the land of his fathers or the land of his birth? Now he knew. Patriotism was not enough, and what was his patriotism anyway? Japan or America? Perhaps neither. His was a loyalty to humanity.

He headed off towards the colonel's quarters.

'He's with the She Dragon,' the lieutenant called after him.

If this hadn't been such a serious occasion he would have smiled at the remark picked up from the women inmates. But these two were far from being figures of fun; one of them at least was less than a military man and far more of a murderer.

In answer to his knock, Yamoto bid him enter. Genda stiffened himself for what he had to say. Punishment, even death would be preferable to letting Nadine die. Without her mother the baby would die too.

Subservience was in his mind when he pushed open that door but was swiftly replaced by horror.

Yamoto was kneeling on the back of a naked Madam Cherry. He saw the belt around her neck, her tongue protruding between bruised lips. Her eyes were staring and vacant.

There was a look of triumph on the colonel's face. 'So. You have returned to meet your fate. You sullied my property. You will pay for that. You will pay for it in great measures.'

Genda's hand slipped onto his sword.

Yamoto laughed. 'American! Put that sword away. You sully its tradition; you dishonour Bushido and your ancestors. I spit on you. American and cowardly you were born and American and cowardly you will remain!'

Making a sound like the wind piercing a narrow gap, Major Genda Shamida's steel blade split the air.

Blood poured from the colonel's throat, spurting in time with the pumping of his heart. His expression of triumph turning to surprise.

Slowly he fell forward, his body covering that of his most loyal admirer. One leg kicked out and hit over the lamp, scattering its consort of moths.

The flames licked at the rush matting and, in the search for more fuel, began to climb the walls and lick at the roof.

Genda threw back his head and closed his eyes. 'Shamida, what have you done?'

There was no time to waste. He pulled woven mats from the floors, hemp hangings from the walls and heaped them onto the flames. The fire would destroy the cause of death, but there was bound to be suspicion. The finger would point at him, but at least it would give him time.

Tongues of flame licked hungrily at the makeshift funeral pyre.

Genda headed for the door, accompanied by the moths that had fluttered around a single flame but now fled the conflagration.

Outside he grabbed a rifle from the nearest guard and shouted for his men, for his sergeant and the young lieutenant.

'The colonel is dead and so is the madam. The rebels have killed the colonel,' he shouted. 'All men over here. Search the perimeter fence.'

He ignored the unspoken questions: how did they get through? Why did we not hear gunfire? What were you doing there, Major Shamida?

Later for the questions; later, when it would be too late.

One warlord had replaced another. Such was the tradition that allegiance was swiftly transferred from the dead colonel to the living major.

'Did you not hear me, you fool? Leave the woman. Find the rebels.'

He used his sword to point in the direction he wished them to go.

The men who had been ordered not to let the major through into the women's camp now flooded towards the perimeter fence and the main gate, their focus now on apprehending the non-existent perpetrators.

'Go with them,' he said to the sergeant and the lieutenant.

They obeyed. Later they might question why he had gone in the opposite direction, but for now he was their superior officer. They knew their place and assumed he knew his.

Shamida ticked off a mental list. Food, water and a boat. But first, Nadine and the baby.

29

Inside the hut, the night sounds had consisted of a cough, a child's cry or a series of barely suppressed sobs disturbed the night air. Outside, the leathery wings of flying foxes whisked through the darkness. A gibbon shrieked, jarring nerves, fooling senses.

Betty was awake and bathing Peggy's swollen face. Every so often her gaze drifted in the direction of the post and Nadine's forlorn figure. Her head had fallen onto her shoulder. Her arms strained against the single rope that held her there.

'Is she still alive?' Peggy whispered through cracked lips.

Betty nodded. 'Barely.'

Peggy tried to raise herself on her elbows. 'We have to do something. And that poor baby. She hasn't stopped crying.'

'You're hearing things. The baby's been asleep for hours.'

Peggy looked up at her accusingly. 'What did you give it?'

'Never mind. Rest.' She lay both hands on Peggy's shoulders, pressing her back onto the thin reed filled mattress which was barely two inches thick and all that lay beneath her tortured body and hard wooden slats.

Betty bit her lip. If there'd been enough liquid in her body she might have cried, but like most of the women, she was all cried out. Despair and dehydration had wrung them dry.

The big, bold Peggy she loved was only half the woman she had been. Starvation and sickness had seen to that.

She stroked the damp hair back from Peggy's forehead and lovingly bathed the sores at the sides of her mouth. Was now the time to tell her how much she loved her? Other women lay together, hugging purely for comfort. Others sought a more physical pleasure, losing themselves in one shivering moment of nervous release.

Betty envied them. Heaven knows, even a hug was small substitute for a beloved husband or sweetheart who might never be seen again. People lived as they could – in their minds or in the real world. It didn't matter. They all needed to lose themselves in mutual solace.

Suddenly the whole hut was disturbed by men shouting and the sound of crackling wood and palm leaves.

Peggy tried again to raise herself from her bed. 'What's all that shouting?'

'There's a fire. I think it's the She Dragon's place.'

Peggy grinned and chuckled. 'That's bonza! Probably caught it alight with her breath!'

Everyone rushed outside to cheer the flames. A bigger cheer went up when someone said the colonel and Madam Cherry were still inside.

'They're both burned to a crisp,' Marjorie conveyed to Betty before collapsing onto her bed mat. 'Oh joy! I'm sure I will sleep tonight. More than my usual four hours anyway.'

Betty's gaze wandered in the other direction from the burning house. Marjorie saw her. 'Get some sleep, Betty. You must be tired out. I'll keep an eye on Nadine.'

Dawn brought a heavy downpour. A cool breeze drove the

wetness through the bamboo curtains and whipped palm leaves from the roof.

Betty was up before roll call to tend to the emptying of the night slops for those too weak to see to it themselves. Afterwards she would wash the receptacles out with earth and as much water as could be spared, though the pouring rain would help. Birds and monkeys were already screaming at the dawn. She paused and listened, sensing she was missing something. She shrugged. Whatever it was, it couldn't be very important.

Ducking beneath the dislodged palm fronds hanging from the eaves, she straightened and looked immediately to the post, expecting to see Nadine closer to death than to life.

The mix of blood, excreta and urine slopped from the pail as it slid from her hand. Was she dreaming? She blinked. No. She was seeing what was really there. The mound at the base of the post had become an island amongst muddy puddles and newly hatched flies and mosquitoes. The ropes that had bound Nadine trailed like water snakes, partly on land and partly in water.

Nadine was gone.

Abandoning her task, Betty ran back into the hut.

'Nadine's gone!' She called excitedly. 'Nadine's gone.'

Women wondering what all the fuss was about stirred all around her.

'She's gone,' she shouted again as she raced down the ward heading for Peggy.

Now she knew what the sound was she'd been missing. She ran to Kia who was curled up in a foetal position, her head resting on her hands. Betty nudged her.

Kia groaned and her eyes flickered open.

'Where's the baby?' Betty asked her.

Kia sighed and snuggled more comfortably onto her hands. 'Gone.'

'Nadine took her?'

The girl nodded vaguely and kept her eyes closed. 'Now I can get some sleep,' she muttered. 'If you leave me alone.'

Betty was desperate to ask her more but Kia refused to make further comment.

Betty ran off, her excitement lending new vigour to her scabbed, tired legs.

Kia opened one eye and watched her go. It would be easy to go back to sleep. Shanti's constant crying had kept her awake all the previous night. Nadine had warned her not to tell anyone anything, and she didn't intend to. Not until she'd had a decent sleep.

Betty went to tell Peggy. 'Nadine's gone,' she said, wanting to kiss her dearest friend, and hoping, just hoping that it would be all right.

So great was her delight and her love that chancing a rebuttal she kissed Peggy's forehead and her cheeks, pausing just inches from her lips.

Should she or shouldn't she?

The question melted away as she realised that there was neither sweet nor rancid breath. Nothing. Nothing at all.

'Oh, Peggy! You silly cow! You silly, lovely cow! Why did you have to go and die now? Why now?'

She kissed her mouth shut and cried her only tears since leaving Singapore.

* * *

Shanti's crying rose, fell and rose again. The jungle drooped in the windless night and the smell of the truck they travelled in was rank with gasoline and men's sweat.

The burning hut in which the colonel and Madam Cherry lay

had been a godsend. Sparks flying up into the night sky had inevitably fallen again and, despite the recent rain, had set fire to the palms of other roofs turned crisp by the burning sun. Panic led to confusion, and confusion led to more panic; perfect as far as he was concerned. He'd headed for Nadine but hid until the fire had died down and the women had returned to their troubled sleep.

Most of the women had been cheering the flames enveloping the two most hated people in the camp so didn't see the major untie Nadine, toss her over his back and tuck the baby beneath his arm. He'd whispered amen to their comments.

'Hope they all get fried,' said one of the few who had witnessed their departure.

'Amen to that,' added Sister Agnes in her soft brogue and made the sign of the cross whilst raising her saintly eyes to heaven. 'Forgive me, Mother of God, but it seems befitting that the likes of them should fry on earth before frying in hell.'

The young girl who had been looking after Shanti was bleary eyed through lack of sleep.

Genda had amassed the things he thought they would need for their journey, most of it such as maps, a compass plus a bottle of whisky, taken from the colonel's office.

The Lieutenant who had told him of Nadine's punishment accompanied them half way to the fishing village.

'Food,' he said. 'I've had water and more food taken to the village and you should be able to find more.'

Genda thanked him. 'Goodbye my friend. How can I ever repay you?'

The lieutenant bowed. 'It is karma, Shamida *san*. My grandfather was vassal to your grandfather. My loyalty too is with the Shamida clan.'

He bowed to both of them before leaving.

With Nadine now leaning on his arm, Genda brought his small family to the village.

Rain hammered on the roof of one of the abandoned fisherman's huts. Her own milk long dried up, Nadine drip-fed Shanti coconut milk through a ragged square of mosquito net.

Genda eyed the threatening dawn rising behind the mountains behind them. 'No way can we wait for this rain to stop. We have to leave now.'

He chose what he thought was the strongest boat. Nadine climbed in, followed by the supplies; a few coconuts, a little cooked rice and some tins of biscuits and bully beef he'd stolen from Madam's storeroom a few days before.

'Some stuff the camp won't be getting,' he explained in answer to her questioning expression.

He also added the truncated remains of an oil drum. The rain hammered down and the drum began to fill with water. They found the supplies left by the lieutenant and the guards loyal to Shamida.

'We'll need all the water we can get,' he said as he pushed off from the shore and clambered aboard once the vessel struck deeper water.

A flock of roosting birds took off from the blue-black treetops skirting the beach.

Soundlessly they peered through the darkness. The beach was a strip of white behind them. From out of the blackness that fringed the beach, a figure emerged, waving long, spidery arms.

Nadine answered his unasked question. 'I don't know.'

The figure became recognisable once the shadows were left behind. Lady Marjorie's lanky frame whipped towards the sea.

Genda began rowing more vigorously.

'Genda! We can't just leave her.'

Even in the half-light, she could see his face was grimly set.

'We haven't got enough food for three. We've barely got enough for two.'

Shanti mewed in Nadine's arms. Soon she'd be crying and once she started, she wouldn't stop.

Nadine stared at the beach. 'She must have escaped somehow. They'll kill her if they catch her.'

Genda surrendered a huge sigh. 'Nadine, we can't take her.'

Nadine struggled to her feet. 'Then I'll go back with her. I'll swim if I've got to.'

'You're jeopardising everything! Think of the baby!'

'Genda, I couldn't live with myself if we leave her there.'

To Genda's ears, the tone of her voice was as powerful as the words. He leaned on the oars and rested his head on his hands. 'OK. OK. Now will you please sit down?'

He used the oars to turn the craft round. 'I only hope the old bird can row,' he grumbled.

Seeing them turn, Marjorie waded into the water. It was waist high by the time she reached the boat.

'Help me.'

Genda stopped rowing and pulled her aboard. She was awkward and took all his strength. Her limbs and arms seemed too long for her body though that too lacked flesh. Eventually, it was as if her body had folded like an awkward deckchair.

'I got out last night in the midst of that hullabaloo,' she said, though they hadn't asked her. 'Don't know how long they'll take before they know I've scarpered. Can't say I care. Nice to get one over on the Nips. Damn the lot of them.'

Genda got in first. 'No offence taken.'

'I was going to say with the exception of American nips. They don't count.'

'Thanks a lot,' said Genda.

His grimace spoke volumes about his attitude. He had not

wanted any other passengers. The boat was small, supplies a lot smaller.

Dawn broke incredibly crisp and sweet, the clouds scudding before a fine North Easterly wind. Genda prayed it would stay with them all the way to Australia.

'We'll stop for water on one of the smaller islands,' he explained, his eyes narrowed against the light reflected off the sea. 'They're scattered like stepping-stones between here and the coast of New Guinea. Each of us rows a little every day.' He closed one eye as he looked up at the clouds. 'Pity we don't have a bigger sail.'

The fishermen of the village had cast their nets in the shallows no more than two miles off the coast and had not needed a bigger sail.

The responsibility weighed heavily on him. Though he did his best to appear confident, the tension was not always easily hidden. 'We must be mad,' he muttered. He'd intended the exclamation to be purely for himself, but Nadine heard him.

'We're free,' she said simply, and turned her face to the breeze.

Lady Marjorie turned out to be a much quieter person when she wasn't in charge of anything. She caught Nadine looking at her questioningly.

Nadine explained herself. 'You seem different than back in the camp.'

Her ladyship smiled. 'Someone had to be in charge and it fell to me. Just because we're not in England doesn't mean to say that the formalities are not still present. It was expected that I should take charge, so that's what I had to do.'

Silently they gazed into the distance. 'I wonder what they're doing now,' said Nadine.

Lady Marjorie sighed. 'Dying, I suppose. Mrs Davies isn't expected to live much longer. Dysentery. Her bowels have collapsed. Dengue, Beriberi and goodness knows what else, and that's besides starvation. And of course, Peggy's gone. What a collection!'

Nadine blinked back her tears. Peggy had been a pillar of strength. Her death was not unexpected, but the world seemed a sadder place already.

'Must be a few thousand miles to safety,' said Marjorie. She was shaking the baby up and down to stop her crying. The baby cried a lot now, her naked little body strangely still, her mouth wide open.

They took it in turns to row. At the end of a period of three days their hands were blistered and sore. Genda managed to hoist the small sail. In the meantime they bandaged their callused hands. The sail would take them forward of the wind when it was blowing behind them. If it wasn't behind them, then they would have to depend on the oars and the rudder to give them direction.

Genda was resting. He'd rowed far longer than either of the two women and the strain was beginning to tell. Energy levels evaporated quickly in the torturous sun. Faces reddened and were crisp with a layer of salt even though none of them had been in contact with the sea.

The level of water in the oil drum tasted greasier. Genda pronounced that soon they must go ashore and search for fresh. The little food they'd managed to bring was also diminishing.

Genda tried fishing using a bird feather as a lure on the end of a string extracted from a net. He was unsuccessful.

He shook his head mournfully. 'If I'd been born a fisherman, I'd have starved to death.'

They all laughed far more than the comment and Genda's pathos warranted, a little light amusement in a sea of sameness.

'I'll give it another go. I'll use the net, but it's heavy. I'll need help.'

Nadine aided him in casting it, dragging it behind them in a wallowing pocket that tended to slow their speed. They caught one fish.

'Hmmm,' grimaced Genda, and they laughed again, though with more despair this time, as if it might be the last.

Perhaps it was the laughter, or perhaps the shade thrown by the boat and the net, but suddenly they were surrounded by flying fish. A sudden gust threw the sail across away from the side of the boat, then just as quickly back again. A host of flying fish came with it, flopping into their laps.

Lady Marjorie clasped her hands together, threw her head back and closed her eyes. 'Thank you Percy,' she shouted.

Nadine and Genda looked at each other. Genda mouthed, 'Who's Percy?'

Nadine shrugged.

'My husband,' said her ladyship. 'He's up there keeping an eye on us.'

'I'm sorry,' said Nadine. 'I didn't know he was dead.'

'Neither do I... well... not for sure. But I think he is.'

Nadine recognised the resigned pragmatism of the camp where death and disease had been ordinary and despair a luxury.

'There's plenty,' said Genda excitedly. He prepared some of it raw for immediate use. The rest he lay out in the sun to dry. 'We need moisture, but it has to last.'

Once every drop of moisture was gone and the fish was dry, he wrapped it in a strip of cloth torn from his shirt and laid it in the bottom of the boat.

* * *

Like the sea and the sky, the days melted into each other

Nadine never tired of looking at the nothingness, the unadulterated spaciousness of the blue-green ocean. The misted outlines of islands clung like clouds to the horizon. She imagined the ocean without sight of land. It would happen once they'd reached the end of the chain of islands. Between New Guinea and Northern Australia were miles and miles of emptiness. Nothing but ocean. There was no guarantee they'd reach safety. They were depending on the wind and also on the currents. So far they were both in their favour, but might not remain so. They might never make it.

Her empty stomach churned at the thought of failure and the hugeness of their journey. Despite their precarious situation, she was filled with the joy of being alive. On those sweet occasions when Lady Marjorie and the baby slept, her eyes met Genda's. Something would spark between them, not a smile exactly, not even love. Satisfaction. Whatever they did they did it freely. No one was insisting they choose sides.

At those times when Lady Marjorie slept, they talked about the night they'd spoke of poetry and other things.

'How is the Honourable Miss Nadine Burton today?'

'She's well. And how is Joseph Smith Junior the Third?'

Salt spray covered her face. The wind filled the sail. Genda used the compass to check their course three times a day, firstly at daybreak, then noon, then sunset.

The skies at dawn and dusk were glorious great sweeps of gold, salmon pink and purple. The days were hot. The nights rarely cool. Midday was the worst, no shade, little breeze and a merciless sun.

A day came that was different. Marbled clouds of purple and grey were building like mountains. The air was humid.

Nadine rubbed at her prickling skin.

'A storm,' said Genda, his eyes red with fatigue.

Just as he said it, the sky exploded with sheet lightening. The air rumbled with thunder.

Nadine instantly took the lid off the oil drum, licking her lips at the prospect of fresh water, unadulterated by essence of gasoline. It would be good to get rid of what was left. Even now she swallowed, the thought of the greasy taste lingering on her tongue. The first raindrops caught on her eyelashes, heavy as coins on her head.

She turned her face skywards. The droplets stirred the sleeping Lady Marjorie. Even the baby pursed her lips and sucked it in.

Genda had fallen asleep at the oars, and although the raindrops pelted his bare shoulders, he did not stir.

The smell of gasoline drifted up from what remained of the water. She looked at Genda, opened her mouth to ask his opinion. The rain turned heavier, the clouds darker.

Nadine took the initiative. What was left of the stinking water sullied the rising sea with a slick of blue, red and peacock green.

She tipped the drum upright again and let the rain thud in.

Genda slowly raised his head, tendrils of black hair sticking to his face as he blinked away his sleepiness.

'It's raining,' Nadine shouted excitedly. She tilted her head backwards and opened her mouth, swallowing each droplet that landed on her tongue.

Suddenly, as is the way of tropical storms, the heavy downpour subsided.

Genda got to his feet and peered into the drum. Delight turned to disappointment. 'It's almost empty.'

'It tasted...'

She didn't finish what she was going to say, about the taste, the stink of the water.

He guessed what she'd done. The veins in his neck stood out like twigs. All the strain of the last few days exploded.

'You stupid woman!'

Marjorie startled awake. The baby began to yell.

'I thought it would go on raining,' she shouted back.

'Well it hasn't!' Genda shook the drum. 'There's barely a cupful in there!'

'I didn't know it would stop, and what was left there tasted so awful.'

Now he shook her. 'Do you realise what this means? Do you? Do you?'

Marjorie interrupted. 'Stop being so silly. What's done is done. I think you should take a look at this child. I believe it's not very well.'

Marjorie's tone was as it had been back in the camp, commanding but sensible.

Whilst Nadine felt Shanti's hot little body, Genda stood in the bow of the boat, staring at the misted islands. So far they had avoided landing to replenish their stocks. They were too close to Sumatra and the places they knew had been conquered. 'Better to push on,' Genda said. 'That water has to last us as long as possible, so go easy on it.'

They had gone easy, drinking right down to the stagnant, oily base.

He looked up to where the clouds had earlier formed a thunderhead. It had vanished as quickly as it had formed. The air had cleared and the first burning rays were torching the ocean.

'We have no choice now. We have to go ashore. We need water.'

He frowned as he eyed the nearest island. Even if the Japanese were not in residence, the islanders might not be loyal to the allied cause.

He looked at Nadine. She did not return his look but gazed into the distance, the sleeping baby making funny little snuffling sounds against her breast.

Marjorie's pale eyes regarded him calmly. 'What's done is

done. We always think it's for the best at the time. Fresh water not tasting of engines would have made a nice change. It was God that turned off the tap – the faucet as you Americans say – not Nadine.'

Somehow he wanted to still feel angry, but he couldn't. Suddenly he could see the funny side.

'I have heard people praying for God to release them from prison, pain and dying. I have never heard Him being referred to as though he was a plumber.' He did say it, but he was also touched that Lady Marjorie had referred to him as an American.

'It shines through,' she said in her matter-of-fact way. 'You decided what was right and did it regardless of family or tradition.'

Worries about how he would explain himself if they got picked up by the Allies had crept into Genda's mind the moment he'd untied Nadine from that stake. They'd diminished now and so had his anger at Nadine tipping the remaining water into the sea. The island and fresh water lay ahead.

30

The black pumice of a long-forgotten eruption formed a crescent of breakwater between the thundering waves and the deep turquoise of a calm lagoon.

Native huts built on stilts and above the reach of snakes and sea huddled like parcels at one corner.

Men working along the water line looked up from mending nets and repairing fishing canoes. The canoes had high prows and wide bellies. Waves rippled gently around them before spilling onto the beach.

'Leave the talking to me,' Genda whispered. 'I know a little Malay – enough to get by anyway.'

He stood tensely in the bows of the boat readying his words, his eyes fixed on the shore. He'd taken the precaution of wearing labourers' clothes in the hope that he would be taken as a native, not Japanese.

Nadine rowed, visions of fresh water and food giving her the strength to go on.

A flurry of action and excitement broke out among those

hammering new bits of timber onto boats. Once they'd taken in what they were seeing, they ran shouting into the sea, some brandishing the hammers they'd been working with.

Strong hands calloused by hard work clung to the bow, fingers graduating along the side.

The boat began to rock wildly from side to side. The baby began to cry.

'Listen,' Genda shouted in Malay. He was drowned in angry shouts.

The boat steadied then rocked again, though only slightly. The baby cradled in her arms, Lady Marjorie stood up. Her shadow seemed almost as long as the mast.

'*Salamut*!' Her commanding voice carried above them all. Once all faces were turned to her, she spoke to them in fluent Malay. 'I pray thee be kind to us. We are weary *memsahibs* without our *tuans* who have been killed by the Japanese. This man, although he is of enemy blood has helped us escape. I beg thee be merciful to him and leave him to our care. He has been of much use to us and will be of more use still.'

An older man, his wrinkled face betraying his great years, walked into the surf. He addressed Lady Marjorie.

'We do not want his kind here. One will be followed by others.'

Marjorie handed the baby to a surprised looking Genda and stepped off the boat. The water reached her waist and although she struggled for breath, she succeeded in reaching the village headman. She bowed respectfully.

'Honoured *tuan*, we are but two women caught up in a conflict we had no part in. We desperately need water and a little food. Coconuts would be nice. Rice wrapped in palm leaves would last us quite a while.'

He eyed her cagily. 'Can you pay for this?'

She bowed respectfully, even more deeply than before. 'The Japanese took all we had. They are thieves and scoundrels as thee, *tuan*, must know well. We have nothing left but our determination. All we can do is begging that you treat us mercifully.'

The headman's eyes narrowed as he looked beyond her to where Genda was holding the baby.

'We do not want this man here.'

'We can leave him on the boat with the baby,' Lady Marjorie offered.

She overdid the usual formalities and bowed again. 'If you will allow two humble women to come ashore.'

The headman nodded thoughtfully, turned and regained the sand. The other men waded after him before they all huddled in a group on the shore.

Nadine was amazed. 'You know Malayan?'

Marjorie looked over her shoulder at them both and winked. 'Lucky my husband was military attaché in Singapore for ten years. He worked hard. You don't get knighted for no reason you know. I had to find something to do with my time.'

Lucky indeed. The headman gave permission for all of them to come ashore, even Genda. The women were allowed to wander the village, gather coconuts and pick fruit. They also washed and changed, the village women generously donating clean sarongs. They washed their old clothes with a particular leaf that produced a soapy lather, the dark-eyed women proudly giving of their knowledge. The washhouse was the women's place. The men stayed at a distance.

Genda had less freedom; wherever he went, two men followed a few paces behind. He ignored their presence, preferring to concentrate on scrubbing the oil drum prior to it being filled with fresh water. Fresh fruit, vegetables and packs of cooked rice and dried fish were stored at the stern of their tiny craft.

They stayed there for one day and one night.

'This is heaven,' said Lady Marjorie, relishing the luxury of lying full stretch on the warm sand. 'My limbs are just too long for that little craft.'

What she said was quite true. With the exception of the baby, none of them had ever been able to lay full stretch.

Shanti still cried a lot and Nadine was getting worried.

Nadine jiggled her up and down in her arms, washed the hot little body with fresh water and fed her coconut milk. Nothing seemed to placate her for long.

Holding Shanti against her shoulder, she walked along the beach to where the black pumice pointed like a huge finger into the sea.

The sun was a blood orange staining the water with its dying rays. Tomorrow they would have to leave. The headman had insisted. But she didn't want to go. Crossing the sea was a daunting task. They'd all talked about how they might break the journey up; hopping from one island to another once they were sure it was safe. The unspoken truth was that none of the islands were likely to be safe. If the Japanese weren't in residence, the islanders themselves, wary of strangers, might chase them away.

The sun was still hot on her face and arms but a cool breeze blew and the surf pounded the shore.

'Paradise.'

Somehow she'd known he was following her so was not startled by the sound of Genda's voice.

He stood next to her watching the sun go down.

'And what is the Honourable Nadine Burton thinking?'

She sighed. 'I wish we didn't have to leave.'

'I know.'

'I wish there wasn't any war out there.'

'But there is.'

They fell to silence.

Nadine thought of Genda's reaction to Lady Marjorie referring to him as American.

'Will you ever go back to Japan?'

'I don't think I can. In the eyes of my relatives I have dishonoured my family.'

'Wouldn't they want to make it up?'

'No. They would want me to commit *seppuku.*'

She was frowning when she turned round. 'What is that?'

'Ritual suicide. Like the Romans, they would prefer me to fall on my sword. Though some might say I've already done that. I have chosen sides, though I'm not too sure either would fully accept me.'

'You rescued me. That might have some bearing on their attitude.'

He smiled at her. They were the same height, same dark hair. The eyes were different in shape, the colours similar.

'I'll remember this time and this place,' she said, turning back to the view.

'I too appreciate beauty.'

She smiled. 'You're looking at me and to be quite honest, I look a mess.'

He smiled, sighed and leaned back beside her.

They walked a little further, finally sitting down with their backs against the rocks, their feet dangling in the sea. The rising spray fell over them. Even Shanti's breath seemed taken away. The child slept.

'She feels cooler,' she said hopefully. 'Perhaps she'll get better out here. The camp was no good for her.'

'The camp was a bad place – most of the time.' Suddenly he began to laugh.

She eyed him with a quizzical smile on her lips and waited for him to explain.

'I was thinking,' he said. 'I was remembering that time when you pretended to faint and was given water and a seat in the shade.'

She raised her eyebrows in mock indignation. 'How did you know I was pretending?'

He grinned. 'I used to do the same when I was a boy. My brother was a bully and bigger and stronger than me. He loved swimming and would challenge me to race to a certain rock about a mile off the beach. He would always get there first, because he cheated, starting before me. Then one day I pretended to drown. A terrible thing to do. I shouted and waved my arms, then slid beneath the surface. By the time he got back to where I'd been panicking, I was already swimming underwater towards the rock.'

'And you won?'

'Of course.'

'What happened to your bullying brother?'

A more melancholy look replaced his cheerfulness. 'I understand he was killed at Midway.'

Nadine dipped her feet more deeply into the sea. She didn't want him to be sad.

'Joseph Smith Junior the Third, would you like to lie down with me?'

That night they slept beneath the stars. Shanti's crying awoke them just as dawn was chasing shadows. Marjorie was warming some chicken and rice the women had given her.

'Bliss,' murmured Nadine, but it didn't last.

* * *

Four days later, they were over one hundred miles further east and the weather had changed.

The surface of the sea undulated with a heavy swell. The waves did not break but heaved into hills, rolling them gently down its slopes into deep gullies before rising to the summit again.

Even though there was little food in any of their stomachs, they all experienced sickness.

'I think we're near land,' said Genda swallowing his nausea and bracing his legs. 'I can smell it.'

The tiny boat balanced on top another surge of water.

Before the boat fell headlong into yet another gully, he glimpsed a small hump of an island. The women saw it too.

'Land. Precious land,' said Marjorie.

Nadine's spirits rose and the soreness of her aching stomach tightened in hope. 'Can we make it?'

Genda eyed the onshore current with worried eyes. 'I'm no sailor, but I feel we should stay out at sea.'

Nadine gripped the sides of the boat. 'No! Land. Please can we set foot on land? I can't stand this boat any longer. I feel sick. I want land!'

Genda didn't answer. He wanted land too, but the current was strong and if there were rocks... The responsibility lay heavy.

They surged skywards on six-foot waves and more swiftly fell into their valleys. Up and down, again and again.

Nadine retched what remained in her stomach over the side of the boat.

The clouds hung low. The wind began to gust.

Genda blinked the salt spray from his eyes, wishing he knew more about the sea, the weather and what he should do. But he didn't.

The frightened eyes of the two women veered between him

and the sea. He wanted what they wanted, but should he chance it?

A storm, a *tai-fun* threatened. A typhoon. The boat was small and the sea was as dangerous as rocks.

The decision was taken out of his hands. No matter how fiercely he rowed, the wind and current were taking them towards the land. Surf began spilling from the tops of the waves. The wind driven spray soaked faces already encrusted with salt.

The current was swift and strong and carried them into the lee of a headland. The little boat swerved and tossed, spinning like a top then slowing as they gained respite and slid into calmer waters.

'Thank God,' called Marjorie.

Nadine hugged Shanti tightly against her breast. The child was crying again.

Genda tumbled from the boat and dragged it further up the beach. Once it was entirely on dry land, he fell flat on his face, totally exhausted.

They found a small niche in the rocks. Water dripped from a craggy overhang. First they drank, and then shivered, totally worn out.

Genda turned his face skywards, the back of his head resting on the rock, his eyes closed.

Marjorie's head fell sideways. She too slept.

Shanti cried. Bleary eyed and aching to rest, Nadine dipped a strip of cloth into one of the coconuts salvaged from the boat. The tiny pink lips fluttered as a droplet of coconut milk fell on her tongue.

Nadine persisted. Shanti had always been a slow eater, almost as though she knew there wasn't much to be had. She tried to reassure herself that Shanti didn't take much milk anyway, but a heavy ache pressed on her chest.

'I should never have brought you here,' she murmured.

In her heart of hearts she knew she didn't mean this place, this island in the middle of nowhere. She meant into this world, into this war.

Feeding her was a long and arduous task. Eventually her tired arm fell into her lap. Shanti mewed in the crook of her arm, her eyes moving restlessly behind paper-thin eyelids.

31

Lady Marjorie Selwyn-Kendall opened her eyes and gave silent thanks. The storm had abated. Branches broken by the wind surrounded them. Less angry now, the surf hissed against the sand.

In the bleary light of a silvery dawn, she looked across at her companions. They were still asleep.

They're young, she mused. Young people have more energy when they're awake, but they sleep more than old ladies like me.

Smiling ruefully, she reminded herself that even in her youth she'd only slept six hours on average. Now she was older – certainly since she'd turned sixty – she slept even less.

If you're awake, you get up. No point lying in bed. Back in Singapore it had been her habit to rise with the sun and find something useful to do. That's what she did now.

Shanti's clenched fists punched at the air and her mew of dissatisfaction was edging towards a fully-fledged cry.

Marjorie rubbed at her bony hips as she got to her feet and unfurled her aching spine. Her joints were always the same in the morning but got better once the warmth of the sun was on them.

She smiled down at the mewing child. Nadine was holding her slackly. If the baby had wriggled as much as some she would have slid from her grasp. But Shanti never moved much. Something was seriously wrong with the child. She'd never mentioned it to Nadine sensing that she already knew the little scrap of humanity wasn't destined to stay long in this world.

Reaching down, she took the baby from Nadine's arms, careful not to wake her. 'Come to Auntie Marjorie,' she said softly.

Nadine's arms fell into her lap. Her eyes remained closed.

Genda also remained still and sound asleep.

'Let's go for a little walk,' Marjorie whispered to the painfully thin child. Like Shanti's mother, she wished the baby would take more nourishment.

Sand warm beneath her bare feet, she set off along the beach. Raising her eyes to the treetops she noted the whereabouts of ripe coconuts. Some had fallen to the ground. Satisfaction flooded over her. They would need them and other food on their journey. Perhaps Genda would be lucky with his fishing line. She beamed at the thought. Coconuts and fish, not much better than they'd had at the camp. It just seemed more. Freedom made you feel like that. And Genda used every ounce of strength to keep them going; she could almost forget that he was Japanese.

The sound of trickling water led her to a narrow gully. A small stream had carved its way from somewhere inland and onto the beach. She dipped a big toe in and gasped at its coolness. Fresh water. They would need plenty of that too.

The sun was getting hotter. Beyond the stream the shade was deeper and promised coolness.

She was getting hot and Shanti's cheeks were turning red, the child fretting.

'I know, I know,' she said, jiggling the skinny baby against her own scrawny frame. 'Let's cool down, child.'

She followed the stream. The shade deepened, the dampness falling over her like a cold mist.

The source of the water tumbled from a fissure in a rocky outcrop into a small pool. Grass and tropical flowers grew around its edge. Sighing happily, she set the child on the grass and lay down beside her.

'This is nice,' she said, folded her arms beneath her head and closed her eyes. 'And your mummy could do with a rest.'

Behind her closed eyelids a vision of the beach came to mind. Genda and Nadine still asleep, the sand littered with branches, the supplies and the boat...

Her eyes flashed open. The boat! The boat was gone!

Suddenly worried, she picked up the baby and got to her feet. She had to get back. If the boat was gone then they were trapped here. But where was the boat? Not properly secured, she told herself. It's probably miles out to sea by now. Hopefully not. Hopefully the sea had taken it and the current had deposited it in some nearby cove. As she headed back to the beach, she told herself that was indeed the case.

* * *

'Wake up! Wake up!'

Nadine blinked into wakefulness and the realisation that Genda was shaking her shoulder.

She became aware immediately that her arms were empty and that Shanti was gone. It wasn't the first time Marjorie had taken her from her arms so was not unduly worried. She presumed Genda was. 'Where's Marjorie?'

Genda, on the other hand, looked very worried indeed. 'Never mind Marjorie. The boat's gone.'

Instantly awake now, Nadine struggled to her feet.

She looked out at the sea. 'Where do you think it will be?'

He wiped his hands against his hips, his eyes fixed seaward. 'It could be miles away, but I'm hoping it just bobbed away on the wind and once the wind dropped, the current took it into another bay.'

A terrible thought suddenly occurred to her. 'You don't think Marjorie sat in it with Shanti...'

'And fell asleep...' He shook his head and pointed at the trail of footprints leading off along the beach. They set off after her.

The storm of the night before had completely abated. The turquoise sea lay like silk, the surf a frill of tumbling lace.

A cool breeze rustled the leaves of the coconut palms. It turned cooler when they began following the same stream Marjorie had followed. Once the sand ended and the vegetation took over, all trace of her footsteps disappeared.

A flock of birds took off from the treetops somewhere to their left.

Nadine and Genda exchanged looks. Without a word being said, they took off in that direction.

Nadine cupped her hands around her mouth, ready to call out.

'No,' Genda whispered, and stopped her.

He didn't look at her.

'I hate it when you do that,' she whispered.

'What?'

'You're not looking at me. You're looking straight ahead. What is it? Why can't I call Marjorie?

Genda swallowed. Even now he couldn't look at her. He knew his eyes would betray his fear. If they were careful... All the same, she had to know.

Carefully, he took a step back. Using both hands he divided the low growing vegetation that surrounded them.

Nadine frowned. What was she supposed to do?

She looked down and saw what Genda had seen: the firm print of a heavy boot.

Genda signalled her to cower down. She did so.

His heart was beating so fast that the sound of his own blood thudded in his ears. Sweat trickled into his eyes. He swiped it aside. He had to see. He had to hear. And smell. Soldiers in a war zone seldom had chance to change their clothes. Uniforms stunk. He knew that from experience.

He got down onto all fours and signalled for her to do the same.

They crawled forward. Every ten yards or so he paused and listened.

The earth was dark and damp beneath their hands. He paused abruptly at one point as a snake slithered across his fingers.

Nadine held her breath. He shivered like a man in a fever before fixing his eyes forward and moving on.

Their sight grew accustomed to the differing depths of shade and shadow. The sound of birds, insects and chattering monkeys filled the air.

The trees were black silhouettes against the red glow of the rising sun shining through them. The path was wet beneath their feet.

Ahead of them a shaft of sunlight poured through a gap in the treetops like the spotlight on a Broadway stage. Rather than bathing the area with a better light to see by, it formed a fierce glare, too bright to see through.

Genda urged her to keep down and move forward.

Giant leaves formed a frame around the light. If it wasn't for those leaves quivering suddenly he would have straightened and walked forward. As it was, he hesitated, listening as the sound of a baby wailing carried through the forest.

And such a strong cry!

Shanti?

She tugged at his arm.

Genda nodded.

He wanted to say that the baby was the least of his priorities. Let's get through this. Let's see if we can stay alive.

Army training and an instinct for survival handed down through generations came to the fore.

He checked in all directions: Forward, each side and behind. Behind was where he saw something move.

He pushed her down and held a finger in front of his mouth in warning.

Carefully, so as not to be seen, he peered through the ragged leaves of a large forest plant.

They came slowly, pale grey shadows at first creeping out of the glaring brightness.

Nadine listened for the sound of a baby crying, not exactly sure where it had come from. She promised herself she would go in that direction sound if she heard it again.

Genda had read her thoughts and was gripping her arm very tightly.

By way of protest she screwed up her face and wriggled.

He could smell her fear seeping from her pores and feel it trembling in the tendons of her wrist, the quaking of her hip against his.

The sound of parting foliage and twigs snapping underfoot became louder.

With his elbow he forced her to the ground.

The sound of bodies pushing through bushes came closer. Her heart was in her mouth. Her face, like Genda's was pressed into the earth. She breathed in the scent of earth and dead leaves.

Something moved much closer than the patrol; she felt Genda

tense and looked at him in time to see another snake, a thin, green one, slither across his neck.

Joseph Smith Junior the Third hates snakes.

Silly, but the thought eased her tension and almost made her giggle.

Fixing his gaze with her own, she held onto his hand, willing him to cope, not to move until the creature's tail had whipped like a leather cord over his shoulder and away.

A twig snapped nearby before their attention reverted to the greater threat.

Genda's hand was flat out on the earth ten inches away from the top of his head. Nadine's was on top of his.

A boot, then another appeared; a rifle was laid down on the ground. A cloud of dust drifted from a pair of dirty trousers being pulled down to ankle level.

Genda managed to slither to a more respectable distance, Nadine tight to his side.

Suddenly an order was shouted.

Swiftly the trousers were pulled up over the muscular calves. Earth kicked up from his hurrying boots scattered over them.

The sound of the patrol receded.

Nadine looked questioningly at Genda.

He said nothing, not until it was safe. The sound of a disturbed forest vanished with the patrol.

32

'Marjorie, darling, you have no sense of direction whatsoever.'

The words her husband had said to her long ago popped into her mind. They'd been staying at their estate in Devon and had gone for a walk in the copse to check on the pheasant chicks being raised there.

Whilst he'd chatted with the gamekeeper, she'd wandered off in search of wildflowers to press between the leaves of her journal. Two hours later she'd realised she was lost.

There'd been servants to search for her back then. In the here and now she could only rely on Genda and Nadine coming to look for her: Hopefully it wasn't that far back to the beach. But she wasn't sure.

Somehow she'd taken a wrong turning. Trees and bushes surrounded her and nothing looked familiar.

Bushes rustled to her right. Wild boar? Weren't they dangerous? God, but her limbs were weak enough, too weak to run for her life that's for sure!

'Hide. That would be best,' she said to the restless baby. 'Don't cry. Please don't cry.'

It suddenly occurred to her that Shanti hadn't cried for quite a while. Hopefully she would remain merely grumbling for a while longer. Funny, but she couldn't hear her doing that either.

She looked around her for a place to hide. There was nothing but trees and shrubbery.

'Here,' she murmured, unable to stop talking to herself even though she knew the boar, or whatever, might hear.

The tree's broad trunk provided something to rest against as well as somewhere to hide.

She slid down against it, the baby caught between her body and her folded legs.

'We'll be all right,' she whispered. Her gaze lingered on the little face. Not as bonnie as my babies were, she thought worriedly. They had had round, plump faces. Shanti had a thin face, a little pointed chin like some old people – herself included. Her limbs and torso were scrawny

The small fists were not clenched like most babies. Her hands hung loosely. Marjorie frowned and pursed her lips. 'You're a very sick baby. I wonder whether your mother knows how sick you are. You're not even crying. You used to cry a lot.'

Panic overtook her. Shanti had cried almost incessantly. And she was so thin, she thought as she re-wrapped the piece of cloth around the baby's tiny body. In her heart of hearts she knew the baby was dying. Surely it was best if she died in her mother's arms? A sense of duty overtook her. She must find Nadine. She must.

Putting aside her fear of a wild animal, she got to her feet, her old joints crackling like kindling as they knotted into place.

She heard a sound. That rustling again!

'Don't you come near me,' she shouted, still convinced she had a wild animal to contend with.

The bushes parted and her old heart missed a beat. She

blinked hard when her cataract got in the way. 'Damn my eyes,' she muttered. 'Never had them before I came here. Bloody Japs!'

The bushes divided. Uniforms! Japanese!

They pointed their rifles at her and said something, a word she recognised but couldn't quite place. Now where had she heard that word before?

She'd picked up a few Japanese words back in the camp. Back there she would have understood and responded immediately. But here, the urge to get the baby back to her mother overruled both her fear and her memory.

She lifted the baby up and attempted to explain.

'The baby! The baby is dying.'

They barked another order and jabbed their rifles in her direction.

'Damn your foul language,' she muttered peevishly: The fact that they were thrusting their bayonets at her failed to register. As well as cataract trouble, she was feeling tired and confused. Old age was catching up with a vengeance. Her mind was set on a course of action and nothing else mattered.

She eyed them disdainfully, just as she had back in England when she'd had a house full of servants at her beck and call. 'I can't stay here chatting to you. I have to get back.'

She made a move to hurry away.

Again they barked orders.

Back in the camp she would have recognised the words for 'stop' and 'stay where you are'. The journey had taken its toll.

She chattered to the baby as she hurried back the way she'd thought she'd come. 'We'll get you back to your mother, my sweet.'

The ground was soft and sprigs of groundcover grabbed at her clothes. Not that it mattered. Even what she called her best sarong – a pale green with a silver frieze, hung in tatters around her lean limbs.

In her fear and determination to reunite mother and child, the enemy were forgotten.

Even a shot fired over her head failed to make her reconsider. Instead it made her more single-minded; only the baby mattered. Still running, she shouted over her shoulder.

'The baby is dying. Do you hear me? I have to take her to her mother.'

The order to shoot cracked out before the two shots that hit their target.

She spun like a top when the bullets hit her, a look of surprise on her face. Overhead, a flock of birds took off screaming in panic.

The Japanese stood over her. Marjorie lay face down and quite still, Shanti's small body trapped between her and the earth.

* * *

Genda pressed Nadine's body tightly into the earth, his hand across her mouth. Her heart was breaking. Her eyes were streaming with tears and she was shaking. It was an hour before he allowed her to move. It no longer mattered that the snakes and centipedes slithered around them.

They had crept carefully through the undergrowth. Nadine had obeyed Genda's signals. Genda himself had been thankful that his eyesight was excellent. He'd seen the footprint. Now it was his ears rather than his eyes that he was depending on.

He listened for the slightest rustle of leaves, the snapping of a twig beneath a clumsy footfall, the sudden scattering of birds.

The moment they'd spotted Marjorie, Nadine had attempted to cry out but Genda had slapped his hand across her mouth and dragged her to the ground. She had not heard what he had heard.

Keeping his hand tight over her mouth, he looked deeply into her fear-filled eyes, willing her to understand that whatever happened was meant to be. They heard Marjorie cry out that the child was dying and had to be with her mother.

The shots cracked out like breaking bones.

Nadine struggled. Genda tightened his grip and shook his head.

Not until he was sure the soldiers had gone did he take his hand away.

Nadine's face was soaked in tears. She shook her head at him. 'Why,' she mouthed almost soundlessly. 'Why?'

He failed to offer any logical explanation. 'Karma. What will be, will be.'

Genda felt as though his insides were ripped into shreds. Much as he wanted to give her solace, he knew there was no time.

'Come on,' he whispered, hauling her to her feet. 'But be quiet. All right?'

She attempted to run to where Marjorie lay. Genda jerked her back.

'No! I will do this,' he whispered.

She looked at him before jerking her chin in an abrupt nod.

Slowly, he walked over to where Marjorie lay and turned her body over. Her lifeless eyes stared skyward. Genda shut them.

He thought about trying to prevent Nadine seeing Shanti's body: an absurd thought. How could he?

She stood silently, her face paler than usual, if that were possible.

'She's dead,' he said. Again he thought how absurd to say that, but his mind was in turmoil. He'd feared hysterics, but this was worse. There was a dead look in Nadine's eyes.

'I heard her. I heard her just now.' Her voice was as dead as the look in her eyes.

Genda shook his head. 'Wishful thinking.'

He also thought he'd heard her cry, but he was tired; they both were. The timing of seeing the patrol and hearing the first shot were muddled.

Nadine fell to her knees and began to scrape at the ground with her hands, her tears forming damp dots on the dry earth. 'At least I'll give her a decent burial.' Her face was tearstained; her nails broke and bled as she scratched at the earth.

Genda attempted to snatch at her hands. 'No! There's no time.'

In vain she attempted to fight him off. 'Leave me alone! Leave me to bury my baby.'

Catching her flailing hands with one of his, he clasped them to his chest. With his other arm he held her close, his face close to hers.

'Brutes!' she sputtered. 'All Japanese are brutes.'

She might just as well have stabbed him. He knew what she meant and felt her despair throbbing through her body. 'I hate you.'

'No.' He shook his head. 'I may look as they do, but you know I am not as they are. The culture of centuries is ingrained in their minds. They cannot think any other way. In time things might change. But not now and now is what we have to deal with. Remember, Shanti was my child too'

She shook her head, caring for nothing except to see her child properly buried. Marjorie too.

He thought quickly as he spoke. 'We have to hide. They'll check with the local village – if there is one.'

Even though her body quaked beneath his hands, he could tell that she understood, but still he was desperate for confirmation. He shook her.

'Understand?'

She nodded miserably.

Devastated by what had happened, he let down his guard. From the corner of his eye he glimpsed a figure.

Had the soldiers come back?

Drawing his sword half out of his scabbard, he turned to face the threat.

He heard the baby cry before he saw the native woman, a child in her arms. She looked startled, turned and disappeared. Within seconds she was replaced by three dark skinned men, their torsos bare above native sarongs. Their expressions were hard to read.

Genda reminded himself that some natives were in the pay of the Japanese. Hadn't he paid some himself?

Nadine noticed the woman and baby. 'Her baby has a strong cry,' she said.

Genda knew she had understood.

Palms together, he bowed respectfully and addressed the men in their own language.

'Greetings to thee. Please forgive our intrusion into thy domain. Our boat was driven ashore in the storm. It has drifted somewhere and we cannot find it. Our honourable old one and the baby are dead at the hands of the invaders. We beg leave to bury them in a respectful manner.'

The three men looked at each other. Wordlessly, they seemed to come to an instant decision. The tallest and eldest of them stepped forward, his palms together and bowing as Genda had done.

'We greet thee to our home, but advise you do not linger. Thy boat has come to rest in a small cove where the current is strongest.'

Genda straightened. Amazing, he thought how full the stomach feels when it isn't sick with anxiety.

'They know where our boat is,' he translated to Nadine, hardly able to control his childish relief.

He addressed the personage he presumed to be the headman of the village.

'I beg thee take pity on a destitute traveller. I have little to give but this sword in exchange for water, fish and coconuts. We need these things for sustenance on the rest of our journey.'

The three men conversed for a short time. They spoke quickly and softly. Genda strained to hear. He thought he heard contempt in their voices. They did not want his sword. His hope faltered. If they couldn't get supplies they would not survive the rest of the journey.

The headman turned back and bowed to him. 'We have no need of thy sword. Thou hast lost the oldest and the youngest of thy family. The compassion of Allah be upon thee. We will provide thee with everything thou needest.'

The Sumatran's quick eyes glanced tellingly at Nadine. She was standing as wooden as a tree trunk, her features frozen and fixed on the dead Shanti.

The headman's voice softened as he respectfully bowed his head. 'Despair not over the last resting site of your loved ones. They will be buried with respect in our own cemetery. Allah grant them peace everlasting.'

Genda bowed and thanked them. 'May Allah bless thy compassion, thy house and thy village.'

That night they hid whilst the villagers loaded the boat with fresh water and provisions. A crescent moon hung low in the sky, just enough light to see by, but too little to be seen.

Numbly, Nadine watched the proceedings. She'd barely spoken to Genda since the killings. Something inside her blamed him for it happening. Logically he'd had nothing to do with it, but her emotions were in turmoil. Everything Japanese was suddenly extremely hateful and that included him. Her dear little baby was dead. She could only guess as to how and why. Inside, she was numb.

She felt his eyes on her, knew they were filled with sorrow, but couldn't bring herself to face him. She wandered off and found a high spot far up the beach among the palms. She didn't know how long she sat there staring out over the sea. Her loss was like the deepest hunger, a hole in her stomach that threatened to suck in her heart. Strange that I can't cry, she thought, but at least the sickness is gone.

Genda's shadow and that of the headman suddenly fell over her.

'Come,' said Genda, and held out his hand.

She looked at it as though she'd never seen such a thing before and declined to take it.

The headman said something. Genda replied. She understood none of it.

Genda crouched low. He smelled differently. She saw it was due to the fact that he had fresh clothes. He must have seen her flicker of interest because he went on to explain why he was wearing a fresh uniform.

'An officer left it with one of their women. He never came back for it and my clothes were in rags.' He chanced a wry smile. 'Couldn't arrive in Australia half dressed now, could I?' He explained further. 'When we come across an allied patrol they will arrest me as a prisoner of war if I'm wearing a uniform. If I'm discovered to be Japanese and wearing civilian clothes they will shoot me as a spy.'

She found it impossible to return his smile. Her gaze continually strayed in the direction of the village and the thought of Shanti buried in the sandy earth. The headman said something else. She didn't know what and didn't care.

Genda touched her arm. 'Sulieman asks if you would like to see the last resting place of your child and your grandmother.'

'She isn't my…'

Genda's smile was touchingly sad. His voice was soft. 'Deep down we are all family.'

He stepped back from her, knowing without her saying that of course she wanted to see her daughter's last resting place.

The village was in almost total darkness except for the faint glow of a kerosene lamp in the headman's lodge. The smell of cooking fires lay pungently sweet on the air, and in the shadows dogs snarled over scraps.

Keeping to the very edge of the village, they came to a cleared plot. Grass and flowers grew on longer established graves. One new one had been added.

'Together,' Genda said before she had chance to ask. 'I think they'll be less lonely. I hope that's OK with you.' He passed her some wild blossom he'd plucked from a tree along the path.

'It doesn't smell particularly special, but it looks pretty,' he said apologetically.

'It doesn't matter. They won't smell it.'

She took it and laid it on the freshly turned earth.

He reached out to touch her shoulder but stopped himself. Perhaps not, he thought. His fingers curled into his palm. His hand dropped to his side. Her sorrow was like a great open wound. He had to give her time to recover – even if she remained silent all the way from here to Australia.

33

The immensity of the sea was clouded in darkness when they left the island. Within an hour of daybreak both of them were staring dumbly at its infinite expanse.

Needing mutual comfort, they'd lain together, cramped but desperate in the bottom of the boat. Neither of them voiced words of love or cried tears; this was sexual contact born of deep emotional need. They had lost a child and were dealing with it as best they could

Genda asked himself why he'd ever entertained the idea that they could possibly make it to Australia. The sea was so big.

Nadine's thoughts were still back on the island and the last resting place of her daughter. She'd laid flowers on the grave along with the imprints of her knees. Genda had had to drag her away.

Genda attempted to show her their position on the tatty map that he kept wrapped in tarpaper and tucked into his waistband. She eyed it vaguely as he told her the coordinates.

'I'm going to come back here when the war's over and put flowers on their grave.'

'Yes. Yes. Of course you are. I've marked it on the map. See?'

The ragged edges of the map quivered when he looked at her. 'And you'll remember the longitude and latitude?'

She nodded wearily. 'I've got a good memory. I'll never forget where that island is. Never.'

She didn't return his look but narrowed her eyes. It was true that she had a good memory, especially for maps; her geography teacher back in India had commended her on it. No, she would not forget.

A string of islands trailed westwards from the one they'd left. Each one drifted past on their left; on their right there was only sea.

Day after day she spent stared at it, feeling empty of emotion and even of hatred.

On those days when the sky was totally devoid of clouds and the sea of waves, there seemed no delineation between water and sky.

'It's like living in a great blue bowl,' Genda remarked.

Nadine did not respond.

Genda was exasperated and deeply worried for the woman he loved. He forced himself to sound cheerful – anything to raise her spirits. Inside he was choked with sadness. The look in her eyes was impenetrable, like sea fog, and her thoughts impossible to read. Not that he needed to. He knew it would take her some time to recover.

In the meantime, he talked and rowed, and rowed and talked, his muscles protesting at the continuous torture.

He never asked her to take over and she never offered. Gritting his teeth, he kept going, punishing himself for everything: for leaving America, for joining the army, for setting out on this crazy journey.

The uniform given him by the villagers was in good condition but he'd kept the civilian clothes, the shirt of which he attached to the puny mast for use as a rudimentary sail, sometimes merely for shade.

Nadine remained silent even when he made notes on the back of the map and told her what he had done. 'I've made notes about what happened at the camp. There'll be a debriefing once we're in Australia. They'll want to know what was happening there.'

'Of course.' She looked away. It was the first time for days that he'd got a reasonable response.

He looked down at her well-shaped feet and remembered watching them as she'd danced for Yamoto. Suddenly, he felt her eyes upon him. Her features were rigid. Her eyes glowed the way they'd used to.

'I had to do it.'

It was hot, midday, and he rested on his oars. His voice was gentle. 'What do you mean?'

'Yamoto! I had to do it.'

He tried not to stare at her, but there was precious little else to look at, just the sea.

It came to him then just how deeply she'd buried her true feelings. She'd always seemed so stoical about what had happened, but now...

'You were forced to do it. There was no dishonour. Life is precious no matter what it is.'

Nadine was momentarily stunned to silence. Although he did not know it, Genda had repeated the words her mother had so often said to her.

'My mother used to say that.'

'Your mother was a very wise woman.'

She nodded.

'You killed Yamoto.'

He nodded.

'Not the She Dragon?'

'No. Yamoto did that.'

On the journey, Nadine told him more about India and the woman with two children selling her body for sex in order to survive. 'That is what I did, but I bought comfort with my body. I had more food than the others, and lived in far better conditions. Plus I only had one man abusing my body. I wish now I had stayed with the others.'

Genda didn't understand. 'Why?'

'Because I am one of them.. Now I am heading for Australia.' She shook her head forlornly. 'They won't understand, Genda. They will just not understand.'

'You don't need to tell them,' he ventured earnestly, beaming because it was such an obvious conclusion. 'Hell, they'll be none the wiser as long as you keep schtum!'

At some time during the night, he fell asleep at the oars, barely feeling someone lift off his arms and slide into his place.

Silently, he fell backwards and snoring the instant he laid his head against the prow of the boat.

Up until then he'd only managed to catnap. Now he dozed more deeply, but the respite didn't last.

Nadine was getting weaker. He woke up one morning to find her slumped across the oars, and yet they were still moving.

'Nadine! Wake up!'

She was sluggish waking.

'You promised you would stay awake' he said angrily. 'I need some sleep, damn you! Are you listening to me?'

She wiped her forehead with a backward sweep of her hand.

'I'm sorry. It's just that I feel so hot and...'

Genda stood up in the boat. 'What about me? Don't you think I'm hot too, sweating my ass off, rowing day, noon and night?'

Shaking her head, she buried her face in her folded arms. Her knees were bent and her toes poked out from beneath her sarong.

She continued to shake her head as though she were kneading it into her arms.

'I can't help it. I feel so tired.'

'Yeah, yeah.' Genda buried his face in his hands, wiped away the sweat and rubbed it into his trousers.

He shook the water barrel. There was enough to get them to the next island whose outline he could see rising from the sea.

'I'm sorry.'

She didn't seem to hear him. Her head was thrown back and her eyes were closed. Her lips were cracked and split at the corners.

He judged she hadn't done that much harm. Luckily the current was carrying them in a south-easterly direction.

Miles and miles of rowing. She took over when she could and he avoided sleeping as long as he could.

They lost count of the days as each one drifted into night and back into daylight.

Nadine stirred in her sleep. 'I'll take over later...' Her voice drifted into a sigh.

'Sleep. I can manage,' he said to her, all the anger gone from his voice.

Hours later, he was still rowing.

He nudged her toes with his boot. 'Hey. Want some coconut milk?'

She opened her eyes. They were red rimmed. He knew she'd been crying again. How long, he wondered, until she could cope with the death of her baby?

'Go on. Drink.' He passed her a coconut in which he'd already made a hole. 'Drink,' he said again.

She looked at him blearily.

He touched her hand. Her flesh burned with fever. He frowned. 'You're sick. Why didn't you tell me?'

She shook her head, curled up and buried herself back down in the boat.

Genda looked at the water barrel. They'd need more – a lot more if they were to continue their journey. He ripped off a piece of his shirt, opened the barrel and poured water over the ripped rag. Gently he dabbed it on her face. 'We need to cool you down.'

'Water,' she said softly, her tongue licking at the dryness of her lips.

He allowed her to drink her fill. Up until now he'd rationed the water to one cup per day, and then not all at once.

'More,' she said, swallowing and still licking her lips.

He shook the barrel and heard the dismal sound telling him it was less than a tenth full.

'Milk,' he said, offering her the coconut again. 'Drink some milk.'

She drank the entire contents. He shook other coconuts. All of them were empty.

'Shit,' he muttered and put the one she'd emptied with the others. They were only fit for food now, not drinking.

Tendrils of wet hair clung to the dampness of her face. Her eyes sometimes flickered, but never opened. Sometimes she wept in her sleep and when she did, he let his own tears flow

It was days later that Genda eyed the island he had seen initially as a pale mauve blob. He rowed with superhuman strength, praying that there was a village on the island and someone to help them.

The force of the sea against the oars was formidable, but still he persisted. Every so often he glanced at her, willing her to wake.

The current was favourable, but the surf crashing onto the only beach he could see looked too powerful for such a tiny craft.

The boat began to prance up and down like a mettlesome

horse. Waves rose and curled over into themselves; most over four feet high and strong enough to tear the boat apart.

If there'd been an alternative, a smaller beach, or more supplies to chance journeying on, he would have done that. But there was nothing else and he had Nadine to think of.

Feathering one oar and rowing frantically with the other, he manoeuvred the tiny craft so that the bow faced the beach.

'Here goes,' he muttered to himself, his eyes fixed on the strip of sand beyond the surf.

The boat crashed on, held aloft by an avalanche of foaming surf.

Despite his best attempts, the boat veered sideways on, her left side facing the beach.

Genda attempted to turn her, but the little craft was no more than a soap bubble tossing on a heaving mass of water.

One last wave tossed the boat skywards, until with a breathless sigh it surged onto the sand. Although the boat filled with water, it journeyed far enough up the beach for Genda to jump out, take a rope at the front, and pull it further.

Every muscle in his body begged for rest, and his eyes for sleep, but he forced himself onwards. Remembering the last occasion he'd pulled the boat onto the beach, he secured the rope around a rock, using it like a winch to pull the craft even further up the beach.

Drenched in sweat and burning with fever, Nadine was only vaguely aware that she was no longer being pitched around. She welcomed the respite, though soon fell back into a feverish sleep.

Gently he took her from the boat and laid her on the sand. She needed more water, but for now there were coconuts lying around. Although tired beyond belief, he gathered up a few and laid them next to her head.

He searched in his pocket for the penknife with which he'd

made holes in the other coconuts. He found it empty and swore. Out there somewhere, he thought, eyeing the sea with undisguised malice.

There was no time to rummage about for anything else – perhaps a nail from the boat – with which to make holes in the bounty he had found. His sword was still hanging at his side but it felt achingly heavy. Usually he could raise it above his head with one hand, but he was tired. It took both hands and all his strength.

Nadine woke up. She saw a man in silhouette against the brightness of the sun. Sunlight glinted on steel. His face and figure was indistinct, but the sword... There was only one that had stayed in her memory, the same one that had sliced off Lucy's head.

Genda was surprised by her scream, but not as surprised as when he looked up and saw a group of uniformed men running towards him.

Something hard hit him in the base of the neck. Something else hit him in the mouth. He fell forward, blood spurting from his nose and mouth, even his ears. Although he tried to speak, to explain his intention but nothing came out but bubbles and garbled incoherency.

'Did you see that? He was going to cut off her bloody head!'

'Is he dead?'

'No. I don't think so. Shall we chop off his head like he was going to do to the Sheila?'

Nadine heard their voices. 'Australians?' Her voice was little above a whisper. Why couldn't she open her eyes? Why was she so hot and where was Genda, where was Shanti?

'Marjorie?'

'Into the sea?'

'Marjorie? Is that you?'

She found enough strength to get up on her elbows. The world was a blur but she saw the men, saw a bloodied body being swung backwards and forwards.

'Genda?'

The horror of what she was seeing chilled her fever. She staggered to her feet, fingers clawing the sleeve of the man beside her.

'He was going to chop your head off,' someone said.

'No! No! He wasn't.'

The sound of her voice reverberated in her head, yet the men did not seem to hear her or they did not understand.

The sun was blindingly bright, the figures elongated and blurred against the sea.

Someone close and smelling of sweat tried to hold her back.

'The Jap's gone. He's dead.'

She tried to scream, but no sound came out. Her throat was dry. Her tongue burned her mouth; the words had to be forced onto her lips.

'He was... American!'

The world went black.

34

In a ward at the Australian hospital in Darwin, inquisitive eyes gazed quizzically at the girl who'd been imprisoned by the Japanese. There was pity, there was curiosity but there was also embarrassment as they weighed up how best to deal with her.

Because of her condition, she'd been kept in hospital for a long time whilst her wounds healed and she gradually weaned onto a normal diet.

'Where were you born?'

'Benares. India. My father was a government official. My mother was Indian.'

Some of those questioning her registered surprise. Others merely wrote down her details as though it were no more than a shopping list.

'My baby died,' she said to one of the doctor's attending her.

He exchanged looks with the nurse standing next to him.

'You gave birth in the camp?'

She nodded.

'Was this very long after your capture?'

'Quite a while. I buried her back on one of the islands we passed.'

More surprised looks before the doctor cleared his throat.

'But your husband wasn't with you.'

'No. The father was Japanese/American – mostly American,' she added with a small smile that brought tears to her eyes and an ache to her heart. 'Is he all right? The man I was travelling with?'

'I'm afraid we don't know that.'

'I need to see him,' she said pleadingly. 'Please.'

She half raised herself away from the crisp whiteness of the hospital pillows piled behind her head and tried to reach out for his hand.

'We know nothing of the man you were travelling with. We must presume that he is dead. Under the circumstances you must concentrate on getting well again.'

Once they considered her relatively healthy, she was transferred to a refugee station where she was interviewed by an officer from one of their nursing corps, and someone from the War Office.

'So. You were captured just after the fall of Singapore?'

'Yes.'

'Were you alone?'

'No. I was with my husband. The Japanese killed him.'

'And then you were taken to Sumatra. We believe the camp you describe was on the south western side of the island, not too far north of the straits separating Sumatra from Java.' The woman pushed an open atlas across the table and pointed to where the tail end of Sumatra almost met the most western point of Java.

Nadine stared at it blindly as though searching for a distinct point that would not come into focus.

The questioning continued. Urgent voices affecting gentleness though not understanding. Not understanding a thing! And always returning to the same questions

'So you were imprisoned by the Japanese.'

'Yes.'

'How horrible for you.'

'It wasn't pleasant.'

'You were starved?'

'We were hungry for most of the time.'

'And they beat you?'

The bald-headed man from the government department seemed to await her answer with undue relish.

'Such things happened.'

'My dear,' said the woman, dropping her voice. 'I'm afraid I have to ask you about the child. I presume you were raped.'

Nadine raised her eyes from the map. She took in the woman's chill blue eyes, the crisply curled hair covering her head like a tightly fitting cap. With a patience born of anticipation, the two of them stared back at her, pens poised, ready to take down the details.

'I don't understand. I've already told you. My baby, Shanti, died. We buried her.'

The nurse shook her head and smiled kindly. 'I don't mean the one who died. I mean the child you are expecting now. Didn't you know that?'

Speechless that she hadn't noticed herself, Nadine shook her head. Her thoughts raced and she felt a great wonder deep inside. This time she knew the identity of the child's father.

'I didn't know.'

'Did he rape you?'

She shook her head. This was just too much to take in.

'If you were raped we will see that he's punished,' the man said gently. 'And please don't be embarrassed. You're far from being the only one. We've heard quite a few stories of what these terrible people have been up to.'

They eyed her expectantly, aching to write down that she had answered in the affirmative. She also knew their attitude to her would change drastically should she tell them the truth.

She agonised. Genda would not suffer. He was probably dead, but even so the urge to preserve something of his memory, of the man that he had been, was too strong to ignore.

'No. He did not rape me. The Japanese I was with helped me escape. He had to escape too.'

She could sense their disbelief, no, their disgust that she had willingly lain with a Japanese major and that he was the father of her child.

'He was of Japanese descent but in effect an American citizen and in danger of being executed.'

'Ah!' said the man hiding his discomfort by fiddling with his glasses and searching his paperwork for the correct place to insert this worrying information.

The woman looked perturbed at first but swiftly readjusted her lipstick smile and poured out condescension. 'You were under great strain, my dear. It's perfectly understandable that you excuse what happened by believing he wasn't really Japanese at all...'

'He was a good man! He helped me escape. If he hadn't, I would have died. He would have too. He killed the colonel. The colonel was responsible for a lot of deaths in China. Genda – Major Genda Shamida hated him.'

She stared at them, hating the way they looked at each other, as though she wasn't quite sane or lesser than them in some way.

'Right!' said the woman. 'You can put all this behind you and rebuild your life. Have you written to your parents?'

'My father's dead.'

'And mother?'

'She's dead too. I've got nobody.'

'Under the circumstances that's just as well. They'd probably be shocked and reluctant to accept a mongrel child. We can of course arrange to have him adopted and...'

'No.' Nadine sprang to her feet. 'As my father is dead he won't know that his mongrel daughter had a mongrel baby as you put it!'

The woman looked shocked and unsure quite how to interpret Nadine's tight-lipped declaration.

'Yes,' she snapped, placing her palms face down and leaning on the desk. 'I'm a mongrel myself! My mother was a Hindustani *nautch* dancer. Did you know that Christians and converts regarded the *nautch* dancers as prostitutes? No! Of course you didn't! And they weren't – not until they were forced into it because their dances were banned. And that's the whole point. They did what they had to do in order to survive. Even the *devadassi*, the temple dancers who sold their bodies as an act of faith. Just as many did in that terrible place I have recently escaped from – just to live, to survive and return to the life we once had. I owe Major Shamida my life – so I'll keep my baby thank you very much.'

* * *

It was in the autumn of 1944 when she was told of her pregnancy, which fostered in her a great determination that this child would survive.

The Japanese were in retreat on all fronts. US forces were pushing ever closer to the islands of Japan though fatalities were high and it was feared would go higher.

She fervently hoped that he or she would not be born into the cruel world as her poor little daughter. This child would have a far better chance. She would make sure of it.

She was lucky enough to find accommodation in a large old house in Darwin, Northern Territory. A widow whose sons were away fighting owned the house. Both women were in need of companionship and somebody to confide in.

'You can stay here as long as you like,' said Mrs Worth, a likeable woman with twinkling eyes who confided in Nadine that she'd always wanted a daughter but had only had sons.

Whilst awaiting the birth of her child, she wrote letters to her father, his solicitor and other people she remembered from both Benares and Singapore. Her father's solicitor wrote back to say that her father had died in her absence, leaving everything to her. He also advised that he would forward letters of credit giving her access to funds he would transfer personally into a Darwin bank of her choosing.

The only sadness she felt at the passing of her father was regret that they had not got to know each other better. Perhaps there might have been some kind of reconciliation. Perhaps he might even have enjoyed the company of grandchildren, though bearing in mind what she remembered of her childhood, perhaps not.

The baby was born in the summer of 1945. Germany had already capitulated in May. Following the dropping of atomic bombs on Hiroshima and Nagasaki, Japan surrendered in August.

Following the tremendous news, Nadine smiled down into the face of her baby son and told him the news.

'The war's over, Joseph. The war is over at last and we're going home.'

It was perfectly possible to wind up her father's affairs in Darwin, but something was drawing her back to India. There would be no closure, no moving on until she saw her place of birth one more time. She took Joseph with her.

* * *

Joseph was a year old by the time she returned to her home in India. The house in Benares was little changed except that the roses needed attention, though not so much as the pergola where she had once danced with her mother.

The old gardener who had talked to his plants was no more, taken in an outbreak of cholera some time back. Her father had caught the same disease. No definition between race or colour there.

The sun was still as hot, the city still as bustling, seemingly unchanged, and yet she knew it had changed; India had changed.

The drive for independence had been fuelled by the weakening of the British Empire, the changes wrought by a war that had redrawn frontiers, fuelled aspirations and shifted alliances. There was a new restlessness in the air, a thirst for something more. India would govern herself.

Regardless that this was the country of her birth, it did not feel like home. Even the possibility of returning to her husband's plantation in Malaya did not appeal to her even if the new constitution there would allow her to take charge of it. In effect, she did not know where she belonged, and of course she had Joseph, her son, to think of.

She asked one of her servants about the future of India and her place in it.

'You will go home, madam.'

'Home? This is my home.'

'No, madam. Your home is in England.'

England! She had never been to England in her life.

'I only know India. My mother was Indian.'

He was an old man who had served her father for many years.

Keeping secrets had been his duty. She could see that her blurted exclamation troubled him.

'You are a *memsahib*, Missus. You were brought up as a *memsahib*. You cannot be anything else but a *memsahib*.'

'I'm sure it will happen.'

'I am sure too, madam. We will have a good Hindu government.'

'And Moslem surely?'

His heavy eyelids flickered like the wings of a trapped moth. 'I will not vote for a Moslem. Only Hindu.'

'But you're both Indian.' She couldn't help the dismay in her voice. Surely millions of civilian war dead counted for something?

He pursed his lips. 'Their culture is not my culture, their traditions are not my traditions, and their religion is not my religion.'

Hearing him say that was disturbing and brought back a host of memories. She instantly thought of Genda the only person she knew whose views matched hers.

Even though she had the pergola repaired, the garden tidied and the roses pruned, the house where she had danced with her mother and with Zakia and her sister, was not where she wanted to be.

She was aimless and waiting, but she didn't know for what. The house held many memories of a different time and of the person she used to be. The only reason she clung on was to ensure that Joseph had a stable home life and could grow in comfort from a baby into a toddler.

She spent her mornings dealing with her dead husband's plantation in Malaya. There was a lot of paperwork to deal with and the country itself had achieved peace but its constitution was changing. What with that and dealing with the final winding up of her father's affairs, and looking after Joseph, she was glad of the respite. Sometimes she stood in Shanti's old room with Joseph in her arms. Even though he was far too young to understand, she told him about her mother and how they used to dance together.

Sometimes she fancied she could still smell her perfume and hear her bracelets jangling on her arms.

Then one day she went in there and smelled and heard nothing. Everything was gone. There was only the sound of scuttling lizards and the smell of the dusty lime wash covering the walls.

It felt to her as though everyone was finally gone, their spirits flown to eternal rest. The house was empty, even of memories, and she didn't want to stay here.

But where did she want to be?

She looked at her small son chasing a lizard around the room, falling to his hands and knees as it scurried into a crack in the wall. His hair was very black, his eyes almond-shaped and his face a perfect heart. He did not look English. Neither did he fit into the mould of being Indian. The only place he might fit in was the place where his father had been born, California, but before that there were ends to tie up. Most of all, she had the vague notion that she had said goodbye to this house and her life in India. For that reason alone she was glad she'd stayed here a while. She was now ready to move on but first there were two other places she wanted to revisit. One was the island on which she'd buried her daughter, Shanti, and Lady Marjorie. The other was the island where she'd last seen Genda alive.

Her mind was made up so she wasted no time in contacting a solicitor, telling him she wished to sell the place as quickly as possible. To her delight he told her he knew of somebody who would be very interested.

The solicitor was true to his word. With peace and the possibility of independence, India was changing rapidly. The house was sold to an Indian merchant who was growing wealthy on the purchase and smelting of scrap metal. 'The war has made much scrap metal and I have bought lots of it,' he'd told her proudly. 'I need a house that suits my more elevated standing in my community.'

* * *

She took a boat from India to Singapore, taking Joseph Genda Burton with her. At first she had agonised over what to name him, but he was all that was left of a very fine man.

In the distance, Singapore rose from the sea like a reclining goddess shrouded in heat-induced mist. It seemed a lifetime ago since she'd last seen it, back when she'd been a married woman.

She'd arranged to stay in a hotel and give herself time to sort out her dead husband's estate.

Singapore looked battered and she was in no doubt that the estate would also have suffered.

Martin himself seemed like a leftover from another lifetime. To her great shame she could barely remember what he looked like. Their time together had been fleeting though not exactly unhappy, merely mundane.

Lawyers she'd hired to administer Martin's estate informed her that the government would be taking it over. Pre-war foreign businesses were being nationalised.

The lawyers hinted that selling it to the government did not have to be done immediately. She could negotiate the price and stay in her old house until everything was finalised. She told him she had no intention of hanging around for the 'right' price. Harvesting rubber did not appeal to her. She remembered seeing hardworking figures flitting like spectres through the mists of morning, tapping the resin from one tree then another. The sight of them had unnerved her. She had no intention of being part of it.

Mr Levine, the lawyer handling the will and other matters,

greeted her warmly in the stuffy office overlooking the congested traffic around Kavanagh Bridge. The sight of the bridge was also unnerving; she had been in the company of Doreen and her children and Lucy Lee van der Meer the last time she'd seen it. Lucy was dead. She didn't know about Doreen but presumed she was either dead or gone completely mad.

She turned away from looking at the bridge and concentrated on what Mr Levine was saying. He spoke slowly, looking up at her frequently to make sure that she understood.

'Mr Levine, I do understand what you are saying.'

He looked surprised at her interruption, his bottom lip drooping in dismay.

'My dear young lady, I feel I have an obligation to point out every salient point. After all, you have no experience of owning or running such an involved business as that constituting your deceased husband's holdings.'

'Mr Levine. It's true I am only in my early twenties, but I should point out to you that I have lived a lifetime during the past few years. I spent much of the war years in an internment camp in Sumatra. During that time it felt as though I'd lived twenty years in the space of three. 1942 until 1945. The end of the war has been over for some time. Now please, I am only interested in doing my duty to my dead husband. I am not interested in rubber. I wish to sell.'

He nodded sagely as though his opinion had been jolted by distinct and relevant information. He steepled his fingers. Nadine's attention was drawn to the swollen joints of his knuckles.

'Mr van der Meer, the buyer is Dutch and I think may be known to you.'

'Van der Meer?' Nadine couldn't believe her ears. 'Indeed he is. I knew his wife. Lucy was…' Her voice fell away. 'She was executed for trying to escape.'

'He has a new wife now.'

'How dare he!'

The lawyer regarded her with amazement. 'He is, or rather, was a widower I believe.'

Nadine's hand flew to her forehead. Her fingertips traced the sweat there.

'I'm sorry. Do excuse me.'

She felt a fool. Lucy was dead. Life must go on and Lucy's husband surely had plenty of his own demons to contend with. She wondered if the new wife was Chinese. Should she seek them out? She decided not to. Things had changed. They'd all changed.

The lawyer resumed his speech.

Once he'd imparted all the information, she made ready to leave.

She smoothed her skirt down over her hips as she got to her feet. The room seemed suddenly clammy. She was desperate to go.

'I'll leave you to draw up the papers and send them to me. I'm staying at Raffles Hotel with my son until everything is complete,' she said to him.

He nodded, the bustle of the street outside reflected in his spectacles.

'May I ask if you intend to stay in Singapore?'

'I will not be staying.'

Something about the way he picked up his pen drew her attention back to his fingers and the swellings on his hands.

He saw her looking.

'They look painful,' she said. 'Have you always had joint problems?'

He put his pen down and took off his glasses. 'No. Not until the Japanese broke them for me. I was interned in Changi during the war and resorted to keeping a diary, which was of course strictly forbidden. Another inmate betrayed its existence in exchange for an egg and a small fish.'

'Oh!'

He picked up his pen. He was halfway to putting his spectacles back on his nose when she asked, 'Do you hate the Japanese?'

He gave it the briefest of thoughts, his gaze spilling out of the window to the building opposite, as though the answer was written there. 'Only the one who broke my hands.'

Something changed in the way he looked at her. 'The war is over; some things have changed, and some things will take some time to change further, principally for the better one hopes. There is gossip afoot. I heard about your son. I hope he is well. Where will you go?'

Nadine looked down at her gloved hands. They were white gloves. All *memsahibs* wore white gloves when living in the tropics. *Memsahibs.* Suddenly she tore them off and threw them on to his desk.

'I'm leaving here. I'm going to find my son's grandparents. They live in California in the United States of America. I think that's where my son belongs. I think that's where his father really belonged too. He was the victim of circumstance.'

'I wish you luck. Will you fly direct or go by sea?'

She shook her head. 'I don't know yet. First I'm going back to where I buried my daughter and Lady Marjorie.' She fell silent as she remembered.

In her heart of hearts she was imagining staring out at the sea where Genda had drowned.

Sensing she was gathering up her memories, Mr Levine waited for her to recommence.

'I know it sounds crazy, but I'm hoping that my child's father was washed ashore on another island nearby and kind people buried him. If it is so, then I need to let his parents know.'

'I wish you good luck.'

She thanked him and left. He knew he would never see her again and wondered how it must feel to love so strongly, so deeply. He found himself wishing that someone had been waiting for him when he'd got back. He'd been a confirmed bachelor. Now he wished it had been otherwise.

35

Going back proved more difficult than she'd realised and she was grateful that Mr Levine offered to help.

The trip was not easy to arrange: a plane from Singapore to Jakarta, from there another, smaller plane and a boat trip to the island she remembered as being like a pearl drop falling from the underbelly of Sumatra. Her stomach churned at the thought of looking on her daughter's grave, but the feel of her son's hand in hers helped her cope. She was offered the services of a woman to look after Joseph by the people she was staying with whilst she visited his grave. She opted to take her son with her.

'He needs to know his sister's last resting place too.'

The heat was as sultry as she remembered; the sky and sea just as blue. But something was different. There was no threat in the air, no danger from an invading army. The sun seemed brighter.

Native people in the village close to the cemetery eyed her warily. The man who had brought her explained the situation to the village headman whilst the populace, mostly children, examined his outboard engine with small prying fingers.

The headman recalled the incident and the man and woman

who had pushed away from the island to journey south. He welcomed her and together with the boatman and a number of other villagers, accompanied her to the cemetery.

There were flowers growing wild close to the cemetery and the earth was dark and moist underfoot. The flowers were bright and beautiful and attracted her son's ardent attention. She waited for permission before entering the cemetery proper.

She addressed the boatman. 'Sulieman, would you ask the headman's permission for me to pick these flowers so I may place them on the grave of my child and my friend?'

Sulieman nodded and accordingly asked the headman.

'He says you are welcome.'

Joseph peered up at her. He was getting tired. 'Are we going to see my sister and Aunt Marjorie now?'

'Yes. Yes, we are.' The familiarity with which he referred to people he'd never met made her smile.

The cemetery was less overgrown than the last time she'd seen it, possibly because more villagers had died in wartime fighting and disease. She counted her footsteps from the old wreck of the banyan tree, its trunk more jaded and dried, the last of its branches rotting into the earth.

The mound will be gone, she told herself, and I will not find her. The cross too will be rotted away.

She was almost right about the cross. There was little left. She would have passed it by if it hadn't been for the flowers. Someone had already laid a colourful bunch on Shanti's grave.

She crouched down and tucked her own bunch beside them. Joseph stood close, eyeing her with a child's curiosity.

'Is my sister still there, mummy?'

'Yes,' returned Nadine softly. 'She's still there. So is Auntie Marjorie.'

Had someone in the village placed flowers there? No. It wasn't possible. The remains of the cross were indistinct. In an effort not to arouse either suspicion by the Japanese or the villagers, she and Genda had been purposely vague with their marking. Whoever had placed flowers on the grave had to know a body was there. After placing the flowers Joseph had picked and brushing the dirt from her hands, she went back to the boatman. He was smoking and talking with the headman. He looked surprised to see her back so soon.

'Can you ask who put the flowers on the grave?' she asked him.

Sulieman, who spoke quite good English, did as she asked. He shrugged.

'He says the grave lay untended until the Australians brought prisoners here. Your man was one of those prisoners. One of them had gone overboard and was washed ashore but they recaptured him.'

Nadine felt an instant fluttering in her heart.

'My man?'

'Yes. He says the one you came with then travelled south with. He remembers him. Half Japanese, half American. His memory is not too clear, but now you have reminded him of these events, he is quite sure.'

'What happened to him?'

'He was very sick for a while. So were some of the Australians. They went away and were going to execute him before they left but he escaped.'

She forced herself to stay calm, to gather her thoughts. He'd been brought back to this island. She could hardly believe it. She then asked him to repeat what he had said. The boatman did so.

The heat of the sun did nothing to quell the shivers that ran through her body. Did she dare hope? She had assumed the worse, thinking she needed to travel on further to the island where they'd encountered the Australian patrol. Now it seemed he had been brought back here.

'This man. Are you sure he was the man who had been with me?'

The question was relayed and answered in the affirmative.

Nadine sucked in her breath. Suddenly the heat of the day was ten times more intense than it should be. Her clothes stuck to her body. Her tongue cleaved to the roof of her mouth. Eventually she asked, 'What happened?'

The headman did not understand what she said. He spoke to the guide and chewed happily on a mouthful of betel nuts.

'The man was caught in our nets and dragged from the sea.'

'He's alive!'

'He is alive.'

Her heart raced. 'Where has he gone?'

The men, even the guide, barely acknowledged her.

'Sir! I wish to know where the man has gone. Where is he staying? Pray forgive the headman for my presumption, but I thought this man was dead. He was a good man and saved my life. I must know where he is.'

Unnerved by her outburst, the boatman felt obliged to convey her question.

'The headman says that Genda Shamida was indeed a good man. They had thought to throw him back into the sea when he became tangled in their nets after escaping from the Australians, but he would not let go and besides a good catch came with him. He was injured and near death, but once recovered he stayed and hid. He helped with fishing and planting crops. Then the Americans came and he went with them.'

Nadine was beside herself. 'Where did he go? Where did he go?'

'The headman says there is a naval fleet in Jakarta and many doctors and nurses of the Red Cross. He says you will find him with them.'

* * *

The journey to Jakarta seemed to take even longer than the one from Singapore. Joseph was tired and needed to eat and to rest.

'Where are we going?' he asked on the last stage of their journey to the one decent hotel in the whole of Jakarta.

'To find your daddy,' she said softly.

She expected an exuberant reaction from him, but there was none. When she looked down at him he was fast asleep.

To her astonishment, most of the guests were Red Cross and other people working for various agencies attempting to cope with the resettlement of military personnel and refugees.

A room was arranged. Even if she found out Genda's immediate whereabouts, she could not possibly go to him. Joseph needed to rest.

She got him settled and a woman to sit with him before going back down to reception.

'I'm looking for a friend of mine,' she said to the slim young Malayan behind the reception desk. 'I think he may have been staying here with the American Red Cross. Can you check for me?'

'Of course, madam.'

She gave him Genda's name.

'I'm sorry, madam, but Mr Shamida has already left for the airport. I believe he is booked to fly out on an American Air Force civilian plane to California.' He glanced up at the ancient and very large clock ticking like a time bomb high on the wall. 'I believe he takes off in about one hour.'

One hour!

Nadine began rummaging for dollars in her handbag. 'Give

this money to the woman looking after my son. Ask her to stay a little longer. I'll be back as soon as I can.'

'She will want more money'

'I will pay her double. Just ask her to stay.'

* * *

The smart American with the firm but searching look in his eyes shook Genda's hand. 'I can't imagine how long it would have taken to get a decent interpreter if we hadn't found you. I hope you'll find your folks OK and that you'll return to help us out.'

Genda's smile was both sincere and sad. 'I hope so too.' He sighed. 'Still, there are plenty of folk who have less to go back to.'

Major Ford, who had been responsible for rounding up the last contingents of Japanese resistance following the surrender, then carrying out endless interviews with those though to be responsible for war crimes, slapped Genda's shoulder. 'Have a safe journey.'

The process had been a long one and Genda Shamida had enjoyed some hard-won vacation back in the States. This time, having revisited places that had invoked painful memories, he was at last going home.

He had tried to find Nadine Burton's whereabouts, but possibly because he did not know her married name, he drew a blank. Nearly three years since the end of the war; she could be anywhere by now.

Major Ford left Genda to move towards the queue of civilian and military personnel, all waiting to board the first of a number of flights heading home.

Heading home. Genda couldn't help feeling saddened by the words and also slightly nervous. Would he be able to resettle in the country he'd grown up in? Being there on a permanent basis was bound to be different than merely going back for two or three months.

The queue edged towards the departures door and the aircraft waiting on the baking tarmac. There was a three sided 'go down' to give shelter: three walls, a fragile roof that was little more than a canopy. Only those at the head of the queue were sheltered from the strong sun. If it rained they'd be drenched.

A bunch of officers and civilian men were loitering close to the door.

A few would be passengers were watching some brown-skinned native girls dancing for pennies.

Genda craned his neck.

'Ain't they something?' said a guy beside him whose attention was fixed on the girls so had not taken in Genda's features.

He said nothing but something stirred inside. In his head he could hear a flute and see a girl dancing.

'Pretty girls,' said the man.

'Yes,' said Genda.

The man's smiling bonhomie melted on seeing Genda's Japanese features. Grumbling something about the enemy within, he turned away.

Better get used to it, thought Genda to himself.

He came level with the dancing girls. A deep longing came to his heart. Surely her arms had been more sinewy than theirs, her movements more fluid?

He blocked the thoughts from his mind. They were too painful. What was the point in tormenting himself?

* * *

Nadine ran across the baking tarmac. It was only a small airport. There was only one queue, mostly military but a few civilians, paper pushers working for the military.

It had occurred to her that she wouldn't recognise him, but there he was, wearing a navy-blue suit, white shirt, dark tie and a trilby, every inch the corporate American. He'd put on a little weight, though not too much. He'd always been broad shouldered, she remembered – but that was before they were hungry – before they'd fled the camp.

Slowing to a walk, her heart quaking, she came up behind him. Like others in the queue he was watching some native girls dancing. They had a silk scarf on the floor into which those waiting were tossing money.

'Say, how can they dance like that without music,' somebody said.

An official asked for Genda's passport. Taking it out of his wallet, a piece of singed, ragged paper fell to the floor.

The queue moved forward and a breeze blowing in from the sea carried it out of his reach. The man who had spoken to him earlier picked it up.

'It's mine,' said Genda politely, and held out his hand.

The man was surly. 'What is this? Hey, I didn't know Japanese read poetry!' He began to read. '"How do I love thee"...?'

Genda curbed his anger. 'Please.'

The man sneered then with great deliberation and even greater delight, he tore it into pieces. Like petals, the pieces fell to the floor.

'Hope you learned them words off by heart,' said the man, his eyes chinks of blue in his pink, plump face. 'Go on, Jap. Tell us how it goes – if you can remember.'

Not yet seen by Genda, Nadine stepped forward, her voice clear and melodic. 'Like this. It goes like this:

'How do I love thee? Let me count the ways...
I love thee to the depth and breadth and height
My soul can reach, when feeling out of sight
For the ends of Being and ideal Grace...'

He turned and saw her, his mouth gaping, his eyes wide enough to drown in.

Nadine smiled through her tears of joy. 'Joseph Smith Junior the third, I presume.'

His jaw dropped before he managed to pull himself together. The words came easily.

'The Honourable Miss Nadine Burton. It's you. It's really you?'

There was space between them, and yet there was nothing. The world was in a mess, people displaced, people dead, people lost, but they knew where they were. It was as if they were back on that beach, a ragged cloud across the moon and the sound of surf kissing the beach.

They cared not at all for the strange glances of those around them. Neither did they care that the queue divided and moved forward. They were an island in a human wilderness, a silent wilderness. Nothing else needed to be said.

MORE FROM LIZZIE LANE

We hope you enjoyed reading ***Women in War***. If you did, please leave a review.

If you'd like to gift a copy, this book is also available as an ebook, hardback, large print, digital audio download and audiobook CD.

Sign up to Lizzie Lane's mailing list for news, competitions and updates on future books:

http://bit.ly/LizzieLaneNewsletter

Want more gritty, heartbreaking historical sagas from Lizzie Lane? Why not explore her brand new *Coronation Close* series...

ABOUT THE AUTHOR

Lizzie Lane is the author of over 50 books, including the bestselling Tobacco Girls series. She was born and bred in Bristol where many of her family worked in the cigarette and cigar factories. Coronation Close is her latest saga series for Boldwood.

Follow Lizzie on social media:

facebook.com/jean.goodhind
twitter.com/baywriterallat1
instagram.com/baywriterallatsea
bookbub.com/authors/lizzie-lane

Ingram Content Group UK Ltd.
Milton Keynes UK
UKHW042250040423
419601UK00005B/72

9 781837 518463